BLOODLINES

CONVERSION BOOK TWO

S.C. STEPHENS

ISBN-13: 978-1494450663

ISBN-10: 1494450666

Dedication

Thank you to all of my readers! I wouldn't be here without your passionate support. And thank you to everyone who helped me get this book published—Lori, Becky, Nicky, Sam, Nicola, Debra, Sarah, Julie and Janet. I would be lost without your help!

Chapter 1 – A New Life…or Two

Seven months. That was the last time my life had been completely normal. So much can change in such a short amount of time. Back then, I'd been relatively content with my life—great friends, great family, and a great job. Okay, a good job with the potential to be great. But an emptiness had been with me too. To be honest with myself, I was lonely. Very lonely. Not that I'd never dated, I had, but I'd never felt connected with any of them. Not the investment banker, who only talked about the changing stock market climate, not the yoga instructor, who tried to convert me to veganism daily, and definitely not the pretty-boy model, who, as I discovered one day when I walked in on him, wasn't aware of the definition of monogamy.

Yes, they were all normal and none of them were for me. My knight in shining armor had ended up being a vampire. Well, a little bit vampire, as he liked to put it. His great-grandmother had been turned into one while she was nine months pregnant. That change had brought on labor and she'd birthed her baby before the change had completely affected the infant. His grandmother was born half-vampire. She had then gone on to marry a human and conceived and birthed a baby, before the vampirism had stopped her human heart and she'd become one of the walking dead. That baby, his mother, had also married a human and had a child, before her mortality was claimed. Her baby had grown up to be the man of my dreams, my partial vampire, who could walk around during the day in full sunshine and suck a cow dry at night—Teren Adams.

That man was now, unfortunately, part of the mysterious undead world along with his mother, grandmother, and great-grandmother. His "conversion" had happened recently, and it had been terrifying for both of us. We'd been abducted by some deranged lunatic who'd assumed that Teren was devoid of all humanity, just because he was partially a mythical creature, a mythical creature that had a reputation for being dangerous to humans—a reputation not completely undeserving. Vampires *were* dangerous and they *did* prey on humans. Full vampires were extremely dangerous—faster, stronger, and with extra abilities that the mixed breeds didn't have, like "trancing", a form of compulsion that could bend a human's will to their own. But taking a life was still a choice, even for full vampires, and Teren's family chose not to. Well, most of his family did. His grandmother had made a couple mistakes in her vampiric youth...and his great-grandmother, well, she killed because she wanted to. She killed people that most of society would deem as deserving of such a death, but still, it was one thing to think that, and quite another to know it was happening...and who was doing it.

Not that I had room to talk anymore. I'd taken a life. It had been the only way to get Teren and me *both* safely away from our abductor. It had been survival—us or him—but it haunted me nonetheless. And, being honest with myself again, I'd struck an incapacitated man, exposing his blood to the air so my near-death, starved vampire would eat. I'd made the choice between a madman and the love of my life. And while the act itself walked my nightmares, the choice did not. Given the same situation again, I'd choose to take the same actions. I'd choose Teren Adams every time. No contest.

And I *had* chosen him...for the rest of my mortal life. We were engaged. I was going to walk down the aisle and marry this amazing man who no longer had a heartbeat. But that fact didn't bother me anymore. It was inconsequential. I didn't know where love came from, but it didn't come from that organ. Teren's heart might be still and lifeless, but his love for me truly knew no bounds. We'd do anything for each other. We already had. I'd killed and Teren had chosen not to. Even though every part of his body had been screaming at him to take my blood, he'd chosen not to.

That was one quirky little side effect of his conversion...hunger. No, that wasn't a strong enough word to describe the level of thirst attacking his body. It wasn't that he could use a little something to eat. No, it was a primal, animalistic need to devour—to consume everything in his path until he was satiated. And I'd been forced directly into his path. Yet somehow he'd resisted that life or death urge to drink my blood. He'd refused me...he'd even refused our attacker, instead choosing to die. Choosing death over taking the life of another. That was my man, and that was why I had no fear of becoming his wife...and the mother of his children.

That was another obstacle that had been placed in our way. He could only give me a child while he was still human, still producing human hormones and nutrients that were vital to giving life, even on the male end of things. I'd resisted his family's pressure for us to conceive at first, and really, I don't think I could be blamed for that. They'd practically shoved the idea of a baby down my throat upon our first visit to their home, a sprawling ranch near the base of Mount Diablo, an "open air pantry" as Teren referred to it.

I'd been angry when I first heard their plan for us. Of course, the way I'd found out hadn't exactly been subtle or welcoming. The idea had practically been an ultimatum—*do this or we'll find someone else who will.* But Teren and I had only been together one month at the time and I may have been dating a vampire, but I wasn't crazy. I wasn't having a kid with a virtual stranger just because some insistent, black-haired bloodsuckers told me to.

I'd broken up with Teren after that. The news, combined with the fact that he was slated to die within the year, had just been too much for my sensible head. I couldn't process it and I'd left him. That hadn't lasted long though. The pull I'd felt for him was entirely too great. I hadn't even made it a week before I was rushing back to his arms. It had taken a couple months after that, but I'd eventually agreed to have his child. And boy, once we had agreed to it, we attempted to make it happen with zealotry. Of course, being under the proverbial gun will do that to you. We'd only had a few months until he would be incapable of making a baby, so we didn't waste any precious time trying.

Even still, we thought we'd failed. I hadn't known I was pregnant when Teren had been injected with some strange liquid that had forced him to change. At that moment, I thought I'd lost Teren, and any chance of having his baby. But through some miracle, or maybe fate, I *had* been pregnant. It was weeks later when Teren had first realized it. In a moment of intimacy, he'd heard the tiny, fast and fluttery heartbeat with those amazing, perceptive ears of his. Two heartbeats, actually. My amazing man had not only managed to knock me up in time, he'd knocked me up twice.

So here I was—a twenty-five year old human girl, hopelessly in love with a twenty-six year old dead vampire, a fact that no one besides my sister knew. And I was getting married to him within the month, so that I would be his wife in every sense of the word before our vampiric twins arrived, a fact that absolutely no one outside of his family knew about.

Should be interesting.

"Teren?" I shouted over my shoulder, pushing aside my sudden flood of memories.

He instantly breezed into the room, a toothbrush in hand and a disgruntled expression on his face. "You don't need to yell, Emma."

I smiled at his irritated look, realizing that he was right. If I needed to speak with him, I really didn't have to put much effort into it. I could talk as if he were in the room right beside me, even though where he *had* been, was the opulent bathroom adjoining his parents' "guest" bedroom. Super ears. One of his many vampiric traits, and one that made living in a house full of vampires feel sort of like we all shared one communal bedroom. Not exactly an aphrodisiac.

"Sorry," I whispered.

He shook his head and smiled at me. "What is it?" he asked, before sticking the toothbrush back in his mouth and continuing to brush those pearly, pointy whites. I watched him for a second, amused that even the undead cared about oral hygiene, and wondering if he flicked out his fangs when he brushed. I'd never seen him do it, but that didn't mean he didn't.

Remembering what I wanted to talk to him about, I frowned. "Are you sure about this?" I sat on the edge of the most luxurious king-sized bed known to man and put my hands back on the satiny sheets. We'd just gotten up from a recent tumble, and I hadn't gotten around to making the bed yet. As Teren gave me a curious, confused expression, I briefly considered dragging his athletic body down for another tumble on those sheets, super ears be damned.

Teren zipped to the bathroom to get rid of his toothbrush, and I heard the water run for a second as he rinsed. Then, in the blink of an eye, he was back at my side. Sitting down next to me, he put a hand on my knee and furrowed his brows. "What do you mean?" His hand went to my stomach and his incredible, pale blue eyes followed the movement. His fingers traced a wide oval over the top of my t-shirt and I smiled at the look of peace on his face.

Since we'd found out I was pregnant a week ago, on Teren's birthday, he'd started touching me like this all the time. He looked almost reverent whenever he did it. He'd initially resisted the idea of having children, of bringing more partial vampires into the world, but now, I think he was more in love with the idea than I was. And I was pretty in love. As my eyes dropped to watch his fingers lovingly caress my soon-to-be expanded stomach, I started to wonder what our children would look like. Would they have my wavy, brown hair and light brown eyes, or would they stick to the Adams' genes and have pitch-black hair and startling blue eyes. As I considered that every child born into Teren's family had inherited the dark hair/light eyes combo, along with pointy teeth and a penchant for plasma, I started to think that the odds were pretty good that they'd look exactly like Teren. I was completely fine with that.

Teren raised his eyes and his calm gaze swept over my face. "Do you mean having children...or getting married?" He cocked an eyebrow and crooked a grin. "Because, it's a little late for both. Or so I've been told."

I grinned at the reference to the sort-of ultimatum I'd given him when I'd found out I was pregnant. In not so many words, I'd basically told him if I was having his kids, he was putting a ring on my finger. He'd been fine with that, as I knew he would be. I pushed his shoulder away from me, and he laughed. I frowned, remembering, yet again, my real question. "No, going back to San Francisco, going back to work and people and...life."

He leaned back and blinked, confused. "Yeah...why wouldn't I want to go back?"

I gave him an incredulous look. "Um...because you died?"

He gave me a sexy, self-assured grin and I resisted the urge to pull him on top of me. "It will be fine, Emma." Laughing, he shook his head. "No one will know my heart isn't what is keeping me upright."

I frowned as I wondered what exactly in his vampire blood *was* animating him, but then I shoved the thought aside. It didn't matter.

Something was keeping him here with me and that's all I needed to know. I sighed and hoped rejoining the world was as seamless as he made it sound.

His hand left my stomach and came around to my hip, giving me a gentle squeeze. "You're stressing…it will be fine." I sighed again, knowing he could read my body without me even having to say a word. My pulse, my sweat, my smell, everything about me gave me away, especially now, since his already sensitive senses were heightened. He'd only changed a few weeks ago, but he'd already gotten good at homing into my moods, memorizing what the different indicators meant when combined together. That helped to skip a few steps when I was ready for some loving, but it could be a little annoying when I wanted to stress without him bugging me about it.

He sighed and brought his hand to my cheek. As always, his cool skin gave me a slight shiver before I adapted to it. "What do you see when you look at me, Emma?"

My lips twisted into a wry grin. "A sexy, baby daddy corpse."

He rolled his eyes and shook his head, his hand on my cheek moving to run through my hair. "If you didn't know about the walking dead part."

I laughed and bit my lip as I studied the attractive man beside me. Finally, I smiled and ran a hand down his chest; his skin was cold to the touch, even through his t-shirt. "I see a smart, successful, funny, attractive, twenty-something-year-old man, who nearly glows with life and vitality." I cocked my head at him. "You're quite a catch."

He chuckled and leaned into me, placing his lips gently on mine. "You are too," he whispered, his cool lips brushing against my warm ones. My heart started beating faster and he smiled wider at hearing it. Looking satisfied, he pulled away. "It will be fine."

I frowned, both at the nagging doubt in my head and the absence of his lips. "But…what *are* you going to do at work?"

Teren worked for Gate magazine, as a writer in the life and style section. Several San Franciscans were learning how to enjoy day-to-day living in the beautiful City by the Bay from a dead man. I loved the irony in that. He appeared to love it too as an amused smile lit his face. "Well, I'm going to write fascinating and entertaining articles about daily life in beautiful San Fran."

Funny. Teren had a bit of a smartass streak in him, something that I generally found amusing, but as I was currently trying to have an earnest conversation with him, it was starting to irritate me. He tilted his head and twisted his lips as he read the emotion on my face. "Everything will be just like it was before we left, Emma." He smiled and shrugged his shoulders. "Well, that's not entirely true. I may tell everyone that I'm engaged...and about to be a dad."

I stiffened like someone had shoved a rod down my spine. Grabbing his hand, I squeezed it tight. "No, don't do that."

He frowned and pulled away to look over my rigid posture as I sat on the edge of the bed. "Why not?" He leaned in, a devilish smile on his face. "Embarrassed?"

A small laugh escaped me against my will and I relaxed. "No," I sighed, resting my head on his shoulder. "But, they'll want to shake your hand or something, to congratulate you." My hand tightened around his even more. I really didn't want anyone feeling that cool skin and getting suspicious.

Not sharing my concerns, Teren laughed. I glared at him, and he grinned and shook his head. "So...?"

I frowned at his amusement. "Well, you're not exactly room temperature. People are going to notice that."

He pursed his lips. "I'm not going to be lovingly caressing my coworkers, Emma. It's mainly just me alone in an office all day, writing or researching."

My expression deepened into a scowl at yet another smartass comment interrupting my semi-serious conversation. "What if they want to do that guy hug thing?"

He raised his eyebrows. "Guy hug thing?" I crossed my arms over my chest, annoyed at the humor on his face. He continued, ignoring my stance. "It's still winter, I can explain the coldness away with the weather." I opened my mouth to object and he raised a hand, stopping me. "I know, we live in California, it gets warm here, but, Emma, some people are just naturally cold. It will raise less suspicion than you think."

I shook my head. "Still, even for a regular human, you're a cold man."

He smirked at me. "Only on the outside."

I sighed, remembering how his relaxed attitude about his secret had nearly gotten us killed before. Looking over my face, his expression turned more serious. "I know, Emma. I'll be careful. I won't touch people more than necessary. I'll fake breathing. I'll act completely human, just like I've always tried to." His hand came back up to my cheek as my eyes started to water. Teren getting exposed again scared me more than I ever thought it was possible to be scared. "I will be careful." He shook his head. "But I need this. I need to feel normal." He squatted down to look me directly in the eye. "You know that."

I sniffed, but a tear ran down my cheek anyway. I still had nightmares of that terrifying man who'd taken us, and what I'd done to escape him. A part of me never wanted to go back home. A part of me wanted to stay here, at his parents' ranch, safely surrounded by vampires who would die to protect me, and the children inside of me. But a bigger part of me wanted to be stronger than the scared little girl I was starting to sound like.

Teren's thumb brushed away my tear and I exhaled a long, slow breath. I nodded and he leaned in to kiss me. As he pulled away, one final objection poured from my mouth. "What if you need to eat?" That was one thing he definitely couldn't do around humans.

He gave me an easy grin. "I can get food, Emma. And I don't need to eat at work. I can wait until I get home." His hand came down to rub my stomach again. "When I'm with you."

A spike of excitement zipped through me at the thought of moving in with him as soon as we got back. That definitely made leaving here a bonus. Another thought struck me though, and, knowing it was better to have my fears verbalized than bottled up inside, I let it out. "What if you have to eat *with* humans? A business lunch or something?"

Teren frowned and turned his head away from me. Maybe he hadn't thought about that yet. He didn't exactly have a functioning digestive tract anymore. He couldn't scarf down the bloody steaks he used to enjoy before his conversion. Standing, he ran a hand through his hair. "Well…" He twisted to look at me still on the bed, watching him, and put on a tired smile. "I'll think of something."

I bit my lip in frustration, but let it drop. I couldn't expect him to have all the answers, but I did expect him to think of all of the questions. My hand drifted to my stomach, wishing I could hear their heartbeats like Teren sometimes could. I wished I could feel them move already, so I'd know they were okay. We had so much more to lose now, we both needed to be careful.

I stood and wrapped my arms around his trim waist. He sighed in contentment and pulled me in closer. I had to imagine that to him, I was sort of a heat source. I probably felt pretty good wrapped around him. That's what I liked to think, anyway. I closed my eyes and laid my head on his silent chest, happy that we were still together, despite all the odds.

I leaned up to kiss him, torn yet again on staying here a little longer, and tossing him down on our impressive bed, or getting back to the real world. I exhaled in delight as our lips moved together; the light stubble that he preferred to keep along his jaw was wonderfully scratchy against my sensitive skin. It really wasn't much of a choice. We had to go back. For one, my "vacation" was over. I'd exhausted every amount of paid time off I had, coming out to the ranch to help Teren through the scary process of converting. I needed to be back at work tomorrow morning.

It was going to be weird to go back to work. I'd been gone for over six weeks, just over seven, really. From what my friend Tracey had told me over the phone, my boss had been going through temps like Kleenex. The most successful one had only made it a week. While it made me happy that I had been missed at the accounting firm where I worked, I was not looking forward to the mound of work I'd need to catch up on. I had a feeling I'd need another vacation soon.

Oh well, at least I had a wedding to look forward to planning. An impromptu wedding. A few weeks away from *now* wedding. We'd decided to get married the week before Christmas…which meant I had just about a month to get everything ready. But, since I did have a household of eager vampires on hand to help out, I was pretty sure it would go smoothly. Well, the planning part anyway, I was still a little unsure of the actual ceremony. My family and a few close friends would be staying at the ranch for the wedding weekend. The ranch of mixed-vampires and that one impertinent full vampire. She was the one I was most worried about—Halina.

While Teren's cool hands slipped under my shirt and ran up my bare back, I worried about the eldest vampire being in proximity to people close to me. I wasn't worried that she would hurt them, I was pretty sure she'd be on a tight leash, well, as tight of a leash that you can keep a vampire on, but I was fairly certain she'd get a huge kick out of scaring the crap out of them. She immensely enjoyed intimidating people, and she sure intimidated the heck out of me.

And how would the vampires eat while my family was here? They usually sat at the table with Teren's human father, Jack, and drank blood from a carafe that kept it warm. They couldn't exactly do that with my mom and friends in the room. Especially since the tiniest amount of blood on their tongues made their fangs drop down. That was a clue that even my mom would pick up on.

So, if eating at the table was out, I guessed they'd be roaming the countryside for food, picking off some of their cattle in the farthest away fields. I felt bad about making them do that, although, it probably wasn't too big a deal for them. Even if Teren liked to deny it, all the vampires had an instinct to hunt, buried deep inside them. I'd seen them all do it, the night of Teren's conversion. Sure, they'd been hunting stupid cattle that hadn't even moved, but the look on their faces as they'd circled and attacked, well, watching them had been terrifying *and* exhilarating.

Teren pulled away from my mouth, his cool tongue breaking apart from mine. At the abrupt absence of his caress, my mind snapped back to what we were currently doing. He twisted his lips and cocked an eyebrow at me. "Am I…bothering you?" he asked, annoyance and amusement in his voice.

Laughing, I pulled him tighter. "No, I'm sorry. Just…being reflective today."

He sighed as he looked me over; the crystal-clear blueness of his eyes was in stark contrast to the darkness of his hair. "You're really still worried? Don't you want to be home?"

He looked down at the floor, to where I'm assuming his mother was, and then across the hall, to where I knew his grandmother was hiding out the daylight. Another vamp trait, or maybe it was just an Adams trait—they could all sense each other. It was more profound the closer they got, and while he stayed in the same house as them, he always knew exactly what rooms they were in. It came in handy sometimes, like when I needed to know where he was on this massive ranch; I only had to find the closest vampire and they could point me in the right direction. It also came in handy if say, we were kidnapped and driven to the middle of nowhere and I needed to drive us back to the ranch, only I had no clue where it was. Yeah, unfortunately, it also came in handy then too.

Teren's eyes came back to mine. "Wouldn't you like to be somewhere more...private?"

My arms around his waist tightened as I smiled. "Yes, I would. I know...I'm stressing. It will be fine."

He kissed my nose. "Yes, it will be." He released me, grabbed our bags, tossed them on the bed, and started the process of packing. And it *was* a process. I'd brought a lot of stuff with me. Over his shoulder he tossed, "Besides, it's not like I'm going to be letting the guys at work lovingly rest their heads against my chest." He turned his head and grinned at me.

I smirked. "Funny. You better not let any of the women at work do that either." I raised an eyebrow at him and then playfully walked up and smacked his ass.

He fully turned to me, his fangs dropping down as he did. "Careful, human." His eyes flicked up and down me in a way that made my body heat, even standing a foot apart like we were. He cocked his head, listening to my heart start to beat faster. He was so strong, powerful and just plain sexy, all vamped out like that, that I couldn't help but get a little turned on watching him. Of course, the pregnancy hormones flooding through my body may have had something to do with that too. He closed his eyes and inhaled. "Emma...we really should get going."

He opened his eyes and I could clearly see the passion in them. It made my breath quicker. "Maybe you should go wait downstairs with my mom. I'm sure she'd love to make you something to eat."

I smiled at his reaction to my reaction; we were both feeding each other's desires. "Maybe I'm not hungry for food just yet. Are you?" I stepped up to him, pressing my entire body along the length of his. He sucked in a quick, unnecessary, breath as our parts lined up.

Slowly, and with a level of seductiveness that would have made any stripper proud, I pulled down the loose neckline of my shirt. It was stretchy enough that I successfully pulled it off my shoulder. I was talented enough that I grabbed my bra strap with it. Teren eyed my bare shoulder with a desire derived from two instincts—the need to eat and the need to have sex. I lifted my shoulder to him, encouraging both.

A low growl came from deep within his chest; it sent an ache straight through me. His eyes lifted to mine and he exposed his teeth as the edge of his lips curled into a cocky smile. I felt fire flooding through me, and I was pretty sure that if he didn't put his hands on me soon, I would explode. Finally, one palm came around to my backside, pulling me even tighter to his oh-so-ready body. The other, came to the corner of my shirt, pulling it back even farther. His lips lowered to my skin, then his teeth pierced the flesh. He groaned deep and sucked hard, his hands pulling me against him. That was when I decided every thought in my head could wait until later…much later.

When our second tumble for the day was finished, and I was spent and satisfied, I laid my head on his chest and listened to the echo of my still-surging heartbeat through his skin. As his body was slightly warmer after so much prolonged contact with mine, it was almost like he was alive again. I smiled as I listened to the reverberation. He stroked my hair, equally spent, but having no physical sign of exhaustion. I peeked up at his face, memorizing the soft, satisfied smile as he lay with his eyes closed. I rubbed a trace amount of blood off his lip, noting and immediately disregarding the slight ache in my shoulder. So worth it.

Teren's smile widened at my touch and he kissed my fingers before I pulled them away. I traced a lazy circular pattern in his chest as I debated getting up and getting ready for the day…again. Instead of doing it, I stretched in the silky sheets and debated staying in this bed forever. Eventually, Teren opened his eyes and stirred, seemingly torn as well.

Grinning, I propped my elbows on his chest, holding him down, symbolically, if not physically. Physically, I had been no match for his strength before his changeover. Now, my gesture was as meaningless as a fly trying to hold down a horse. He stayed on his back and smiled up at me however, willing to play the role of captive, if only for me.

My long hair brushed over his bare skin as I tilted my head in question. "Do you feel different?"

He chuckled and tucked a piece of hair around my ear. "Yes. Now I feel tired…and very satisfied." He practically purred those last words and a shiver went through me.

I twisted my lips at his remark. "I wasn't talking about the sex, smartass. I was talking about your conversion. Do you feel different, now that you're dead?"

He laughed at the look on my face. He'd known full well what I'd been talking about. Biting his lip, he looked up at the ceiling, his face more serious. "Actually, I do." He shook his head before bringing his eyes back to mine. "I wasn't expecting that, but, I feel…" he shrugged his shoulders, "more alive."

My face scrunched in confusion and he laughed again. "I know, that sounds weird. But, it's true. I feel everything around me more intensely." His eyes looked past me as he examined the world in a way I would never really be able to. "I can differentiate every particle of the air. I can see colors I didn't even know existed before. I can hear sounds that have never been audible." His eyes came back to mine. "And I can taste…" he inhaled and closed his eyes, "everything." He reopened them and gazed at me with a look of wonder on his face. "You wouldn't believe how beautiful the world is like this, Emma."

While I stroked his chest and tried to grasp how he saw the world, how he saw me, he looked around the room like he was seeing it for the first time. How odd that a being no longer living in the world, could feel more connected to it. I felt a little like old technology compared to him, like how a black and white TV must feel when it's placed beside an HD flat screen. If inanimate objects had feelings, of course.

He shook his head. "It's strange. It's like the senses swap around with each other. Like I can taste sound, hear color, and touch emotion." His eyes came back to mine, wistful. "I wish you could experience this."

I sighed and sank my chin to his chest. Sometimes I wished that too, but there was just no guaranteed way to make me a partial vampire like him, and giving up all of my humanity, having to live in shadows and darkness, just wasn't something I was willing to do. Plus, I couldn't right now anyway. Not with two lives inside of me, depending on my still beating heart to keep them alive and nourished.

I kissed his cooling skin, feeling the hard muscle encased beneath it. Laying my cheek down on that solid chest, I smiled up at him. "I'll just have to experience you. That's enough." Teren smiled and kissed my forehead.

Eventually we did pick ourselves up and keep our hands off each other long enough to get all our stuff together. Hand in hand, we walked down an elaborate dual staircase, the kind of staircase that debutantes would be paraded down when they were announced to the world. The seemingly simple vampires had a taste for the finer side of life. The contradiction made me smile, but I sort of understood it. In a way, Teren's family was kind of reclusive, keeping to themselves and away from almost everyone else. If I never really left my home, I'd want it to be the best home money could buy, too.

Smiling at each other, Teren and I walked into a sunny and bright-with-life dining room. Teren's father, Jack, was sipping his coffee at the table and reading a paper. He looked up at us when we entered the room. "Morning, kids. Just get up?"

Knowing Jack was the only one awake in the house who was not aware of just how long Teren and I had been "up" made embarrassment flash right through me. I could only nod in response. Teren chuckled and squeezed my hand as he pulled out a chair for me with his other one.

Jack smiled at his son's gallantry and then went back to drinking his coffee, happily oblivious to our bedroom antics. I loved that about Jack and felt even closer to the man I considered a father figure. He didn't look much like Teren, what with his brown but graying hair and warm brown eyes, but he was as warm and gentlemanly as his son, and Teren's manners were no great surprise to me after spending a little time around his role model.

Teren kissed my neck but didn't join me at the table. He usually didn't, not since he'd stopped eating. Being around food didn't bother him or anything, he just usually took the time while I was eating breakfast to visit with his mother or his grandmother, since just sitting there and watching me eat was a little boring.

I hadn't been seated for more than ten seconds before Teren's mother, Alanna, whisked out of the kitchen with a plate of food for me. She loved playing hostess and since she'd lost a human to feed when Teren died, I think she'd started making up for it with me. Even before she'd known I was expecting, she'd piled on the food, and now that she did know about it, the habit had gotten even worse. The plate before me was mammoth, loaded high with pancakes and a rich-looking molasses syrup. A mound of fresh fruit and about three sides of bacon made up the rest of the platter-sized plate. I knew better than to object, though.

"Thank you, Al...Mom." Alanna had insisted I treat her like family from day one. It was still an odd thing to do, but I was trying. I supposed it would feel more natural once we shared a common last name.

Alanna gave me a brilliant smile. Her eyes were the exact same shade of blue as Teren's. They caught a shaft of morning light and sparkled in the rays. The sun didn't bother her too much. She could be in it for short periods of time with no adverse consequences, unlike the other women. Teren's grandmother could tolerate being in a hazy-with-light room, but it was painful for her. Halina, on the other hand, would fry to a crisp in sunlight. She couldn't even be in a room with rays of light and stayed holed up in her underground lair until sundown. One of the downsides of vampirism. And one that faded with each mixed generation. It made me obscenely happy that our children would get to play in the park in the afternoons, just like all the other kids. I wanted to give them as normal a life as possible. I understood Teren's need to be like everyone else, so much better now.

Alanna swished over to her son's side, locking her arm around his. Her long, black hair was free down her back except for two long strands in front that were pulled back from her face. Her black-as-night hair also perfectly matched her son's, and as Teren smiled down at her, I could sense the deep connection they had. It was more than just a close mother/child bond. It was a species bond as well. Alanna completely understood her son, because she was exactly like him. She knew what it felt like to changeover. She understood his thirst. She shared his desire to keep their secret hidden. She saw the world in the same amazing way he did.

Their bond was so tight, it might have made an ordinary wife-to-be jealous. I suppose I wasn't ordinary, though. For me, it lightened my heart. I knew I wouldn't be a part of Teren's life forever, not with how long he could potentially live, and I wanted him to have strong bonds with other people, especially other people with an equally long lifespan. I didn't want him to be alone...ever.

Which meant I also had to play peacekeeper sometimes. For, as close as they were, Alanna and Teren were also a lot alike, and that meant they occasionally butted heads. Usually, it was because Alanna was trying to protect Teren, and he didn't feel like he needed to be protected. I tended to agree with Alanna on that one; Teren could be a stubborn ass sometimes.

Looking up at him, Alanna spoke a phrase in perfect Russian. All the vampires could speak it. Halina had taught them. She'd been born and raised in Russia, but had moved here as a little girl. I guess it had pleased her to keep her native tongue alive, and she'd taught her daughter who had taught Alanna, who had in turn taught Teren. Jack had told me that he could pick out certain words and phrases, but foreign languages weren't as easy for him to grasp as it was for the vampires, and he'd never really felt the need to learn it. "Let them have their secret language," he'd jokingly told me once.

Not liking secrets, I was determined to be fluent in the complicated sounding language. I'd been picking up words and phrases as well, and from what I could tell, Alanna had just told her son "good morning" and then something that included the word "blood". I'd picked up that one early on, as they talked about blood a lot, for obvious reasons. He nodded at her and I figured she was just being a mom and letting him know there was food in the fridge, if he wanted some. Some things never change, regardless of the species.

Turning back to my plate, suddenly ravenous, I picked up my fork and started, in a very unladylike way, shoving forkfuls of pancake into my mouth. Teren chuckled and bent down to kiss my chipmunk-like cheek. "You're hungry *now*, I see," he whispered in my ear.

I choked on my food, knowing his mom had just heard that…and knew exactly what he meant by it. I shot him a glare, my full cheeks feeling hot. He gave me an innocent expression and I heard Alanna lightly laugh as she walked over to give Jack a kiss. Jack looked up at her laughter, but not understanding it, went back to reading his paper. I took the opportunity to smack Teren on the thigh.

He swiftly kissed my cheek again. "I'm going to get a little snack." He gave me a not so innocent look. "I find myself completely drained this morning."

I rolled my eyes and shook my head as he laughed again and turned to walk into the adjoining kitchen. I watched him leave, his body as lean, muscular and appealing in his worn-in jeans and long sleeve t-shirt, as it had been completely bare. I thought about him drinking blood in there. It didn't bother me like it used to. Obviously, since I let him do it from me. But I did worry about him getting enough to eat when we were back at home. I knew he'd never hurt anyone. His will power had been tested to the extreme a few weeks ago and he'd proven without a shadow of a doubt that he had an extraordinary level of control, but I didn't want him to go hungry. I was a mom now, too. Well, almost. But those instincts were there, and I didn't want him to suffer. It's not like we'd be living on a ranch with plenty of opportunities for him to feed. He'd pretty much have to rely on buying small livestock at farmer's markets. He'd be eating a lot of chickens.

Returning my focus back to my plate, I tried not to worry about it. He could always run out here if he got really hungry. The ranch was about an hour from our home—in a car. On foot, Teren could probably make it in fifteen minutes.

Teren was still in the kitchen, and I was halfway through my massive stack of cakes, when something weird happened to me. My stomach started to churn. I set my fork down and pressed a hand on my belly. A horrible, familiar sensation swept through me and I stood up. My head started to swim as well, and I began to panic a little bit.

I knew the sensation rising in my stomach and throat—every person over the age of four recognizes it. My stomach was calling a halt to the act of eating, and was now going to "evacuate the pool," so to speak. I looked around as my hand came up to clamp my mouth shut. My mind went blank. I could only comprehend that I didn't feel good. I couldn't think past that to where the damn bathroom was in this massive home. Suddenly getting scared that I'd lose it on the expensive dining room table, I started backing up…and lightly crying.

Jack had just started to look up at me, when Teren instantly blurred into the room. His fangs were still out, his teeth slightly red from his breakfast, and his face was extremely concerned. "Emma?" I knew he could sense my body's discomfort, but he didn't know why. He looked a little terrified.

"Bathroom," I squeaked out from under my hand. He heard, understood, and picked me up and swept me down the hall to the other end of the house, where a bathroom fit for a queen was situated. I barely had time to note the stale air in the room that was obviously hardly ever used, before I dashed to the bowl and noisily launched the entire contents of my stomach into it.

Teren's cool hands came up to my back; they felt like heaven-sent icepacks on my suddenly overheated skin. He pulled aside my hair as I lost it again, and then he cupped my cheek, and cleaned me off with a towel.

"Thanks," I muttered, as I leaned my face into his cool, wonderful skin.

"You all right?" The concern was thick in his voice, and I opened my eyes to look at him. He sat on his knees beside me, looking like he wished he could do more. I understood feeling helpless. I had certainly felt that way when he'd been horribly injured. Of course, that had been much more serious than morning sickness.

I smiled as my stomach settled. Slinging my arms around his neck, I straddled his lap. He held me tight and I relaxed into the calming coolness. "Morning sickness," I whispered, loving those words and hating them at the same time. I didn't enjoy throwing up, but I did enjoy the *reason* I was throwing up. I looked up at him and grinned. "I don't think the kids like pancakes."

He laughed and kissed my forehead, squeezing me a little tighter than he usually did. I must have looked pretty awful, because he still seemed pretty worried. "I'm fine, Teren...all normal pregnancy stuff."

He rested his head against mine and nodded. "I know...I still worry about you, though."

I pulled back and put a hand on his cheek, understanding that too. I constantly worried about him. "I know."

He helped me stand. As we opened the elaborate door handle of the marble and gold leaf room I'd just spewed in, Alanna stepped into the doorway with Teren's grandmother, Imogen, right behind her; she was cringing in the too-bright-for-her sunlight.

I smiled at their show of concern. "I'm fine," I immediately said, feeling a little stupid at everyone jumping up because I got sick. "Imogen, go rest upstairs, please. You shouldn't be down here. I'm fine, really."

Imogen didn't look to buy my bravado. "Are you sure, dear? Is there anything we can do for you?" She wrung her hands as her face winced. The light in the hallway had been subdued with heavy curtains, most likely thanks to Alanna, but it was still causing the vampire pain.

To reassure her, and a nervous looking Alanna beside her, I quickly muttered that I was fine again and threw on a tired smile. With Teren supporting my elbow and helping me walk through the door, like I was partially an invalid, I thought I probably looked pretty pathetic. Wanting them to feel okay about me, I straightened and stepped away from him. He made to reach for me, but I gave him a warning glance. He understood and let me be; he knew I was no damsel in distress who needed my hand held because I'd gotten a little woozy.

Alanna and Imogen looked a little less concerned as I walked as confidently from the room as I could, but I was feeling a little dehydrated and my hands were shaking. They all followed me back to the dining room, Alanna darkening the area for her mother. Jack, most likely wondering what all the fuss was about, looked up as the assemblage paraded me back to the table. While I went from standing to sitting, Alanna swept away my plate and came back with a tall glass of water. I downed it, wishing they'd all stop worrying, but understanding why they were. What I carried inside me was important, as important as a child was to anyone, but also important, because I carried the last of their line. Teren's dead body could no longer contribute to the making of new life, and these children would be the last I ever carried of his, the last I ever carried, period. If I lost them...

I couldn't even think about that.

After my glass of water, my color came back. With reassuring pats and belly rubs, the vampire women finally left me alone. Teren squatted in front of me, his hands on my cheeks as his sky blue eyes searched mine. "Let's go home," he whispered. I nodded into his hands, thinking that was the best plan I'd heard all morning.

Chapter 2 – Back to the Real World

After a couple more large glasses of water, followed by a couple more visits to the bathroom—the regular kind of visits, not the upchuck kind—I felt like myself again. Teren stuck close to my side, his eyes rarely leaving me. The concerned look on his face never really left him either, even when I sat at the table, making small talk with his father, both of us laughing over one of Teren's childhood tales.

A few minutes later, Teren excused himself to pack the car. A couple of minutes after that, when he was done, he came back for me and insisted that he should take me home so I could rest. I rolled my eyes at him, since I felt one hundred percent fine, but then I grudgingly agreed, since I did have unpacking, washing, mail, bills, phone calls and ugh…maybe I *would* just lie on the couch.

With swift hugs for Jack, Alanna and Imogen, and apologies that we couldn't stay to say goodbye to Halina, who was sleeping downstairs, we made our way to Teren's Prius and began the bumpy journey down their super-long gravel driveway.

It felt odd to be leaving, especially since I hadn't even been in a car in nearly two months. The last time I'd been in Teren's car flashed through my mind, but I immediately pushed the memory aside. I didn't want to connect Teren's vehicle to that awful event. I didn't want to be reminded of it every time we went somewhere.

As we pulled onto the highway that led home, I sighed contently and put my hand on Teren's thigh. He placed his hand over mine and laced our fingers together. Even though the movement was a tender one, I could feel the rigid way he held my hand. If I didn't know any better, I'd say he was being protective, or possessive.

I brought my other hand over to lay it on top of his, making a Teren hand-sandwich. "You all right?" I asked as I clamped our skin together.

He looked over at me, a tight smile on his lips. "Sure, I'm fine."

As he returned his eyes to the road, I could see the tension in his jaw and neck; whatever he really was, it was not fine. "Teren…"

My tone clearly indicated that I didn't buy his answer and I wanted the truth. Sighing, he looked over at me again. His eyes watered, and concern washed over me at seeing his emotion start to bubble up. He shook his head. "What if something happens to you?"

I scrunched my brow, not making the conversational leap with him. Seeing my confusion he explained himself better. "Pregnancy is hard…some women don't make it…" Still looking sad and worried, his eyes drifted back to the road.

Understanding, my hand went to his cheek and brought his eyes back to mine. Knowing his vampiric reflexes could handle driving without both eyes on the road, I made him meet my gaze. "I will be fine. This morning was completely normal." I couldn't help but note the contradiction of me assuring him that everything was fine, now that we were talking about my safety and not his. Things were different when your concern was for another's life, and not your own.

He shook his head free from my grasp and looked towards the road. He didn't need to. He knew this highway so well he could probably drive it blindfolded. "I know, Emma. I know today was fine. But what about tomorrow, or the next day? There is so much that can go wrong, and I can't… If I lose…" He stopped talking and swallowed his painful thought; his eyes darted to my stomach and then back up to me.

I swallowed back my own emotion and leaned over to kiss his shoulder. "I know, Teren. I know." He was terrified of losing any of us. That was the downside of loving someone so much. You throw your heart out there and hope nothing will yank it away and tear it to shreds. Teren couldn't predict what would happen to me, and he was right. Pregnancy wasn't always a cause for celebration. Sometimes pregnancies ended badly. But you couldn't go through life waiting for bad things to happen. I was pretty sure that was how people went mad. I also noted the contradiction in that, and made a mental note to not worry about Teren being exposed so much. Well, I'd try not to.

I rested my head on his shoulder. "Today I'm fine, Teren. Today, we're all fine." I sighed and felt him nod. That was all we had to go on, all any of us had to go on…and it was enough.

Before I knew it, we were back at my adorable, slender home. It was a Victorian townhouse. One of those that was wedged right up to its neighbor, so you could easily walk across all the roofs, if you were so inclined. It had been my grandmother's home, and she'd left it to my mom when she'd passed away. Mom had kept it, for the investment and the sentiment, and I rented it from her at an outstanding rate. It was blue with quaint white shutters and a charming red door. I'd miss it when I eventually moved in with Teren.

He helped me bring in all my stuff and even ran a load of laundry for me while I put the clean clothes away. As I listened to him bustling around downstairs in my laundry room, I thought he was a pretty amazing boyfriend and would surely be an equally amazing husband. Feeling content and happy, and not worried for once, I whispered, "I love you, you know."

Just as I was putting away my last pair of slightly soiled boots, Teren breezed into my doorway. His cool arms slipped around my waist and his chin, rough with stubble, scraped against me as he rested his head in the crook of my neck. "I love you too, you know."

I grinned and a small laugh escaped me as I twisted in his arms. Looking over his handsome face, a frown came to my lips. "I'm going to miss you."

He frowned as well, as he tried to understand what I meant. "Miss me? Am I going somewhere?"

I started to smile, but then I sighed and ran my hands down his shirt. "Yes, you're going home, to get ready to go back to work."

He tilted his head as he thought about that. "Yeah, I suppose I should. You're not coming with me?"

I bit my lip at seeing the clear disappointment on his face. It was endearing how much he wanted me with him. I shook my head though. "I can't. I should get ready too…and I've got a lot of stuff around here to catch up on."

He looked around my bedroom, but his eyes were focused beyond the walls. He was probably thinking about all the things he had to catch up on as well, including picking up his pup from my mom's house. Remembering that, I put a hand on his cheek to return his attention to me. "I could come with you to pick up Spike though? Divert my mom's attention, in case she wants to hug and kiss you to death." I laughed at my joke and a huge grin erupted on my face. I couldn't wait to see my mom and sister again. I'd talked to them often, but hadn't actually visited them in a while.

Teren grinned and ran a finger down my cheek. "Actually, I talked with your mom before we left." He chuckled as he shook his head. "She asked if she could keep Spike until we all got together for dinner on Tuesday. I think she's fallen for him." He gave me a playful wink.

I laughed and then leaned back in his arms as that sank in. "Dinner? Tuesday?" Mom, Ashley, and I, all got together for weekly dinners at a local café that we really loved. We'd been doing it for years and once Teren and I had started getting serious, he'd joined the party. But things had changed recently.

Nodding, Teren said, "Yeah...she assumed the Tuesday night dinners would continue, once you got back." He narrowed his eyes at me, his brow furrowing while he studied my reaction. "I assumed they would too. Was I wrong?"

I shook my head, clearing my expression. "No, no of course we'll start doing that again. I just..." I looked up at him. "What are *you* going to do?"

He looked at the floor, his arms around my waist tightening while he considered his options. Finally, he lifted his head and sighed. With a shrug he said, "I guess I'll be running late at work, and join you just after dessert."

I stared at his face for a moment, a sudden sadness hitting me that we couldn't have a normal, happy meal with my family, not if he'd just be sitting there watching everyone else eat. How would we explain that? I brought a hand up to his face. He closed his eyes at the contact and leaned into the warmth of my skin. "That won't work forever, Teren."

Opening his eyes, he sighed. "I know."

We both stared at each for a moment longer and then he leaned in to give me a goodbye kiss. I allowed myself to get lost in it, to forget the downside of dating a vampire and remember that there were advantages too. And Teren made forgetting pretty easy—he was an unbelievable kisser. His mouth and tongue could do things that I was beginning to believe were part of his supernatural ability, for no human I'd ever kissed had made me feel it through every cell in my body. As my fingers were sliding through his thick hair and the backs of my legs were bumping up against my bed, he started chuckling. I broke contact with him, a little surprised to find my heart was racing and my breath was noticeably faster. Like I said, great kisser.

His hands came up to cup my cheeks, gently pushing me back from where I'd been attempting to find his lips again. "I should get going." His eyes swept over my room. "Let you get to work on your affairs."

My body could have cared less about my affairs and I knew he was completely aware of that. I tried to kiss him again, but he held me back; a smug look was on his face. I sighed in irritation and pulled away. "Fine." Using all my willpower to step away from him, I gave him a scathing glare. "You don't play fair."

Laughing, he reached out for me. I ignored the gesture. Smirking, he shook his head and walked over to give me a platonic kiss on the cheek. In my ear he whispered, "You drive me crazy, every second of every day. You have no idea how much I'll be missing you tonight." He stepped into me, his body pressing against my side. I closed my eyes and held my breath. His breath, cool on my ear and neck, gave me delightful shivers. "If I can make you feel, just once, what I feel constantly…well, I think that's very fair."

His lips closed around my ear lobe, and I groaned and turned my head to find him. He wasn't there. Feeling like I was in some weird, semi-drugged state, I blinked and looked around my empty bedroom. Faintly, I could hear laughing coming from downstairs, and then I heard my front door opening.

"Jerk!" I yelled through the doorway where my honey had just blurred away, leaving me all riled up and alone. Only soft chuckling answered me as my front door closed.

I let out a frustrated sigh, then decided to forego all of the things on my to-do list and do the one thing my body really wanted to do right now. I took a bath.

Monday morning began with me fighting the urge to throw my alarm clock across the room. It had been a long time since I'd needed to use one. While Teren's and my time on the ranch wasn't exactly Club Med, it had been a true vacation in the sense that we hadn't needed to be awake at a certain hour. We'd usually woken at breakfast time, so I could partake in Alanna's wonderful cooking, but it had been a leisurely, relaxing wakeup. Not the jarring, forced-from-sleep annoyance that was an alarm going off by my ear.

Grunting some sort of nonverbal objection, I turned it off and got up to go get ready for the day. I changed into my work clothes, a nice formfitting pantsuit with an adorable, fitted jacket, and curled my wavy hair, leaving it loose around my shoulders. With a nice pair of heels and my jacket open, showing off my deep cut, lacy top, which was about as sexy as I could dress at work, without getting a warning from the HR department, I grabbed a quick breakfast and hopped into my cute little yellow VW bug. I smiled as I drove it to work; I'd missed my cheery little car.

I started feeling a little less cheery as I pulled into the parking lot and my stomach started questioning my meal choice. I sat in my car, breathing slowly and carefully through my mouth. I prayed for my stomach to settle down and accept the food I'd given it. Seriously…we needed to work together on this, or this pregnancy was going to be a long one.

Finally, my body agreed with my head and the nausea passed. With one last quick exhale, I slapped on my professional face and headed for the doors. I was assaulted long before I ever got to my cubicle. A striking blonde squealed and wrapped her arms around me. The sudden movement jarred me back a step and my stomach firmly objected to the quick shift in direction.

As my face surely went through several shades of green, I hugged the woman embracing me for dear life, and prayed, yet again, not to lose it. The beautiful woman pulled away from me, a happy glow on her pixyish face. "Emma! God, we've missed you. How was your vacation?"

I breathed as nonchalantly as I could through my mouth, as I quickly threw on a bright smile. "It was great, Tracey. How were things here?"

She tossed her hand out in a casual manner. "Oh, the same." We continued down the aisle way to my desk, and my stomach thankfully relaxed. Tracey subtly pointed at various people that we worked with as we walked. "Stressed over a bad investment. Wife had a baby last week. Bitchy…just 'cuz. Having an affair…" she pointed at a petite brunette and then looked around until she spotted a middle-aged man near the break room, "with him." She turned back to me and barely contained a giggle. "I totally heard them going at it in the supply closet last week."

I quickly looked away from the woman as she met eyes with me. As we reached my "home away from home," Tracey's stream of gossip died and she leaned against my wall. "How is Teren's dad?" she asked, her face shifting into an adorable frown.

I turned into my cubicle here at Sampson, Neilson and Peterson, and opened the bottom drawer of my desk to shove my full purse in it. I hadn't gotten any better at not carrying my life around with me. I smiled at Tracey's question, as I straightened and turned back to her. Teren's dad falling ill was the excuse we'd given everybody for our extended time away. It had worked pretty well as a reason for Teren to be gone for such a long time. I mean, it wasn't like we could tell everyone the truth, that Teren was dying and reanimating, and he'd needed to be away from innocent people when he'd done it.

"He's…as good as new." I shrugged and Tracey smiled. "You'd never even know that anything had ever been wrong with him." I started to giggle, as I thought of Teren and not his dad. You really wouldn't know he'd passed away, at least, not by looking at him. Tracey cocked her head at my seemingly inappropriate laugh, but she didn't say anything. I had a habit of laughing at odd times and my friends were just used to that about me.

"That's great, Emma. Tell Teren I'm glad his dad is all right."

A loud throat cleared, and Tracey and I both shifted our attention. Behind Tracey was a large, dowdy woman who always reminded me of an unpleasant version of a fifties sitcom wife. She routinely dressed in long skirts and shapeless blouses, and there was even a large string of pearls around her plump neck. Her brown hair, that had mostly turned gray, was always pulled into a tight, unforgiving bun that complemented her general attitude. She tended to have a perpetual scowl plastered on her face, and seemed to look at everyone as if they were doing something inappropriate.

Clarice. Unfortunately, she was my boss. She was currently looking at Tracey with undisguised malice. She was *not* Tracey's boss. "Don't you have somewhere to be?" she grumbled at her.

Tracey grinned at me. "Have fun. Glad you're back." She smirked at Clarice and then left me alone with the sour woman.

"So, you remembered where the building was. Kudos." She handed me what had to be a two foot stack of paperwork. As I grabbed it, she pointed to an equally large stack of papers already sitting on my desk. "These are all new clients that came in while you were gone." Her flat lips turned up into a tiny grin. "Familiarize yourself, and get them all entered into the system."

And with that, she turned and left. No, we missed you, welcome back. No, did you have a good time? No, did everything turn out okay? No, did your boyfriend knock you up while you were gone? Nope, nothing but professionalism from Clarice.

I sighed and sat down, adding the large stack to the stack already there. I knew coming back would be a lot of work, but damn. The accounting firm I worked at was an up and coming one and it seemed like they'd taken off, right as I'd left. As I started sifting through the paperwork, I hoped I'd run into an interesting file—maybe a celebrity or a socialite or something.

Just as I was wondering how Teren was faring at his first day back at the magazine, I heard my phone chirping in my purse. Clarice tended to frown on cell phones at the desk. I quickly looked into her office directly across from mine. She was absent, most likely helping her boss, Mr. Peterson. I took advantage and opened the drawer to rifle through my bag and find my cell phone.

Pulling out my cute, pink flip phone, I saw a text from Teren. *'Miss you. How's it going?'*

I glanced up at her office again and then quickly typed back a response. *'Miss you too. I'm drowning in paperwork. You?'*

My phone chirped in my hand, a second after I'd hit send. *'Good, just finished my article. No fondling yet.'* I smiled and shook my head, both at the fact that he'd already whipped out an article, and that he was still teasing me about my overcautious fears. Just as I was about to respond, my phone went off again. *'Are you coming over tonight? I can't sleep alone again.'*

I quietly giggled and bit my lip as I responded with, *'Yes.'*

His response was again a quick one, and I smiled at the image of him sitting at his desk, speed-typing messages to me. *'Good, I missed you…and the kids. Anymore sickness?'*

His loving concern for me warmed my heart. *'No…almost threw up on Tracey, but luckily didn't. She wishes your dad well.'*

I pictured him laughing at my answer as his reply flashed on my phone. *'I would have loved to hear how you'd explain away ralphing on her. I'm glad you're okay. I'll add Tracey's wishes to my coworkers. My dad will get a big head, with how much sympathy he's been receiving today.'*

I let out a happy sigh as I thought of my tall, dark and dreamy, undead man. Just as I was going to tell him I should get back to work, the phone alerted me again. *'So…what are you wearing?'*

I laughed out loud and was startled to almost incontinence when a stack of even more papers slapped down on my desk. Breathing heavier, I raised my eyes to Clarice. Hers were narrowed. "Since you have free time," she nearly sneered, "here are some reports I need copied…now."

"Sorry, yes, Clarice." I gave her an apologetic smile as she sauntered back to her desk in a huff. Typing Teren a quick goodbye, I shoved my phone back into my purse, and got back to my expanded work pile.

By the end of the day, I couldn't believe how tired I was. I'd nearly forgotten what a full eight hours of work entailed. True, Teren and I had helped out on the ranch, and I'd fallen asleep from exhaustion more than once during our stay there, but there was something vastly different about being outside in the fresh country air, helping to wrangle cattle with an assortment of super-speedy, unnaturally strong vampires, than being in a small, fluorescent-lit office space with paperwork up to your eyebrows. I knew it would get better as I got more caught up, but, at the moment, shoveling cow poop again sounded fabulous.

Tracey popped around to my side of the cubicle with no sign of fatigue on her sprightly face, and asked if I'd be coming back to the gym as well. Tracey and I had been taking kickboxing there a couple times a week for the last few years. While I loved the workout, and the feeling of self-assurance it gave me, I was really too tired to contemplate moving that aggressively right now.

"No, I think I'll pass tonight." I yawned halfway through my sentence and Tracey laughed at me.

"All right. Ben will be bummed." She winked at me. "He's subbing tonight."

I grinned at the look of love on her face. She had met Ben while he'd been subbing for our regular teacher during a kickboxing class. They'd hit it off right away and, despite a rocky patch, they were still together.

I yawned and grabbed my purse. "Tell him I said hi. Teren too." Ben and Teren had hit it off too, and they were friends, I guess. As close as Teren was friends with anyone who didn't know his secret. He had a natural tendency to keep people just slightly away from him. Honestly, he did that with me too sometimes, which had led to some pretty spectacular fights in these last seven months, but I did understand his reluctance to let people in; he never knew for sure who was going to stick around.

Tracey nodded. "I will. See you tomorrow, Emma."

I watched her leave and yet another yawn escaped me. Wondering why I was so exhausted, I looked down at my still flat stomach. "Are you guys making me tired?" I murmured to myself.

A throat clearing made me look up. Thinking that someone had heard my comment made my heart surge. I wasn't prepared to tell the world I was pregnant. I sort of wanted to get through the wedding part first...and I was still a little reluctant to bring that up, too. Not that I was embarrassed, no way, but we were getting married fast, and I was only too aware that superfast weddings usually meant one thing. And I was fairly certain that if anyone asked me directly if I were pregnant, I'd blush, giggle, and squeal like an imbecile.

Clarice narrowed her eyes at me as she shook her head. "You didn't get as much done as I'd hoped...but you did a good job with what you managed to finish, I suppose. Don't be late tomorrow." With that, she waddled down the hall to the exit.

Pleased that she hadn't heard me talking to the embryos in my belly and that she'd just given me a compliment, I couldn't help but smile. True, it was a very backhanded compliment, but that's what you got with Clarice—a tiny drop of honey with a huge dollop of vinegar. To keep working here, and remain sane, you learned to grasp that sweetness wherever you found it.

Still smiling at the rare words of approval, I drove myself directly to Teren's place. His car was in his half-circle drive when I got there, and I'd no sooner shut off my vehicle than he was standing at my door, opening it for me. I smiled at his super senses and his super sweetness, and let him pull me into a hug. I sighed as his arms wrapped around me, glad that our first days back had gone well. And considering that he hadn't been staked at work, I'd say they went very well.

We pulled apart from each other and my eyes traveled down his well-dressed body. It had been a while since I'd seen him in anything but worn jeans and boots, and while he looked amazing in those clothes, I'd almost forgotten how nicely he cleaned up. His khaki slacks and crisp, light blue dress shirt hugged his body perfectly. He was...yummy.

I bit my lip as I studied the man who would eternally look yummy. His hand cupped my cheek as my gaze traveled farther down his body. "You okay?" he whispered. That brought my attention back to his face and I looked up to see him frowning at me; concern was clear in the blue depths. "You look exhausted," he added.

I leaned in to give him a quick kiss. "Yeah, I guess I am." My fingers resting along his neck started threading through the shorter layers of his hair. He smiled as he gazed down at me. "I've been on vacation for too long. There was just a lot to take care of today."

He cocked his head at me, then swiftly swept me into his arms. I squeaked in surprise as I hugged him tighter. "Well, let me take care of *you* now then."

I settled my head into the crook of his neck and sighed contently. "Okay..."

He walked with me to his impressive, two-story home. It wasn't as impressive as his parents' spread, but still, for highly sought after San Francisco real estate, it was a nice place. He stopped at his wrought iron and wood front door and effortlessly held me with one arm, while opening the door with the other. It made me laugh that he hadn't had to adjust me at all while he did that. Being around his strength made me feel weightless, and that was a very good feeling for a soon-to-be-mammoth girl to have.

Teren kicked the door closed behind us and walked me to the most comfortable couch in the world. He laid me down on the massive, white leather behemoth, kissed my forehead, removed my shoes, and wrapped me in a blanket. Smiling at his sweetness, I grabbed his arm as he started to move away. The chill of his skin crept up my fingers, but the thrill of touching him made that iciness feel warm as it traveled up my arm.

He smiled as he looked down on me all snuggled on his couch. "I'm just going to make you something to eat," he softly said.

I nodded and tilted my head up. He obligingly leaned down to kiss me. "What about you," I muttered as his lips pulled away.

"I was hungry after work, so I already ate," he said as he straightened.

I cocked my head, wondering what he'd had for dinner. His family generally seemed to only eat a few pints once a day, but Teren was still pretty new, and needed to eat a couple times throughout the day. It wouldn't hurt him or anything if he didn't, he just got…grumpy, and tired. At the ranch, that wasn't a big deal, there was lots of food, but here? He smiled at my silent concern. "Mom sent me home with a care package. I'm good for a while."

A smile graced my lips. Of course his mother would take care of him. Actually, it wouldn't surprise me if she came by weekly with a stash for him. She was just a caretaker like that. I instantly stopped worrying about what he'd find to eat. His family would never let him starve. Happy, I relaxed back into the couch, closed my eyes, and let the feeling of exhaustion sweep over me.

I was awakened from a particularly steamy dream a while later, by the smell of pasta directly under my nose. I cracked open my eyes and saw a plate of something rich, creamy and incredibly fattening piled high in front of my face. Teren gave me a half-smile as he watched me come alive again.

"I was wondering whether I should wake you or join you." His half-grin turned a little devilish. "That sounded like a good dream."

I took the plate from him as I straightened on the couch. Immediately plowing into the food as my stomach rumbled, I smiled around the fork in my mouth. "It was. Maybe I'll show you later."

His eyes widened with interest as he took a sip from the goblet in his hands. I watched him drink a few swallows of what looked like really deep, red wine. I knew it wasn't wine though, especially with how his teeth had dropped down. Leaning back on the couch, he watched me eat as well. Sighing in contentment, I placed my shoeless feet on his lap. He grinned and began to rub them while he drank his blood.

I pointed to his glass with my fork. "You saved some?"

He shrugged and pointed at my plate. "I told you once before that we'd still eat together. I meant it." Smiling, he took another small sip.

I shook my head at the cute look on his face and continued shoveling food into my mouth, conscious of the fact that I wasn't nearly as cute. I didn't care though—I was starving. Before I knew it, the pasta was gone and I was considering licking the sauce from the plate. Teren could cook; even dead he was amazing.

He laughed as he gauged the hungry expression on my face. "I'm glad you liked it." His brows drew together as he took my empty plate from me. "I only hope you can keep it down."

He said that with concern in his voice, and I put a hand on my stomach as I smiled. "Yes, I think they're very happy with Daddy." He gave me a breathtaking grin and leaned down to kiss me. When he pulled away, I was suddenly equally happy with him, but in a very different way.

He tilted his head, taking in my body language, then lightly shook it as he straightened. "I'm gonna clean up." He pointed at me with his empty glass. "You...rest." Smiling to himself, he turned and made his way through the arch that led into a kitchen most women would die for.

I sat on the couch, snuggled in my blanket, for as long as my body would allow, but he was right when he'd said my dream had been a good one. And he was really right when he'd offered to join me. With my stomach full and content, and my body feeling awake and carefree, I decided I'd rested enough. I wanted to be a little more...active.

Hoping to catch him by surprise, I stealthily got up and crept into the kitchen. Although that was pretty improbable, he didn't react to my entrance. He only continued absentmindedly rinsing dishes before putting them in the dishwasher. Thinking I'd actually done it, I tiptoed across the tile floor. I was just about to throw my arms around his waist, when he spoke.

"Aren't you supposed to be resting?" Amused at my attempt to sneak up on him, his lips twisted into a smile. I grunted in irritation and casually slung my arms around his waist, since my element of surprise was gone. Darn super ears.

"You're no fun," I muttered into the back of his shirt; I could feel him softly laughing.

Suddenly, he twisted around to face me. "I'm plenty of fun." He raised an eyebrow as he slipped his arms around my waist. "You're just noisy."

I smirked at his comment, but then his lips lowered to mine and I remembered what I'd come in here for in the first place. Eager, I leaned into his embrace and deepened our kiss. His hands tightened around my waist while mine ran through his hair. He angled his mouth, sweeping more of that marvelous tongue along mine, and a groan left me as my body started to heat.

His fingers reached down to cup my backside and a low rumble sounded in his chest. Loving what that noise did to my already aroused body, I pressed my hips flush to his; he was equally aroused by me. Our lips never stopping, my hands slid down his shirt and casually popped open the buttons. When I had the last button free, I slid the fabric over his cool shoulders. Helping me, his fingers came up to pull his shirt free from his slacks.

We pulled apart and I took the opportunity to appreciate his muscled perfection. My fingertips lightly trailed along his tan skin. While nothing happened physically, by the quick intake of breath, I was sure he'd have goose bumps if his skin were normal.

As his lips lowered to my neck, his hands pulled off my jacket. I sighed at his caress and tilted my head, to give him all the access he needed to explore the surging vein he loved so much. He growled again as his tongue flicked over the surface, stoking the already unbearable ache building in me.

My hands ran up his back as his fingers ran over my lacy camisole, feeling my breasts through the thin, seductive fabric. Suddenly, he pushed me back into the island counter. I gasped as the hardness of his body pressed up against me, trapping me against the hardness of the counter behind me. Wanting him inside of me already, I brought my leg up his thigh. He pulled back to look at me, passion clouding the perfect paleness of his eyes. He took a split second to tear off my shirt and then a slow smile lit his lips as he stared unabashedly at the black, lacy bra I was wearing.

Watching his eyes drink me in, I calmly reached around and unclasped the bra, letting it spring free and drop to the floor. His smile fell and his expression turned wondrous. I smiled at his reaction, even after all this time, and urged his face down to me, to feel what was his. He went freely, his lips closing over a nipple and gently sucking. My leg clasped him tighter as his name fell off my tongue. My hand in his hair tightened as he switched sides. His hand firmly pulled my hips into him. I swear he was even harder, as hard as the granite counter pressing against my ass.

Oh hell…

As I closed my eyes and let my head fall back, I was vaguely aware of him lifting me up. My legs automatically encircled his waist. Then I felt air rushing past me. By the time I opened my eyes, we were in his bedroom, and he was pulling back his covers and lying me down on his silky sheets. A slight shiver went through me as the cool fabric hit my back, and his cool skin rested on my stomach. Eager to find his mouth again, I ignored being enveloped by the chill and pulled him tighter to me.

His hands worked on my pants, undoing and removing them in a matter of seconds. Mine worked on his more clumsily. He pulled away from my body for a fraction of a second and when he returned, I could feel the cool, naked length of him pressed against the warm length of me. Desire and a surging rush of anticipation shot through me at what I knew was coming. My breath came faster, and my lips on his were more insistent, as my fingers tugged at the last barrier between us, the tiny scrap of material around my hips that was passing for underwear.

He looked down my bare body, groaned, and his fingers joined mine in tugging my underwear off. In our eagerness, the delicate fabric ripped and I cringed at the slightly painful sensation, then groaned at the hotness of him destroying my underwear. He chuckled and tossed the ruined pieces aside. "Sorry," he muttered, before his lips lowered to my breast.

I was about to say don't worry about it, when a couple long fingers slid between my thighs. I lost the ability for coherent speech after that. Making vague erotic noises, I closed my eyes and reveled in that wonderfully chilly touch. He eventually warmed to my considerably hotter temperature and those talented fingers began working into a rhythm that was quickly going to bring me to climax. Just as I was panting and clutching at his shoulders, he removed them.

I gasped and sought his lips, needing him now more than ever. He ferociously kissed me, his cool body pressing into mine. Separating from my mouth, he ran his lips down my shoulder. He glanced up at me with an almost feral passion in his eyes, then he dragged his tongue over the healing wounds on my shoulder. Closing his eyes, he shuddered and his teeth dropped to sharp fangs at the memory of drinking from me.

I bit my lip and squirmed as I watched him. I wanted him to bite again, but I knew he wouldn't, not so soon after feeding on me. He opened his eyes, and his teeth automatically retracted. I grabbed his cheek. "No, leave them out." He tilted his head at me and in a low, breathy voice I added, "It's…hot."

He dropped his fangs, and then he crashed his lips back to mine, careful to not hurt me with his sharp canines. I was less careful and nearly attacked him with my need. Then he blurringly fast flipped us over, so I was straddling him. With his superhuman strength, he deadweight-lifted my hips and lowered me directly onto him. An animalistic growl escaped him and a loud moan left me.

I still wasn't used to the coolness of him filling me. It was such a shockingly erotic experience, that every time it brought me right to the edge of climaxing—and on occasion, it did. His body would eventually acclimate to mine, but that first thrust was something so incredible, it nearly did me in every time. Sometimes I wished his body wouldn't warm with mine. The hot/cold sensation was *that* remarkable.

He sat up with me as I straddled him, my knees along his hips. He laid his head against my chest as I rocked against him, slow at first and then with a growing urgency. As his body warmed along the outside of me, my body heated to near inferno levels from the inside. His strong hands grasped my hips, pulling me onto his body even more. He filled me so deeply that I almost couldn't take it. My release came hard and fast, and I clenched around him, inside and outside. The cry escaping my mouth hardly did the explosion within me justice.

Just as I hit the very peak of it, when I was sure I actually *would* explode, his body stiffened under me and he let out a long, low groan. His head rocked back and forth along my chest as he came inside of me. Clutching him tighter, I kissed his cheek and whispered how much I loved him as I came down off my high.

Afterwards, we slumped against each other, almost holding the other up. Then he exhaled and lifted his head to look at me. His earlier passion was replaced with a calm, deep love, and his fangs were still extended. That was either for my benefit, or he'd simply forgotten about them at this point. "I love you," he whispered, before kissing me.

"I love you too," I whispered back.

He gently helped me off of him and I rolled onto my back. Settling onto his silky sheets, I held my arms open for him. He smiled, his fangs retracting, then he laid on top of me and intertwined our legs. I cradled his head and pulled him down to my chest. He exhaled a cool breath, making my skin pebble, as he nestled between my breasts. With a contented, purring noise, he wrapped his arms under me and held me tight.

Just when I felt my heart shifting back to normal, my breath following and sleep beckoning, Teren popped up on his hands, and crouched low over my body. I started at his sudden movement and furrowed my brow, puzzled. Teren wasn't looking at me though; his head was tilted to the side and he was staring past me, listening. Just as I was going to ask him what was wrong, his eyes shifted focus and he stared at me.

"Did you hear that?" he whispered.

I twisted my face into an expression that had to be comical. Aside from my own breath, I heard nothing. "What?" He suddenly sat up straight, and I shivered as his warm-compared-to-the-air body was ripped away from me. "Teren?"

He looked at the door and then back to me. With a serious face he whispered, "Stay here," and then he blurred from the room, grabbing his pants as he streaked away.

Irritated at my post-coital bliss being snatched away from me, and worried about what could have riled him, I sat up and pulled the sheets around me. "Damn it," I muttered, to no one in particular.

Chapter 3 – Some Secrets Are Just Hard to Keep

The sun had set outside, but a nearby streetlamp cast a reddish light through Teren's open windows, bathing everything in his room with an almost fire-lit glow. I stood and debated if I really should stay where he'd told me to, or if I should leave and investigate as well. I knew I wouldn't be able to pinpoint the mysterious sound like Teren could, but I was pretty handy in bad situations, if that's what this was.

A knot tightened in my stomach and I started to worry. Sure, Teren was stronger now than before his conversion, and he was much harder to kill, since he could do the super-healy thing, but he wasn't invincible. And we knew with certainty that there were whack jobs out there who wanted him removed from this world, just because of what he was. Some people couldn't look past the prejudices.

Shivering and rubbing my bare arms, I walked over to his closet and pulled down one of his dress shirts. It was long on me, completely covering my backside and hitting my legs mid-thigh. It cut the slight coldness in the air considerably though. I glanced around his closet, our closet soon, and looked for anything weapon-like. All I saw were clothes; Teren really didn't have much in the way of self-defense.

I tiptoed back to the bedroom, not sure why I was being quiet, but feeling the need to not make a sound. The red-orange light of the lamp outside flashed on various hard objects around the room—the TV remote, a particularly thick book he was reading on his nightstand, his laptop sitting on a chair tucked under his window. I didn't see anything great, but if we *were* going down tonight, we were going down swinging. I ended up grabbing an umbrella propped up by his bathroom door. With a hand on my stomach, I decided that I would do what my vampire fiancé had requested of me, and stay put, for the children's sake. Wanting an easier spot to defend, I backed into the bathroom, crouched down low, and held my cheap umbrella like it was a sturdy baseball bat.

I wasn't sure how long I waited there, but it felt like an eternity. Teren could search every nook and cranny of this house in a matter of minutes, so the longer I waited, the longer I was positive something horrible had happened to him. As time ominously ticked by, and my legs started protesting the rigid posture I was keeping them in, tears started stinging my eyes. It couldn't end like this. I couldn't have just made love to him and then lost him, all in a matter of moments. He was supposed to be mine forever. That was the deal. We were fated. We were destined to have a long life full of love, happiness, children and grandchildren. That was what getting through his hard changeover had meant for us—that we were free to love each other peacefully, for the rest of my life. Not for him to be whisked away forever because he "heard something."

I felt the tears brimming as my overactive imagination started playing out all the different scenarios in which some intruder might have gotten the best of him. In my head, I watched him die a hundred times over. I felt the tears course down my cheeks as I listened for any sound that he was okay.

Just as my arms were beginning to shake from the tension I was holding in them, the bathroom door started to swing open. Panic and fear made me cock back my makeshift weapon; I swung it around as soon as the figure walked into my sanctuary. In my self-riled turmoil, I didn't even register who I was swinging at until he reached up and calmly grabbed the stupid, fragile umbrella. It bent a little as he yanked it out of my hands.

"What are you doing, Emma?"

Teren was standing right in front of me, half-dressed and staring at me, like he thought I'd possibly gone mental in his absence. As I felt a sob rising in my throat, I started to think that maybe I *had* gone mental. I brought my hands to my face as the relief mixed with the icy edge of fear still lingering in my system. Concern broke over Teren's face at seeing me on the verge of hysterics, and he instantly had me in his arms. Sweeping me up, he cradled me like a child.

"Baby, it's okay. You're okay. You're okay." He repeated it over and over while he walked me back to his bed. He continuously stroked a hand down my back while he placed dozens of kisses along my forehead. I tried to hold back the stupid tears, but they were coming regardless. Teren laid me down and got in bed next to me. I embarrassingly clenched him tight when he moved to cover me with his blankets. Once I was safe and cocooned in his bed, with my arms firmly around him, his hands came up to cup my cheeks. Sweeping his thumbs across them, he tried to dry my concerned tears; on his face was an expression of confused compassion. "Emma?" he whispered.

Between hiccups and stuttered breaths, I managed to get out, "I thought...something...happened...to you."

Understanding, he swept me into a tight embrace and rubbed my back. "Oh God, I'm sorry, Emma. " Pulling away, he searched my eyes. "I'm fine, baby. Okay?"

Willing my body to calm down, I nodded. Before I could protest or stop him, he zipped out of bed, securely closed his heavy curtains, then returned to me. He kept his eyes open, staring at me, and the phosphorescent glow of the whites of his eyes became brighter as the room darkened. That was another vampire effect—the glowing eyes. It was only apparent if they were somewhere really dark, say hunting their prey late at night. It had an almost hypnotic-like effect, to relax their prey into submission...as if they needed the extra help getting humans to submit to their power.

It did have a calming influence though, and my mind started blanking out as that light absorbed me into its peace. I felt my heart even and my breathing slow to the low and long breaths people take while they're sleeping. I was so relaxed, that if he had told me to close my eyes and go to sleep, I probably would have. But he didn't try any hypnotic parlor tricks on me—he knew better than that. Instead he twisted to turn on the lamp on his nightstand.

"Better?" he asked, as I blinked in the sudden brightness.

Taking in his back-to-normal blue eyes, I nodded. "Yes, sorry I freaked out."

Shaking his head, he kissed my nose. "I'm sorry I worried you. I just thought I heard..." His voice drifted off and he bit his lip. After a second he shook his head and let out a soft sigh. "I must have been hearing things though." He shrugged. "I searched everywhere, inside and outside, but I couldn't find anything...out of place." He shrugged again and held me close, cradling my head to his chest. "I'm so sorry I worried you, Emma."

I nodded against his skin, amazed at how quickly I'd imagined the worst. "You didn't do anything wrong, Teren. I guess I'm still a little...frazzled...by what happened to us." I said that last part barely above a whisper. I hated to even talk about it.

Pulling away from me, Teren rested his forehead against mine. "I would never let anyone harm you, Emma. You or the kids. Ever." He practically growled the words and I relaxed as the strength in his voice gave me confidence. He wouldn't, and things were different now. He was different—stronger. Any hunter we encountered from here on out would have their hands full with Teren Adams.

Leaning up, I gave him a soft kiss. "I know, baby. I feel safe with you." I whispered, as I laid my head back down on his chest.

"And you *are* safe with me," he said as I closed my eyes.

My earlier exhaustion crept up on me, adding to my emotionally draining last few moments. I was half-asleep when I responded with, "I know..."

Then I was fully asleep.

The next morning I awoke when the scratchy stubble of Teren's jaw rubbed against my neck as he kissed me. He whispered that he had to go to work, but I could stay and sleep in a little if I wanted, since he'd run to my house and picked up some stuff for me...including another pair of underwear. I chuckled, thinking about our romp last night and considering the fact that when he said "run," he probably meant that literally.

With a swift kiss, we parted ways for the day. Teren worked an hour before me; he was a much nicer alarm clock than I'd had yesterday. I smiled as I stretched out on his luxurious bed and thought about what waking up like this every day would be like.

After a while, I got up and walked to the bathroom. Flashes of freaking out in this room came to me, but I tried to push them back to the farthest recesses of my brain. As strong as I tried to be, what had happened to us had been traumatic, and the side effects still showed themselves sometimes. I knew I wasn't alone either. As strong as Teren tried to be, when he said things like he had last night, the conviction in his voice betrayed his true fear. He was worried that he wouldn't be able to stop someone from hurting me again. In a way, I suppose he felt like he'd let me down before. I didn't feel that way though. There was no way either one of us could have been prepared for what that maniac had put us through.

I dressed for my day, smiling at the rose Teren had placed upon my stack of fresh clothes, and pursing my lips in amusement at the tiny scraps of fabric he'd picked out for my undergarments. With a shake of my head, I put on the red thong with its matching demi-bra and garter belts. That's right, he'd picked out garter belts. Then I covered up all the sexiness with a relatively chaste long gray skirt and fitted black blouse. Fixing my hair and makeup, I was on the road, snacking on a bagel, in no time.

My day at work was just as exhausting as my first day back, with Tracey asking more questions about life on a ranch. I gave her pretty honest answers, since the day-to-day activities there really had nothing supernatural about them. As we conversed throughout the day, I considered telling her about the wedding. I imagined how excited she'd be, and how much of a help she'd be in the whole planning process. Of course, she'd be a bridesmaid and of course, she'd have an opinion on her dress. I held off though. I wanted to tell my family first, and since tonight was our weekly dinner, it would be the perfect opportunity to tell them.

I spent the rest of my shift daydreaming about dresses, flowers, and Teren all decked out in a tux. Before I knew it, Clarice was grunting some sort of a goodbye, and murmuring that she wished I'd get caught up already, and Tracey was calling out goodnight and telling me to say hi to my sister for her.

I called Ashley before I left, to make sure tonight was still on and to let her know that Teren would be late. Of course, she knew the real reason why he wouldn't be joining us for a meal—she knew exactly what Teren was—but she also lived with Mom and could let her know for me, thus sparing me a direct lie. As I pulled into the café a short while later, I called Teren, to let him know I was here and meeting with everyone, and to tell him I wished he was here too.

He shared my sentiment and told me he'd wait an hour or so and then join us. I sighed as I hung up the phone with him and cracked open my car door. It wasn't that I couldn't handle being without him for an evening or anything. I just liked having him around, and wished he could partake in things that normal guys could, like dinners with the soon-to-be in-laws.

The hostess, Marie, greeted me by name, told me she was glad I was back, and then gave me a brief hug. My family had been coming here for a while and everyone here knew us. It made me happy that my absence over the past few weeks had been noticed, and I'd been missed.

I'd beaten my mom and sister to the café, so she ushered me back to our usual table and set me up with a glass of water while I waited. I sighed and took a long drink, suddenly feeling parched. My eyes aching, I leaned my head back on the cushion of the bench seat and listened to the soothing jazz playing softly in the background.

I felt the cushion beside me compress and opened my eyes as I turned my head. "Rise and shine, sleepy." A beautiful, scarred face was giving me a warm smile, and an ache went through me. I'd gone too long without seeing that face.

"Hey, Ash." I exclaimed as I gave her an eager hug.

The effects of the horrible fire that Ashley had survived as a child were lasting ones. Even after dozens of surgeries, she had scarring over most of her body. But her physical appearance was only that—physical. It did nothing to dampen her spirit or dissuade her from her dream of being a nurse in the burn unit. She was in her second year of school and nothing would keep her from that goal— not the stares, not the whispers, and not the lack of a love life. But, as she pulled apart from me and I saw the glow in her warm brown eyes, I couldn't help but see what Teren had very correctly informed me of once—that despite all that life had thrown at her, she was happy.

"I missed you," I softly said, as I ran a hand down the side of her head that could still grow hair. Like her eyes, her hair matched mine too. I couldn't help but think that if the fire had never happened, we'd be near twins.

She snuggled into my side. "I missed you too."

Our mother, a plump, happy woman, took the seat opposite us and beamed at her daughters. I beamed right back at her, missing her just as much as I'd missed my sister. Phone calls were great and all, but they weren't the same as being face to face with someone, and I was used to seeing these two weekly, if not more. I reached out and grabbed Mom's hand, thinking that her graying hair had gone a little grayer in my absence.

"We missed you, honey. How was the ranch?" Her eyes lit up at the romantic notion she had of life on a ranch. I instantly remembered the time I'd scraped dead skin from between a cow's toes, but decided not to burst her idyllic picture.

"It was great, Mom, and Teren's dad is doing so much better."

She leaned back and grinned at me, pride clear on her face as she thought about her daughter stoically helping out an ill man and his young wife. I felt a little guilty that my mom had to be told the cover story, but she didn't know the truth and couldn't know it. Unlike my sister, she wouldn't handle me being with a vampire very well. She was a mom, and she'd always be a mom, and I didn't want her hair going white over constantly worrying about my safety. And even though I now agreed that her fears were justified ones, letting her in on the secret would only hurt her. In this case, the lie was better, so I slapped on a grin and committed myself to telling it.

I told her about the aspects I could talk about, while our usual waitress, Debby, came over to take our orders. She joined our conversation, and everyone laughed, enjoying my stories. A general "aah" went over the crowd as I reminisced about Teren helping a cow deliver her calf. Tears may have sprung up as I thought back to a certain night a couple weeks ago. Not him birthing cattle, although, that had been awfully sweet. Gross, but sweet. No, my tears were over the tiny growing babies in my belly, and the thought of Teren helping to birth them. At least he'd have experience.

I shockingly ordered something other than my standard Panini, which caused a moment of stunned silence to go around our group. After Debby left with our orders, the conversation drifted back to Teren. When my mom asked what had held him up at work, I gave her a vague response of "a deadline." Since he worked for a magazine, that excuse came in handy, even though I didn't think Teren had ever been under the gun for a deadline in his life. He was…fast.

We all dug into our food when it arrived moments later. My stomach rumbled at the heaping plate of pasta in front of me, and then it churned for just a second. I slowly inhaled through my nose and stared at a circular stain on the table to distract myself. I could not throw up here; that would certainly raise some questions. And as Ashley was seated on the edge of the bench and probably wouldn't be able to scoot out of the way quick enough, if I was going to vomit, I was going to do it right here at the table. I closed my eyes and begged my body to return to normal.

"Are you all right, Emma?" My mother asked from across the table.

I made myself open my eyes and look at her as confidently as I could. I was sure I was paler, but I hoped my smile was distracting enough that she wouldn't notice. "Of course, Mom." I also made myself pick up my fork and dig into my food, even though my rumbling stomach was warning me not to. Praying I wasn't making a tactical error, I swallowed a huge mouthful of pasta.

Mom nodded, went back to her French toast, and continued on with a story about her friend's daughter running off with a married man. I listened to her, concentrating more on the sounds of the words than the details of the story, and eventually my stomach stopped protesting. Then, as if something had switched inside of me, my stomach became ravenous and I inhaled my food. Mom and Ash both cocked an eyebrow at me. "I missed lunch," I murmured between swallows.

Moments later our plates were taken away and we relaxed with cups of coffee. Well, two cups of coffee. Having given up caffeinated treats while trying to get pregnant, I was now more partial to hot chocolate. We were sipping our beverages, chatting about Ashley's school load, when we were distracted by a squeal down the aisle. We all turned to look, and my mouth fell open as my heart shifted into overdrive.

Teren had just shown up and Debby was thrilled to see him. Personally, I think she was always a little too thrilled to see him, especially considering the fact that she was married, but what had me full-on alarmed was the fact that she had thrown her arms around him like she hadn't seen him in ten years. All I could think was—*she's touching him…she'll know.*

Feeling panicked and on edge, I started to stand at the table. My stomach rose into my throat when, after commenting how great it was to see him, she proclaimed, "Boy, but you're cold."

I unconsciously tried to squeeze past my sister, so I could free Teren from Debby's grasp. In my nerve-heightened state, I didn't even realize I was squishing Ashley, I was only aware of something getting in-between Teren and me.

"Emma, ow." I heard Ashley say. My focus was locked on Teren though, and I ignored her.

My mother's firm voice broke through my panic. "Emma, sit down. You know Debby's a flirt, but Teren wouldn't do anything with her. See."

I glanced down at Mom staring over her shoulder at Teren and Debby. My gaze drifted back up to Teren and our overeager waitress, and I could see what Mom meant. Teren had successfully separated himself from her and was laughing as he gave her a playful warning gesture with his finger. Feeling a little stupid at my overreaction, I slowly sat back down into my seat while Teren slipped around the boisterous woman.

Mom and Ashley stood to greet him and I tensed again; more people were about to touch him. With a dazzling smile and apologies for being late, Teren gave my mom an oh-so-brief hug before engulfing Ashley in a huge bear hug. Mom accepted her brief embrace and smiled widely at his show of affection for Ashley. Teren had a natural kinship with my sister and their connection was a deep one. Ash also knew that Teren had died, so he could touch her for as long as he wanted. Within reason, of course.

I relaxed as everybody broke apart and started to sit back down. So much for my silent promise to not worry so much about him. Oh well, tomorrow was always another shot. Ash shifted to sit with Mom and Teren sat by my side. Leaning close to kiss my cheek, he whispered his agreement to my silent goal. "Stop stressing. It's not good for the babies."

I bit my lip, giggled, and reflexively put a hand on my stomach. Teren laughed with me as he grabbed my free hand and interlaced our fingers. I heard Mom sigh and I looked across the table at her. "You two are so…" she sighed again and lightly shook her head. "True love….it's so nice to see. It reminds me of my own."

I swallowed and looked down. She meant her and my dad. Even though he had been gone for years, over ten of them, she still considered herself married to him. She even still wore her wedding ring. I'd already given up on trying to convince her that Dad would be fine if she moved on. She just wasn't interested.

Teren squeezed my hand while Mom asked him if he was hungry. I looked over at him as he shook his head and met eyes with my mother. "No, thank you. I slurped down a quick meal earlier." He crooked a grin and flashed a glance at Ashley. She giggled into her hand. Mom shrugged and let it go, not understanding what he really meant by that. I discreetly rolled my eyes.

We settled into small talk, with Mom asking him even more questions about the ranch, and I started to get a little antsy. I didn't want to make small talk about ranch life, now that he was here. I wanted to tell them. I wanted to finally let everyone know we were engaged and getting married within a month.

Teren, maybe super-sensing my growing irritability, shifted the conversation for me. Placing our laced hands on the table and looking at me in adoration, he calmly said, "Since we're all together again, Emma and I have some news."

I peeked at my mom and sister; they both looked equally confused and intrigued. Letting me break the news to my family, Teren didn't expand on his sentence. He only tenderly stroked the back of my hand with his thumb and continued to stare at me. Mom and Ashley shifted their gazes to me accordingly. "Well," I looked at each one, savoring the moment and feeling tears well up as I did. "Teren and I are getting married," I whispered.

My mom practically erupted in her joy. Her hands stretched out for me, engulfing me in as much of a hug as she could across the table. My sister clenched Teren's arm and told us both congratulations. My mother's theatrics got the attention of Debby and she sauntered back to see what the fuss was about. With tears dripping down her cheeks, Mom told her that I was getting married. The way she put it, Teren was almost inconsequential—it was her *daughter's* wedding. I couldn't help but grin at Mom's happiness.

Debby smiled, a little halfheartedly if you asked me, and congratulated us. Offering a round of wine on the house, I politely, but firmly told her no. Joking around, she muttered, "What? You pregnant, honey."

I bit my lip and felt my cheeks go bright red. I started shaking my head no, trying to laugh off the question, but I hadn't been expecting someone to ask me that right now and I was a little thrown. Teren squeezed my hand and looked at me with curiosity, maybe wondering if I wanted this part shared or not. I met his eyes, not sure what I wanted either.

Finally, Mom broke the building tension. "Oh my God, you are!" I looked back at her, a denial ready on my lips, but tears were streaming down my cheeks and a huge smile was on my face. I heard Ashley gasp beside Mom and Teren started to chuckle. I hadn't even really had a chance to refute the accusation yet.

Sputtering on any sort of coherent refusal, I ended up sighing and saying, "That's not why we're getting married." My mom brought her hands to her face and Ashley's mouth dropped wide open. Both of their eyes drifted to where my stomach was hidden under the table and I started laughing. Debby congratulated us again and went off in search of some sparkling cider to celebrate.

Mom and Ash were still dazed when she left. I cocked an eyebrow at their odd, silent reactions. "Mom? You...okay?" I slowly asked. I always thought Mom would be a little shocked by it, but okay. Her silence was starting to unnerve me.

Finally she dropped her hands and stood up. "Get over here, I need to hug you."

Ashley came out of her startlement and stood up; she was crying now as well. Teren quickly got out of our way, a small smile on his face as he stepped back from the table. My sister attacked me when I stood up. "I can't believe you made it in time," she whispered in my ear. I nodded into her shoulder, disbelieving it as well. A sob escaped me when she rubbed my back and said, "I'm so happy for you, Emma."

I could only tearfully nod again as she pulled away. Then Mom was engulfing me. I had to take a step back from her ferociousness. She started weeping and I laughed as I held her. "Mom, really, it's okay."

Pulling back, she cupped my cheeks. "I know, dear. I'm just so happy for you, the both of you." Her eyes flicked over to Teren and then back to mine. A huge grin broke across her face. "I can't believe I'm going to be a grandma!"

Mom hugged me while Ashley gave Teren another squeeze, then Mom let me go, so she could hug Teren as well. This hug was not a brief one, as Teren firmly and warmly, wrapped his arms around her. When she pulled back, she muttered, "Wow, you are cold," as she wiped her eyes. Then her focus was on me again and she didn't mention anything more. Teren raised an eyebrow at me and I sighed that he was right, once again; no one was suspicious about his temperature.

Debby found some cider and gave us each a glass. Taking one for herself, we all toasted Teren's and my new life together. I secretly watched Teren, as he faked taking a sip, then discretely poured some of his drink into a pot behind him. I smiled into my glass at his deception.

"So you two crazy lovebirds, when's the wedding?" Debby asked as she finished her glass.

I took the last sip of mine and shrugged. "December 19th."

Every female head in our congratulatory circle twisted to stare at me. "What?" They all said together.

I looked at each one in turn, not sure why they were all more shocked now than when I'd admitted I was pregnant. "What?" I asked cautiously.

They all shared a brief glance, and then Debby responded for the group. "You cannot plan a decent wedding in a month. Trust me on that." Debby had been married a couple times, so I suppose she would know these things.

I smiled and shook my head, thinking that the majority of the details were probably already being handled by Teren's super-efficient family, a family that also had impeccable taste and would lavish me in a fairytale wedding that would outdo whatever I could have come up with. "It's fine." I looked over at Teren and stretched out my hand; he took it with a smile. "Besides, we have a lot of help anyway." I shrugged. "I'll practically only need to show up."

Before Debby could respond, my sister gave me a sly grin and added, "Yeah, and she wouldn't want to be all huge at her wedding anyway, so quicker is probably better."

Teren laughed as I reached over and smacked my sister's arm. "Thanks, Ash." She grinned, laughed, and then hugged me again.

We sat back down and talked about wedding details, then baby details, then more wedding details. It didn't take long before I was yawning, exhausted, and ready for bed. Teren put his arm around me as we all made our way out of the café. I smiled and nestled into his side while we followed Mom to her car to get his beloved pooch.

We found Spike with his head out the window, merrily panting. The collie's entire body started vibrating with happiness when he saw Teren. Mom reluctantly opened the door and Teren clapped his hands and squatted to Spike's level, calling his name. Spike dashed over to him...and then stopped. My heart started surging as I considered that Teren's temperature might not be what gave him away. His dog might. Collies were smart, and Spike could clearly tell that something was off about his owner. I wasn't entirely sure what he would do, but I pictured him biting Teren, and leaving him with a vicious wound that my mom would want to inspect. I then imagined that wound healing right before Mom's eyes. That...would not be good.

Teren frowned as Spike stayed a couple of paces away from him, holding his shaggy body still as he sniffed the air. Mom started to walk towards Spike, but Ash held her hand out and stopped her. I wasn't sure, but Spike didn't look too friendly at the moment, and he might lash out at her by mistake if she spooked him. And she might if she wasn't careful. All of his attention was on trying to piece together the new oddness of his master.

Teren dropped to his knees and patted them as he called to Spike in a soothing voice. He looked a little worried, like maybe he'd lost his favorite pet. With obvious caution in his body, Spike leaned in with his nose, his foot slowly following. He did it a few more times while Teren's encouragement picked up pace. Eventually Spike got close enough for Teren to touch him. He flinched away from the contact for a second, and then his nose practically inhaled Teren's hand. After a moment or two, he gave Teren a soft lick, and then he seemed to relax. He leaned his shaking body into Teren's, and Teren wrapped him in a big hug. Scuffing up his shaggy fur, Teren was clearly elated that his pup hadn't rejected him. Spike was happy too, as he gave Teren a mini bath, licking him profusely everywhere he could reach. I laughed at the sight of a boy and his dog.

When everything with Spike seemed back to normal, Mom came up and stroked the slight curve of his tail. "Wow, I thought he was going to bite you for a second there."

Teren's face twitched, just fractionally, and then he pulled it into an effortless smile. "Yeah, I know." Standing and scratching a joyous Spike's back he added, "It was like he'd forgotten me already. He must really like you. Thank you for watching him for me."

Mom nodded, tears in her eyes as she gave Spike one last quick hug. I shook my head, knowing that visits with Mom from now on would be as much about seeing Spike as they were about seeing us. We waved to Mom and Ash as they took off together, then we piled Spike into Teren's car and planned to part ways.

Teren frowned at me as I opened the door to my bug. "You are coming over, right?"

I grinned and gave him a soft kiss. Glancing over at where Spike was barking at Teren in his closed up car, I playfully said, "Well, I'm not sure. I wouldn't want to interrupt anything between you two."

Teren rolled his eyes and slung his arms around my waist. "You preempt the dog...although he will probably want to sleep between us tonight."

Teren laughed and I bit my lip as I studied his handsome, stubbled face in the orange tint of the parking lot lights. The glow of his eyes was muted to near nothingness in the refracted light around us, but I could see it, or at least, I imagined I could see it. I pictured seeing it in its full glory in his dark bedroom and bit my lip even harder.

Leaning up, I kissed him again. "Yes, I just need to run home and grab some stuff." I pulled away and gave him a serious expression. "We really should get me moved in soon."

He smiled at me and winked. "I could get you moved in, in a couple of hours." He leaned in to whisper into my ear; his cool breath sent a shiver down my spine. "I'm really fast."

I giggled and released myself from his grasp. "True." I let my eyes seductively roam down his body. By the time I'd reached his eyes again, I could see that he'd stopped faking his breathing. "But you do know how to take your time too." My voice was intentionally husky and his mouth dropped open a little. Inwardly, I smiled that I could still do that to him. Outwardly, I sucked on my lip and kept up the foreplay.

Teren took a step towards me, looking like he wanted to take me right there in the parking lot. Although it wouldn't be our first time having sex in a sort of public place, I was more in the mood for a nice, big private bed. I put a hand on his chest and stopped him, then quickly dropped down into the seat of my car. He frowned and leaned on my door frame. "So, you'll be quick?" he asked, a little impatiently. I nodded and pulled on my door to close it. He stopped me at the last moment, cracking open the door. "And you'll keep on what you're wearing now?"

His lips curled into a devilish smile and I shook my head at how darn attractive he was. I gave him a devilish smile in return and pictured his delight in seeing me in the underwear he'd picked out this morning. "Oh, yes." I tilted my head and leaned forward, he leaned in as well. "Although, I may come back with a little less on than before."

I wiggled a piece of my shirt and his eyes darted down my body. "And you say I don't play fair," he muttered. I laughed and successfully managed to close my door.

Once I got home, I packed the largest bag that I could pack quickly and trudged it back to my car in record time. When I showed

up at his door a half hour later, I surprised him by doing what I said
I'd do. While he blurred my bag away to his room, I slipped my coat
off and hung it up in his entryway closet. When he blurred back
down, he nearly fell over, which made me happier than I should
probably admit. He openly stared at my body, only clothed in black
high heels and the racy little red number that he'd picked out. His
eyes drifted from my breasts to my heels and then locked onto the
garter belts. They stayed there for a total of five seconds, and then he
snatched me up and blurred me away to his monstrously comfortable
bed.

Chapter 4 – Plans and Proposals

Now that the cat was out of the bag and my family knew, both about the upcoming wedding and the upcoming baby, the planning process began in earnest. Mom wanted to help out, so I put her in touch with Alanna. The two of them started making plans for flowers, music and food. I smiled at the fact that they were bonding over such a happy event, and tried not to worry about my mom meeting Teren's family. It would be fine. Both sides were filled with good people, and they would surely get along, despite their differences.

The only thing that had started to bother me was the guest list. It kept getting bigger and bigger. I nearly fought with Mom over wanting to keep it just immediate friends and family, but she swore that she'd promised such and such a cousin that they could come to my wedding, since we'd gone to theirs. After a dozen or so incidents like that, the guest list had grown to nearly a hundred. That started giving me panic attacks. The more people that came to the ranch, the greater the risk of exposure. Alanna and Teren kept assuring me that it was fine, that the bulk would only be coming out Saturday evening for the actual ceremony and then they'd be leaving. But it still made me nervous.

So much so that I'd started considering changing the location. But trying to reserve a spot somewhere with only a couple weeks' notice was surprisingly difficult, even in December. After a dozen or so phone calls, and Teren complaining that I'd hurt his mom's feelings, I gave up. It would just have to be at the ranch and I'd have to find a way to relax. Teren reminding me that Halina could do mind wipes, if needed, helped a bit with that.

When the wedding planning looked to be on track, my mother shifted to baby planning. Insisting that prenatal care was vital, she bugged me about getting in to see a doctor. She said I should have gone in as soon as I'd suspected. I sighed and told her everything was fine and I didn't need to go, but she'd given me the *This is my grandchild and you will go* face and I'd told her I would make an appointment as soon as I could.

Honestly, I did want to make sure the babies were okay too, I just didn't feel right about nurses and doctors poking and prodding

my body. Teren assured me that it was fine, that as long as they didn't
directly test the embryos, everything would look normal to humans,
as my blood had no trace of vampirism in it. It made me anxious, but
I conceded to the expert and made an appointment. I really was
looking forward to hearing the heartbeats like Teren could. Plus, I
could finally tell everyone that we were expecting twins. I couldn't
exactly spill that fact without seeing a doctor first. I couldn't tell
everyone—*How do I know? Oh, well, Teren can hear the different heartbeats.*

Teren came with me on the first visit and held my hand. We did
get to hear the heartbeats, and of course, I cried. Teren smiled at
clearly hearing what he could sometimes hear anyway, and he was
very happy that my senses could experience it now too. The doctor
surprised us both by doing an ultrasound. Even though I was only a
couple of months along and the babies were only about the size of
kumquats, or so the doctor told me, they had a machine that could
take a look-see from the inside. It was cold, but then, I was used to
that, and slightly uncomfortable, but when the image popped up on
the screen…it was beyond any feeling I'd ever had before.

I looked over at Teren. His eyes were glued to the black and
white monitor, his mouth dropped open in awe. The doctor pointed
out a section of the grayness that was moving, fast and fluttery—a
heartbeat. I knew Teren could still hear the heartbeat in the near
silent room and I knew his mind was connecting the sound to the
image. His faintly glowing eyes started to water as he watched the
screen. Then the doctor twisted the device and confirmed what
Teren already knew, that there was indeed a second heartbeat. We
acted surprised, which wasn't hard for me, since I was a blubbering
mess anyway. Then the miraculous doctor measured something on
the screen and told us I was around ten weeks along, putting my
conception date in October, right around the time of our abduction.
My due date was near the end of June. He also told me that
everything looked normal. I cried again after hearing that. Not that
I'd been worried something wasn't normal—aside from a little nausea
and more tender than usual breasts, I felt fine—but hearing a trained
professional say everything was okay was wondrously calming.

After we left, I immediately called my mom to tell her the news,
and to tell her that she was right—going to the doctor had been one
of the best ideas she ever had.

Trying to not let ourselves get overwhelmed by all the newness in our lives, we resumed our weekly get-togethers with Tracey and Hot Ben, so nicknamed because he was Abercrombie and Fitch model gorgeous. He was surprisingly sweet though, and definitely a good match for Tracey. I was still nervous, the first time we were all slated to meet up. Maybe the flood of hormones was making me a supernaturally strong worrywart?

"Are you sure about this, Teren?" I flopped down on his bed—our bed, as we'd officially moved in all my stuff last weekend—and stretched out on the covers.

He glanced back at me, his bare back sexy and inviting as he rummaged in his drawers for a casual shirt. I smiled at his new dresser set. Since all of my clothes had pretty much taken up his massive walk-in closet, we'd had to go buy him some new furniture. Smiling at my smile, he tossed back, "Sure about what?" before continuing with his quest.

I sighed and flopped over to my stomach. I lightly banged my feet together as I rested my head in my hands. "Hanging out with Tracey and Ben. I mean, you're only a couple months old, isn't it a little early to be socializing?"

Finding a shirt, he straightened and gave me a wry look. "I'm not an infant. It will be fine." He slipped the shirt over his body, hiding that magnificence from me and I sighed again. Flattening it out over his chest, he added, "Besides, we're not going out to dinner. It's just a movie." He walked over to sit on the bed.

I stretched out one hand to him and he grabbed it. I brought his knuckles to my cheek and shivered as his skin gave me a momentary chill. "Yeah, I know…but still."

Leaning over, he gave me a kiss. "Remember about that stressing thing? It will be fine." He pulled back and smiled. "And, we have something important to ask them, remember?" He tilted his head and raised an eyebrow. I smiled. We hadn't told them about the wedding yet, or the babies. We'd wanted to wait until they were together, so we could ask them to stand up with us when we got married.

I rolled over to my side, bringing the back of his hand to my heart. He smiled wider and I imagined that he could probably feel my heartbeat through his sensitive skin. "I know, it will be great. I guess I'm just nervous about the hugging and congratulating part."

He smirked at me. "It's not like I'll be running my hand up Tracey's shirt, she'll barely notice."

"You better not." I smirked as well and then a thought struck me. I grabbed his hand with both of mine and started vigorously rubbing the dead skin.

Confusion altered his features as he watched me. "What are you doing?"

I grinned as I continued applying friction to his hand. "An experiment. You tend to warm up the more you touch me, so I thought maybe I could warm you up before you touch Ben and Tracey."

He rolled his eyes, then gave me a lopsided grin. "I could think of warmer places to shove my hand," he told me.

I stopped rubbing his hand and debated whether I should smack him or kiss him. Deciding we didn't have time for the latter, I rapped him on the arm. He laughed while I brought his hand to my cheek. I sighed at the slightly warmer feel and he smiled watching me. "There, nearly human."

There was adoration in his eyes as he murmured, "That's my motto." He kissed me and I let myself get lost in it for a moment. But then we started getting too lost in it; I had to push him back when he started to move over the top off me. Pulling away from his mouth, I told him, "We have a show time to make." It came out a little breathlessly.

Pressing against me he muttered, "We have time."

I laughed and shoved him away from me. He gave me a disappointed expression and I laughed harder, pushing him all the way off me. "You really are so incredibly easy," I giggled as he helped me stand.

He made an affronted noise and grabbed his wallet from his nightstand. "I'll have you know," he pointed down to his jeans, "these are actually very difficult to get into." He gave me a lopsided grin. "In fact, only one girl can."

Walking over to him, I slipped my arms around his neck. "Good," I said, giving him a soft kiss.

His pale eyes sparkled with mischievousness when he pulled back. "Yeah, I promise I won't tell her about you."

I gasped and brought my arm back to smack him soundly in the chest, but he blurred out of the room. "Chicken," I yelled out the open door. I heard laughter answer me, but he was probably already downstairs. "Smartass," I muttered, knowing full well he could hear me.

We pulled into the theater parking lot a moment later and holding hands, we strolled into the lobby. We spotted Tracey and Hot Ben instantly, as they had their mouths all over each other. Grinning, we walked over to say hi.

Tracey waved hello when she noticed us, and I clenched Teren's hand tighter as we approached the eerily attractive couple. Ben's sculpted face and highlighted hair was a complement to Tracey's curves and blonde flowing mane. The two of them were almost more pleasing to look at when they stood together. Tracey's big blue eyes brightened when she took in Teren; she hadn't seen him in a while. Ben hadn't either, for that matter, and, as Ben and Teren were sort of friends, he was the first to greet him.

"Hey, man, glad you're back." One arm still around Tracey, he clapped Teren on the shoulder. I exhaled and relaxed a smidge.

Tracey giggled and leaned over to give Teren a quick one-armed hug. "Oh," she squeaked, "cold outside, isn't it?" She brought her hand to Hot Ben's chest and rested her head against his shoulder. "I'm glad your dad's okay, Teren," she said.

Ben nodded. "Yeah, if he ever needs help again," he put on a dazzling smile, "I'd love to try working on a ranch."

Teren grinned and shot me a look. "Thank you, but I think that, uh…problem, won't come up again." I started to laugh, and switched it to a cough into my hand. Teren squeezed my waist and I relaxed into his side, happy that everyone was oblivious to what he really meant, and happy that the horrid moment he'd just joked about, was finally a moment that we *could* joke about. A moment that was gratefully over.

"Shall we?" Teren indicated the ticket line and, laughing at all being together again, we bought our tickets.

After the movie, we headed to a bar where we sat in a noisy corner and Teren faked sipping his dark bottled beer. As you couldn't see through the glass at how much was left, no one suspected that he wasn't actually drinking it. Relaxing even more as our deception started getting easier, and honestly, Tracey and Ben started getting drunker, I decided it was time to up that joyous feeling.

To interrupt the conversations around me, I clinked a spoon from a nearby table against my glass of Shirley Temple. Tracey and Ben stopped giggling into each other's sides and turned their heads to look at me. Teren grinned; he knew what I was about to do.

"Um…guys." They both blankly blinked at me, and I thought we might have to give them a ride home. "Teren and I have some news." We looked at each other, and Teren smiled softly and grabbed my hand. Not looking back at Tracey and Hot Ben, I said to Teren, "We're getting married."

I heard an incredibly loud shriek from Tracey. Teren winced and closed his eyes; that had probably been exceedingly loud to him. Twisting my head, I watched a half-drunk Tracey try and maul me over the table. Laughing, I stood up so she could hug me. She jumped up and down, squealing, and every head in the bar turned at the commotion. Trying to shush her, I added, "We'd like you guys to stand up with us."

At that point, she collapsed into my arms and started sobbing; I took that as a yes. Ben, more calmly than his girlfriend, stood up to hug me. He had to put his arms around Tracey to do it. Then he clasped Teren's hand. Teren stood at my side, watching Tracey sob in my arms with an amused grin on his face. Ben congratulated us both and said he'd be honored. Tracey finally pulled herself together and said that she'd be honored too. Then she looked behind me at Teren and started sobbing all over again. Letting go of me, she reached out for him. I tensed, but honestly, she was so tipsy, he could have had icicles dripping from his nose and she wouldn't have noticed. She clung to him, crying onto his shoulder and murmuring congratulations, until Ben finally pulled her back to her seat.

Sniffing and wiping her nose, she hiccupped and asked, "When are you guys going to do it? Spring? Summer?"

I grinned in my excitement. "The nineteenth."

She looked at me blankly. "Of which month?"

I frowned and furrowed my brow. "Of this month."

Her face dropped as her mouth fell open. "This month? Jesus, Emma, that's only a couple of weeks away. How about a longer heads up?" She shook her head and took a sip of her drink. Pausing, she muttered, "Why so fast? You pregnant or something?"

I flushed and attempted to shake my head, but Tracey saw the color in my cheeks and sputtered on her drink. "Holy shit, you are!"

I sighed that I was a complete failure at keeping my secret off my face. I guess I was just too thrilled about it. Giving up, I grinned as idiotically as I wanted to. "Yes, I am."

Her earlier exclamation was near silent in comparison to her new one. I thought we might get kicked out with the angry glares we were getting, and Teren actually brought his hands up to rub his temples. I suspected his hearing might be slightly less supernatural after tonight.

She didn't even give me the chance to let me stand again before she stumbled over to my side and sat on my seat with me. Flinging her arms around me, she started crying again. "I knew it was weird that you were drinking a Shirley Temple."

I laughed and hugged her back, glad that most of our secrets were out. Ben stood up to give Teren a brief hug, not commenting on his chilliness, and then we spent the rest of the night going over the upcoming nuptials.

Not too much later, Teren and I decided that we should take the sloppily drunk Tracey, and the slightly less drunk Ben, home. As our foursome was walking to the car, Teren suddenly stopped and looked down an alley. Furrowing his brow and cocking his head, he ignored the sounds of the two giggling people in our group and focused on something down the alley. My heart started beating harder as I whispered, "What is it?"

"I don't…" His eyes narrowed, and he took a step towards the dark crack between the two buildings.

Panicked, I grabbed his elbow. He twisted to look at me and I shook my head at him. "Don't you dare, Teren. You stay here…with me." I searched his eyes until he finally nodded.

Looking back to the alley, he shook his head. "I don't hear it anymore anyway."

As Tracey and Hot Ben laughed and bumped into the back of us, I asked him, "What did you hear?"

He grabbed my hand and we starting walking down the street to his car. "I'm not sure, it was really faint." I swallowed—really faint to Teren was *really* faint. He noticed my reaction and gave me a nonchalant grin as he brought me closer to his side. "It was probably nothing." His other hand went to his head. "I'm practically deaf now anyway." He made a motion like he was trying to clean out his ear and I laughed, my fears momentarily tempered by his humor.

I drove Teren's Prius with Tracey beside me while Teren followed us in Hot Ben's SUV. Tracey chatted the entire time we drove to Ben's house. She briefly talked about my pregnancy, and was more than a little upset that I hadn't told her immediately, and then she switched to the wedding. She had seen a bridesmaid dress last week that would be perfect. She wanted to go buy it tomorrow. I told her that was fine; I didn't care what she and my sister wore, I didn't even care what colors they wore. Tracey giggled as she described it in detail. I laughed when she told me it was blood red. How perfect. I told her I'd call Ashley and we'd all go and find one for her too.

We dropped them off at Hot Ben's apartment, and stayed a few minutes to make sure the drunken couple would be okay for the rest of the night. When they started getting handsy in the entryway, I thought their night would be just fine, and Teren and I made our way home. We got a little handsy in the entryway as well, and ended up stumbling half-dressed into his obligatory piano room, where we had an intimate moment of our own on the bench in front of his baby grand.

We fell asleep there, with our feet up on the bench and a blanket from a nearby chair draped across our bare bodies. Once the intensity died down, Spike found us and nestled against us. I sighed in my sleep, happy with our odd little family.

The next morning, I awoke to a steaming cup of cocoa placed on the floor by my head. Teren was squatting behind it when I cracked my eyes open. His expression was amused as he indicated where I was sprawled on the floor; half of me was underneath the piano bench with Spike sleeping close into my side. "You move all this way...to have a slumber party on my floor?"

I chuckled as I stretched out the kinks in my body. Spike stirred beside me and licked my shoulder. "I didn't hear you complaining last night," I muttered between yawns.

He leaned down to kiss me. "I had nothing to complain about." He sighed as he pulled away. "I have to go...I'll see you tonight."

He kissed me again and I playfully pulled him down to me. He grunted as he lost his balance and the top half of him fell on the top half of me. He started laughing as Spike yelped and darted out of the room, but my appetite had sprung back up and I wasn't in a laughing mood. I wasn't letting up with the affectionate kisses either. His laughter died away as well, once his humor switched to something else. He eagerly returned my ardent touches, his hands moving under the blanket to caress my bare skin. One hand went straight down between my thighs and slid against me. I was ready for him again, already, and I moaned in his mouth as he worked his fingers over me. Dropping his head to my shoulder he muttered, "Emma...I don't have time for this..."

My response was a nonverbal one as I groaned and arched against his hand. I could feel the heat his icy touch created rising in me already. His body leaning against mine shifted position so he could press his hips against my leg. His mouth came back to mine, nearly attacking me, and his hand continued stoking my fire. Then he brought his thumb into the equation, circling it around my sensitive core as his fingers slipped inside of me. I gasped and pulled at him. My hands were everywhere—in his hair, tugging on his clothes, trying to pull him on top of me, even though that stupid bench was in the way.

He murmured something about really needing to go, but as I was close to exploding, I breathlessly begged, "Please, don't…stop."

His breath fast in my ear, he panted, "This is killing me. I need…something, Emma."

Without thinking about it, I brought my wrist to his mouth. He didn't hesitate at what I offered him. His free hand held my arm and he bit down, easily puncturing the skin. That was all I needed too. My release instantly burst through me, and I cried out with the force of it. He made several short moaning noises as he drank while I came. When his fingers and mouth slowed, I felt drained and satisfied, on multiple levels. Eventually he licked the wounds closed on my wrist and removed his fingers from inside my body; he licked those too. Still breathing heavy, he pulled back to gaze at me with unfocused eyes.

My own breath heavy, I ran a hand down his face, wiping a speck of blood off his lip. "Holy hell, Teren. Can we wake up like that every day?"

He grinned and laughed, leaning in for a quick peck as his teeth retracted. "Now, I really do have to go. I love you."

My fingers trailed down his arm as he stood. "I love you too." He grinned as he gazed at me, shaking his head in wonder, then he turned to leave the room. He called out another goodbye before I heard the door shut. I sighed as I reached over for my surprisingly upright hot chocolate. I really, really loved living here.

Later at work, I broke the news of my upcoming wedding to Clarice and the rest of my coworkers. I broke the news because a bubbly (even with a hangover) Tracey wouldn't shut up about it. Clarice overheard us talking about dress shopping later so I confessed my plans. She gave me a three second smile before flatly saying, "You don't have any more vacation time, so I hope you weren't planning on a honeymoon."

Mentally I rolled my eyes, but I only replied with, "No, we sort of already had our honeymoon." I smiled at the memory of all the weeks we'd spent at the ranch. Clarice walked away, muttering something about that being a good thing. I didn't mention to her that I'd be taking maternity leave before the year was up, and I made

Tracey promise to do the same. I sort of had the feeling that news would drive Clarice over the edge.

After work, Tracey and I took my car and picked up my sister before heading to the dress shop. It was a quaint little wedding boutique and I had to hold in tears as we walked past the pure white beauties in the window. Tracey and Ashley both laughed at my reaction and Ashley muttered that it was sort of hypocritical for me to wear white, since I was already pregnant. I pinched her arm while Tracey laughed in agreement.

Smiling, we all entered the shop together. Ash and Tracey quickly found the dress Tracey had picked out, and both women squealed in delight when they found a similar one for Ashley to try on. I was a little nervous for my sister, but the floor length dress had long sleeves and a high neckline, and would cover most of her scarred body. I was kind of surprised that Tracey had even liked the conservative style when I saw it on the rack, but when they both tried them on, I understood. It was very form fitted, and clung to their bodies in such a way, that they both might as well have been naked. We had my sister's altered, so it was just a tad looser on her, and then I started trying on wedding dresses, just for fun.

When I got to the third one, I knew it was *the* one. A short train trailed on the floor behind it, and the sleeves were an intricate, see-through lace design with pearls stitched along the seams. The front almost looked like a corset, but the respectable kind, with crisscrossing strips of satin emphasizing all of the assets that Teren adored, especially now that those assets had started to swell. The back had a cutout shape of a heart between my shoulder blades and a row of pearls lining my spine. The whole thing was elegant and a touch sexy, and cost more than all my pantsuits combined. But it was perfect, and already fit me with no real adjustments needed. It seemed like a no brainer to me, so I ended up leaving the boutique with dresses for the girls and a dress for me.

I had Ashley hide the dress at her place, which was my old place. After I'd moved out, Teren and I had helped her move in. My mom objected at first, claiming the steep stairs were too challenging for Ashley, as some of her joints were a little stiff, but Ash had rolled her eyes and told Mom that she was nearly twenty and she wanted to try

66

living on her own. Mom couldn't really object to that, so she'd halfheartedly helped us change her over.

Ashley loved it. She loved the independence and loved having friends from school over at any hour, loved not having to worry about waking Mom up, and she'd confessed that she hoped to have a boy or two over. I hoped she did. I hated the idea of her looks keeping her from the love she so deserved. But as I listened to her talk and heard the growing confidence in her voice, I suddenly heard a woman emerging, and I was positive that someday, some man would hear that woman too, and love her with all his heart, making her scars just what they were—irrelevant.

I was smiling over that thought as I came back to my new home, a modern two-story building, with a breathtaking view of the ocean out the wall of windows in the living room. Sunsets here were truly spectacular and I couldn't wait for the late days of summer so Teren and I could sit out here every evening and enjoy them together. A thrill shot through me as I realized that Teren and I would be married by then, we'd be husband and wife. Then a frown hit me. I'd also be the size of a house by then. We'd have to check the weight limit on his deck.

Teren disrupted my negative thoughts by easily picking me up and carting me off to the kitchen. He plopped me down at a chair by the table and asked about my shopping trip while he prepped a plate for me. My stomach rumbled as I eyed the steaming pile of lasagna he set in front of me, and not waiting for him to join me, I hungrily dug in. I told him all the details about the trip that I could; I mentioned that I found a dress for me, but kept back the details of it. He could wait.

Teren laughed at my hunger as he poured a glass of blood for himself from a steaming carafe. It was eerily similar to the kind his mom used at the ranch. He sat next to me, casually leaning back in his chair as he sipped his dinner. I watched him while I ate, and wondered how a liquid diet could possibly be as satisfying as the calorie-leaden food currently plopping into my stomach. Teren eyed me with an odd grin while I watched him. Taking a break from inhaling my food, I asked, "Do you miss it?"

He tilted his head as he took another sip. "Miss what?"

Bloodlines

I raised a forkful of cheesy goodness. "Food. Real food. Well, human food." Human food which I continued to shovel down my throat with abandon.

He gave me a lopsided grin as he shook his head. "No." His pale eyes moved away from my mouth to look into mine. "Surprisingly, no, I don't miss it." He shrugged and indicated my plate with his glass. "It doesn't even sound good anymore."

I smiled that at least he didn't miss something that he couldn't have anymore. I mean, he couldn't exactly digest the incredibly heavy food I was starting to get full on. "Well, that's good that you don't have to endure a lifelong...yearning." I laughed at my choice of words.

He laughed, too, and took a long drink of his blood, closing his eyes as he relished it. Slowly he opened them; the blue depths looked as satisfied as mine probably did. "No, I don't yearn...for *that*." His grin was devilish. His fangs only intensified the look, and I felt a flush of desire sweep over me.

After taking a long draw of his drink, Teren switched to a content smile. "Besides, you wouldn't believe how good this is." He closed his eyes and inhaled a deep breath. Concern entered his expression as he cracked an eye open. "Not as tasty as you, of course."

I laughed around a mouthful of food. It was kind of funny to me that he was actually concerned that I'd be offended if he enjoyed his cow drink more than he enjoyed me. I raised my wrist, the bandage on it vividly reminding me of this morning. A slow smile spread on his face as he remembered it too. "Oh, I know that, Teren. Don't worry, you make that painfully clear." I smirked and he chuckled as he took another sip.

Then his eyes grew speculative. Slowly he asked, "Do you...? Would you...want to try it?" He extended his glass to me.

My eyes widened and my stomach tightened. Ew. Why would he think I wanted to try that? "No, Teren...gross." His eyebrow lifted and I quickly amended with, "No offense." He laughed, and started to pull his glass back.

As he did, a fragrance hit me that I'd never smelled before. I grabbed his hand, and pulled the glass back to me. I inhaled the top of it while Teren scrunched his brows again. It smelled better than the meal I was ingesting. My mouth started to water as I imagined that thick, warm, fragrant liquid running down my throat. Grossed out by my own desires, I shoved his hand away from me and plugged my nose to keep that delicious smell back. "Oh my God, Teren."

He tilted his head as he took a sip. "That bad?" he asked.

I shook my head. "No…that good." I made a disgusted face and he laughed at seeing it.

Extending the glass again, he said, "Are you sure you don't want to try it?"

I forcefully shook my head. "Ew, no." He chuckled at me while I frowned at his reaction. "Hey, it's not me who wants it." I placed a hand on my stomach, hoping the hormones in my body were really what were causing my craving. "These little bloodsuckers are the culprits."

He busted out laughing and then stood at the table to lean over and give me a kiss. The blood on his tongue…was fabulous, and I hated myself for enjoying it. Pulling away, he sat back down and tilted back the rest of his dinner. "You're adorable, Emma." He gave me a love-filled gaze. "Don't ever change," he whispered. I smiled shyly as I finished the rest of my meal.

When I was done, Teren cleaned up after me, sweeping my plate away as speedily as his mom did. Before I could stand to join him in the adjoining kitchen, he'd blurred back to the table and set a box right in front of me. I froze as I stared at a small, velvet encased container. I knew exactly what fit inside boxes that size. My eyes started to water as I continued to stare at the thing.

Teren squatted by my side, his voice soft in my ear while I was entranced. "It has occurred to me, that in the rush of all of this, I've missed a step." His hand reached out for mine but I still couldn't tear my eyes away from that box. My heart was hammering.

"I love you so much, Emma. I know we've rushed things, but I wouldn't change a second of our time together." I finally tore my eyes away to look at him, and a tear finally dropped to my cheek. His eyes were wet as he gazed back at me. The level of love on his face took my breath away.

He rubbed the back of my hand as he searched my face. "I know we don't have the kind of time together that I wish we could have." He shook his head. "I would keep you for all of eternity, if I could, if I could keep you just like you are." His other hand came up to rest on my heart and I understood the reference. He meant if he could keep me human, like I was now, but immortal somehow, like him. I swallowed back the emotion as more tears fell to my cheeks. A tear fell from him as he continued. "But, even still, I will live every day that you have, trying to make you happy. And I won't ever take our time together for granted."

He swallowed as another tear dropped from his eye. With an achingly beautiful smile, he moved his hand from my heart and opened the tiny box. In it, was the most incredible ring I'd ever seen. The diamond was round, flawless, and huge. The platinum band it was set in was lined on either side, all the way around the band, with small, blood-red rubies. I let out a soft sob at the symbolism. The ring was the perfect representation of him and me. Gently sliding the ring up the finger of my left hand, he whispered, "Will you marry me, Emma Taylor?"

I could barely speak through the sobs, but my nodding and throwing myself onto his lap was pretty much answer enough. I was a little startled at how emotional the actual proposal was to me, to both of us really. I mean, we'd already decided to get married, we'd picked a date, and I'd even picked out a dress today. But him placing that ring on my finger…something about that act, made it all finally seem real, and I couldn't stop the torrent of tears.

I could not wait to spend the rest of my life with this man.

Chapter 5 – What Some People Will Do To Appear Normal

Between my mom and Ashley stopping by three to four times a week to go over wedding details, and visit Spike, finally catching up on the backlog at work, tracking the twins' progression on a baby calendar (they were the size of limes now), and somehow fitting in Christmas shopping, the first couple weeks of December flew by, and my wedding was right around the corner.

Teren and I went out to the ranch the weekend before, to help Alanna make sure everything was prepped, but upon arrival, we realized that our visit really wasn't necessary. Well, I realized that. Teren had been telling me the whole trip up that we were just going for a friendly visit, that they'd have everything good to go already. And they did. Alanna showed me the rooms containing all the decorations, just waiting for the following weekend. She showed me the flowers that she and the girls had arranged, that were being stored in their massive fridge, since they didn't need to keep a whole lot of food in there. They even told me that their hired hand, Peter, had become an ordained minister…just so he could marry us. They really had thought of everything.

We spent the entire weekend just relaxing, visiting with his family and talking about the two biggest events upcoming in my life—the wedding and the children. They all took turns with their heads against my stomach, relishing the sound of life within me. I again felt a little jealous that they could hear what I couldn't, but I pushed it back. I'd hear their heartbeats again soon enough.

The last week before the wedding weekend was filled with tracking RSVPs, getting the final accessories, and having everyone's dresses fitted one last time. As I felt like I was bigger than when I'd tried it on, I worried that my dress wouldn't fit me. Luckily, it did, and Ashley carefully packed it in her bag for the trip.

Before I could really stress about the upcoming ceremony, it was the Thursday morning before the wedding. It was also my last day of work before the wedding. Much to Clarice's annoyance, Tracey had gifted me one of her days off, and the two of us were done for the week in eight short little hours. The entire wedding party—Ashley, Tracey, and Hot Ben—were going to spend the entire weekend out at the ranch with us. I was a touch nervous about that, but what had my stomach in knots on this beautiful, crisp December morning, was the fact that the girls were taking me out for a bit of "last time you're single" girl fun. And Ben and some of Teren's coworkers...were taking him out.

I wasn't the least bit worried that Teren would try to do the whole "one last casual fling before you're tied down" thing. Teren was much too loyal for that. But I *was* worried about him "drinking" all night with a group of guys. I obviously had an excuse not to drink, but Teren didn't, and bachelor parties had a habit of not stopping until the groom passed out in his own vomit.

I had no idea what he was going to do.

When I asked him about it before he left for work, he shook his head at me and said, "I've been acting human for a really long time, Emma." With a raised eyebrow he added, "I even know how to play drunk." I sighed as he left, but mentally smiled and wished I could watch Teren act like an idiot to fool his friends. Brushing off my concerns for the moment, I prepared for my last day of work as Emma Taylor.

Clarice made no comment over the fact that I was getting married. No surprise, really. I wondered if she even remembered why I was taking a long weekend. Tracey however, brought it up every five minutes. She was giddy as she described the club she wanted to take me to tonight. Ashley went to lunch with us, and turned bright red when Tracey started gushing about these male dancers she'd seen there a few months ago. I sighed and rolled my eyes, already a little tired at the prospect.

But I should have known that Tracey would make the night...memorable for me. She brought veils with her for us all to wear—her, me, Ashley, my mom, which really made the night interesting for me, a few other friends from work and a few from the gym. Then Tracey positioned all of us right in front of the stage.

Now, I wasn't one to get all hot and bothered over a guy thrusting his hips in my face...even if the body was ridiculously defined, but watching my friends and family get drunk, and be more and more friendly with said guys, was enough to have me in an almost constant state of gut busting laughter. It got especially funny, when the tallest, darkest-skinned man I'd ever seen, came over with a cute Latino, and started dual grinding on my mom. Oh my God, I'd never laughed so hard.

When the most attractive man in the place focused his attentions on my blushing sister, I nearly cried for her. I could tell from the way her eyes never left him that she liked him, and he never once looked at her any differently than any of the other women, even gorgeous Tracey. He treated Ashley the same, or maybe even a little better, as everyone else. I tipped him obscenely well for that.

As the night went on, and I took my bachelorette attentions with as much dignity as I could, I started to wonder how Teren was fairing with Hot Ben and the guys. I thought about texting him, but then decided against it. That might look like I was checking up on him to his friends, like I didn't trust him or something. And I couldn't have trusted him more. My concern for him had nothing to do with a woman.

After we piled into the limo Tracey had rented for the night, I checked my phone to check the time. There were several awaiting texts that I'd missed while in the loud club. With nervous knots in my stomach, I opened them as Tracey plopped down beside me.

"Who's that from?" she mumbled, slurring a little, as she looked over my shoulder.

I tried to shield the phone, but I was too worried to do it very well. I just knew something was wrong. I opened the first one without answering Tracey. It simply read, *'I love you. Have a good night.'*

I smiled and relaxed as I opened the second one. *'Love you, just got to the club.'* They had gone to a strip club, of course.

The next one made me smile. *'Ben bought shots…and lap dances. I turned down the latter.'*

"Hey, what's that say about Ben?" Tracey asked over my shoulder. I quickly opened the next one.

'Miss yuo…' I grinned at his purposely misspelled message. Tracey frowned. "Either I'm drunk, or he's drunk." She giggled at his next message. *'I cnnot wait be you husbnd.'*

She jokingly bumped against my shoulder as the rest of our group clued in on what we were doing. "What's up, Em?" Ashley asked.

Tracey answered for me. "Teren drunk texted her." Ashley raised her eyebrows. She knew perfectly well that Teren couldn't get "drunk." I lightly smiled and shook my head at her, before reading the next one. Tracey busted up laughing and I turned bright red. *'Cnt wait to fuk you.'*

Oh, I was so smacking him for that one. Teren didn't generally talk to me like that. While I kind of liked it, I knew he'd mainly done it to amuse my girlfriends. Drunk texting. Just another form of his constant charade to convince the world he was just a typical guy. How little the world knew.

Tracey doubled over with laughter as she repeated the text to the entire car. Everyone joined in on the laughs, my mom included, which was mortifying. I considered reading the rest of the texts when I was alone, but Tracey jerked the phone away and typed in a quick reply. I could only imagine what she'd just told him. Before I could get the phone back, she opened and read the last one. *'Ben's sick…going home.'*

I smiled when I saw the message was just ten minutes ago. He'd be home when I got home. Tracey frowned though. "Ben's sick?" She looked over at me, peeved. "How am I supposed to have drunk sex, if he's sick?" She stuck her lip out as she handed me back my phone. "Jerk off," she muttered, crossing her arms over her chest.

The laughing car turned their attention to Tracey and I relaxed. Teren was right, he *could* fake being drunk, and, except for Hot Ben's queasy stomach, everything was fine.

When I finally got home, I found Teren in our bedroom with his head tilted to the side, like he was intently listening to something. I knew it wasn't me, since I was in the room with him. I furrowed my brows, wondering what he was listening to. Then he shifted his attention to me, and the look of concentration faded as he grinned at me like an idiot. My confusion fell off of me as I took in the adorable, eager expression on his face. He was clearly excited about something. I lifted an eyebrow in curiosity, as I set my purse down on my nightstand. "What?" I asked quietly.

His grin not leaving him, he raised the phone in his hand; the text Tracey had sent him was open on the screen. Not looking the least bit drunk, since of course, he wasn't, his smile turned playful. "Really? You're gonna do *that*, to me tonight?"

I causally walked up to him standing next to our bed and glanced at his phone. Seeing what Tracey had told him I'd do, my cheeks heated, but looking back at his face, I tilted my head and gave him a seductive grin. Not answering him, I dropped to my knees.

Teren had the cutest smile on his face the next morning. I really wasn't sure if his grin was because we were getting married tomorrow, or because of what I'd done for him last night. I couldn't keep the grin off my face as I thought about our evening. Tracey would be so proud of me for following through with her sexy text.

We picked up my sister and then met the others at a gas station on the edge of town. Tracey had on the darkest sunglasses I'd ever seen. Her face had the glazed look of someone who'd already thrown up a couple times. I sympathized with her; I'd thrown up a couple times this morning too, just for a completely different reason. We companionably leaned against each other as Teren put gas in his car.

Ashley slung her arm through mine, looking tired, but not nearly as green as Tracey; she hadn't overdone it as much as Tracey had, or Hot Ben for that matter. The three of us girls watched Teren laugh at Ben and pat him on the shoulder in greeting. Ben winced in pain. His eyes were covered by equally dark glasses, and he had a hand on his stomach, like he was going to lose it on Teren's shoes. I laughed, remembering what Teren had confessed to me this morning. He'd switched out all of his full drinks for Ben's empty ones. The rest of the guys had either been so drunk, or distracted by the semi-nude girls, that no one had noticed.

Ben had unknowingly drunk all of his drinks and Teren's as well. It was a miracle the boy could still stand. I told Teren it was a good thing Tracey was never going to find out about that; she'd stake him for sure.

Teren explained to Ben the general area of where we were going. Ben blinked, but I think he understood. He shuffled off to his car with Tracey. They both looked a little slow. As Ashley and I got back in Teren's car, I hoped that Ben could maintain focus long enough to not lose Teren on the highway.

Surprisingly, we all made it to the ranch together. Both cars drove down the super-long gravel driveway, and as we passed under the huge, white wooden arch proclaiming the family name, I sighed contently. I'd soon be a part of that family. Maybe guessing what I'd been thinking, my sister reached up from the backseat and slung her arms around my neck. We both giggled while Teren smiled.

As we got closer to the spread, I marveled at the beauty of the Adams Ranch. Sitting between the foothills, at the base of Mount Diablo, it was as close to idyllic as one could get. Green trees filled in the cracks between the valleys, where water gathered in streams and pools. Teren and Ben would probably be spending some time this weekend fishing in those watery spots, regardless of the chill in the air. Boys would tolerate all sorts of adverse conditions for their hobbies. Men were weird that way.

Cows of various colors lazily munched on some long tan grass. Some of the closer ones watched us as we passed. Farther out in the fields were even more cows basking in the early morning rays. That was one thing the family kept fully stocked on at all times—cattle, food for more than one species.

As we pulled into the driveway, I heard Ashley let out a low whistle. "Wow, I don't think I'll ever get used to this place."

I smiled at her while Teren parked beside Halina's sporty European car. I knew exactly what Ashley meant. The place was breathtaking...and huge. It consisted of three buildings, forming a U shape around a pool area in the back. The side buildings were low and long one-stories, while the main building was a huge two-story dwelling that dwarfed Teren's place. Every building was capped with Spanish roof tiles that gleamed blood-red in the sun, symbolic and perfect. The rest of the building was made up of warm, honeyed wood, and white stucco walls. They were embedded with smooth river rocks along the bottom, so it resembled a seamless stone wall, sort of castle-like. Also perfectly symbolic. If any of the humans visiting this weekend realized what kind of people lived here, they'd have found it as humorous as I did, I was sure.

We stepped out of the car as Ben parked beside Teren. When he and Tracey stepped out of their car, they both had comically slack jaws. Teren grinned, and I giggled at their faces. I suppose I'd looked like that on my first visit, too. Locking arms with Ashley, I walked over to a still stunned Tracey. She gave Teren an odd look, then turned to me and whispered, "You never told me Teren was loaded."

I saw Teren's lip twitch and knew he'd heard her. Grinning, I shook my head at her bewildered face. "Because it doesn't matter, Trace." I watched him smile as he flashed his eyes to me in-between a conversation with Ben.

Ashley laughed at Tracey's still confused face. Finally Tracey shook her head and said, "Why the hell are you still working for that bitch? You could probably buy the company."

Teren laughed, then switched it to a cough mid-chuckle. Grabbing Tracey's arm, I led her to the house she couldn't seem to get over. "They're not *that* rich…besides, it's his dad's money." I wasn't entirely sure how his family had amassed such an amount, or whose it was technically. They seemed to live a communal lifestyle though, or a "nest" lifestyle, to put it in vampire terms, so they probably considered whatever they had to be everyone's. It was sort of a sweet way to live. Assuming everyone liked each other, which luckily, his entire family immensely loved each other, nearly worshipped each other. That was sweet too.

We followed the granite steps to the huge wooden overhang above the front doors and I noticed the potted white roses trailing up each one of the massive support beams. I grinned at the beauties that the vampire women had put up for me. Nervous-excited energy flitted through me at the thought of tomorrow. Having heard my body's changes, Teren reached over and grabbed my hand. He knew that I was nervous, excited or maybe both, and he gave me an encouraging smile as he started to open the door. It swung in before he had a chance though, and I suppressed a grin at his mom's impatience. The unexpectedness made Ben take a quick step back. His face went a sickly shade of green with his sudden movement, and he put a hand on his stomach as he groaned. I held my breath and prayed that he didn't toss his cookies on my beautiful new roses.

He kept it together though, and slapped on a gorgeous smile that almost made him seem normal. Relaxing, I turned to greet Teren's...*my*...family.

"Emma," Alanna beamed, as she, for the first time ever, ignored her son and swept me into her arms before him. Her long black hair swished around me as she slowly wrapped me in her cool embrace. I returned the gesture, feeling tears sting my eyes already. Oh, boy, I was never going to make it through this weekend.

Eyeing me warmly, she pulled back from me, then shifted her attention to Teren. He grinned and greeted her just as warmly as she'd greeted me. Yes, one thing this family had in spades was love for each other.

When they separated, Teren gave his dad a swift hug, then swished his arm out to indicate our friends. "Mom, Dad, this is Tracey and Ben, and of course, you remember Emma's sister, Ashley." Ashley had visited me at the ranch not too long after Teren's conversion. Alanna and Jack gave her a soft smile of acknowledgement before Teren finished his introductions. "Guys, this is my father, Jack, and his wife, my step-mother, Alanna."

Tracey and Ben threw on polite smiles as they shook Jack's hand and I mentally reminded myself about Teren's cover story. Alanna, Imogen and Halina, all looked too young to be his mother, grandmother and especially, his great-grandmother, so, to the outside world his birth mother had died a few years ago and his father had remarried, to a younger woman no less. Imogen and Halina were being "sold" as Alanna's sisters. That story would work for several years, until eventually Teren's never-ending youth ruined the tale. Then he would have to be sold as Alanna's sibling as well. That would be a weird lie to say; she was too much a mom to me.

Tracey was alternating her gaze between Alanna and Teren. There was a clearly confused look on her sickly face. I understood. Alanna and Teren were almost carbon copies of each other; the resemblance was eerie. But he'd just established that he and Alanna weren't blood related. Tracey was trying to figure that out. I smiled, picturing her astonishment when she met the other vampires; they were all eerily similar. That was one unfortunate part of the story. You just had to buy that they weren't related to Teren, even though they looked just like him. Again, I supposed Teren could be changed in the story to be their brother…and again, weird.

Jack looked ecstatic to have another fishing partner in the house. He clasped Hot Ben on the back, which made Ben wince, and then we were all led into the foyer. Tracey let out a low "wow" as she looked around the house. I smiled as I looked around too. The grand double staircase, the beautiful French doors that opened up into the impressive living room, the art along the walls, including the stunning sunset that Halina had painted, and the naked, crying woman fountain in the center; it was beautiful, meticulous and classy, much like Alanna.

Alanna had set more potted roses along the banisters; the pots were a swirled black and white marble, with faint streaks of red in them. The roses themselves alternated between a deep red, and a white as pure as snow…or vampire skin. The roses had been strung along the railings, so they looped around them, all the way to the top. The colors mingled beautifully. White and red pillar candles lined the edges of every single step, and when they were lit, I imagined that the entire staircase would glow. Even more candles and roses were spaced throughout the room, and a few petals floated in the fountain. I shook my head as we left. It was impressive…and it was only the entryway.

Alanna started walking us to a side hallway that led to one of the different buildings. The guests weren't staying in the main building apparently, which was probably for the best. We passed through a covered breezeway into one of the wings that the vampires never really used. I supposed that they planned on eventually filling all the rooms with grandchildren—great-great-great-great-etc-grandchildren. That was one of the things about living eternally—you had to plan for events *really* far in the future. It sort of blew my mind. I wasn't even sure what I'd be doing in the next six months, let alone the next sixty or six hundred years, although that last one wouldn't really be a problem for me, as there was no way this human girl would live that long.

Alanna showed us into a room she'd set up for Tracey and Hot Ben. They both thanked her and lay down on the bed, face first. I chuckled at our tired, hung-over friends. As Alanna left with Ashley to show her to her room, Teren laughed at Ben, smacked his feet and told him he'd go get his bags for him. Ben muttered something about Teren being an ass for not being hung-over too, and then he started snoring. I shook my head at the pair, and wished them both a speedy recovery from last night's festivities.

Teren lickety-split got their things and then rushed to get Ashley's as well. He blurred into her room, since he didn't have to hide any of his abilities from her, and she grinned and thanked him as she experimentally bounced up and down on her luxurious bed.

Teren set down two black dress bags and cocked an eyebrow at me. "Don't you worry about that," I told him. Knowing my dress was in one, he grinned. I smiled as I studied the gorgeous man I was about to marry—the jet black hair and pale blue eyes, set off by his impossibly sexy stubble. He was supernaturally perfect.

He leaned in to kiss me and then excused himself so Ashley and I could talk about the wedding. Alanna joined us. After she assured me that Teren was bonding with his dad at their favorite fishing hole, I showed Alanna the dress. She "oohed" and "aahed" and started crying pinkish tears in her joy. She hugged me again and patted my slightly larger belly. "You're going to look so amazing, Emma. I'm so excited that you're joining my family." As I clasped her chilly hand, I felt exactly the same way.

Eventually, Tracey and Hot Ben woke from their "nap" and stumbled out to find everyone. Alanna pointed Ben toward the general vicinity of where Teren was fishing with Jack, and Ben's face brightened considerably. Looking like his normal handsome self, he grabbed some spare equipment and gave Tracey a quick kiss goodbye before following Alanna out back, to where the jeeps were located.

Tracey had taken one look out her window after resting, and knew exactly what we girls were going to do while the boys played in the chilly waters. She'd decided that we were all sipping mojitos in the hot tub. Okay, she and Ash would be sipping mojitos in the hot tub. I would be sipping caffeine-free soda and dangling my feet over the edge. The doctor had told me that anything hotter than bath water wasn't good for the kids, and after all I'd gone through to get knocked up, I wasn't taking any risks.

Ash would normally never wear a swimsuit in a situation like this, but she felt so comfortable around Tracey and the vampires, that she gleefully changed into a modest one piece. Tracey changed into tiny scraps of material that I was sure were illegal in several States.

They ducked out to the pool while I headed to the kitchen to prepare their drinks. From all the way inside, I could hear Tracey's exclamation when she saw it. I giggled, remembering how impressed I'd been with it, too, when I'd first seen it. The pool area was exquisite. Flat river rocks made up a patio that seamlessly surrounded an Olympic sized pool, hot tub, and barbequing area. There just weren't enough words to describe how natural and incredible this place really was. I hoped the ranch stayed in their family forever.

Alanna joined me after seeing Hot Ben off. She slung a cool arm around my waist while I opened the fridge to look for some beverages that humans could drink. Alanna smiled and opened a cabinet above the fridge, where several bottles of alcohol were tucked away. I was a little surprised at first, until she explained that Jack liked to have a drink or two with the hired hands, and Teren used to join them sometimes, back when he could drink.

As Alanna automatically started making mojitos, having heard Tracey's request, I leaned back on the counter and watched her lightning fast hands work. "Are you guys going to be okay this weekend, Mom? I mean, you won't go hungry or anything?"

She smiled that I'd used her preferred form of address without having to correct myself, and then turned back to her work. "Of course, dear. We have ways to eat in secret."

I worried my lip and looked out the window, to where I could see the rolling hills full of herds of cattle. "Yeah, well, I really appreciate all of the trouble that you've all gone to."

She stopped and placed a hand on my shoulder; her youthful face was warm and open. "It's no trouble, Emma. You're family." My hand automatically went to my stomach and her eyes tracked the movement. With a small smile, she shook her head. "That's not what makes you family, sweetheart." I was confused, until she continued. "You have my son's heart...that's what makes you family."

She removed her hand and picked up a tray to put the drinks on. I felt my eyes watering over her words. The feeling only intensified with her next statement. Picking up the tray, she said, "You have no idea how long he looked for you."

I swallowed, and a tear fell down my cheek. "Probably as long as I looked for him." A goofy grin broke out on my face, along with more tears, and I silently cursed my hormonal body. My current state didn't mix well with these darn emotional vampires.

Alanna had pink tears in her eyes too, and she gave me a swift hug with her free arm. Both of us swiped our eyes, then we headed out to the back. Finally seeing the area for myself, I gasped and felt my mouth drop open. A large, white wedding tent had been stretched out between the two buildings and dozens, no, hundreds of twinkling lights were strung underneath the canvas. Outdoor heaters had been set up around the perimeter, ready to warm up the humans who would be bothered by a chilly December evening. A Plexiglas floor had been constructed over the pool, effectively creating a huge open area where once only swimming had taken place. You could see the calm water under that glass, highlighted by blue underwater lamps. Walking on that glass would seem like you were walking right on top of the water.

Dozens of balloons in reds, whites and black were tied off at the four corners of the massive tent, and to every available surface around the patio. Candles and roses, also in the weddings colors, covered nearly every other flat surface. Tables lined the area on the edges of the pool and the pool-floor itself was already set up with rows upon rows of folding chairs. The far end of the tent held a low bench with candles and roses. A wooden arch directly over it was draped in twining flowers. I blinked away more tears as I realized what I was looking at—the spot where Teren and I would be married.

Feeling Alanna's encouraging pat on my back, I closed my mouth and muttered something along the lines of "it's beautiful." It was all new, too—none of this had been here when we'd visited last weekend. The hot tub was behind the tent, and as the sides of the canopy were tied open, I could see through it, to where Tracey and Ashley were laughing in the massive tub of near-boiling water.

Tracey noticed me walking up and exclaimed, "Isn't this amazing, Emma!" She shook her head in delight. "Your wedding is going to be so beautiful." Her eyes misted, and I saw a brief moment of wistfulness pass her features. I started to wonder if she and Hot Ben would get through this weekend without "the talk."

As I took off my shoes and rolled up my pant legs, Alanna handed the girls their drinks. I watched Tracey, amused, as she took it and cautiously took a sip. She had to still be hurting from last night. As the searing water hit my feet, I sighed in contentment. Alanna finished by handing me my pop, and then she cocked her head to the side, listening to something, or someone. I strained, but couldn't hear what her super ears could. Tracey took no notice, but Ashley watched her as intently as I did.

She smiled at me. "I'll be back to check on you girls in a bit."

The day was cold but clear, and a flash of sunlight played on her dark hair as she turned to leave. I wanted to ask her what it was, but she couldn't really explain it in front of Tracey, so I didn't ask. I would just have to trust the vampires.

As I was banging my legs against the back of the tub and reveling in the mixture of chilly air and hot water, I started to truly relax. Everything was going perfectly…and everything would end perfectly. This weekend was going to be fabulous. And I was going to come out of it an Adams.

The cause of Alanna's earlier distraction became apparent when maybe ten or fifteen minutes later, my mom showed up in the backyard. I bounded up to greet her, while Alanna excused herself to get something to drink for her. I also knew that Alanna needed to get away from the bright sun. It was probably starting to get uncomfortable for her.

"Mom, you're here!" I exclaimed, hugging the plump woman tight. Mom hadn't been going to show up until tomorrow morning, to give us "kids" a chance to celebrate alone.

She grinned and hugged me back. "Yeah, I ducked out of work early. I know you're having a bonding moment with your friends," she pulled back to look at me and tears were in her eyes, "but I wanted my girls."

Tears were in my eyes now too. "It's fine. I'm glad you came." I felt the tears sliding down my cheeks, and thought that maybe the vampires weren't the only emotional ones. "I'm so glad you're here." I nearly sobbed that and rolled my eyes at my overreaction.

Mom only sniffled, then laughed. Pulling apart from me, she swiped underneath her eyes. "You're a little emotional, aren't you?" Everyone laughed at that, me included.

"Yeah, darn pregnancy," I muttered.

Mom patted my stomach, a broad smile on her face. "And that only gets worse."

I sighed, then hugged her again. A little while later, Tracey and Ashley had had enough of the steamy water, and they scrambled out of the tub and into thick, warm robes. Mom looked around the fairytale backyard and kept muttering, "It's so beautiful, Emma."

I nodded, agreeing with her, and then I showed her the areas of the house that I could, while Tracey and Ashley changed back into regular clothes. She was amazed at the spectacular view of Mount Diablo from the living room, and she gaped at the stone fireplace; the stones along the flue were meticulously positioned in such a way that they resembled a flame. But those reactions were nothing to the reaction I got when I showed her the kitchen.

Alanna's kitchen was to die for, especially if, like my mom, you loved to cook. She opened every dark mahogany cabinet, examined everything in the double fridge, that was mainly holding flowers at the moment—no blood, thank goodness, and let out a loud exclamation when she saw the walk-in freezer, which also thankfully had no visible blood in it. Alanna joined our tour and pointed out all the intricate details of the kitchen that only a fellow cook would appreciate. I tuned them out when they started going over recipes.

If my mom thought Teren's step-mother was odd, or a little too identical to him, you'd never know it by her body language. She leaned in close to the woman as they animatedly debated casserole recipes. I tensed when Mom touched Alanna's shoulder, but then I relaxed. Mom was too caught up in the conversation to note Alanna's "differences."

Mom didn't bother with the rest of the tour after that. She was content with Alanna in their favorite room. The two of them started preparing a feast for dinner, just as the boys came back from fishing. Tracey mauled Hot Ben and I embraced Teren. Jack gave Alanna a warm hug and handed her the few fish the boys had managed to catch. It wasn't much since it wasn't fishing season, but Alanna looked like he'd just handed her a diamond bracelet. She gave him and Teren a huge hug.

"Thank you, boys," she proclaimed brightly, then she and Mom started talking about ways to prepare it.

I smiled and relaxed into Teren's arms, completely comfortable.

While Alanna and Jack kept Mom occupied in the kitchen, the rest of us slipped into the living room. Tracey and Ben felt the need to make sure Teren and I got started in our marriage the "correct" way. I tried to pat my baby-filled stomach and explain that "we got it," but Tracey was having way too much fun describing, in detail, every kinky act that she felt we needed to try on our wedding night. My sister blushed and sipped her drink, silent, but intently listening. I felt flushed, knowing every vampire could hear Tracey, but not knowing how to tell her to shut up in front of my in-laws.

Teren only laughed, occasionally looking embarrassed, occasionally giving me sly glances. I wanted to smack him at those eager looks, but resisted, especially when those sly glances started affecting me. Ben laughed at our obvious discomfort, and then interjected a few ideas of his own.

Just when I'd had enough of their outlandish, and in some instances, painful sounding, suggestions, a cool voice sounded over our shoulders.

"No, that position is better if her legs are held higher."

I tensed, but every head shifted to look at the newcomer. Halina sauntered into our midst; the sun must have set while we were talking. The entrance to her underground lair was actually in the living room with us, hidden as a closet, but no one had noticed her opening the door. They'd been too engrossed in Tracey's latest suggestion. They all gaped at her, both at her sudden appearance, and her startling similarity to Alanna…and Teren. Her outfit probably didn't hurt either, at least in Ben's case. She was wearing a form-fitting, long-sleeved dress that stopped just below her ass. It was really provocative and not at all appropriate for ranch wear. It was completely Halina.

Hot Ben's eyes drifted down Halina's long, snow-white exposed legs. He'd probably get smacked if Tracey was paying more attention. She wasn't, though. Her eyes were drifting between Halina and Teren, trying to figure out the familial connection.

Teren stood and gave Halina a swift hug. He was happy to see his great-grandmother, but he needed to look as if he was only greeting his step-mother's younger sister. Ah, the never-ending charade.

"Guys, this is Alanna's little sister, Halina." Teren grinned, barely suppressing a laugh, and I could instantly see why. Behind his back, where only I could see it, Halina had pinched his thigh, hard. On a human, it probably would have incapacitated him. The oldest woman in the house apparently did not like being referred to as the "little" sister.

Hot Ben instantly stood and extended a hand to her. That got Tracey's attention, and her eyes pulled away from Halina to glare at Ben. As he had a stupid *Wow, you're hot* look on his face, I thought they might have more than one uncomfortable conversation this weekend.

Halina crooked a smile at him, obviously enjoying his reaction. And I supposed it would be even more apparent to her. Since she was one hundred percent vampire, she had the most acute senses of all of them. And she enjoyed men. She enjoyed their attentions, just as much as she enjoyed terrifying them. As she listened to Ben's blood flow increasing, while shaking his hand and purring his name back to him, I could only imagine how satisfied she was.

"A pleasure," she drawled out, her eyes dragging over his body.

Tracey immediately stepped between them, breaking their contact. Not wanting to touch Halina, she only waved at her. Tracey looked a bit afraid under the mask of bravado she had on, and I wondered if maybe some part of her was sensing what I'd sensed the first time I'd met Halina, that she was dangerous. It was an almost primal desire to not want to be in her presence. Of course, Tracey wouldn't understand why she felt that way, so she'd probably brush it off as jealousy or something, but it was so much more than that.

"Hey…Tracey. Ben's other half," she added with a slight smile.

Ben made some sort of noise behind her and Tracey nonchalantly elbowed him. Yeah, they were definitely having a conversation later. I cringed when I realized that Halina would hear it…and she would love them arguing about her. Halina's eyes drifted to my sister, and her entire demeanor changed. The cold, calculating vixen that had just mentally undressed Hot Ben, was suddenly a nineteen-year-old girl, embracing her long lost best friend. She swept Ashley into a warm hug, and both of them giggled like they were reuniting at summer camp. I shook my head in amusement as I watched them.

They had bonded when Ashley had visited. In a surprising way, Halina had taken a shine to my sister. She had nearly the same protective instinct towards her that Teren had. Halina hadn't chosen this life, and had lost a lot when it had been forced upon her—the normalcy of working hard on the farm with her beloved husband, watching the sun set together, the possibility of filling their farm with children. Although she hid it well, the absence of her old life crushed her daily. My sister had also had a fate not wanted thrust upon her. Her life-changing scarring and the death of our father had set her on a path that most people wouldn't wish on anyone.

The two brutal fates had bonded the women, almost tighter than blood could have.

Tracey was openly glaring at Hot Ben while my sister and Halina caught up. I was about to go over and tell Tracey not to fret too much about it, that Halina just had that effect on men, but the last vampire in the house made her appearance before I could take a step.

Teren and Halina both looked over a few seconds before Imogen entered the room, but no one noticed their precognition. Halina slung an arm around my sister and turned to watch her daughter enter the room. Imogen walked straight up to me and swept me into a hug. In her exuberance she actually lifted me a good foot in the air. It looked a little odd, considering the woman was no bigger than I was, but my friends were too busy staring at her appearance to notice. She set me down and I pulled back to look at her. She had on the long skirt and modest blouse that she preferred to wear, and her hair was neatly pulled back into a braided up-do. Her face was perfect, ageless, and yet another copy of the family genes.

Teren walked up and gave her a polite hug, again downplaying their closeness, then he introduced her to the group, "This is Alanna's twin sister, Imogen." I started at that, before smoothing my features. I hadn't known the story involved the mother/daughter being twins. I imagined the two of them loved that, they were very close. Irritation blossomed in me that I hadn't known all of the lies I'd have to tell, and then I was a little irritated that I had so many lies to memorize. Oh well, it was the life I'd signed up for.

Teren pointed out Ben and Tracey, who greeted Imogen with friendly waves. Imogen was attractive, they all were, but she exuded an older vibe, like the grandmother she was, and not the raw sex appeal that seemed to effortlessly drift off of Halina. Hot Ben's eyes didn't stay focused on Imogen for very long. After his greeting, he was back to ogling Halina, who played with a strand of her wild, free hair and gave him a look that clearly said, *I have chains in my room, wanna see?*

Under my breath, I muttered, "Stop it right now, Halina. Tracey is my best friend. If you try and sleep with him...I won't let you come to the wedding." No human in the room heard me, but Imogen cracked a smile and Teren chuckled.

Halina openly pouted. Then she fixed her face into a wry smile and adjusted her super-short dress. Raising an eyebrow at me, she said, "There is no 'try' about it, but...fine." She gave him a brief glance, then sighed as she turned to leave. Ben and Tracey looked really confused by her seemingly random statement, but Ash looked over at me and cracked a smile; she could guess what I'd said to her.

Halina got to the doorframe and paused. Putting a hand on the wall, she seductively leaned into it. Ben openly watched her and Tracey finally smacked his chest, returning his attention to her. Halina smirked at the exchange and looked over at me. "Plenty of other fish anyway," she muttered. Shifting her gaze to Imogen and then Teren, she brightly said, "I'm going out to eat. Have fun at…dinner." She gave them an odd smile, then left the room.

My face went pale white, and I clenched Teren's hand. I didn't like the thought of her "going out to eat." That usually meant exactly what it sounded like, and I didn't want her anywhere near my hometown when she was hungry. "Teren," I whispered, stress in my voice.

He leaned over to kiss my cheek, and whispered in my ear, "She won't kill. I made her promise." Pulling back, he gave me a serious expression. I swallowed, but nodded.

She wouldn't kill. I knew that stipulation was only a temporary one. Halina enjoyed what she did, and even though she only took the lives of people she deemed dead already, i.e., child molesters, rapists, general scum bags, it was still taking a life and it still knotted my stomach. I knew Teren had somehow coaxed a promise out of her to please me this weekend, and I also knew that the "promise" wouldn't extend as long as I'd like it to.

Imogen gave me a soft smile and shrugged her shoulders. She had deep regrets over her own few kills and wouldn't do it again, but they each sort of took an "it's your choice" stance on the matter. Especially when it came to Halina. But then again, as Teren had told me once before, "Have you ever tried to stop a full vampire from doing something they *want* to do?"

As I relaxed a bit, and accepted that some poor schlub was going to lose a pint or two, but at least not his life, the second part of Halina's statement started to worry me. Dinner. I'd completely forgotten about dinner. Not long after Halina left, Alanna and my mom came into the room and announced that it was ready. Crap. Three non-eating vampires, faking eating dinner, around three not-in-the-loop humans. I had no idea what they were going to do.

It turned out that what they were going to do, was sit down at the table with everyone else. I looked over at Teren seated beside me and nervously squeezed his hand, but he only looked back with perfectly calm eyes. Whatever they had planned, it was something they were all in on, and all comfortable with. As I glanced from him to Imogen, sitting next to Ashley, to Alanna, setting the table with my mother, I saw no tension in the vampire faces, only a calm peace.

I shifted my eyes to Jack, the one human who knew that something was up. He looked content sitting back in his chair and making polite conversation with Hot Ben. I watched the middle-aged man, with the graying hair and the warm brown eyes, but I didn't see any stress in his features. Not until Alanna put a hand on his shoulder as she set down his glass of water.

When she did that, he looked up at her, and a brief look passed between them. The look in his eyes worried me some. It wasn't the nervous tension that I was feeling; no fear was in his face that they'd somehow be discovered. No, the look in his eyes was one of deep sympathy. Like he knew she was about to do something that was going to be unpleasant for her, and he felt badly about it. She briefly smiled at him, leaning down to kiss his cheek and whisper in his ear.

Imogen and Teren looked at her. Teren took a deep, calming breath, and I felt tears sting my eyes. Whatever they were going to do, was not going to be fun for them, and they were all still resigned to do it anyway. For me.

I wanted to stand up and beg them not to. I wanted to tell Alanna to bring out the carafe. I wanted them to feel comfortable in their own home. And I again debated moving this entire event somewhere else. I didn't want them hurting themselves for me.

As my hormonal tears started to spill over, Teren turned my face to his and began kissing me. The humans at the table whistled their encouragement, but I still felt like sobbing. His fingers discretely wiped away my tears as he whispered in-between our lips. "Don't stress. We do this for you willingly. We love you." He pulled back and his knuckle swept down to dry my face. As Tracey hollered her approval, he leaned in and whispered in my ear. "We will be fine. Just enjoy your evening."

I gave him pleading eyes, wanting to know exactly what they were "willingly doing for me," but I couldn't speak. He sighed at the look on my face and leaned over to kiss the other side, whispering in my other ear, "Please, make what we're about to do…worth it."

He gave me a pointed look and raised an eyebrow. I swallowed and nodded, looking at him, then Imogen, and then finally Alanna, as she and Mom finished setting the table. I suddenly realized why Halina was really skipping this meal. She didn't want to partake in whatever they were about to do.

My mom chuckled as she sat down beside me and I slapped on a bright, fake smile. She patted my knee and looked around me to Teren. "Just can't keep your hands off each other, can you?" She let out a dreamy sigh. "It was like that for me and your father before our wedding too."

Imogen perked up and gave my mom a sympathetic glance. Imogen didn't mention her own husband's death, her "character" had never married, but maybe living vicariously through her grief, she encouraged my mom to talk about her long lost husband. Mom did, and the entire table shifted to follow the conversation.

My eyes drifted around everyone at this mammoth, elaborate table. The platters of steaks, freshly caught fish, mashed potatoes and green beans, slightly separated everyone. During a pause in the story, Alanna began dishing up plates of food, brushing aside my mom's attempts to continue helping her.

My mouth dropped open as every vampire in the room was given a plate of food…human food. I couldn't even conceal my astonishment as I watched them in horror. They were all given a steak, a spoonful of potatoes, a small helping of the fish Ben and Teren had caught earlier, and a forkful of beans. Once they were all served and Alanna had seated herself at the other end of the table, they all began cutting their food. My eyes were as wide as saucers as Teren grabbed a fork loaded with a hunk of meat and held it in front of his lips. He looked nervous, but his voice was steady. "Eat up, Emma." He popped the food in his mouth and gave me a quavering smile. "It's delicious."

When I still hadn't done anything, he pointedly glanced at the plate of food Alanna had set in front of me. I tore my eyes away from the sight of him eating, and made myself concentrate on my meal. Oblivious, my mom and Tracey talked while Jack watched his wife with worried eyes. Ben went on and on about how good the fish was, and Ashley looked around at all the eating vampires with a look of puzzled amazement that probably matched mine. But unlike me, she shrugged, assumed it was just something they could do, and joined in a conversation with Mom.

I cut my food and woodenly popped some in my mouth. I really wasn't sure if it was something they could do or not. I watched Teren and the girls eat, and felt a knot of apprehension at the disgusted look on their faces. I wasn't sure what human food tasted like anymore to him, but I knew he had no desire for it. I imagined it was much like eating a plate of dog food, or maybe worse, dog vomit.

Tears stung my eyes again, but I pushed them back. They seemed to be eating just fine and if it really was only that it tasted bad, well, they could handle that for one night, right?

As the meal progressed, and everyone finished their wonderful food, a light and happy feeling fell upon the table. It would seem that dinner had successfully gone by with no one the wiser to my new family's situation. I relaxed into Teren's side, but he held himself rigid and upright in his chair. Alarmed at the tension in his body, I subtly turned to study him. He was trying to keep his face smooth, but I could see the way he clenched his jaw, the way he winced every once in a while. He was in pain. He was sitting there, calmly having a conversation with Ben, in pain. I clenched his hand, but he didn't look at me.

That was when I noticed the faces on the other vampires. They were all in pain, horrible, horrible pain. I could see it in their body language. To me, it was written all over their tense faces. Seeing the sadness on Jack's face, his eyes moist, his smile forced, I could see he saw it too. It was a little miraculous to me that the rest of the room couldn't tell.

As Alanna hadn't moved to clear the table yet—a startling indicator all by itself, my mom offered, and began clearing things away. Alanna smiled softly and thanked her. It was at this point that Imogen stood and politely excused herself. No human took notice of her leaving, but my eyes couldn't stay off of her. She walked slowly and stiffly from the room; she sort of resembled the way Ashley walked. She was gone for just a few moments before Alanna and

Teren closed their eyes at the same time. A look of compassion passed their faces.

That look terrified me. They were hearing something I probably wouldn't want to hear, something Imogen was doing that they would each have to do. I suddenly closed my eyes, understanding. The vampires could eat food, obviously, they still had mouths and stomachs after all, but they couldn't digest it. So…the food had to come out. The same way it came in.

I squeezed Teren's hand as my eyes watered. He opened his and looked down on me with a tight smile. He nodded and I nodded back. We both knew now, we were both on the same page.

Alanna excused herself as Mom started bringing in pie. I wanted to cry at the sight, tell Mom that no more food was needed, but I made myself smile and thank her. Made their sacrifice worth it.

Teren sat there the entire time we ate, no longer talking, his eyes closed, his brow scrunched in pain he could no longer disguise. I wanted to scream at him to just go and get rid of it, since it was hurting him, but no one else would understand, and I was way too riled up to secretly whisper it to him. Finally, it was Hot Ben who noticed his discomfort. "You all right, Teren?" He raised an eyebrow and tilted his head. I could have kissed Ben for bringing it up.

Teren cracked open his eyes. "Actually, I feel a little…odd. I think I'll turn in." He slowly stood and calmly said goodnight to everyone. I watched him leave the room and had to force myself to not run upstairs to be with him. I looked over at Jack and saw the same level of restraint on his face.

None of the vampires returned to the table after that.

As Mom and Ashley and Tracey cleared the dishes and made some coffee for Ben and Jack, I excused myself to check on Teren. Jack gave me a sympathetic look and briefly nodded at me. He knew what I'd find, and he knew it would be bad.

My stomach clenched with each step to our room. I hated what he'd done to himself, all to maintain the image of humanity. I hated that he had to hide. But at the same time, I understood it. As I reached the top of the dual staircase, I put a hand on my stomach and wondered if this was the future I was condemning our children too. I suddenly understood one of the reasons why Teren hadn't wanted to continue this…trait.

Softly and cautiously, I opened the door. I wasn't sure what to expect. Looking around our opulent guest room here at the ranch, I blinked in the soft lamp light, surprised. It was empty. Just as I was wondering if maybe he went somewhere else, I heard him.

It wasn't hard. I could clearly hear him cry out, although it was coming out muffled, like he was screaming into a pillow or something. It was coming from the bathroom, so I ran in there. My heart leapt into my throat when I saw him. He was covered in blood. Panic seized me, as I watched him heave a pile of blood onto the tile floor. It wasn't coming from a wound, it was coming…from him. Adrenaline surged through me as I knelt beside him. I wanted to yell for help, but there was no one to yell for. All of the vampires were going through this, and the humans that knew the secret, were entertaining the humans who didn't. There was no one to help Teren, but me.

In-between vomiting up more blood, he curled into a fetal position, clutched his stomach, and groaned into a blood soaked towel. His fangs were extended, having dropped down at the presence of blood, even his own. I'd never imagined so much blood could leave a person's body. I started crying and shaking as I held him. He was so out of it he couldn't speak, only continued screaming into anything that would muffle the noise, and heaving up more blood, the food having long ago left his system.

His body apparently had a severe reaction to food being put inside it. His sickness was about quadruple what my morning sickness was. As blood ruined his clothes and mine, I held him tight, stroking his back and murmuring that I loved him, and everything would be okay. I wasn't even sure if he heard me. I wasn't even sure if everything *was* okay. I had no idea how to help him.

Worrying that my family would come check on us, and then understanding why Jack wasn't immediately at Alanna's side—someone had to run interference—I cried into Teren's back as he continued his muffled screaming and heaving. I didn't know what else to do.

Although he was still shaking uncontrollably, the vomiting eventually stopped. A while later, the cries stopped as well. I held him in my arms, our bodies coated in the blood he'd released—it was cold and sticky, and smelled awful, all pooled together like it was. I fought down my own nausea as I stroked his hair and kissed his temples. I wasn't sure how long I held him in that chilly, bloody bathroom, as he shook in my arms, but eventually a body breezed into the room.

"Teren…how long did you let it go?" I startled as Halina knelt beside him, her face was both irritated and worried. She lifted his weak head and his eyes rolled back before he could focus on her; his fangs were red from his own blood.

"Will he be okay?" I whispered, hope filling me that someone who understood what was happening to him, could help him.

She muttered something in Russian as she examined him. "Yes." She looked back at me. "We're harder than *that* to kill." Running her hand over his face, she muttered, "But he didn't have to let it get this bad." With a wry smile, she added, "And he could have made this mess in the toilet."

A soft laugh escaped him and I nearly sobbed in relief. He hadn't responded to me once since I'd been in here.

Halina started cleaning him up and then helped him stand. He was weak, but he managed to get on his feet. She started walking him away, more carrying him than helping him. They walked into the bedroom and then she surprisingly turned to the window. Picking Teren up, she slung him over her shoulder, like he weighed nothing. I watched as she opened the window and prepared to jump. Confused, I exclaimed, "Wait, where are you going with him? Shouldn't he rest?"

She paused and looked back at me, her face hard. "No, he needs to eat. They all need to eat. Now."

Deep understanding rang through me, as I suddenly saw the real reason Halina had skipped dinner. It wasn't that she wanted a bite in town. It wasn't that she didn't want to go through what Teren and the others had gone through. It was that one of them needed to stay strong, to help the others. Their love for each other was overwhelming, as was my guilt, that they'd felt the need to do this in the first place. I couldn't imagine having the foreknowledge of how painful something you were going to do was, and then doing it anyway. It would be like knowingly shoving your hand into a fire. But, as my fingers automatically drifted down to the twins in my belly, I reconsidered. The end result of my situation certainly wasn't going to be easy, but sometimes, the ends justify the means.

I nodded at Halina as I watched her step up onto the window ledge; they couldn't really just walk out the front door, what with Teren soaked in blood like he was. Before she jumped, she turned back and looked me over. Shaking her head, she muttered, "Shower, change, and then go tell your friends that he's fine and he's sleeping." She pointedly raised an eyebrow at me. "You're going to be a member of this family. You must now play your part."

I nodded again, and then she turned back to the window and jumped. They were gone by the time I looked outside.

Chapter 6 – Pre-wedding Jitters

I stared at the ceiling of our bedroom, waiting. I mentally traced every raised section of the textured walls, making images out of the patterns where there really wasn't any. Anything to distract my mind. Anything to stop myself from wondering how Teren was doing, if he was feeling any better. That last image of him covered in blood wouldn't leave me. Several of the patterns on the walls reminded me of the pool of red liquid we'd been huddled in. God, I hoped he was okay.

As I shifted for the thousandth time in the too-quiet room, I finally heard the door crack open. It was late, several hours past the time everyone had called it a night, and the hallway behind Teren was dark. His eyes glowed at me until he walked into our dimly lit room. I sucked in a sharp breath when I saw him.

Closing the door, he stood beside it and let me take him in. He looked like something straight out of a Steven King novel—splotches of dried or drying blood covered him; his jeans and shirt were saturated with it. His face had deep red smears and smudges, both from the act of being sick and my bloody hands caressing him. He stood with a hunch and his face was worn, close to exhaustion, if not already there. His pale blue eyes were slightly unfocused as he looked at me, but a small smile was on his lips.

"Hey," he whispered, his voice hoarse.

My eyes instantly watered at the sight of him, and I flew out of bed to throw my arms around him. My forcefulness made him stumble back a step, and I choked back a sob at how frail he seemed. His arms swept securely around me though, as he held me tight.

"Teren, what were you thinking?" I murmured in his ear.

He didn't answer, only softly stroked my back. I pulled away, my hands going to his blood smeared cheeks. Cupping them, I searched his eyes. He gave me another small smile in response. Hating the evidence of his painful night all over him, I grabbed his hand and pulled him into the bathroom. He willingly followed, his feet shuffling on the padded carpet as he forced his body to move.

I closed the door behind us, not really expecting any distractions, but wanting to play it safe anyway. Teren watched me, almost blankly, and I thought only sheer will power kept him standing. I came back and gently swept his shirt over his head. His chest was smeared with dried blood from where the wet shirt had stuck to his skin. Some sections of his shirt were still wet, and I threw it in the corner of the recently cleaned bathroom. Bringing my eyes back to his chest, I bit my lip and fought back the tears.

His fingers came to my chin, lifting my gaze to his. "I'm fine, Emma." He shrugged in a tired, but casual manner. "Just a little…discomfort, but it's gone now."

My mind filled with the remembered sounds of his muffled screams. *A little discomfort?* I shook my head. "You didn't have to do that," I whispered, my voice sounding loud in the quiet room.

His fingers, still tainted red, brushed over my cheek. He tilted his head as he regarded me. "Yes, I did. We couldn't have all walked out on dinner with your family, especially Mom and me. We had to appear normal."

My hand grabbed his and I flattened his cool fingers against my cheek. "No, none of you should have had to do that." Wanting him to feel the comforting heat I provided, I stepped into him and brought my warm arms around his cool body. Looking up at him, I bit my lip. "We could have gone somewhere else, or eloped. I was so selfish to ask for this."

He immediately grabbed my cheeks and shook his head. "No, Emma. We wanted this. We all wanted to give you this." A warm smile lit his tired face. "You deserve a normal family dinner. I wanted to give you that, we all did. We crave normalcy too." He stared intently into my eyes. "And we want to give you a *normal* wedding experience."

I sighed, then pointedly cocked an eyebrow at him and rubbed a smidge of dried blood off his chin. He crooked a grin and shook his head. "Well, as normal as we can give you." He shrugged, then, looking too tired to keep standing, he sat on the edge of the tub.

I watched him sitting there, staring up at me with a content expression, and sighed again. Turning from him, I stepped over to the shower and turned on one of the dual heads. Under the sound of the water, I again said, "You didn't have to do that."

As I turned back to him, he smiled, and I knew he'd heard me. He didn't comment though, only slipped his stained shoes off. I helped him remove the rest of his clothes and then helped him get into the shower. It felt a little odd to help him, when he was usually the supernaturally strong one, but the evening had sapped a lot of that strength. As he sagged against the shower wall, I slipped my pajamas off and hopped inside, to continue helping him.

He laid his head back against the wall, his eyes closed and his face pale. The spray of water hit his chest, droplets landing on his face and mine. The dried blood started to break apart and run like rivulets down his body. Hating the sight of the red streams, I grabbed some soap and got to work. I was determined to see that bloody mess gone. Teren exhaled contently as I lathered the soap and spread the bubbles over his chest, pausing to scrub harder in the more concentrated areas. The bubbles forming on his body turned pink from all of the blood, and the water streaming around us went through various spectrums of the shade.

Noting the haggard look on his face and the shallow way he was breathing I scrubbed his cheeks, I lifted a corner of my lip and wryly said, "You finally look hung-over."

He cracked an eye and smiled. He glanced down at my naked body, then closed them again. "Totally worth it," he muttered.

I ran some soap in his hair; my fingers turned pink as the dried blood in the blackness came clean. "I don't see how anything could have been worth that," I muttered.

Hearing me, he opened his eyes again. He grabbed my hips and pulled me into him. "You're worth it. You're worth anything."

I sighed at the sight of my fiancé covered in pink bubbles, and laced my arms around his neck. I ran my fingers through his wet hair and just took a moment to appreciate him. For me, he and the women had willingly done something that they knew would cause them pain. And as Halina had explained, when she'd cleaned up the bloody mess he'd left, Teren had made the situation worse, by allowing the nearly toxic food to stay in his system much longer than was necessary, or healthy. She'd explained that anything but blood in their system now had an almost acidic effect on them, and what Teren had done had literally eaten holes in his body. If it weren't for his super healing ability, it would have killed him. Sort of brought new meaning to the word allergic. Well, I guessed we had a viable excuse for him to not ever eat out with us again—extreme food allergies.

I smiled, kissed him, and rested my wet head against his. He grabbed some suds on his chest and teasingly plopped them on my hair. I laughed and he smiled, then, too tired to keep them open, he closed his eyes again.

While he continued to lean against the wall for support, I cleaned the rest of him, paying close attention to his fingers, ears and neck, anywhere where blood might have pooled, and could be visible to someone else. After he was sparkly clean, I gave myself a quick rinsing, then shut off the water and patted us dry with some nearby towels.

Looking half asleep on his feet, Teren crawled into the oversized bed with me; both of us were still naked. His body was lukewarm from the shower. He wrapped it around me, and rested his head in the crook of my neck. Sighing contently, he snuggled himself further into me. I cradled his head and kissed him softly before shutting off the lamp and closing my eyes.

Before sleep took me, I started replaying the evening. Again I marveled at what he'd done for me. As I smiled and stroked my fingers down his back, I whispered, "Thank you."

Thinking he was already asleep, I was a little surprised to hear him murmur, "You're welcome," into my skin.

I hugged him tighter, then a thought struck me. "When did you guys realize you'd have to do this?"

He stiffened and I adjusted myself to look at him; apprehension was clear on his face. I furrowed my brow at seeing it. He sighed a cool breath, closed his eyes for a second, then met my gaze. "We've always known this would happen this weekend, Emma." He shrugged. "We've been preparing, since you first said you wanted it here."

Horror and guilt went straight though me. I pushed him away and brought my hands to my mouth. "Why didn't anyone…?" I couldn't finish the thought, but Teren understood.

His hands reached up and lowered mine, exposing my face. "We didn't want you to worry about us. We knew we'd be fine…once it was over."

I shook my head, tears forming again. "We could have gone somewhere else. We could have gotten married at a courthouse, Teren."

He stopped my sputtering with his lips. When I was calmer, he muttered, "This is what you wanted, what you deserved to have. Our problems were manageable."

I stared at him, speechless. Then irritation flared in me, like it does sometimes, when I'm really worried. "You could have given me a heads up! I could have been told what would happen, instead of finding you covered in blood and not knowing why. I've had enough of secrets. After you told me everything about your conversion, I thought I was done being kept in the dark!" My tone got especially heated on the end as I replayed my fear.

He blanched and looked guilty again. "You're right…I'm sorry." He shook his head on his pillow, as his fingers moved a strand of hair behind my ear. "I just didn't want to you to worry…and I honestly didn't know it would be that bad. I'm sorry if I scared you."

I hugged him tight, my temporary anger gone. "You did, Teren. You terrified me."

He again murmured that he was sorry. His voice was thick with the need to sleep, and I hugged him tight, needing him close, even if he was slipping from consciousness. When I was sure he was asleep, I playfully muttered, "I wonder why Halina got to be the lucky one? You guys draw straws or something?"

He chuckled in my arms, still awake. "No, she just wouldn't have been able to tolerate it like us, so it wasn't an option for her." I pulled back, surprised.

His eyes lit the distance between us in the dark room as he shrugged. "The side effect of food is less severe for us than for her. Her full vampirism doesn't react...as well."

My surprise turned to shock. *As well?* I didn't think Teren spouting blood all over the bathroom floor was exactly "well." It was worse for Halina? How much worse could it get? He took in my stricken face, then shrugged again. "She probably would have lost it at the table."

I swallowed the sudden lump in my throat. Yes...that would have been worse.

Teren was still asleep when I woke up the next morning. As I watched the sunlight flash on his dark hair, I thought he looked better. His face wasn't so pale anymore and he didn't have any more circles under his eyes. No sign of fatigue was with him at all as he slept beside me. Shifting on my side to watch him, I suddenly realized that this was the last morning I'd wake up beside my boyfriend. Tomorrow morning, he'd be my husband.

He was a stone still sleeper: no fidgeting, no fussing, no snoring. Looking at him closer as he laid on his stomach with his head angled towards me, I realized he wasn't even breathing. Curious, I put my hand in front of his face. Nope, nothing. No breath at all. It was eerie, and too reminiscent of when he'd died. I quickly pulled my hand away.

"What are you doing?" he muttered, his eyes still closed.

I laughed and ran a hand through his hair. A smile cracked his face and the still look left him as he woke up. "Just seeing if you were alive." I giggled at my joke and he peeked up at me with amused eyes.

"Cute."

I giggled again and sat up on my elbow. "I just never noticed that you don't breathe while you sleep." I shrugged. "It's kind of creepy."

Stretching out, he inhaled a deep breath, obviously just for show, then propped himself up on his elbow to face me. "That is just what every man wants to hear on his wedding day." Grinning, he leaned in for a kiss.

I obliged him, and pressed my lips to his. The warmth from his shower last night had worn off, and he was cool again. I tried to not think about that awful moment when I'd found him in a pool of his own blood, and instead I focused on the miraculous things he could do with his mouth. As I let my memories fade, he scooted closer to me, until his cool body was along the length of mine under the sheets. He reached out to pull my elbow out from under me and I gasped as I fell to the bed. He was on top of me in a flash, still kissing me intently, purposefully.

Gently pushing him back, I playfully muttered, "What do you think you're doing?"

His hands slid over my body as his mouth shifted to my ear. "I really thought you'd have that figured out by now."

Laughing, I pushed him away when his mouth drifted back to mine. "We can't have sex before we get married, Teren."

He pulled back, looking normal, healthy, and…incredulous. His hand rested on my stomach and he gently squeezed while cocking an eyebrow. "Really?" His voice matched his disbelieving eyes and I clearly got the implication—*What does it matter, if I've already knocked you up?*

I laughed and shifted my body out from under his. Standing, I stole the sheet and demurely wrapped it around myself. He frowned and made no move to shield his bare body with the remaining covers. I bit my lip as I took in the sight of him, but made myself stay where I was. "Yes, really. We may have done things backwards, but we'll at least do the wedding night the right way.

I sat down on the edge of the bed and he smiled and scooted over to me, covering himself in the process. "All right, love," he said, kissing my cheek.

He looped a lock of hair behind my ear, and I again thought of being his wife. Immediately after that thought, the image of him covered in blood returned to me. I frowned, wishing I could keep that thought away. He frowned too. I tried to fix my face back to happiness, but he'd already seen it. "What's wrong?" He stroked my cheek with his knuckle while he looked over my face.

I could feel my eyes water as I gazed at him, and I hated that I was nearly crying already. "I'm just glad you're okay," I whispered.

He sighed and pulled me to him. "I'm sorry I worried you. I'm fine...we're all fine." He pulled us down onto the bed. Lying on his back, he securely wrapped me to his chest. I heard my heart through his body and made myself believe it was his.

He held me for what felt like an eternity, and my worries left me as peace flooded me. He probably would have held me for an eternity too, except he cocked his head, started chuckling, then began covering his body with the bedding between us. I raised my head, curious, but he only grinned.

Just as I was going to ask him what was going on, our door busted open. I gasped in surprise and cinched the sheet wrapped around me as Tracey and Ashley bounded into our bedroom. Teren didn't even flinch, and I had to assume he'd heard them coming.

Feeling every spot of skin on me heating, I sat up and glared at the both of them. "We could have been having sex, you guys!"

Ashley blushed and giggled, looking away, but Tracey pouted. She looked at Teren like he'd completely let her down. "I know," she muttered gloomily, and I thought that she'd actually been hoping to catch us. Teren laughed at the look on her face and snuggled farther into the bed, slipping his arms under his head. I was pretty sure he wouldn't have let us get caught like that, not with those super ears of his, although, sometimes he did get a little lost in the moment.

"Good morning, girls," he said, looking completely relaxed and comfortable, even though I knew he was probably a touch embarrassed; if his skin could still do it, he'd probably be blushing.

Ashley giggled as she sat down on the bed and greeted him. Tracey gave him a sly grin; she was probably picturing the thick quilt over the top of him being gone. I rolled my eyes, kind of wanting to smack her, but then she grabbed my hand and helped me pick out some clothes for my big day.

Teren and Ashley watched me get dressed under the sheet. I managed to slip my clothes on without ever revealing my naked body. Sheet dressing was an art form that really only girls had mastered.

Ashley turned to Teren on the bed. "Are you feeling better?" she politely asked him.

I caught the curiosity in her voice, she had to be wondering what could possibly make a vampire not feel well. Before Teren could answer Ashley, Tracey asked, "Yeah, you getting cold feet or something?"

I inadvertently laughed—Teren's feet were actually very cold. Teren shook his head at me and Tracey, then answered my sister; his tone was just as polite as hers had been. "I feel much better, thank you."

When I was dressed, I leaned over and gave him a kiss. This might be the last I saw of him for the afternoon. As the kiss deepened, a giggling Tracey and Ashley pulled me off of him. All of us were laughing as they held me back. Playfully, I told him, "I guess I'll see you later. Don't be late."

Grinning, he shook his head as the girls literally pulled me through the door. When we were in the hallway, I heard him respond with, "I wouldn't dream of it."

Once we were several steps down the hall, and the giggling girls seemed assured that I wouldn't rush back into that gorgeous, naked man's arms, they finally loosened their grip on me. I was tempted to run back to him anyways, but laughing along with them, I let them lead me down the gracefully curving staircase to the kitchen.

Holding hands with my two best friends, I came across my two moms. My birth mother was humming to herself as she scrambled a pan of eggs on a ceramic burner. Her grin was wide and happy while she worked, and her brown eyes sparkled when she looked up at me. Mom was in hog heaven here. My second mother, Alanna, was frying up a batch of bacon, the maple smell mixed with the telltale hiss of frying grease and my mouth started to water. I prayed my stomach stayed down today.

Alanna looked up a second after my mother, and they both nearly greeted me in unison, "Good morning, Emma."

Feeling giddy, anxious, and eager for today, I giggled as I sat on a stool at the center island. Ashley and Tracey took stools on either side of me, the chairs creaking as they experimentally twisted them back and forth.

"Good morning, everyone," I chipperly said, sort of feeling like a princess from a fairytale, especially since Tracey had made me put on fuzzy white slippers with the word *bride* in big, black script on the front of each one. She'd wanted to buy me the matching jacket too, but I'd put my foot down on that one.

Mom beamed at my enthusiasm, her eyes already misting. Alanna gave me a warm greeting. I eyed her more carefully than I had my mom, to see if any of her sickness was still with her. But her skin was the normal olive color it always was. Her pale blue eyes showed only happiness, and her perfect, lineless face was only giving me a warm look of reassurance. I was sure that if I could have asked her how she was, she would have told me that she'd never felt better.

Just as I was about to ask her anyway, Tracey asked me a question. "Teren's got amazing pecs, does he work out a lot?"

Ashley giggled into her palm while my mom gave Tracey a blank look. She was probably wondering when Tracey had seen Teren's chest. I smacked Tracey across the arm while Alanna softly chuckled as she studied the bacon she was cooking. Tracey made an offended noise and scowled at me. "What? I'm just saying…he's deceptively defined." She shrugged and ran a hand through her long, blonde locks. Her lip turned up into a wry grin. "That's not a bad thing."

I closed my eyes, picturing Teren busting up laughing in our room right about now. There was just no way he hadn't heard her. Alanna pretty much confirmed that for me, by glancing upstairs and smiling. Shaking her head, she went back to cooking her bacon. I shifted the conversation by asking everyone what the plan was for today. Mom shook off her confusion over Tracey's accurate knowledge of Teren's body, and started animatedly going over her plan with Alanna to prepare all of the food for the guests.

Surprise made me sit up straight. They were going to spend all day cooking for, at last count, one hundred and fifty people? Alanna chuckled and assured me that most of the food was already prepared and in the freezer, they simply had to heat them up. They were going to spend today preparing the finger foods—cookies, dips, mini-sandwiches, and various forms of pastries. That did not sound like much fun to me, but I wished her and Alanna well.

As the girls and I dug into the steaming plate of food Alanna set before us, I began to wonder how I'd pass the time today. The nervous energy in my body was only building, and the actual ceremony wasn't until seven o'clock at night; we were having it well after dark, so Halina and Imogen could fully enjoy the festivities. As the still steaming eggs burnt my tongue with my excited shoveling, I started to think that maybe I should find a more constructive way to taper off this feeling. Besides, I couldn't spend all day eating. I did have a dress to fit into tonight. Unfortunately, the only other thing I was coming up with involved Teren's aforementioned pecs, and while that would be wildly entertaining for me, it sort of left out the other members of my wedding party.

When I finished my food and started in on my sister's, Tracey came up with a good idea. She suggested we spend the day getting mani/pedis and having our hair twisted into fabulously intricate up-dos. I really didn't want to leave the ranch, but I was buzzing like a woman who'd just downed six shots of straight espresso. When Mom emphatically agreed that they'd get more done without me around, I was finally convinced we should all get pampered. It was my day anyway, right?

Tracey thought it would be a lot of fun to not tell the boys we were leaving. I didn't spoil her fun by letting her know that Teren was well aware of everything we'd just talked about. She also thought it was great fun for me to leave my "bride" slippers on. I let out a dramatic groan, but I secretly loved it. I wanted everyone to know that I was getting married today. Hell, I felt like announcing it on the radio, or interrupting the scheduled programming with breaking news. Something big—because that's how I felt today, like something big was happening. Something big and wonderful…and eternal.

After the seventh hug and kiss, my mom practically shoved me out of the kitchen so she could get down to business with Alanna. While hugging Alanna, I secretly asked her if she was okay, and as I'd predicted, she told me that she felt great. I knew that's what she'd say, but at least by my asking, she knew that I had been worried about her. I had been worried about all of them.

I whispered a goodbye to Teren, then the three of us girls scrambled into Alanna's sedan that she was letting us borrow. The solid black car was sleek and luxurious, with cream leather seats that were so soft, you almost felt like you melted into them. Tracey ran her hand over the edge of the cushions and sighed as her head dropped back. "This is the life." She looked over at me. "Now I seriously wish I'd met Teren first."

She winked, so I knew she was kidding—she was hopelessly in love with Hot Ben, after all. I gave her a humoring smile as I suppressed a laugh. If she knew that the owners of all the fineries she was enjoying this weekend no longer had heartbeats, she'd never come near this place again. Luxurious or not, Tracey wouldn't deal with the idea of vampires very well.

As I drove us back into the city, I wondered if we'd even find a place to accommodate three of us on such short notice. Then Tracey pulled out her cell phone and speed dialed her salon. That clued me in that maybe it wouldn't be a problem. Five minutes later, we all had reservations at Bella Sole. I had to smile that the name of the salon meant Beautiful Sun. If they only knew the irony of them doing hair for a vampire's wedding.

Tracey kept us occupied for hours. Time flew by as we were pampered—our toes were painted in a girly shade of pink, our nails were dipped, buffed and French manicured, and our hair was curled into long spirals and twisted into elaborately done up-dos. All except Ashley, who had her hair curled, but left it down. Since only one side of her head would grow hair, I think she felt more secure having it the way she was used to having it.

After a late lunch at a small café close by, we grabbed coffees and cocoa, and headed back to the ranch. I was eager to start dressing for the big event. Pulling up to the drive, we could see that even though it was still hours away from the actual ceremony, a few guests had arrived. Some people just really like weddings.

Giggling the entire way, the girls pulled me into Ashley's room. We sat on the edge of the bed and talked about all the things girls talk about when they get together: catty girls at work, or at school in Ashley's case, the current mystery running through our favorite television show, the most unusual sexual requests, positions and/or places. I kept my mouth shut on that one, thinking that Tracey would not want to know the things my bloodsucker liked doing. While Tracey and Ashley gabbed and changed into their dresses, I started to wonder what my vampire was up to.

I wasn't sure how he'd spent his day, or how he was feeling now. I wondered if, like me, he was feeling anxious butterflies swarming around his stomach. My stomach was also starting to feel something else, something not so wonderful. It was starting to veto the BLT I'd eaten at the café. Either that or the gigantic hot chocolate I'd just finished tilting back.

As Ashley and Tracey adjusted the clingy, blood-red fabric of their dresses, I put a hand on my stomach and exhaled slowly and carefully. Hopefully pure willpower would be enough to convince my belly that everything was fine. It wasn't working though. I closed my eyes as my stomach churned. I felt a bead of sweat on my professionally done makeup, but I knew that was the least of my concerns now. Clamping a hand over my mouth, I shot up off the bed and ducked out the door, muttering, "Be right back," as I ran for a bathroom.

Running blindly down the hall, I began to wonder where the bathroom was on this side of this ridiculously huge house. I ran into an open door that looked promising, and nearly groaned in frustration when I saw it was just another stupid bedroom. Then I noticed a door in the room that was cracked open enough to reveal a bathroom. I exhaled in relief. I would have done the happy dance if I'd had the time. I didn't though. The only thing keeping down my lunch was the hand covering my mouth.

Running into the room, I dropped to my knees, and lost it right at the toilet. Knowing I was pretty much ruining my makeup made a few tears fall. I hated getting sick. When my body was empty, I weakly stood up and shuffled over to the sink. Careful to not look in the mirror, so I didn't see how awful I looked now, I rested my head on the side of the sink, turned on the water, and rinsed out my mouth. I felt myself sniffling, and more tears formed. Not wanting to be alone in my discomfort anymore, I suddenly wished Teren was with me, and not out bonding with the boys somewhere.

As if on cue, cool arms wrapped around me. I was pulled into a muscular chest and twisted into a carrying position. As Teren turned off the water, I sighed and wrapped my arms around his neck, just happy to have him near. He kissed my head as he walked me back to the bedroom. I buried my face in his cool shirt, and the smell of the outdoors filled me—water, grass, and nature—all with a light hint of his cologne underneath. He was manly and wonderful, and his mere presence had a calming effect on my queasy stomach.

He laid me down on the bed and rested beside me. I lolled my head over to look at him as he propped up on an elbow to watch over me, almost protectively. I smiled at the look of concern on his face. "You found me," I whispered.

He half-grinned at me as a finger came out to wipe off my smudged mascara. "I heard you," he said, his smile shifting to a pout. "Are you all right?"

A small laugh escaped me at how trivial my sickness was in comparison to what his had been. "I'm fine, Teren, really." I shook my head and my smile felt huge to me. "This is nothing at all." My hands snuck out to clutch his body and I pulled him into me, like we were two magnets that couldn't bear to be apart.

He laughed as I clung to his body, then he sank down to the pillows and held me just as tight. "Good," he murmured, his nose sliding along my neck. I shivered at the cool touch and felt him smile as he pressed his lips to a vein there. I had to imagine that vein was pulsing faster than normal. "Why did you run into this guest room anyway? There is a bathroom right by Ashley's room at the other end of the hall."

I rapped him on the shoulder. "Because this house is too damn big, and I have no idea where everything is." He chuckled, and I pulled back to look at him; his pale eyes caught a flash of sunlight streaming through the window next to us. "Why were you in the house? I figured the boys would be off in the wilderness somewhere, hunting vicious trout."

He laughed at my comment, then gave me a sheepish grin. "I've been feeling edgy, anxious. I was scaring the fish away." I laughed at that while he shrugged. "I thought I'd get something to eat, thought maybe that would calm me down."

I raised my eyebrows at him, happy that he was feeling what I was feeling. I wanted to tease him some though. "Oh, nervous?"

"No, excited." He smiled, then leaned over to kiss me.

I relaxed into the feeling of his cool mouth on mine, and let myself indulge in this man I was going to marry, just a few hours from now. My hands threaded into his hair as he shifted his weight over my body. My fingers moved to slide up his cool t-shirt as he palmed me through the outside of my button-up. I groaned and rocked against him as his lips moved down to my neck; his course stubble sent tiny waves of pleasure through me. As his tongue found the sensitive spot in the crook of my neck, I pulled his hips directly over mine.

He groaned a little as he instinctually pressed against me. "You know cold cow's blood won't satisfy you right now," I whispered in his ear. He growled low in his chest and pressed against me again in answer. I suppressed a moan, quickly inhaling my breath instead. He was ready for more than just a love bite, and I sort of was too. Breathily, I added, "You can snack on me, if you like?"

"I always like…" He rumbled a low growl again and the lips pressing heated kisses into my skin turned into the pinpricks of fangs, ready to plunge inside me. I gasped at the thought, but pushed him back.

"What do you think you're doing?"

He blinked, his eyes full of passion and hunger. His fangs were extended to drinking length, and his brows were furrowed in puzzlement. "You said…"

I rolled my eyes. "I'm getting married in a matter of hours." I pointed to the glaringly obvious vein in my neck that he'd been about to puncture. "I don't need to go down the aisle with the world's worst hickey." Or circular fang wounds.

He looked down, embarrassed. "Oh, right." Peering back up at me, he asked, "Then, where?"

The look of desire on his face, made me feel supernaturally sexy. With a quick glance to make sure the door was closed, I gently pushed him to the side of me and began slowly unbuttoning my white long-sleeved blouse. Teren's breathing stopped as he lasciviously watched my fingers exposing my skin, button by slow button. When the shirt was completely opened, his breath started again, heavier than before. With my newly perfect, French manicured nails, I drew a line straight down the middle of my chest. Stopping just above my bra, I grabbed a section of the cup and pulled it back, exposing the creamy skin on the top part of my breast, the part my bra and dress would easily cover.

"Here," I whispered, my other hand reaching up to his neck and pulling him to me.

He exhaled a cool breath across my skin, his eyes closing just before contact, and then he sunk his teeth in. He was gentle, tender, and yet at the same time, commanding. I gasped at the tremor of pain, followed by the warm heat of my blood being pulled from me. His cool lips desensitized the skin around the area, and the cool brush of his tongue soothed me, just as surely as it ignited me. He made a purring noise, his hands clenching and unclenching my hips as he drank from me. I smiled. This was the last time he'd do this from his girlfriend. The next time, I'd be his wife.

I was in a euphoric, connected, peaceful state of mind, when everything suddenly took a drastic turn. Somewhere in my haze, I registered the one sound Teren and I really couldn't afford to hear right now—the sound of a door rapidly swinging open.

"Teren, you in here?"

Hot Ben stepped into the room, closing the door softly behind him, just as Teren and I both shifted to look. Teren's super abilities hadn't registered that Ben was opening the door, until it was too late; he did sometimes get caught up in the moment when we were like this. And we'd definitely just been caught. My mouth dropped wide open and my whole body tensed. Teren lifted his head to stare at Ben, his mouth was also open in startlement. In the brightly lit room, the blood on Teren's tongue and dripping down his chin was startling. As were the all-too-apparent fangs.

Ben, at first, didn't notice. "Oh, hey, sorry guys. Trace said she saw Teren go in here, but I didn't...know you...were both..." His voice trailed off as what he was seeing started clicking together in his mind. I could almost hear the gorgeous boy's thoughts out loud—*Oh,*

I caught them almost screwing, cool. Wait, why is there blood on Emma's chest? Wait, why is there blood on Teren's mouth…and holy shit, are those…fangs?

Teren sucked in a sharp inhale as the realization of what had just happened struck him. His teeth immediately retracted with his breath. Ben's eyes widened and he scrambled to open the door. "How did you…? Oh my God." He managed to open it in his fumbling, but it was quickly slammed shut by Teren, who was instantly standing at Ben's side holding the door closed.

Hot Ben stepped away from him, like he had the plague. "How did you…?" he said again, clearly confused by Teren's speedy abilities. "Stay back," he muttered as he bumped into a dresser.

Pulling my shirt tight to my body, I sat up. My white bra and shirt were now bloodstained and ruined; Teren hadn't had time to close the wounds. "Its okay, Ben."

Ben looked at me, frantic. "Run, Emma, I'll hold him off."

I smiled, warmed that Hot Ben was willing to take on a vampire for me, but I shook my head again. Teren answered Ben before I could. Walking toward him with a hand outstretched, like Ben was a terrified dog who might bite him, Teren calmly said, "I can explain. Please…calm down."

Ben tittered, sounding on the verge of a panic attack as he nervously laughed. "Explain? You can explain your teeth? What the hell was that, Teren?" His eyes shifted to mine. "What the hell were you doing to her?"

Teren cocked his head, looking flustered and embarrassed, not to mention scared that he'd just lost the closest thing to a friend that he had. While he floundered for something to say, I said, "He was hungry, I told him he could bite me." Still clutching my shirt, I walked over to Teren's side and put my hand on his arm. Teren looked back at me, sadness in his pale eyes.

Ben flicked glances between the two of us, like we were both mad. His eyes darted to the door behind us and I could clearly see him calculating the odds of getting around both of us lunatics. I sighed and wondered when the screaming would start. Ben opened his mouth a few times as he ran a hand through his blonde highlights. "Bite you? Hungry? He's what…? A…a…"

"Vampire," Teren calmly stated, raising his chin a little.

Ben snorted, gave us disbelieving looks, and then swallowed nervously. "You guys are nuts. I'm gone." He moved then, edging around me to get to the door, but Teren moved to block him. Ben pushed Teren out of the way. Well, he tried to. I could see that he put a lot of strength into the attempt, but if Teren didn't want to move, no human could make him.

"Let me go," he said through clenched teeth. He looked like he was torn between peeing his pants or using some of his kickboxing skills on Teren. I didn't know how to tell him that neither response would help him escape.

"He's not going to hurt you, Ben," I quietly said from behind him.

Ben looked back at me. Oddly, panic and fear only made him more attractive. "Then tell him to let me go." Twisting to me, he grabbed my arms. Fear made his grip painfully tight. "Don't let him kill me." I heard Teren sigh behind him, and start to say his name, but my shirt had fallen open when Ben jarred my hands free and my blood-soaked bra elicited a harsh reaction from an already freaked out Ben. He inhaled in sharp pulls and his fingers dug in even tighter. I cried out, hunching over as pain shot through both of my arms.

That was all Teren needed.

He shoved Ben off of me. And when Teren wanted a human to move, that human moved. Ben flew to the other side of the room, smacked into a wall and sank down in a slump. He slowly raised his head and Teren was instantly standing right in front of him. Bent into an aggressive crouch, a low growl rumbled from Teren's chest. Ben shied away from him and I quickly ran over to the pair, and put a hand on Teren's back.

I knew the reason for Teren's overreaction, but poor Hot Ben would never understand. Teren had helplessly watched me be brutally attacked before, and had vowed to never let that happen again. While Ben wasn't exactly harming me like our maniac captor had, the instinct to defend me was still the same. Teren would never let anyone harm me again, even a friend.

I rubbed soothing circles into Teren's back, urging him to calm down. He looked at me—his fangs were still extended and a mean sneer was on his face. Seeing my concern, his entire body relaxed. Closing his eyes, he sighed and lightly shook his head like he was clearing away a bad dream. When he reopened them, he was calm, and his fangs were hidden away. With a sheepish face, he turned to Ben and extended a hand. "Sorry, man. I get a little…protective of her. I didn't mean to do that." I squeezed Teren's arm while he stretched his hand farther out to Ben. "I really wish you hadn't walked in here."

Ben stared at his hand in horror, like Teren might ram it through his chest at any second. Terrified, he whimpered, "Are you going to eat me now?"

Teren retracted his hand when it was obvious Hot Ben wasn't going to touch him. Rolling his eyes, a small laugh escaped him. "Yeah, Ben, I'm gonna drain you dry."

His tone was incredibly sarcastic, but I elbowed him in the ribs anyway. Ben didn't catch the teasing note in Teren's voice; he looked like he was about to be sick. "Oh God…"

Sighing, I squatted in front of him and put my hands on his shoulders. "He's joking, Ben. He's not going to kill you." I rolled my eyes and glared at Teren over my shoulder.

Teren frowned and crossed his arms over his chest. "I'm still the same person, Ben. I'm still the same smartass that goes fishing with you, and jokes with you about Tracey's shoe fetish." He patted his chest as his brows scrunched in frustration. "I'm still me. This is just a *part* of me, but it doesn't change my character. I'm still the same guy that you know. Am I a killer?"

Ben grudgingly looked over my shoulder at him. Inhaling a calming breath, he kept his gaze locked on Teren's. I could practically see the courage building in him, as he considered all the times that Teren could have killed him, if he'd really wanted to. He obviously hadn't, Ben was still living and breathing, so maybe he was piecing it together that being a vampire, didn't automatically make you evil.

With a shake of his head and a much clearer voice he said, "You're…a vampire."

Teren extended his hand to Ben again, his face begging Ben to take it. "Yes…and I'd never kill you."

Ben eyed him for long moments while I moved away from the two friends. Finally, Ben nodded and took his hand. Ben stared at Teren's hand while he effortlessly pulled him up. "I really am sorry about flinging you into a wall," Teren said sheepishly.

Ben didn't respond to that, just kept staring at Teren's hand, even after they separated. Finally he pointed at it. "Is that why you're always so cold?" Teren shrugged and nodded. Ben ran a hand down his face as he slowly shook his head back and forth. "I can't believe this." He looked over at me as I buttoned up my shirt. "And you've known about this?" he asked.

I bit my lip and nodded. "From nearly day one." I walked over to Teren and grabbed his hand. Lacing our fingers together, I gazed up at him in adoration. He looked back at me, love clear on his face too, although, I could see worry there. He'd really loved his time with Hot Ben. I looked back to Ben, my voice as confident as my gaze. "Believe *me*, when I say that you don't have to worry about him hurting you…or me…or any human. He doesn't eat people."

Ben's startled face shifted to the embarrassing stain right over my breast. Damn, I'd really liked this shirt too. Teren followed his gaze and coughed, a little embarrassed. "Um, that wasn't really eating…" He looked back at Ben, a devilish half-smile on his face. "That was more…foreplay."

Ben's eyes widened more, then he shook his head and ran both hands down his face and then back through his hair. He seemed confused as to how drawing blood could possibly be erotic. Oh, if he only knew…

Teren put a hand on Ben's shoulder and Ben looked up at him; his face was an odd combination of horror and wonder. As I thought about his panicked reaction, I started remembering my own initial reaction. Teren had always said I was rare. As I watched Ben's nervous face twitch as he studied where Teren was touching him, I remembered Teren telling me that nearly every other girl he'd ever told, had had much the same reaction as Ben. Seeing that reaction in person, I came to appreciate just how rare and odd my initial response had been, and what a relief it must have been for Teren. I squeezed his hand tighter.

In a soothing voice, Teren spoke to Ben, as if he were going into shock. "Ben, I know this is hard to take, and I'll admit, having you know about this, would make our friendship so much easier…" he shook his head, a heavy sadness in his eyes, "but, if this freaks you out too much, you don't need to remember it." He shrugged and looked resigned that, either way, things would be different.And I supposed they would be. Ben would either remember, and have to come to terms with Teren's reality, or he'd have his mind wiped, and Teren would have to deal with the fact that his best friend couldn't accept him for what he really was. I squeezed his hand even tighter and he lightly squeezed back.

Teren dropped his hand from Ben's shoulder while Ben gave him a blank look. "What do you mean?" Ben backed up a step, like Teren was about to do something to him. "What are you gonna do to me?"

Teren sighed. Turning his head away, he muttered something under his breath. I wondered what he was saying, but figured he was probably speaking to his family. They had to know what was going on. Well, maybe not Halina, since she was probably sleeping. Teren sighed again before answering Ben. "I won't do anything…but when Halina wakes up—"

"Halina?" Ben interrupted, his eyebrows furrowing into perfect points. "Your step-mom's hot sister?" Teren started to speak, but I could see the light go off in Ben's brain as his eyes widened and his mouth dropped. "Oh, God…she's one, too." He cocked his head at Teren. "Did you turn her?" His eyes hardened a bit, like, if Teren said yes, then he was going to kick his ass. I bit my lip to stop the inappropriate laughter that was bubbling inside of me.

Teren gave him a half-smile. "No, actually, she's my great-grandmother, and she's the one that…spawned all of us." Teren laughed a little, and I couldn't help but match him.

Ben gaped at us. "All of…" He stopped talking as more lights clicked on. "Oh God, they're all…the whole family?"

Teren shook his head, still chuckling. "No…my dad is human."

Ben looked pale, and I released Teren to help him sit on the bed. Sitting beside him, I soothingly stroked his broad back. Ben scuffed up his hair, then slumped his head in his hands over his knees. "All of them…" He looked up at Teren. "It's all a lie?" His face was incredulous, and a little hurt.

Careful to keep his distance, Teren sat on the other side of him. "Yes. But you can understand why we have to, right?"

Ben nodded woodenly, still looking lost in thought. He stared at his knees for a moment before looking over at Teren again. "Then, Alanna…?"

Teren smiled widely for the first time since this little fiasco. "Is my mother, my birth mother."

Ben looked bewildered again. "Vampires can have children?" I giggled, and my hand reflexively went to my stomach. Ben caught the movement and flushed with color when he realized that of course they can, since I was expecting. It wasn't that simple, but Ben didn't need to know all the gory details. "Oh," he muttered, looking between my stomach and Teren.

Teren beamed at me, but didn't explain all the facts to Ben either. Ben watched our little love fest for a minute, then turned to me. "Aren't you worried that they'll," he flung his hands at my stomach and shrugged, "you know?"

I cocked my head, completely confused. "That they'll what?"

Ben turned even redder as he shrugged again. "Eat you…from the inside."

Ben grimaced at the thought. I did too, and I thumped him in the chest. "God, Ben! Ew!" I smacked him again as he cringed away from me. Teren chuckled.

Trying to defend himself, Ben muttered, "Hey, I'm just saying, there has to be blood and stuff in there and what if they get hungry and you know…"

I smacked him again, really putting my comparatively frail human strength behind it. Ben made pained noises as he tried to block my hits. "God! No! They are just babies. There will be no blood swilling in the womb. Ew!" I smacked him again as Teren full on laughed.

Ben finally managed to stop me from clobbering him. He apologized and threw a, "She's worse than you," at Teren, which made him laugh even harder. As I watched the exchange, I thought about what Ben had just said and whispered to Teren, "That won't happen, right?"

Hot Ben was busy rubbing his arm from where I'd fisted him. He hadn't heard me, but Teren had. He gave me a *Really?* face before rolling his eyes and shaking his head, no. I smiled and relaxed. That's what I'd thought anyway.

When the laughter died down, Ben looked back at Teren and silently stared at him, like he was seeing him for the first time. Finally, he shook his head and muttered, "I still can't believe it. I mean, we've hung out during the day…we went camping for God's sake." He scrunched his brow. "I've seen you eat…lots of times. Are you sure you're a vampire?"

Teren chuckled and then sighed, knowing he'd have to explain his special brand of vampirism. Taking a few minutes he went over his family line. When he was done, Ben looked even more confused. "So…you can eat, and be in the sun, and you were born, not created, so…you're mainly human?"

Teren sighed. "No, not…anymore."

Ben scrunched his face. His perfect features looked so puzzled, it was charming. "He died recently. Side effect of vampirism," I said while Teren gave me a loving glance.

Ben seemed shocked as he looked from me to Teren. "Oh, sorry, man." He gave Teren an odd, friendly pat on the arm, like I'd just said Teren's dog had died, and not him.

Teren laughed at the gesture and shrugged his shoulders. "It's not so bad." I smiled at his causal answer to being a member of the walking dead. Hot Ben shook his head, still stunned. I patted Ben's back, hoping he'd choose to remember this conversation, for Teren's sake.

As he was still piecing the puzzle together, he looked between the two of us and said, "But…you ate last night?"

I stopped laughing as I thought of that dinner. Teren did too, and his eyes locked onto mine. A moment of shared sympathy passed between us and then Teren answered Ben's question. "I…paid the price for that."

Ben brought a hand to his chin, making a connection. "Oh, that's why you were sick." Teren nodded and Ben looked amazed. "You willingly got sick, to pass as human?"

I nodded, my eyes watering. "Yes, he did." My hand stretched across Hot Ben to grab Teren's knee and he laid his cool hand over mine, gently squeezing before he released it.

As I pulled back, Ben watched our connection break. His face was still speculative. "The club…the drinks?" He looked over at a suddenly sheepish Teren.

"I switched my full ones for your empty ones." Teren's eyes were apologetic. "You never noticed."

Ben suddenly laughed, his face relaxing. "God, I thought I'd suddenly become a lightweight or something." Teren laughed with him. Still studying his odd friend, Ben's face turned serious again. "So, that's your whole life? Playing a role, living a lie?"

Teren sighed and looked past him to me. "It feels like that sometimes." He shrugged. "I wouldn't if I had a choice. But this…isn't a choice for me. It never was." Ben sighed and put a hand on Teren's shoulder. I nearly cried at the contact, so did Teren. His eyes watered some, as he carefully watched Ben's reaction. "So, like I said, we have ways to make you forget, if you don't want to remember this." That last part came out in a whisper, and the moisture in his eyes got dangerously heavy.

Ben looked him over and then looked back at me. "I just…I need a minute to process this." He returned his gaze to Teren. "Do I have a minute?"

Teren nodded, smiling sadly. "Of course."

Ben looked at each of us again and stood; he was shaky on his feet. "I need to go lie down," he muttered.

Teren nodded and stood with him. He placed a hand on his shoulder, and Ben looked back at him but didn't flinch at the contact. I took that as a promising sign. "You can't tell Tracey, you can't tell anyone." He gave him a pointed look. "We're trusting you."

Ben swallowed and nodded. He took a step towards the door then turned to me. "You've know about him from the beginning, Emma?" I smiled and nodded. Ben shook his head, amazement in his face. "Wow, you're a strong person. I don't think I could…" He let that trail off, as he looked back at Teren. My earlier hope that he'd be okay with it, faded.

As he took a step, Teren called out to him. "Ben." Ben looked back and Teren continued. "Halina will make the choice for you, if she knows that you know. You can't let her see that you know the truth." Ben swallowed, looking a bit frightened again. He took another step towards the door when it seemed that Teren was finished. As he got to the handle, Teren spoke again. "I would really rather you make this choice for yourself, so please, be careful what you say…even alone. We have exceptionally good hearing."

With his hand still clasping the metal lever of the door, Ben turned his bleach-blonde highlighted head back to Teren. "How good?"

Teren smirked and took a step towards the door. Lowering his voice, he said, "Good enough to know that last night, Tracey asked you if you would…" Teren looked over at me and then took a step to Ben and whispered something in his ear.

Ben paled. "Jesus, Teren! We weren't even in the same building as you."

Teren raised an eyebrow. "I know…"

Ben's blue eyes grew as wide as lakes. "Oh, that means they all…"

Teren grinned and nodded and Ben flushed with color. "God, I wish I'd known that earlier." He cringed and shrugged. "Sorry."

Teren laughed and patted Ben's shoulder. "Don't worry, I've heard worse." Teren winced and Ben let out a nervous laugh. Sighing at the both of us, Hot Ben shook his head and finally opened the door to leave. I was happy that he was at least not screaming at the top of his lungs. Muttering goodbye, he practically fled the room that had probably just changed his entire view on life.

I walked up to Teren and clasped his hand. He sighed as he looked down on me. Not knowing what to comment on, I playfully said, "So…what did Tracey ask him?" I grinned and Teren grinned with me.

"You don't want to know," he whispered as he leaned down to kiss my cheek.

Feeling a little melancholy for Teren, I rested my head against his shoulder. "Now what do we do, Teren?"

He laid his head against mine. "Now…we get married."

Chapter 7 – I Now Pronounce You…

There are a lot of things that happen when you get married. The first of which is having your friends and family dress you like you're suddenly incapable of doing it yourself. After Teren escorted me from that fateful guest room, he took me back to Ashley's room, where even I could hear the ruckus and laughter emanating. The two girls inside were sipping on glasses of champagne and doing last minute adjustments to their hair and makeup when we opened the door.

Tracey squealed when she saw Teren standing beside me, both giving him congratulations for the upcoming nuptials and admonishing him for confiscating me for a quickie before the ceremony. Since neither one of us wanted to explain what had just happened, we let her think that. Plus, Teren was shirtless, since I was wearing his t-shirt; I couldn't have walked into that room with a blood-soaked boob now, could I? Not without squeals of a different kind. Sex was really our only cover story, since Teren had felt the need to escort me all of the way into Ashley's room, and they all saw him half-naked. He claimed he was worried I'd get sick again, but really, I think he just needed the comfort of my presence after the tension with Ben.

Teren took the commotion, and Tracey's relentless teasing about the absence of my shirt, with an embarrassed grace. His eyes betrayed the true worry he felt over recent events though as he kissed me on the head and told me he'd see me at the altar. Those words passing his lips had a way of making me forget that a friend had just discovered our secret. That was, until he left and I was attacked by Tracey. Having her fuss over me, while I discreetly slipped on a bra of Ashley's—thank goodness we were nearly identical in more ways than one—reminded me that Hot Ben was no longer clueless Hot Ben. While Tracey stripped off my clothes, I hoped Ben wouldn't break Teren's heart.

The second thing about getting married, besides no one letting you do anything for yourself, is the fact you're not allowed any freedom. Once I was in my white gown, I may as well have secured myself in heavy manacles down in the deepest dungeon. True, it was the nicest dungeon on earth, but still, I wasn't allowed to leave Ashley's room. I was a prisoner in white satin and a crystal tiara. Only bathroom breaks were being allowed, and even those were monitored and supervised, the hallway cleared of outsiders like my friends were the secret service and I was some foreign dignitary.

I was allowed a few visitors to help me pass the time though, mainly family, so really, just Mom and Alanna. I had to watch the growing festivities through the window. Through my peephole into the real world, I could see one of the pastures near the front of the house, where Jack and Jack's trusted hired hand, Peter Alton, were having guests park their cars. Some of the more uppity people did not looked pleased about walking through the mud to get to the house. I smiled, knowing their view of the ranch would change dramatically, once they got inside.

The time passed slowly, and my nervous energy dissipated a little in my boredom, as I watched distant relatives and friends of friends walk through the muck to come view my wedding to a vampire. Mom and Ashley regaled me with tales of what such-and-such cousin was wearing, and how the forty-year-old ex of a far-off uncle had brought her twenty-year-old boyfriend. I laughed with them at their stories, and then the group of us started taking candid photographs.

Teren and I weren't doing the traditional posed photos. We'd rather have everyone looking natural and causal, so we could remember people how they really looked. Like Teren had said, "Capture people in their natural environment." After my friends and I snapped at least three dozen "natural" photos, and a couple of risqué ones of me for Teren, it was finally time to face the music. The wedding march music, to be more precise.

That brings me to the last thing that happens at weddings. Your friends become your ability to stand up straight and walk upright, as your body becomes so overwhelmed with love, terror and excitement that the very act of breathing becomes too difficult to do properly. With my entire body shaking, the closest people in my life led me away, supporting me with their arms wrapped around mine. We slowly walked down the hallway to a side door that led out back to the pool. Out back to where my vampire was dressed to the nines, and probably just as anxious as I was, only he had every eye already on him. I let out a nervous titter at the thought of him all antsy out there. I really hoped Hot Ben was still standing beside him.

My nerves shot to panic level when the door opened and the sound of orchestral music and the smell of lit candles, filtered back to me with the swirling air wrapping around my body. As the comfort of my bridesmaids started leaving me one-by-one to set the stage before me, I clasped onto my anchor, my lifeline—my mother.

Once Ashley and Tracey had left me, and mom and I were alone in the hallway, I turned to her. I grasped her upper arms as icy terror flooded through me. "Mom, I can't do this."

She calmly looked me over, tears in her eyes as she gently stroked my cheek with her thumb. All she said was, "He loves you…and he's waiting."

Peace flowed through me. He loved me…and I loved him. That was all that mattered. I nodded, a calm smile breaking over my face as my mom and I hugged. I clung to her, to that last tie of my childhood that I was leaving behind. Tears were stinging my eyes already.

I vaguely heard the music that was my cue, and vaguely heard my mother tearfully tell me that it was time as she handed me my bouquet of flowers. Grabbing them with one hand, I wrapped my other around her arm, pulling strength from the contact. Then she led me out the door, and led me to my future.

The rustle of people standing was what I noticed first. I couldn't really see much, and I was supremely grateful that Mom wasn't leaving my side as tears hazed my vision. I could make out the red of the carpet that was leading me to the white canopy holding every person in this world that I cared about. I sensed the bodies standing around the outskirts of the tent, there were too many people inside for everyone to fit. I felt the heat of the outdoor lamps as we passed by them.

A whispering followed me wherever I went, and I could just make out the words "beautiful", "gorgeous", "wonderful." I tucked the praises away in my brain, storing them for later days, when I knew I'd need the positive reinforcement. Then Mom and I were under the tent and my hazy vision crystallized. The tears in my eyes caught the twinkling lights strung everywhere underneath the canvas and expanded them to glowing snowflakes. The spectacular beauty of them stole my breath as we walked along the red carpet leading me to the altar.

Then the water in my eyes became too great to bear, and the heavy tears dropped to my cheeks. As they did, my vision cleared. Teren was the first thing I saw. Teren was the *only* thing I saw. I was positive more people were in the tent, I could still hear the whispering above the procession music, but I took no notice of them. My soon-to-be husband was waiting. He had tears on his cheeks too as he smiled at me.

I held his pale gaze as more tears dripped off my cheeks, staining my dress. I didn't care. Mom brought me closer to him and my breath came faster with each step. He was mine, he was waiting. His smile was glorious as he stood in a jet-black tuxedo that matched his jet-black hair. His hands were calmly clasped together in front of himself. He stood tall and straight in his sharp tux, with a button collar instead of a tie, and a silver vest peeking out underneath the jacket. The outfit emphasized every enticing thing about him.

He was…perfect.

As my mother handed me off to him, something inside me changed as well. When his cool hand took mine, I felt some instinct buried deep within me ignite, something that told me that everything was going to be fine, because we were now in this together—for life. I would never need to worry about Teren straying on me, nor would he need to worry about me straying on him. Not with what we meant to each other. As his fingers interlaced with mine, a calm assurance filled me. This man would love me, with the same intensity that had driven him to throw Hot Ben against a wall to protect me, until my deathbed. My looks, my body, my mental faculties…none of those things fading from me would keep him from my side.

I turned and faced him, suddenly feeling as if the rest of this ceremony wasn't even necessary. I completely understood what he'd meant when he'd told me that in his eyes, I was his the day I'd saved him. That, to him, I was already his wife. And he was right. We were already married, already bound, in our souls, if not on some legal document.

My eyes lost in Teren's, I heard Peter's gruff voice fill the space of the tent. There were introductions and a poetic rendering on the meaning of love, and, although I never turned from Teren to look at him, the image of the rough and tough cowboy speaking of love almost made me giggle.

When Peter got to the section about exchanging rings, Teren finally pulled his gaze from me. He looked behind him to his dad, who handed him my ring with a beaming smile on his face as he stood next to his son. It was probably a little odd to my distant relatives that Teren's dad was standing up as his best man, instead of some twenty-something guy, but that was just Teren's family. They were close. As Teren turned back to me, I looked past Jack and felt myself sigh with relief. Hot Ben was standing beside him, looking pale and nervous and eyeing Teren with caution. I knew from his behavior that he still knew what Teren was, and he'd decided to stand beside him anyway. Again, I could have kissed Ben.

Finally remembering what I needed to do, I turned to Ashley standing beside me. Her blood-red dress was elegant and beautiful, and the elaborate curls on half of her head were facing the direction of the crowd. From their perspective, she looked nearly normal. To me, she looked perfect. I gave her a quick hug as I handed her my bouquet of white roses. Then I took Teren's unadorned platinum band from her. I flashed a quick smile at Tracey behind her before turning back to Teren; she looked exceedingly hot in her skintight dress and intricate up-do.

Opting for our own words instead of prepackaged ones, since nothing about our relationship was prepackaged, Teren began speaking as he slipped the ruby encrusted ring on my finger. I swallowed a lump in my throat as silent tears ran down my cheeks.

"Emma Taylor, I think I fell for you the moment you dumped your coffee all over my shirt." He grinned and soft laughter went around the tent, followed by a round of soft sniffling. He tilted his head as he gazed at me adoringly. "I would have married you on that first day in the coffee shop, if you'd have had me."

I smiled at his sentiment. Once the ring was in place, he stroked my fingers. "I promise you that I will always love you, that I will always take care of you, and that I will never let any harm come to you." Silence filled the tent as Teren's face intensified on those words. While the crowd didn't understand the meaning, I did, and even more tears slid down my skin.

Clutching my fingers, he added, "I will be *your* husband until the day I die." With tears building in his eyes and falling down his cheeks, he softly said, "I will love you, for the rest of my life."

A sob escaped me and the tears cascaded at hearing those words, at seeing his tears, at understanding what he really meant when he said that. When most grooms say heartwarming things like that, they are assuming that they will live a long life together, and will each die within a relatively short amount of time of the other. With most men, those sentences merely imply that "I will never love another while we are both alive, that I will never stray, and we will still be in love with each other on our deathbeds."

But when Teren said those things, he knew, without a shadow of a doubt, that I would die before him, quite possibly centuries before him. What he was really saying was that he would literally mourn me, miss me, and love me…for eternity. That he would never move on from me, would never marry another. I would always be his wife, no matter how many hundreds of years we were apart. It was a heartbreaking admission and I openly sobbed. I heard others sniffling at his sentimentality, but really, only his family understood our true pain at those beautifully simple, yet horribly complex words.

Knowing I was skipping a step, I reached up and kissed him. The sniffling in the crowd shifted to laughter and Peter coughed and said, "We're not there yet." I ignored them. My man had just said something that deserved a bigger response than me sobbing in front of him. I poured my soul into that kiss, letting him know that I would make the short time we were together worth it. I would give him memories he could take with him, for the rest of his supernaturally long life.

When we broke apart the crowd was openly laughing at us. I sniffled and wiped my eyes, as I muttered an apology to Peter. He smiled warmly at me, looking very debonair in his gray dress suit. Shaking his head, he indicated the ring I was still holding. Turning back to Teren, I slipped it on his finger.

I said something, something warm and loving that brought tears to Teren's eyes and made him smile warmly at me. It wasn't nearly as moving as what he'd said, although the crowd still sniffled. While I couldn't remember the words in my hormonal, emotionally charged vows, the overall sentiment was—*I love you more than words can express, and that will never stop.*

After my vows, we kissed again, and another laugh went over the crowd. Peter finally gave up and simply proclaimed our kissing bodies to be husband and wife. I ignored the thunderous applause and the sound of several bodies standing and clapping; I already knew we were husband and wife. Teren and I kissed, smiled and hugged. Finally we tore our attention off of each other, to take in the crowd of well-wishers.

I didn't know a lot of them, only having heard of them through family stories my mom told, but some were familiar and I smiled warmly at them. At the people I loved, I smiled brightly. My mother, her eyes a red, watery mess. Alanna, her eyes so pink from her tears that she almost looked like she had an infectious disease. Imogen, who was clapping at us and swallowing repeatedly. I could tell she was forcing herself not to cry; vampires cried pure blood, and although that trait had faded away by the time it had diluted to Teren, it was still pretty obvious in Imogen. Beside her, her bare arms wrapped around her daughter, was Halina. No tears were on the vampire's cheeks, nor did she seem to be holding any back, but she beamed at us as she hugged Imogen.

After another moment of clapping, Teren took my hand and led me down the carpet path placed over the Plexiglas floor above the pool. Along the sides of the carpet, I could see the pool water glowing blue, lit from the bulbs beneath it. Combined with all the candles and the twinkling lights above, the space was well lit, and no trace of a glow was in Teren's eyes as he shook hands with my relatives. No glow but a happy one, that was.

The music shifted to a happy beat as Teren and I drifted over to the barbeque area of the patio, where the tables of food were being set up. People congratulated us and gave me hugs. In fact, I hugged so many people that my automatic response to someone walking in front of me was to grab them and enclose them in a teary embrace.

Teren thought that was pretty funny, since I didn't even know the majority of the people's names.

Between the bustle of talking to strangers and having my sister shove some food in my mouth—some sort of teriyaki beef that was to die for—the folding chairs were swished off the pool, and the red carpet was rolled away. As I noticed people starting to dance on the huge Plexiglas floor, I also noticed that the lights under the pool had started shifting colors in time to the music. They pulsed red then blue then a really beautiful green. I smiled around a mouthful of food at the beauty of my fairytale wedding. And I hadn't planned any of it really.

I embraced and thanked every in-law I could find after that. With tears running down my cheeks, I even told Halina I loved her. She smirked and raised an amused eyebrow to Teren, then she proceeded to bump and grind a couple of my cousins on the dance floor, her super short, strapless dress, riding even higher up her toned thighs.

I pulled Teren out to the floor, and much to my mother's dismay, we danced all night long. People were so entertained by the environment, the food, and the music, not to mention the wine and the huge hot tub that a few brave souls jumped in, that no one really noticed that we skipped over the cake cutting, just serving the slices instead, and no one gave any champagne toasts. We didn't need them anyway. Well, my mom noticed. She tried to get me off the floor several times to do the "formally correct" wedding things, but only hugged Teren tighter as he twirled me around the see-through floor, and told her we'd do it later. Of course, I had no intention of doing it later, since my husband couldn't eat or drink. I was not about to subject him to another round of blood-chucking on our wedding night. I had much more appealing plans for him than that.

Eventually, Mom let it die. Alanna helped with that by keeping her occupied on the dance floor with her and Ashley. When it was really late at night, the revelers finally started dispersing. I cried and hugged each one, telling my third cousin, Tyra, that I loved her and we'd get together soon, even though we'd never hung out before and I wasn't even sure of her last name.

When just a handful of us were left, and Teren and I were sleepily slow dancing, Hot Ben and Tracey came up to us. Teren stopped our movement and we broke apart. Both of our eyes were on Ben. Tracey, oblivious and slightly tipsy, congratulated us both with long hugs and sloppy kisses on the cheeks. After pulling apart from Teren, which made Ben clench his jaw, she slurred, "It's getting cold out here." With a grin she added, "You should go upstairs before Teren turns into a Popsicle."

I giggled at her comment, but stopped when I noticed the pale look on Ben's face. Teren extended a hand to the side of the pool and asked Ben to talk to him for a minute. Ben swallowed, but eventually nodded as he looked around at all the human witnesses.

I sighed at his reluctance to be alone with Teren, and eavesdropped without seeming like I was. I turned to Tracey when she muttered to me, "Did you see Ben during the ceremony?" She shook her head, her now freed blonde curls dancing, "You'd think *he* was getting married up there, by how nervous he was."

I giggled self-consciously as Tracey frowned at her seemingly commitment shy boyfriend. I was pretty sure that wasn't the case, since Ben adored Tracey, but I couldn't really explain the reason for Ben's nerves to her, so I didn't comment. Luckily I didn't need to. Ashley joined us and distracted her.

"We're gonna take off, sis," She brightly said.

I cocked my head at her. "You're not gonna stay until tomorrow?"

Ashley shook her head and she and Tracey both giggled. "No way, we don't want to be anywhere near you on your big night."

A flush warmed my cheeks. "God, Ashley. We're in a different building for goodness sake." I wasn't worried about *their* ears hearing us anyway.

She and Tracey exchanged a glance and then they laughed again. "Yeah, we know."

I couldn't hear anything Ben and Teren were talking about, over Ashley and Tracey's giggles, but I figured Teren would tell me later. Wife's privilege, right?

As Ashley and Tracey walked away, to go pack their stuff, Teren and Hot Ben came back. They both looked worn, but had small smiles on their faces. As Ben gave me a hug goodbye, I watched Teren over his shoulder. He tilted his dark head, listening, and then muttered something under his breath. I knew he was talking to his family, and I could easily imagine which member. As Ben and I broke apart, I looked over to the other end of the dance floor. Halina was staring at us. Her eyes were narrowed in disapproval as she stood stone still amid the handful of dancers left.

Ben noticed my gaze and looked over at her too. He sucked in a quick breath as he caught her glaring at him. I think if Halina had made the slightest move towards us, he'd have bolted. "Oh God, did she hear Teren and me talking? Does she know that I know?" he whispered.

I didn't need to answer him, for Halina, several feet away from us, nodded, slowly and deliberately. There was no question that she was answering him. Ben gasped and backed up into Teren. Teren put a hand out to steady him and Ben looked back, a little unsure about his closeness. Teren kept his eyes on Halina, as he stated, "You won't be bothered, Ben. You're free to go home, if you wish."

Halina shifted her gaze to Teren, clearly not happy about that, but she made no move to disagree with his decree. Ben took Halina's distraction as a chance to scramble away from us. I sighed as I watched him leave, both grateful that he'd chosen to remember, and sad that he wasn't as instantly okay with it as I had been. Although, when it came to Halina, even I had needed a minute to adjust. Teren's eyes were still on Halina, and I heard him mutter, "We'll talk about this later."

Halina shot him a vicious glare, then she turned to walk away from the pool, to the back of the patio where she could disappear into the night. I figured a cow or two were going down. I hoped no humans were, deserving or not. Teren sighed as he looked down on me, and wrapped an arm around my satin covered waist.

"So?" I asked, putting an arm around him.

He shook his head. "He says he wants to remember…but I feel like he, just as much, wants to forget." His eyes were sad as he smiled. "I don't know if we'll ever be the same, but I don't think he'll say anything." He looked over to a point off to his right, where he could sense his great-grandmother in the darkness. "And if he does…she'll take care of it."

I patted his chest and leaned into his side in sympathy. I knew what that friendship had meant to him, and I hoped it could somehow survive. Before I could respond, the rest of the guests started coming up to say their goodbyes. My mother was last. She wished us well, but she didn't want to stay and pester us on our first night together. I automatically put a hand on my slightly expanded belly, thinking it was nowhere near our first night together, but I understood my mom's sentiment. It was our first night together as husband and wife.

After she left, Alanna came up to us. With tears in her eyes, she congratulated us both. Then she turned and started to walk towards the darkness where Halina had disappeared. "Where are you going?" I called after her.

She turned and a knowing smile was on her lips. "We are all spending the night at the ranch hand's home." She lifted her hand to indicate the massive, empty spread. "You have the main house all to yourself."

Surprised and embarrassed, I stammered out a thank you. She giggled, the youthful sound matching her youthful appearance, and then she blurred from sight. Teren laughed at seeing her dash away, and then he swept me into his arms with a broad smile on his face. "Mrs. Adams, are you ready to retire for the evening?"

I tightened my arms around his neck, pushing aside my embarrassment as the desire to rip off his incredible tuxedo struck me. "Oh, yes, Mr. Adams." I giggled as I kissed him.

I felt his strong arms tighten, then felt the rush of air as he blurred us upstairs, since he no longer had to hide his abilities in this empty home. For once, no one but Teren would be privy to my moans of passion. I delighted in that fact, just as much as I delighted in the feel of his stubble along my sensitive skin.

He set me down beside our massive bed. A fire in the fireplace was already going and dozens of candles around the room were lit, filling it with the heady scent of vanilla. The multiple flickering lights masked the glow of Teren's eyes and emphasized the desire. He stepped away from me, his hands trailing down the lace sleeves as he took me in. "That dress...is spectacular," he murmured.

His eyes, combined with the feather-light touch down my arms, heated my core and made me start to burn with need for him. He inhaled deep, and his eyes were unfocused when they came back to mine. Stepping toward me, his body lightly brushing mine, he leaned in to whisper in my ear, "Do you have any idea how good you smell...when you're ready for me?" His nose ran up my bare throat, left purposefully unadorned for him, since he preferred my neck naked. A gasp escaped me and my knees felt weak. "When you're wet...because of me?"

Speech not really capable in my brain anymore, I could only groan at his erotic words. His cool lips closed over an earlobe and his hands ran up my back. His chilly fingers traced the heart outline between my shoulder blades, giving me goose bumps. As his mouth shifted back to mine and my fingers traveled up to his dark, thick hair, he started popping open the pearl buttons along my spine.

He opened each one at a slow, human speed, and it took a while; they went all the way down to my backside. With our mouths never stopping, he slipped the satin and lace material off my shoulders. His fingers followed the fabric down my arms, and my breath picked up with each new inch of skin that was exposed. When my arms were free, his fingers explored the ribbon corset highlighting my ample cleavage before he let the dress drop. When all that remained was a white pool of symbolic purity, Teren pulled away from my mouth and gazed at my body. His face was anything but pure as he took me in.

His breath heavier, he trailed one finger along the strap of my snow white bra. Achingly slow, he followed the strap down to the cup. My chest was heaving at this point. He dipped his finger into the cup and twisted it, so he could caress the twin wounds he'd made earlier. I gasped at the sensation and the memory, and attacked his mouth as I ripped off his jacket.

He lifted my body out of the remnants of my heavy dress and set me on the bed. Leaning over me, still kissing, he helped me remove his shirt, vest and other fabulous adornments. When only his lower body was dressed, he straightened and looked down at me. Under his powerful gaze, my shaking fingers went to the buttons of his pants and slowly unfastened them. His hand came up to run through a curl in my up-do. As I slowly opened the zipper of his black slacks, he pulled out the pins keeping my hair in place.

At the same time that I freed his pants and pushed them down his hips, he freed my hair and fluffed out the curls around my shoulders. He left the tiara on. He kicked off his shoes and socks after stepping out of his pile of pants. When he was only in his black boxer-briefs, he leaned over me again, until I laid all the way back on the bed. Teren scooted me up to the middle, pausing only a second, to rapidly toss the mountain of decorative pillows to the floor.

His fingers traveled from my plain white, virginal looking bra to my not-so virginal abdomen, holding his twins safely deep inside. While his cool body explored every inch of my heated flesh, I explored every inch of his. My hand ducked inside his underwear, eager to feel how ready he was. He did not disappoint. He groaned low in my ear, as my hand tightened around him. Then he pulled my hand away and crouched over me.

"Give me fifteen minutes," he said, a playful grin on his face.

I frowned and sat up on my elbows. "Fifteen minutes? What for?"

His smile turned devilish. "It's a surprise, one you'll like."

I kept up my frown, but his playful smile intrigued me. "Fine…but after fifteen minutes, I'm starting without you."

His smile dropped and his eyes dragged down my body to stare at my underwear. I couldn't help but tease him, so I ran a perfectly manicured finger over the most sensitive part of me. He blurred out of the room.

While he was gone, I tossed the covers to the floor, undressed, and spread myself over the luxurious silk sheets. The firelight danced along my bare skin, making shapes and patterns in the hills and valleys. I started to feel my long, emotional day catch up to me, and I hoped that whatever he was doing, he did it soon before I fell asleep. That would not be a satisfying wedding night story to tell Tracey, not that I'd be telling her much anyway.

Just when I was wishing I had his super senses and I could either hear him or sense where he was, he blurred back into the room. I stared at him, just as he stared at me. He looked no different than before, but he was completely naked now and completely ready for me. I was instantly ready again too as anticipation shot through me.

His eyes lingered on my nakedness spread across the bed for him as he walked towards me. "You're so beautiful," he muttered before crawling over me. I started to respond as my hands instinctually reached out to embrace him, but the words froze on my tongue. My eyes widened in shock as he laid down on top of me. A small grin was on his face at my reaction. He was warm.

Every extremity of my body wrapped around him as I tried to process the now odd sensation. He was warm, really warm, slightly above my temperature. While I loved the cool sensation of him against my skin, feeling him this way brought back every memory of when he was alive. My eyes started to water as I caressed every section of skin that I could find. I'd missed this.

"How…?"

He smiled as I continued mauling him. Leaning down, he brought his warm lips to my ear and I shuddered as his hot mouth sucked on a lobe. "Hot tub," he whispered.

It was only then that I noticed that his warm skin, while not damp, had that muggy feeling you get when you've been in water a long time. I also noticed that the edges of his hair were wet, not the top, just around the sides like he'd held his face under the water. I sighed in contentment and brought his mouth to mine. Even his tongue was warm.

"Oh my God, you're so warm…you're so warm." My hand ran down to the lower part of him, still completely hard, and now completely warm. "Oh my God…"

The moisture in my eyes started spilling over and he stopped his chuckling to look at me. Confusion passed his features as he dried my tears. "I thought you'd like this. I'm sorry."

I immediately shook my head. "No, I do…I *so* do. I just…" I swallowed and made myself smile, made myself push back the emotion. "I love how you are…I even like the cold." My hands tightened over his body as I drew him even closer to me. "But like this…" I sighed and hugged his head to me. "You feel alive again, Teren."

He pulled back and gazed at me for a moment, then he shook his head. "I am alive, Emma." He smiled and rested his warm forehead to mine. "I may not be living…but I *am* alive."

He kissed me then, intently, like he wanted to show me through physical contact just what he meant. I reveled in him, in our mouths moving together in unison, our hands clutching the other's warm flesh, our breaths fast, our sounds full of need, our warm, aroused bodies sliding against the other's as our hips rocked together. Just one shift by either of us and we'd officially consummate this marriage.

Getting lost in his temperature, I pushed his head down my chest. "I need to feel your heat…everywhere."

He groaned, obliging me with searing kisses down my body. "God, that's hot," he muttered into my skin. His hands and lips worked over my body, firing every sensitive stretch of skin he passed—a swell of my breast, a rigid nipple, the slight bulge of my stomach, the softness behind my knee, a tender spot on my inner thigh. When his pleasantly warm tongue stroked and tasted the wetness between my thighs, I grabbed his head and cried out, instantly grateful that the house was empty.

As I came down off my climax, he flipped me over and turned his attention to the small of my back, my spine, my ribs, then my shoulder blades. It was incredibly stimulating and I was soon ready for him again. As he sucked on his favorite part of my neck, his hands slid under me to caress my breasts. I pushed my hips back into his, wanting him inside me.

He growled low in my ear as his hands shifted to my hips and guided me onto him. I gasped as his warmth filled me. His coolness was incredible, but so was him feeling alive again. Groaning, he dropped his head to my shoulder. His warm chest rested flush against my back, heating me inside and out. His hips moved against me as I rocked back into him. Moaning, I let him know exactly how incredible he felt to me. His left hand reached out to clutch mine, and our wedding bands clicked together as we grasped each other tight. It nearly felt like we were drowning in the pleasure engulfing us.

As Teren neared his climax, he pulled out and quickly twisted me around. When we were face to face, he entered me again. His mouth came down to mine and he groaned in relief as our bodies resumed their rhythm.

Breathing heavy in my ear, he muttered with a tight voice, "Oh God, Emma. It's so….it's so…"

His voice trailed off, and I grabbed his head, muttering, "I know. I know, baby."

And I did know. We'd made love dozens of times. I mean, he'd already successfully impregnated me, but this, making love right now as husband and wife, it felt completely different and new. It felt like the first time. No, better than the first time, better than any time. I wasn't sure why that was, but being with him like this, as his wife, was such a deeper connection than I had ever expected to feel during sex.

I clutched him tight, almost scared to feel the intensity rising in me; I could even feel the tears close to the surface. His hand reached over to grab mine, left to left again, and he squeezed us tight, his body rigid and shaking with the force of the release building inside of him. Feeling more confident that we were going into this together, I relaxed the hold on my body and let the explosion hit me. And it was an explosion, bigger than anything I'd ever felt before, ever. I let out a long cry filled with all of the love and ecstasy that I felt pouring through me.

He continued to move in me, possessing me, filling me, overwhelming me, and then a moment later, his body stilled and he cried out, his moans matching my own, his release just as intense as mine. With panting breaths and slight rocking movements, we maintained the sensation as long as our spent bodies would hold onto it, then the feeling ebbed and only peace and satisfaction remained. And a whole lot of love. Always that.

He stayed on my chest, stroking my hair and kissing my forehead while I reveled in his still warm body on top of me. "I love you, wife," he said into my hair.

I looked up at him, the tears in my eyes finally rolling down my cheeks. "I love you too, husband."

Chapter 8 – Acceptance and Rejection

I stirred under slick, satin sheets. In my mind, I wasn't in a luxurious bed, though. No, in my semi-conscious state I was floating in a pool of light red liquid. The sun was bright in the cloudless sky and as I experimentally moved, the water, while warm directly around me, became cooler farther away from my body. And unlike any liquid in real life, it supported my weight, cradled me like a waterbed—a tropical fruit punch waterbed. Somewhere in the distance, I heard birds calling and waves lapping. As I basked under the glorious rays of the sun, I trailed my fingers through the odd, supportive red water and beads of it splashed over my bare skin, turning portions of me a speckled pink.

I laughed at the strangeness of it all and a deep laugh answered me. Turning my head, I saw Teren lying next to me; he was supported in the weird liquid as well. He turned his head to gaze at me, his blue eyes and dark hair in sharp contrast to the red water. He smiled, his fangs pure white and casually long, then he rolled over the springy water to lie on top of me. With a soft sigh, he dropped his head to the crook of my neck. His scratchy stubble against the sensitive skin of my collarbone started bringing me to awareness.

He was real. The red lake was not, but *he* was real.

The haze of my dream lifted as my legs stirred in the sheets again. This time I recognized the fabric as our bed, and not a fruit punch pool. My eyes still closed, I also recognized the weight on top of me, and the smell—that light cologne scent that Teren had been wearing yesterday, the day we got married. Inhaling, still more asleep than awake, I let out some sort of mumbled greeting to my husband. His head still buried in my neck, I felt him rumble a response.

Neither one of us being more than barely conscious, I wrapped my arms around him. His body, while not nearly the temperature he'd been last night, was still on the lukewarm side. I sleepily indulged in the feeling of him covering every bare inch of me. His hands wrapped under my body and we held each other as we drifted through phases of light slumber.

As I fluttered in and out, my legs instinctively opened to him. As he fluttered in and out, he instinctively pressed himself against me. Neither of us speaking, one of my hands trailed down his broad back to rest at his hip, while one of his hands slid down my spine and curved around my pelvis to rest on my knee. He gently brought my leg around him as he settled himself over me.

I exhaled as his ready body gently pushed into mine. He let out a deep sigh, sounding more like a man relaxing back into his favorite recliner than a man making love to his wife. Perfectly content. With our eyes still closed, his head still buried in my neck, we began to move together. It was slow and languid, neither one of us really striving towards anything, just enjoying the feeling of being so intimately connected.

We stayed that way, silently and slowly rocking together, between the cool satin sheets and the warm, down-filled quilt, for a long, blissful eternity. Just when I could feel a deep, slow build-up starting, another part of my body decided to speak up first.

One hundred percent wide awake now, I stiffened board-straight underneath him. Confused, he stopped moving and raised his head to blink sleepily at me. "Emma?"

His tired eyes tried to focus on mine, but he was still groggy and slow moving, and I needed him to move much quicker. One hand flew to cover my mouth while the other shoved Teren's shoulder, pushing him off of me. Understanding that I was about to lose it on him if he didn't move, he instantly retreated. Without looking back, I shot up off the bed and stumbled my way to the bathroom. I just barely made it into the private room with the toilet.

I was so ready for this part of pregnancy to be over with.

Almost immediately, his cool hands were there running up and down my back. I looked at him over my shoulder as I panted into the bowl. I sort of hated him at the moment for putting me in this position. He smirked at my expression and then pointed at the swirling water I'd just flushed down. "Sorry, did I do that?" His voice was sweet and innocent, but the twinkle in his eye was not.

Glaring at him as I sat back on my heels, I put a hand on my stomach and raised an eyebrow. "You know you did."

"Sorry." He grinned, not looking sorry at all.

I wanted to complain, but then he swept me into his arms and treated me to a nice, relaxing, soapy shower. As he washed my hair and massaged my back, I just couldn't find the words to complain anymore. When I was clean and feeling human again, Teren wrapped me in a huge, fluffy robe and put me back in bed. Then he blurred away and left me alone. I wanted to complain about that too, until ten minutes later when he came back with bacon, eggs and a plate of waffles. I loved my husband.

He seemed to love me too. While I scarfed down my food, he played with my wedding band. A loving, peaceful look was on his face the entire time he twisted my ring in never-ending circles. When I was full and finished, and positive the food would stay down, I set my plate on the nightstand and proceeded to finish what I'd so rudely halted this morning.

This time, I made it through without getting sick.

His family stayed away for the bulk of the day. Well, for Halina and Imogen it wasn't really a choice, they were stuck wherever they were until the sun set, but Jack and Alanna stayed away, giving us our newlywed space. And we needed it. We didn't leave the room much, or the bed for that matter. We lounged, laughed, talked, made love, napped, played card games and made love again, all afternoon long. It was bliss. Pure, romantic, we-just-got-married bliss.

Teren did slip out of our oasis once or twice to get a bite to eat, dressed only in a pair of loose lounge pants, which was a delightfully yummy sight. I let him leave by himself, taking the time he was gone to call my mom and sister. I sort of wanted to call Tracey, just to talk to Ben, to make sure he was okay, but I supposed that could wait. I mean, Teren and I had already kind of had our honeymoon. Today was all I was going to get, so I was going to enjoy every darn minute of it.

When Teren came back, full and satisfied, he immediately stripped off his lounge pants, and I thoroughly enjoyed every single second of our time together.

Eventually the sun did set though, and Teren and I got dressed and remained dressed. He let me know when everyone was coming back, and we headed downstairs to greet them. As I was hugging Alanna and thanking her for the beautiful weekend, Halina immediately grabbed Teren's arm and pulled him into the library. And let me tell you, when Halina wanted someone to follow her, vampire or not, that person followed. Teren stumbled as she dragged him away.

I eyed where they went nervously and I saw both Alanna and Imogen cringe. At one point, even I could hear the heated voices. After that, Imogen slung her hand over my arm and gently pulled me towards the kitchen. Knowing they were trying to spare me the showdown going on a few rooms down the hall, I let them lead me away. Alanna set me at the table and made a quick meal for Jack and me. Jack studied his plate, but he occasionally looked at his wife and then down the hallway where Teren and Halina were still "talking."

When he did it again, along with Imogen and Alanna, who were sipping their drinks at the table, I dropped my fork and said, "Shouldn't someone go in there?"

The trio looked at each other and then to where Teren was. Imogen finally broke the silence. "He's fine," she said, drinking her blood.

I sighed, and gave Alanna hopeful eyes. She let out a weary exhale as she met my gaze. "He really is fine. He's just…explaining the situation to her."

I looked at the three of them and shrugged. "What situation? Ben?"

They glanced at each other again, then back at me. Imogen answered, her youthful face concerned as she peeked at the hall. "Yes." She brought her eyes back to mine. "We really don't like people to know about us. Teren knows that. Ben should have been wiped immediately."

I blinked at each of them. "I knew."

Alanna and Imogen shared a look that spoke volumes. I suddenly realized that if Teren and I hadn't ended up together, I most definitely would not have been allowed to remember what he was. I had suspected that, but knowing it for sure was startling. Tears stung my eyes at the thought; I couldn't imagine not knowing.

Alanna's eyes were sympathetic as she watched the emotion on my face. "It's just a precaution, Emma. The fewer who know, the fewer who can find out."

I swallowed as I looked over her beautiful but sad, pale eyes. "My sister knows," I whispered, suddenly worried that my confidant was going to be snatched away from me.

Imogen looked down while Alanna glanced at Jack. My heart was in my throat when Alanna spoke to me; her eyes never left her husband. "Halina spoke with her. She won't wipe her mind," her eyes returned to mine, "so long as she stays silent." She smiled. "Halina is quite attached to the girl, as are we all."

Relief filled me that my sister's memory wouldn't be tampered with. A thought struck me as I thought about memories. No one was allowed to know their secret? Did that mean that no one was allowed to even remember them? "How much does she wipe? When she erases someone, how much do they remember?"

The vampires looked at each other again and it was Imogen who answered me this time. "It depends on the circumstance. She won't touch the people who came to the wedding, that meeting was too trivial, must people will have forgotten our faces in a few weeks. For other relationships, she may take everything. Some people, the acquaintances we're around the most, but who can't be let in on the secret, well, when we leave here, they won't even remember our names. They'll only have a vague sense that they knew this person once. Every specific thing about us will elude them though. We could meet them again, give them the exact same names, and they'd never even realize that they already knew us."

The tears stung my eyes as the implications of that hit me. Aside from each other, hardly anyone they met remembered who they were. I supposed, when it was time to move to another region, all traces of them were erased. That must take Halina weeks to scour through all the people. Although, most of the family stayed secluded at the ranch. The only vampire really out there forming attachments was Teren. He was creating a lot of work for her by leaving coworkers and friends who would need their memories dimmed, if not eradicated. No wonder they didn't like him being away from the ranch. How lonely to not have anyone remember the bond they had with you.

And, I supposed, if things had worked out differently for Teren and me...*I* wouldn't even know him. With how close we'd gotten, they would have taken everything. Every cherished memory I had. While I wouldn't know the difference, Teren would. He'd still be in love, but to me, he'd be a complete stranger, just someone I'd spilt coffee on one day. I desperately wanted to hug him, all of them. "That's so...sad," I whispered.

Alanna had a small smile on her fanged face as she sipped her blood. "We have each other."

I shook my head. "But Teren wants more."

Imogen sighed and reached out for Alanna's hand. As one, they turned to Jack when he finally spoke. "He does. He wants a normal life, normal job...normal friends." Jack sighed and shook his head. "The fact that the side effects are so mild on him, that he can pass as human so easily, makes living a life in secret...more difficult." Jack shrugged, his aged eyes looking sad. "He's always wanted to leave his mark on the world...and that just can't happen. It's impossible to not leave some sort of trail, not with how connected everyone is now, but we do what we can. It's one of the reasons Teren writes under an alias."

Jack sighed while that fact sank in. Teren wrote articles for Gate Magazine under the name John Jones. Very generic. I had always assumed he did that for privacy. I guessed in a way I was right. Alanna met eyes with Jack and they gave each other sympathetic smiles. I wondered if someday, Teren and I would share sympathetic smiles over the table, while our children's spouses dealt with the realities of their lives.

"It hurts him, I think, having to hide," Alanna said quietly.

I looked down, hating this conversation, but understanding it too. The constant charade, the self-imposed isolation, the endless lies—all of it to hide the truth from everyone. People who wouldn't be allowed to remember much, if anything, about him anyway. It was heartbreaking for someone who ached for normalcy.

The vampires simultaneously looked up at the hallway, and a moment later Jack and I did as well. Halina huffed through first, heading to the table and pouring a thick glass of blood from the carafe; she immediately downed it. Teren came in a few steps later, looking tired, but happy. He smiled at me as he sat down. When Halina slammed the carafe down in front of him, probably denting the table, he didn't react, only grabbed it and calmly poured himself a glass. I guessed he'd won.

Halina pouted during dinner and both Imogen and Alanna whispered foreign words to her. Afterwards, I tried to help Alanna clean up the wedding decorations still strewn all throughout the entryway and backyard. I should have known better. She shooed me off, loaded Teren down with our presents and as much of the leftovers as he could carry, and then practically swept us out the door.

While Teren packed up our car, I said my final goodbyes and thank yous. Ending up in front of Halina last, I gave her a hug; her cold body gave me a slight shiver in the December air. Her pale eyes were worried when I pulled away, but she wasn't looking at me. Her eyes were attached to Teren's back as she watched him fill the trunk of his Prius. Feeling sympathetic, hormonal, and full of I-just-got-married good feelings, I cupped her cheek.

Shocked, her eyes shifted over to mine. A little shocked myself, I dropped my hand and intently held her gaze. The wind picked up some, billowing Halina's tresses around her like a pure black cloud. "He'll be okay," I told her. "I won't let anything happen to him."

Even *I* knew my promise was an impossible one. I guess I'd said it so that she would know she wasn't alone in worrying about him. I was right there with her. She seemed to understand and smiling at me, she nodded. We hugged again and were still hugging when Teren walked up to us.

He grinned at the sight of me seemingly bonding with the one vampire who had nearly had me running for the hills a few months ago, and then his eyes settled on his great-grandmother. He spoke a long, flowery sentence in Russian to her. She sighed and nodded before reaching up and hugging him. Then she repeated the only line that I'd actually understood—*Ya Tebya Lyublyu*—I love you.

My eyes watered as Teren grabbed my hand and led me to the car. Darn emotional vampires.

I tried to bring up the conversation he'd had with Halina on the car ride home, but he didn't really want to talk about it. He would only say that she was worrying too much, and that he was positive Ben wasn't going to say anything to anyone. I could see the tension in his jaw though, and thought Teren was simply wishing out loud. He *wanted* to believe Ben would choose their friendship over fear, or even over fame. I wasn't sure, but I had to imagine that one of Halina's concerns was that once he was outside of their influence, Ben would gather his courage and speak out. Most reputable news sources would scoff at his tale, but if he looked hard enough, he could probably find one that wouldn't. If he wanted to sell a story and make a little money, Teren's was a good one to sell.

I just didn't see Ben doing that though. Neither did Teren. That's why he'd let him leave. He had faith. Well, tomorrow would answer the question for both of us I guess. If Ben was going to spill, Tracey would be the first one he spilled to.

I put it out of my mind when we arrived at home; there was nothing I could do about it tonight anyway. Teren walked around the car to help me out, as he liked to do, but he paused an inordinately long time at my door. He stared at me through the glass, but I knew he wasn't really seeing me. He was listening. Without opening my door, he straightened and looked across the street. I looked with him, but I saw nothing out of the ordinary.

The neighbor's house was the same large, two-story dwelling that we'd left behind Friday morning. Painted in a sort of bright teal color that I found atrocious, it had high hedges that formed a natural fence around the perimeter. A balcony on the front of the home, highlighting what I'd always assumed was the master bedroom upstairs, was just as empty as it usually was. And In the darkness, I could just make out Goldie, Spike's favorite cat to chase. She jumped off the vacant front porch and dashed underneath the shrubbery before running off down the street. All pretty standard stuff.

Teren had an eerie expression on his face though and a growl rumbled from his chest. I could hear him all the way through the thin metal of the car. I could almost feel it vibrating my skin as I sat safe and sound on the inside. Panic sliced through me at hearing that noise coming from him, but when he took a couple of steps, like he was going to stride over to our neighbor's garish spread to personally investigate whatever was bothering his senses, I opened my door. He started and looked back at me. As I stood from the car, he pointed at the vehicle in a clear command to stay put.

Ignoring my natural instincts to not be commanded, I opted for caution and stayed standing in the open door frame. When it seemed I was obeying, Teren's eyes returned to the street, and he took another step. Lunging forward, I caught his hand at the last second. He looked over at me, and I could see that the desire to stay was warring with the desire to leave. I shook my head at him, commanding him not to go. If I was going to be cautious, then so was he.

"I'm tired. I want *us* to go to bed." I stressed the "us" in that sentence, just in case he'd missed it. I didn't know what he was hearing, but I knew it was something I didn't want him checking out by himself. Besides, hadn't I just promised Halina that I wouldn't let anything happen to him? We were stronger together than apart, he needed to learn that.

He finally sighed and with one last glance, and I swear a sniff, he scooped me up and carried me across the threshold, like we were back in the fifties or something. I giggled, relieved. Running into the house from a newly installed doggy door just off the laundry room, an exuberant Spike met us at the door. He barked and ran circles around the two of us. He ran in-between Teren's legs whenever he could, while Teren attempted to keep moving forward without stepping on him.

Teren set me down in the entryway, and Spike jumped up so he could try and lick my face. Teren walked back outside to get our bags, and I watched him through the open door. While he grabbed our belongings from the trunk, he occasionally glanced over at the neighbor's house. He shook his head, but made no move to go near it. The final remnants of worry left me when he set our stuff down just inside the door and softly closed it, shutting out the world. Then with a wicked grin, he blurringly fast swept me back into his arms. I squeaked and held him tight while my body adjusted to the quick change in position. Laughing at my reaction, Teren held me tighter and gave me a brief kiss. Then our little trio headed upstairs.

Teren laid me down on our bed, then turned to bring our stuff up from downstairs. I gave him a look that clearly said, *You better only be going downstairs, and not outside to investigate whatever you heard, while I'm out of eyeshot.* He stared at me for a second and then, understanding, he nodded in silent agreement.

Trusting that he'd listen to me, I comfortably settled myself on the bed and let the busy weekend overwhelm my exhausted body. Spike hopped up with me, his long tongue lolling out the side of his mouth as he shook with happy energy. He nuzzled into my back and, snuggling into his furry warmth, I was asleep long before Teren returned.

I was so tired that I didn't wake up until Teren kissed me goodbye for work the next morning. Smiling, I eagerly kissed him back. My fingers ran over the metal of his wedding band as our hands slid together; the metal was as cool as his skin. As he straightened to leave, he handed me a calla lily. Amazed at his never-ending romantic side, I took it and inhaled a deep breath. So far, married life was going swimmingly.

Once he was gone, I crawled out of bed and made myself get ready for work. I couldn't help but smile at the fact that I was in my pajamas. I was so out of it last night, that I hadn't even noticed Teren changing me.

Forcing my still-tired body to go through the motions of showering, dressing and doing makeup, I suddenly thought Tracey had a good point when she'd asked me why I was still working. Teren's family had money, seemingly a lot of money. Did I really need to keep trudging to a job every day? I did like it though. It occupied my mind and made me feel like I was contributing to something larger than myself, even if it was an already well-off corporation. It was just the process of getting there that sometimes sucked.

Once I finally dragged myself to work, I was met with multiple little surprises. First, Clarice congratulated me. I think my eyes were as wide as they could go when she said that. Of course, she handed me a stack of papers at the same time, so really, I suppose, she could have been congratulating me for that. Second, someone, and I'm going to assume it was Tracey, had decorated my "office." My tiny cubicle was swarming with balloons, roses and cards stuffed with well wishes. It made my eyes tear up, seeing all the thoughtfulness.

My last surprise was the one that filled me with the most relief. Tracey hugged me and exclaimed over and over about what a great weekend she had, and what a perfect wedding it had been. She was startled that I'd pulled it off on such short notice, but she wasn't startled that my husband was a member of the undead. She was none the wiser. Ben had been worthy of Teren's trust, and hadn't said a single word. That made me very happy.

After a day of warm hugs, endless flashes of my gorgeous ring, and thank yous to anyone who would listen, including the FexEx guy who was dropping off a package to Mr. Peterson, I was worn out. By the time five came around, I was ready for a long bath and a backrub from my extraordinarily strong husband.

But the surprises weren't quite done for the day. Late in the evening, an anxious Ben arrived on our doorstep. Shuffling his weight from side to side, he nervously glanced over my shoulder at Teren, standing a few yards back in the entryway. Then he exhaled a long, slow breath. Seemingly more confident, he asked, "Can I come in?"

Running through all the things he could potentially say that would break Teren's heart, I told him, "Of course," and led him into the entryway. He looked around our home, his blue eyes drifting over all the little luxuries Teren surrounded himself with, and then he followed Teren and me into the living room.

As he took a seat on the leather sofa, he tossed a cursory glance at the wall of windows that showed a magnificent view of the ocean; the expanse of water was as pitch black as the night sky around it. Teren and I exchanged a long look before we joined him. Sitting in-between us on the long, soft-as-a-bed couch, Ben stared at his hands clasped over his knees. His fingers traced the tiny scars and marks a person gets on their skin over the course of their life, but he didn't speak. Knowing that his mind was probably running a mile a minute, Teren and I gave him all the prep time he needed.

Finally he spoke, although he still stared at his hands. "I know, I wasn't supposed to see what I saw the other night," he quietly began. "But I did." He finally looked up at Teren. "And I can't stop thinking about it."

Teren swallowed and nodded. His face was calm, almost resigned. Ben slowly shook his head. "What you are…blows my mind." Looking over at me, Ben shook his head again. "I don't know how you handle it so well, Emma."

Looking back and forth between the two of us, he sighed and leaned back onto the couch; we followed suit. "Watching you two at the wedding though…all I saw was a couple in love." He turned to Teren again. "I didn't see a fictional monster." He turned to me. "And I didn't see a woman who willingly gives her blood to a fictional monster." He stared at his hands again. "I only saw love. A love that makes me believe the world is a better place, because the two of you are in it."

I smiled and looked over at Teren. He smiled with me, although his was tight. Reaching out for Ben, I put a hand on his knee. "Thank you, Ben. You don't know what your acceptance means to us, to Teren."

Ben stopped studying his hands to look up at me. I swallowed when I saw the tears in his eyes. "I'm sorry, Emma." He shook his head. "But that's not what this is."

I felt my own eyes water as I shook my head. "But…you said…"

He swallowed, and flicked a glance at Teren and then me. "I know, and I do feel that way about you," he looked at Teren, "about both of you." He shook his head, and fear was in his watery eyes. "But I can't deal with what I saw anymore."

Ben looked over at Teren, his face deeply apologetic. "I'm sorry. I know you're not a bad person, or whatever, but I can't handle being in a world where things like you exist."

Teren nodded and looked down, but didn't say anything. I found I couldn't be as stoic. "What?" I smacked Ben's shoulder so he'd look at me; he did so reluctantly. "You're his friend! That means accepting him for what he is!" My voice heated, as my hormonal emotions flared.

Ben swallowed and leaned away from me. "I *am* his friend. It's not him I can't handle." He glanced at Teren while I furrowed my brow, angered and confused. "I can't deal with the fact that all the myths are true. That horror stories are real."

I rolled my eyes and sighed. "Ben…"

He returned his eyes to mine, and his perfect face was pale "No, Emma. I'm sorry, but I'm not as strong as you. I need to go back to how I was before."

Irritated, I snapped, "You not knowing won't make it any less real, Ben."

He shook his head at me. "I know that. But, in this case, ignorance is better." Still staring at the ground, Teren let out a soft exhale. Ben ran a hand through his highlights and looked back at him. "I can't sleep, Teren. Every bump, every dark corner…I just keep wondering what else is out there."

With a sad sigh, he put a hand on Teren's shoulder; Teren finally looked up. "It's not you…it's the possibilities you represent." He pointed outside, to the house Teren had been interested in last night. "I mean, just walking over here, I thought I saw something in the shadows." He brought both hands to his face and leaned over his knees. "I'm sorry, I'm really sorry. I just can't live this way."

He stayed bent over while I silently fumed. I was more angry over Teren's loss than Ben's choice. Teren only sighed again and put his hand on Ben's shoulder. "Okay. I'll have Halina fix this. You won't remember a thing."

I straightened in my seat, wondering just how much Teren was planning on taking. If he took everything of Ben's memory, then he'd have to take Tracey's too; we'd spent too much time together as a foursome. I suddenly realized that by marrying him, I'd sort of signed away all of my relationships too. Teren noticed my rigidness, but didn't comment. Cringing, Ben looked up. "She freaks me out, man." Teren smiled and Ben added, "How much will she erase? Will I even remember you?"

Teren looked at him for achingly long moments. I thought he was debating, right now, if he should just end the friendship. I felt a hot tear slide down my cheek. Why couldn't Ben just be okay with this? Finally, Teren softly said, "I'll only take the day of the wedding." He left it at that, but I could clearly hear the part he didn't say. *For now.*

Ben didn't catch the hidden words. He instantly brightened as relief filled his gorgeous face. "Oh, thank you. I was hoping we'd still be…" Swallowing, he looked down, like he suddenly couldn't meet Teren's eyes anymore. "You hate me, right? Think I'm weak."

Teren smiled and patted his back. "No, Ben. I understand. You're not the first person who couldn't handle knowing."

Ben nodded and gave me a sheepish glance before turning back to Teren. "I'm really sorry, you guys. I wish I could…" He sighed and shrugged.

Teren stood and extended a hand to Ben. He stood and clasped it in a friendly shake. Friendly, but businesslike. Teren smiled. "It's okay. I understand, Ben, and I'm not angry."

A part of me wanted to tell Ben that too, but the bitter part of me thought Ben should just man up. For now, I listened to that part. Not wanting to share in the warm goodbyes, I stayed on the couch with my arms crossed over my chest. Teren deserved having a friend that loved him for him, and everything that entailed.

After a swift goodbye, Teren told him, "I'll line up a meeting with Halina. It may take a little bit though. Will you be okay until then?"

Ben smiled nervously, but nodded. I frowned, knowing that Halina would come right now if Teren called for her. He was still giving his friend a chance to change his mind. Still holding out hope that Ben might choose to know him, rather than not know him. Ben sputtered apologies again, then sheepishly backed out of the room. I said nothing as he left, barely even acknowledged his hasty exit. I was too busy being pissed off *for* Teren, since he didn't appear to be.

After showing him out, Teren came back to the living room and sat down in the same spot on the couch. He was silent and composed as he stared straight ahead of himself. I thought I should say something, I just didn't know what. Then a tear dropped to his cheek. After that, it was like he crumbled, and his head dropped into his hands. I was immediately at his side, holding him, stroking his back and murmuring sympathies.

Mentally I cursed Ben for finding us, for ever walking into that room on us. I silently berated him for freaking out and for wanting to forget, for hurting Teren with his rejection. But I couldn't *completely* hate Ben, not even when Teren gave up his stoicism and sought comfort from me, laying his head on my lap as he sniffled back his pain. Even then, I couldn't hate Ben. I couldn't hate him, because I sort of understood him. I understood his fear anyway. Sometimes I even shared it.

I just loved Teren enough to deal with it.

Chapter 9 – Changes

Teren put off dealing with Ben for much longer than I thought he would. In fact, I was well into my fourth month, with an adorably cute baby bump on me, and he still hadn't done anything about it. His optimism that his friend would turn around tore me, especially since Ben asked him every time we all four got together, when Halina was going to see him. Ben was starting to get a little worried that the longer it went on, the greater the possibility was that she couldn't help him anymore.

It visibly bothered Teren that Ben considered memory loss a "help," but he assured him that it didn't work that way. If Halina wanted, she could convince Ben that he didn't even know his own mother. That fact didn't make Ben appear any more comfortable. He actually looked worse and worse every time I saw him. His normally gorgeous face started thinning out, and deep circles started to appear under his eyes. His skin had the sallow look of someone who woke up every ten minutes at night. He seemed to have been genuinely honest with Teren when he'd told him that he couldn't sleep anymore.

Tracey didn't understand the physical or emotional changes in her boyfriend. She started to do what most women in her case would do. She started to think it was her. We had multiple conversations that revolved around me assuring her that Ben was still head over heels in love with her, that he wasn't a liar, and he definitely wasn't a cheater. I was pretty sure she didn't believe me on that last part though. It didn't help the matter any that Ben had a habit of asking Teren about Halina right in front of Tracey. Tracey was convinced that her boyfriend was sleeping with the sensual woman. I really couldn't blame her for coming up with that explanation. Hot Ben was different—moodier and quieter, more introverted, and always looking over his shoulder whenever we went out. I was a little surprised that Tracey hadn't come up with drugs, too, since he was starting to act like some paranoid meth addict.

I felt horrible about the whole thing, especially when Tracey told me about some of their fights. They'd never really fought before this, and now it was becoming a more and more common occurrence.

Honestly, I was getting a little scared for them, for how long they could make it through this stress, but, stubborn as always, Teren still wouldn't call Halina.

"Teren, he looks awful. I know you want his support, but you can't force this." I sat on the bed, rubbing my expanding belly while Teren calmly changed his clothes. He looked at me in the vanity mirror over his dresser, but he didn't answer. I watched his jaw tighten with tension though. I knew him well enough to know that he wanted me to drop this.

I got up off the bed, walked behind him, and slipped my arms around his waist. He'd just taken off his work shirt, and my body shivered a little as I clung to his; the bump of our children touched him before any other part of my torso. Teren smiled, and wrapped one hand over the both of mine. He reached the other around behind him so he could feel my stomach. Laying my head on his shoulder, I met eyes with him in the mirror. "You can't keep avoiding this. It's cruel."

My irritation with Ben's choice had faded away when the physical symptoms of his stress had started to show. He really couldn't handle knowing that the myths were true, and Teren withholding ignorance from him *was* kind of cruel. Teren hung his head, and his fingers over my hands tightened. "I know," he whispered. He looked up at me with pleading eyes. "I just can't yet, Emma."

He didn't say please, but I could feel the word in the air. He wanted time. He wanted Ben to know, and to eventually find peace with it. I bit my lip and resisted the urge to tell him that Ben would never be okay with the knowledge. He should just let him go. Teren eventually had to let everyone go...but, right now, he needed this. Plus, as time went by, Ben had started talking to Teren about Teren's life. They would sit on our couch, Teren's face animated as he went over aspects of what he could do. He wasn't bragging to Hot Ben or anything, he was just relieved to be able to finally tell him the stories he kept bottled up. Like the fish they'd caught last camping trip. Teren had heard them coming up the stream, and he'd plucked one out of the river with his bare hand while Ben had his back turned. Or how Teren knows that the waitress at a bar we frequent, since Teren could fake drinking better than he could fake eating, had a major crush on Ben; apparently her heart started racing whenever Ben was around. Ben listened to all of this with his head in his hands over his knees, looking both intrigued and freaked out.

One of my hands moved to Teren's shoulder, and I rubbed his skin warm, then kissed it. "Okay, but if he keeps asking, you need to do it." I raised my eyebrow at him. "For him, if not for you and the others."

I kissed his shoulder again and then released him. He sighed as we pulled apart, but then he nodded. With a bright smile, I told him, "I'm going to go get a snack." Teren grinned as he shook his head at me. I was starting to "snack" on a frequent basis. I rationalized it as eating for three, but really, I just loved having an excuse to eat nearly a half gallon of ice cream every night.

Massaging my protruding stomach as I walked downstairs, I marveled at how amazing the human body was. Currently, I was incubating two lives inside my own. That was a little miraculous to me. And since I hadn't tossed my cookies in two solid weeks, I had my fingers crossed that the horrible morning—no, more accurately, "anytime throughout the day"—sickness was over with. I was feeling pretty good about this pregnancy thing.

My clothes had tightened up on me once the wedding was over, almost like the twins had realized they didn't need to hide anymore, and they were free to grow like weeds. Teren had taken me shopping for a whole new maternity wardrobe, which was just as much fun as it sounds! So with a stomach that looked like I'd swallowed a cantaloupe, although Teren would say bowling ball, I reveled in my new, comfortable, super-stretchy, and yet still body-concealing clothes—I still hadn't told Clarice yet.

As I made an obscenely huge bowl of peppermint ice cream, loaded up with chocolate sauce, I was feeling really, really good about this pregnancy thing. I grabbed my bowl, sat on the couch, and flipped on the TV to some reality show that didn't require any brain cells to follow. I thought enough during the day, I didn't want to have to do it while relaxing. The creamy goodness hit my tongue and I sighed in contentment. I smiled, knowing Teren would hear my happiness. I liked him knowing when I was happy. And I was frequently happy. Sure, my life was more complicated now that I was married to an undead vampire and all, but the underlying emotion I felt every day, was joy.

I giggled and kicked my feet against the couch cushions like a five year old. Then, above the noise of the TV, I heard a scratching sound. Curious, I set down my ice cream and went to check it out. Walking past the table in the kitchen, I headed to a small hallway that held the laundry room and a bathroom. The sharp, clicking noise was coming from the laundry room, so I stepped in there.

I flipped on the switch, but the room was empty. I couldn't figure out what the sound was at first, but then it happened again and I immediately understood. Spike's doggy door was in this room, and a round laundry basket had been set in front of the flap. The heavy obstacle was overflowing with clothes and impossible for the collie to push back. He was effectively trapped outside. A flash of guilt washed through me that I'd inadvertently blocked Spike's entrance to our warm home. I immediately removed the basket and vowed to do better on keeping up with that sort of thing. No one ever mentions that the signing of wedding papers also commits you to the responsibility of doubled laundry loads. Of course, my husband did make amazing dinners for me, and more often than not he cleaned up afterwards too, so I didn't complain about it…out loud.

Spike immediately bolted into the room and cowered in a corner. Startled at his odd behavior, I went over to him and hugged the shaggy coat to me. He nestled into my side; I could feel him lightly shaking. "You okay, boy? Something out there?"

Feeling protective of my step-pet, I walked over to the door, unlocked it, and stepped outside onto a small concrete slab. The late January air was chilly. A shiver went through my body as I vigorously rubbed my arms and looked over Teren's sloping lawn. It was a big yard and there were hidden areas with deep shadows and dark, menacing trees. When something in the back corner near the garden shed shifted, my heart seized. Then Goldie, the neighbor's cat, hopped up on Teren's fence and I nearly had a heart attack. Thinking I was beyond stupid for being alone in the backyard, investigating strange things just like Teren had a habit of doing, I hurried back into the house.

I closed the door, securely locked it, and encouraged Spike to follow me into the kitchen so I could get him something to eat. Teren instantly breezed into the room with a disapproving look on his face. Oh yeah, I guess if he'd heard me sighing, then he'd also just heard me ask the dog if something had spooked him. Then he'd heard me stupidly go check on what that might be. That really wasn't too smart of me. I wouldn't have been happy if he'd done it. We did need to be more careful than the average husband and wife.

Teren seemed about to scold me, when a strange look suddenly passed over his face and he tilted his head. Then he looked over to the hall where the laundry room was and his features shifted to surprise. "Oh," was all he said.

His face shifted back to normal as he came over, squatted down by his dog, and ruffled his fur. "Sorry to lock you out, boy." He grinned, then kissed Spike's head while Spike thumped his tail.

Confused by his weird reaction, I put my hands on my hips. I'd really been expecting a reprimand; I'd already even prepared my defense, namely that the hormones in my body had temporarily flooded my common sense. "Oh?" I said sarcastically. "That's it?"

Teren looked up at me, still smiling, then straightened and kissed my forehead. "Yep."

He turned to walk away, but I grabbed his t-shirt. "Wait, you can't just say 'oh,' all surprised like, and then not explain." Shaking my head at him, I added, "That's not proper etiquette."

He chuckled and raised an eyebrow at me. "I didn't realize you and I followed the rules of etiquette."

I slung my arms around his waist, trapping him to me symbolically if not physically. "Yes, we do. Everyone does to a certain extent." Smiling, I added, "That's what keeps us civilized."

A devilish grin on his face, he leaned in to place a cool kiss along the vein in my neck. "Was I being civilized then, when I bit you last night in that spot that makes you—"

I cut him off by shoving him away from me. He laughed while I sputtered, "What was 'oh?'" My cheeks heated from the memory he'd just given me and his thumb traced the flush of color.

"I felt you," he whispered.

I cocked my head, confused. "You...felt me? What do you mean?"

He slung his arms around me, actually trapping me, and shrugged his shoulders. "When you went outside, I knew it. At first I thought I'd only heard it, but when you came back inside, I realized that I was wrong." He shrugged. "It was faint, but I'd also felt it."

I sighed, not understanding his meaning. "I don't..."

Smiling, he twisted me back and forth in our embrace. "Like I can feel my family...I felt you. I sensed *where* you were. I'm doing it right now. I see you, I feel you, I smell you, I hear you...and I can sense you."

My eyes widened as his words hit me. His entire family, well, the vampiric part of it, could sense each other's locations, like they'd all been LoJacked or something. And now apparently, he could sense *me* too. "How...?"

His eyes drifted to my stomach, bulged between us. "Them." His eyes went back to mine, joy clear in the pale depths. "I can sense them. Their blood is my blood, my family's blood." He squeezed me tighter, a huge smile spreading over his face. "Now that I know what that faint feeling is, it's very apparent to me, and I think that will only get stronger as they grow." He raised an eyebrow. "As long as they are inside you, I'll know where all three of you are."

Shocked silenced me. I'd forgotten about that vampiric trait. Well, not necessarily forgotten about it, but I'd certainly never considered that he'd have a bond with the children like that before they were even born. A tiny part of me was jealous at the connection he had to them, and a tiny part of me was irritated that even more of my privacy was lost; he'd always know where I was now. My mind spinning, I focused on what his bloodline tracking ability meant for our children's future. "Well, I guess we'll never have to worry about losing the kids at the mall..."

He laughed, and held me as tight as my GPS-spouting stomach would allow.

A couple of weeks later, nothing had changed. Well, nothing had changed in the Teren versus Ben standoff. Plenty of things were changing in my world. For starters, I felt the twins move. At first I thought it was just gas or my stomach rumbling, but one night, when Teren and I were snuggling on the couch watching a movie, I felt a definite and profound kick. Teren looked at my stomach at the same time I did. Both of our hands moved to my belly.

I glanced up at him. "Did you hear that?"

He grinned and nodded as his eyes returned to my tummy. "Yeah, I've been hearing movement for a while now, but that was really distinct."

A second kick greeted our awaiting hands and we both started laughing. Then I started crying. Teren scooped me into his lap and kissed away my emotional tears with a laugh.

Once I knew what it felt like, I started feeling those little kicks and squirms all the time. I started to feel less jealous of Teren's ability to bond with our children pre-birth, and started relishing *my* connection to them. He may be able to sense them and hear them in ways that I couldn't, but I was the one keeping them alive.

Teren started becoming more conscious of that, too. In a move that actually didn't please me, he stopped feeding off me. A week after we'd both felt them kicking, I'd tried to get him to bite me. I'd never really had to try before, not since that very first bite, and it was a little irritating to me to have to beg for it. He worried his lip as he stared at his favorite vein in my neck, but he slowly shook his head. Only his eyes betrayed the fact that he wanted to be piercing my skin more than anything.

"Why not?" I said breathlessly. "I can wear that nice turtleneck you bought me for a few days."

With a sigh, he sat back on his heels. He was still kneeling over me, but resting just below my hips so my growing belly wouldn't get in the way. He shook his head, and his eyes instantly locked onto my stomach. I was getting larger and larger now, as I rolled into the halfway point, the 20th week. My doctor said the twins were growing wonderfully, and every blood draw or pee test I'd taken had showed no inherent dangers. Personally, I wasn't that worried about me passing anything dangerous to them, I knew exactly what condition they were going to end up with, but it was a comforting thing for a doctor to say. We had an intensive ultrasound scheduled in two weeks—the big one—the one where they could tell the sexes. We hadn't decided if we wanted to know or not.

Teren put a cold hand on my naked belly; his chilly fingers automatically elicited a response from the twins. I wasn't sure if they sensed his temperature, even through the layers of skin and fluid separating them from him, or if they just sensed that Daddy was near, but they almost always kicked or moved when he touched me like that. A slow smile broke out on his face, a face full of wonder and love, and his hand circled the now watermelon-sized stomach.

"I can't. I shouldn't," he whispered. I tried to sit up, but failed in getting around my belly. He looked up at me struggling to get closer to him, and shifted his position so he was lying beside me. I rolled onto my side and put a hand on his bare, silent chest, and subtly exposed my neck to him. His eyes drifted over to what I offered, but he shook his head again. "It's not mine anymore, Emma." When his eyes returned to mine, they were content and committed. "You are supporting three lives with that precious blood." He took my wrist and placed a kiss along the crisscross of veins just under the surface. His eyes closed as my pulse vibrated across his lips. "I won't let you support a fourth." He opened his eyes and smiled at me. "I have plenty of other ways to get fresh blood."

I frowned, but I knew full well he meant an animal. Teren would never bite another human, and not just because he couldn't erase the event from them like Halina could. No, he would never bite another human because that would almost be like he was cheating on me. The act of drawing blood was a surprisingly intimate one, and I would be devastated if he ever touched another girl that way. He knew that, and he would never hurt me. So, no, my frown wasn't over fear that he'd "stray," my frown was because…well, I liked it.

He smiled as he followed my thought process. "After they are born, I will drain you until you pass out, but not right now, okay?" He gave me a playful grin, and squeezed my bloated body tight to his.

I sighed, then smiled and kissed him. "Fine…but you better."

He laughed and then rolled me on top of him. I had to bend over my stomach to still kiss him, but I managed. "You're so kinky," he whispered through increasingly heated kisses; my hormonal body quickly started igniting at the seductive, half-naked man pinned underneath me.

"You haven't seen anything yet," I whispered. A low groan escaped him at hearing my words, then I proceeded to show him just how "kinky" I could be.

The next biggest shift in my life was work. Eventually my expanded body became too much for me to hide, especially since my clothes before had always kind of highlighted my figure. When I switched to baggy clothes, I tipped off some of the more observant girls that worked there. Not Clarice though, she didn't clue in until she caught me absentmindedly stroking my stomach one day. Then her jowly jaw had dropped open, and her face went a ghostly shade of white.

"God, are you pregnant?" She asked that like I had some sort of infectious disease. She almost looked like she wanted to put her hand over her mouth and nose as a precaution.

Stopping myself from rolling my eyes or laughing at her response, I threw on a bright smile and said, "Well, I was going to tell you this when I was a bit further along" (say, nine months along) "but I guess you should know as soon as possible." Just to see her reaction, I lifted my shirt and showed her my stretched-beyond-natural stomach. "Yes, Teren and I are expecting. Twins, actually," I tossed in for good measure.

Her reaction was pure gold. Her eyes widened and she went a sickly shade of green. Shaking her head, she backed away from my body like she was witnessing a scene from a scary movie. As she stared at my skin in horror, I swear she expected my abdomen to burst open into a bloody, gory mess. "Why would you do that, Emma?"

Her shocked eyes lifted to mine. Frowning, I covered my body. "We want children," I said, a little defensively.

She looked at me like I'd just set a match to a winning lottery ticket. "Oh, you had such potential here. I was really thinking you'd take over for me, one day." She sadly shook her head; her thick neck barely allowed the movement.

I bristled at that comment. "I'm not leaving. I can have children *and* a career."

The corner of her lip lifted in a smirk. "That's what they all say." She sighed. "When is D-Day?"

As my momentary high dulled, I sullenly said, "June 26th."

She sighed, mentally ticking off how much time she had left with me, then she turned and waddled back to her office, probably to call the temp agency so they could start looking for my replacement. Irritating woman. Once again I thought Tracey was on to something, and Teren's family should just buy the company for me. Clarice wouldn't seem so high and mighty if this pregnant chick was suddenly her boss.

Not long after Clarice discovered my secret, Tracey and I were having a leisurely cup of coffee at a local shop in town. Well, she was having coffee; I was still sticking to hot chocolate. It was mid-morning on a Saturday, and the place was starting to pick up. We sat on luxurious, padded chairs in deep crimson and gold fabric. The fancy chairs could have been just as easily set up in a medieval throne room as a coffee shop. I relaxed into the exquisite seat and glanced around the space while Tracey went over her Hot Ben woes; they were fighting again. Contemporary music softly played in the background and dim lighting was suspended over other groups of plush chairs. Most of them were in sets of two or three, just perfect for relaxing with a friend or two.

A lot of the people who already had their beverages were sitting in other fancy seats, looking as comfortable as I felt. An older man with a head of thick, dark hair was having a pleasant conversation with a woman who looked to be about half his age; he was resting his hand on her knee so I figured they were more than friends. Behind the older man and his young girlfriend, I could just make out a pair of forty-something women, eyeing the couple. They whispered heated conversations as they glared at the woman, not the man, and I thought that perhaps they had each lost a beloved to a younger woman. I hoped that when I reached their age, Teren didn't come to regret his decision to marry me. I immediately discounted that, though. What we had went far beyond physical looks.

Tracey's sigh pulled me back to our conversation, well, her conversation. As she drank her frothy coffee treat, I sipped on my cup of hot cocoa. I savored the chocolaty goodness hitting my tongue while Tracey continued on with her theory that Hot Ben was diddling Halina.

After hearing this theory for so long now, I wasn't sure what to say anymore. I'd already told her that there was no way it was true. And there really *was* no way it was true…Hot Ben was terrified of Halina. But Tracey never believed me, so now I just listened. As one of the twins kicked my ribcage, I brought a hand to my stomach and soothed the youngster, massaging the spot that he or she had been kicking all morning. They generally rotated and twisted, kicking and squirming in different spots, but things were getting tight in there as they got larger, and they were concentrating on one area more often nowadays. That wasn't as much fun for me.

While Tracey absentmindedly stroked a blonde curl and debated whether or not she should hire a private eye, I fixated on the swaying lamp hanging over the table behind her. The shade was a deep, rich red, almost the color of blood. It reminded me of Teren, and the fact that he still wouldn't bite me.

When Tracey mentioned the name and an address of a detective, I finally tuned into what she was saying. She wasn't just randomly joking around that she should have someone trail her possibly straying beau, she was actually researching it.

"What?" I said, a little startled that she'd seriously do it.

She set down her coffee. The smell wafting up reached my nose and made my mouth water a little; I did miss my caffeinated coffee fix. "Well, what else am I supposed to do, Emma? Ever since the wedding, he's been so weird." She worried her lip and shook her head; her pale hair swished around her shoulders. "I know he's hiding something."

Her eyes watered and guilt filled me. I knew so much that I couldn't tell her. I knew exactly what was wrong with Ben. I knew exactly why he was being weird around her and what secret he was keeping from her. I knew…and I couldn't tell her. There was nothing about the situation that I could share, no comfort that I could bring her. Nothing I had to tell her would make her feel better anyway. She'd be just as freaked out as he was. No, she'd be even worse than Ben. She'd be beyond terrified, and would scream to the world that vampires existed. She'd probably end up in a straitjacket.

Doing the only thing I could, I extended my hand and placed it on her arm in sympathy. "I'm sure it's not you, Trace. He loves you, adores you, even."

Her beautiful face held in a frown, she gave me a doubtful look. I set down my cocoa and grabbed her hand. Letting my face look hopeful, I exclaimed, "Why don't you and Ben, and me and Teren all go—"

A woman moving past us brushed up against my shoulder and stopped walking. Tracey and I were sitting on the main path to the counter, and several people had walked back and forth while we'd been talking. But all of those people, even the ones who had inadvertently touched us on their journey for more beverages, had only apologized briefly before continuing their journey. This woman stopped and faced us, and I cut off my conversation to stare at her.

She seemed around my age, with straight, shoulder length hair. She wasn't a drop-dead beauty like Tracey, but she had a certain girl-next-door quality that made men take notice of her, including the male barista that I could see checking her out from the corner of my eye. She was slim and tall, with small features to match her small curves. Her eyes were a grayish blue color and were narrowed in confusion as she looked at me.

"I'm sorry," she said quietly. Tracey finally took notice of her and twisted her head to look. "Did you say…Teren?" I nodded, confused as to what this woman wanted. Her eyes widened and she sputtered on her next sentence. "Teren…Adams?"

My eyes narrowed as someone I didn't know, a female someone I didn't know, mentioned my husband's full name. "Yes," I said slowly, curiosity nearly killing me.

A small curve touched her lips as her entire posture relaxed. "Oh, wow. There's a name I haven't heard in a while." Her hand came to her mouth for a second as she looked between the two of us. "I'm so sorry, I didn't mean to eavesdrop. I just heard you mention that name, and it's so unusual, I just thought, what are the odds, right?" She shrugged as a bright smile lit her lips. I sort of hated thinking that my husband made anyone else smile like that.

"Yeah, it is…different." Curiosity eating me alive, I finally managed to say, "I'm sorry, who are you?"

The woman shook her head, her face suddenly apologetic. "Oh, I'm so sorry, how rude of me." She extended her hand and I lightly took it. "Carrie, Carrie Davids." She smiled bright again, like I should know exactly who she was now. Glancing at the ring on my finger she added, "Are you Teren's wife?"

I smiled. Indeed I was. "Yes, Emma Adams." I stressed my new last name, just to make absolutely sure this strange woman knew who I was. "And…how do you know Teren?" I added as casually as I could. Tracey was silent beside me, but when I flicked a glance at her, I could tell that in her pessimistic mood she had already labeled this woman standing before me as Teren's side action. I ignored Tracey and focused on the girl again. Teren wasn't cheating. I was certain of that. Pretty certain, anyway.

She flushed a bit, and her hand nervously ran through her hair. "Oh gosh, I'm just being all sorts of rude today, aren't I? Sorry, you just caught me by surprise with that name. I mean, I never expected to hear that name here, of all places." She shook her head. "The odds, really?" I threw on a barely contained smile, since she still hadn't answered my question. Noticing, she quickly said, "High school. We went to school together in Virginia."

I immediately relaxed as her relationship to my husband became apparent. Tracey snorted. She clearly didn't buy that, but I still ignored her. Brightening, I threw on a genuine smile. "Oh, I've never met anyone who grew up with him. It's nice to meet someone from his past." A part of me was a little surprised this girl even remembered who he was. Didn't they say that most people would only vaguely remember him? She'd figured out who he was by only his first name.

Carrie smiled at me as she rewound to the past. "Yeah, we had some great times. You're very lucky. He's a great guy." She said that last part wistfully and some tension came back to me. *Just how had she known my husband?* Before I could ask, she added, "Do you live around here?" She looked around like Teren might be here, too. I mentally smiled, knowing he was visiting his family at the ranch. Returning her eyes to me, she said, "Do you think we could all get together while I'm in town?"

Relief flooded through me that she didn't live here. Sighing with fake disappointment, I said, "I'm not sure. He's very busy at work."

She brightened. "Oh, did he become a writer? He was so brilliant in school."

My smile left me. She knew him so well. Too well. "Um…yes. He writes for a magazine here." Not knowing how I felt about this woman, I slapped on a friendly smile. Another child knocked me from the inside and my hand automatically went to my stomach to massage the area. "Well, I'll be sure to tell him you said hello." *You can be sure of it.* I had a lot of questions for that boy.

She didn't react to my clear dismissal. Instead her eyes drifted to my stomach and I swear her face paled. "Are you…? Is that…?" She looked up at me with unnecessarily moist eyes. "Are you expecting…Teren's child?"

My brows furrowed at the look on her face. I couldn't even speak. Luckily, or unluckily, Tracey answered for me. "Yep. He knocked her up good…twins. Right around the time they got *married.*" She stressed married, like she was trying to warn away this could-be home wrecker. I still didn't think that was what this was about though.

Carrie's gaze returned to my stomach. The tears in her eyes filled to flood level, and she hastily brushed them aside. "God, I'm sorry. I'm being so inappropriate today. I just didn't expect to hear about him again…and here you are…and you're…" She looked at Tracey's smug face, then to me. "I should go. Congratulations…to both of you."

She twisted to leave and I reached out and grabbed her hand. More tears fell as she looked back at me, and my sympathetic side kicked in. "Are you okay?" Tracey snorted again and I ignored her again. This woman was hurting for some reason, and it couldn't just be because some boy she'd known in high school had gotten married and started a family.

Carrie sniffled as she stared at me. Her blue eyes glistened with more unshed tears. "I'm sorry. It shouldn't still affect me after all this time, and we were so young, it really was for the best." Biting her lip, she shrugged. "I guess you just never really get over that kind of loss." Tears she could no longer contain fell from her eyes.

She was really starting to lose it now, and I had no idea why. Then her words started floating through my head, and I started to piece together what she meant. Loss. She didn't mean losing Teren; she hadn't seemed much more than curious about him, until she looked at my stomach. That was when pain had reduced her to the blubbery mess she was now. Pain, over my pregnancy. Loss…over her own?

Staring at my stomach, Carrie spoke in a low voice that was both sad and reminiscent. "I wonder if they will have his super dark hair and beautiful pale eyes." She stopped talking and looked back up at me. "Such a great combination, isn't it? The darkness and lightness. So perfect." Her hand went to her stomach in a familiar move, a move I did daily. My eyes widened as I watched her, my suspicions confirmed.

"Were you pregnant?" I whispered.

Carrie looked terrified, like I might strike her. Backing up a step, she pulled apart from me. "God, I'm so inappropriate. I shouldn't be bringing this up with you." She shook her head and started to leave. "Please, tell Teren hello. It was nice to meet you."

I quickly stood up before she could go. Well, I stood as fast as I could from the throne room-like chair. Tracey understood, and helped me. The woman paused as I desperately grabbed her arm again. "Please," I begged. "I need to know. Did Teren get you pregnant?"

She sighed, her expression sincerely apologetic. "It was a long time ago. Please don't be angry." Shrugging off my hand, she took a quick step back. "I'm so sorry I said anything. You just…surprised me. Brought back a lot of…memories." Backing up another step, she muttered, "Please, give Teren my best."

I only nodded. I planned on giving Teren *my* best as well. I couldn't even comprehend the fact that this woman vividly remembered him, right down to his hair, the color of his eyes, and the fact that he loved to write. Her admission over their relationship was so startling, that I was a little numb. Tracey had to physically help me walk outside, for fear I might pass out at any moment. I wasn't the first woman to have Teren Adams' child growing inside her. I felt like my world had just shattered.

I managed to separate from Tracey once we left the coffee shop. I told her I was fine, that it was in Teren's past and didn't concern me in the slightest. She eventually seemed convinced enough to leave. I had to imagine a visit with Hot Ben was in her future though. She was probably even more concerned over what he may be hiding from her.

I couldn't worry about Ben and Tracey any longer, since the hole punched through my gut started to ache. Teren had gotten someone pregnant and never once mentioned it. You would think that was the sort of thing he'd mention while we were trying to have a baby. And what happened to the baby anyway? Carrie had only mentioned loss. She never actually said what kind of loss. Did she not make it through the full pregnancy or did she give the baby up? I couldn't imagine Teren's family letting an heir go, so I tended to think it was the first part. She'd lost the baby. Willingly or unwillingly? How far along? While they were in school? How often had they had sex to get her pregnant?

As I automatically started driving to the ranch to confront my husband, that's the direction my mind went. I knew I shouldn't, I mean, neither one of us were virgins going into our relationship, and I'd had my fair share of dalliances, but as I sped along the highway, the only thing that was running through my head was the various positions Teren and that woman had possibly been engaged in. I pictured them in her car in the school parking lot, under the bleachers during a pep rally, and even up against the wall in the girl's locker room. I doubted any of those scenarios had actually happened, but I pictured them anyway. I also wondered if I'd just met Teren's "first." My stomach felt sour by the time I got to the ranch.

Alanna greeted me at the door. She opened it right as I walked up—she could sense me now too, since the blood in my babies was a homing beacon to all the vampires. She gave me a bright smile. "Emma, I didn't think you'd be by today." She tilted her head as I strode into the entryway. "Are you all right, dear?" She could probably hear my hammering heart.

"Where is he?" I bit out through clenched teeth.

She looked over her shoulder to a place outside, where Teren must be. "He's coming. He sensed you approaching."

I nodded and started pacing the room with my fists clenched tight. Alanna stopped me by putting a hand on my shoulder. "What is it, Emma?"

I started to answer her, to ask if she knew about any of this, and, if she did, how could she not tell me, and what else did she know, when suddenly Teren breezed into the room. His pale eyes took in my body language—my heart, my smell, my stance—everything about me was pissed off. He scrunched his brows as he walked over to me. His cool fingers cupped my cheeks while his eyes searched for clues. "What happened?"

Grabbing his hands and pulling them off my face, I clenched his fingers in mine. Even though I squeezed hard, he made no indication that I was hurting him; I probably wasn't. "I met someone today, someone who knows you…very well." I said it calmly, but an undercurrent of seething anger was there, and he sensed it.

His body stiffened as he stared at me. "Okay," he said it slowly, and it was easy to see that he was confused as to why I was such a different person than the woman he had tenderly made love to just this morning.

Remembering all of the intimate moments we had shared, and unfairly mixing them with all of the intimate moments I'd imagined him having with another woman on the drive over, I shoved his chest away from me. He took a step back, his expression hurt. "Carrie," was all I said. I wanted to see if he'd instinctively know who I was talking about.

I glanced at Alanna, but she looked hopelessly lost. That made me feel a little better. Maybe I wasn't alone in my ignorance. Teren looked lost too…at first. "Carr—" His eyes widened and I knew the exact moment he realized he'd been busted. "Oh God, Emma." He walked over to me and put his hands on my upper arms. "I can explain."

I shoved him away from me again, like he'd just confirmed every intimate act that I'd imagined of them. "You can explain getting another woman pregnant!" Teren took a step back; a hand went to his mouth while the other ran back through his hair.

"What? Teren?" Alanna came over to stand beside me, her cool hand resting on my arm as she stared at her son, incredulous. I put my hand over hers, grateful that not everyone had kept this secret from me. Just my husband apparently. Jack walked into the room that was now filled with tension. He looked between me, his wife and his son, and seemed unsure if he should stay or not. As I was still fuming, I really didn't care which choice he made.

Teren glanced at his mother when she questioned him, then upstairs to where Imogen was probably questioning him too. Keeping his eyes up there he said, "I'll explain." He brought his panicked eyes back down to me. "Just let me explain."

I crossed my arms over my chest and nodded. I wanted to tap my foot too, but that felt a little dramatic, so I stood as still and rigid as I could. Teren made a move towards me, but seeing my clear tension, he sighed and stopped where he was, next to the crying woman statue. His face sort of matched hers.

"We were young, Emma, just kids." He shrugged and glanced at his mother before returning his eyes to mine. "We dated a few months and then…she got pregnant." He whispered the word, like him saying it out loud was somehow worse than me yelling it. And in a way, it was. I cringed as the words left his lips, and swallowed to keep back the tears stinging my eyes. He took in my turmoil, then sighed. "She lost it, Emma. She didn't even make it eight weeks before she miscarried." He shrugged his shoulders. "There is no baby."

My hands flew to my sides; my fingers were clenched so tight my fingernails dug into my palms. "Why did you never mention this to me?"

Looking sad and unsure what to say, he shrugged and repeated, "There is no baby."

I looked away from him as my anger ebbed and surged. I couldn't control the waves of emotion and seeing his torn face was only making the sensation worse. I needed to ride out this tidal wave of anger before I spoke again, or else I might try and tear off his secretive mouth.

Alanna took my silence as a chance to speak to her son. "Carrie?" she said slowly. "Who is Carrie?" I turned to watch her as she walked up to him with her hands on her hips.

Teren sighed and closed his eyes, looking for all the world like he was about to have a conversation that he had never intended to have with his family. He reopened his eyes and with clear resignation, he met Alanna's gaze. "We dated in high school."

Alanna scrunched her brows. "I don't remember a Carrie in high school. I don't remember you being serious with anyone, not until college."

Teren looked at the ground while Jack stepped up to his wife's side. Grabbing one hand from her hip, he held it in his. Her entire posture relaxed. Without looking up at her, Teren said, "I didn't tell you about her. I didn't want any of you to know."

Alanna looked like Teren had just slapped her. With guilt in his eyes, he looked up at her and spoke a long sentence in Russian. Her expression softened and she shook her head and put a hand on his cheek.

Irritated that her irritation was leaving her while mine was not, I spat out, "You should have told *me*, Teren."

His eyes came back to mine. "I know, I'm sorry."

Alanna turned to look at me; her eyes were pink with unshed tears. "You saw her today? In town?"

I nodded. "She's visiting or something. She won't be here long, but she wanted to see Teren once she found out he was here." My eyes shifted to him as my tone dripped with venom. "She says hi, by the way."

He closed his eyes, but opened them immediately when Alanna spoke again. "We'll need to tell Halina. She'll want to see the girl."

"No!"

The heat in Teren's tone shocked Alanna and me. We both turned to look at him; his dad gave him a puzzled look as well. "Teren, she can't be allowed to know—" Alanna began.

Teren shook his head and grabbed his mother's arms, cutting her off. "She doesn't know. She never found out."

Alanna raised an eyebrow at him, surprised. "You didn't tell her what you were, when she got pregnant?"

He shook his head, and anger surged through me at hearing that stupid p-word again. "I thought you wouldn't bring anyone into this unknowingly. Isn't that what you said to me?" I snapped.

He stepped away from his mother and approached me. Cautiously, he put his hands over my arms, sliding them all the way down to my fingers, trying to relax me. All it did, though, was remind me that he'd probably slid his hands down that woman's arms in this exact same way, comforting her when she realized she was with child—his child. I bristled at the contact, and he sighed.

"She's why, Emma." He stepped up to me and my belly brushed his stomach. Clenching my hands, he spoke softly. "When she found out, I realized how dangerous what we'd just done really was. She was the *only* one that I wasn't cautious with. She was the only one that I didn't make sure *one* of us was protected. And I just couldn't tell her what she was really carrying. If she had given birth…" He sighed and rested his head against mine. "I was sixteen, Emma. I was stupid…please don't hate me for that."

I started shaking as I held in my conflicting emotions. Anger still boiled in me, but so did understanding and compassion. Lord knows I hadn't made the smartest choices, especially at sixteen. I'd just managed to dodge the proverbial bullet. Teren hadn't been so lucky, and it had certainly woken him up as to how hard relationships were going to be for him. Even the first few times we were together, he'd been diligent about protection. Come to think of it, he'd been diligent until the day he watched me pop a pill. Feeling the truth in the hard lesson he'd learned, I relaxed in his grip and finally let his fingers interlace with mine. He rocked his head against me as he whispered that he was sorry.

Alanna came up to him and rested a hand on his back. "You should have told us, Teren."

He looked back at her, his eyes sad. "It didn't matter. She didn't know what I was, and she lost the baby." He shrugged, looking like a sixteen-year-old who had just gotten caught doing something really stupid.

Alanna shook her head at him. "No, you should have told us, so you wouldn't have had to go through that alone. We can't start lying to each other, Teren. We're all we have. We need to be honest. Here, if nowhere else, we need to be honest."

Teren swallowed and looked down. "I'm sorry, Mom. I just...I wanted her left alone. It was hard not to tell you, but I wanted her...to remember." Looking up, he spoke another Russian sentence to her. Alanna sighed and lowered her hand from his back.

"I have to tell Halina, Teren. I can't keep something this big from her, and mother won't." Her eyes drifted upstairs to where Imogen was in her room hiding from the sunshine. I was sure that if there were more curtains in the entryway, Imogen would be right down in the middle of this conversation, putting in her two cents worth. As both vampires still had their heads turned to the upstairs room, I thought maybe she was anyway.

Teren started shaking his head as he looked back down at his mom. "Just give it a few days. Emma said she was only visiting, just wait until she's left town before you tell Great-Gran. Please?"

Teren's hands tightened in mine as he begged for his ex-girlfriend's memory. Thinking back to her tears in the coffee shop over their lost child, I had no idea why he wanted her to remember that tragic event. Alanna seemed equally confused as she looked at him.

"Teren, we removed the memory of your face from every other person in that school." She blinked as she thought about it. "I don't know how Grandmother missed her, really."

Teren twisted to face his parents, his face sheepish. "Carrie's mom removed her when she discovered what had happened. She pulled her, and took her to another school, to get her away from me. Since you weren't aware of how close she and I were, I never told you that she left."

Alanna's eyes widened. "Teren, we rely on you to tell us everything, so we can get everyone. It was the only reason we let you attend a regular school in the first place. If you've held back…" I could see Alanna's eyes calculating all the people they'd have to track down. It was daunting, even to me.

His head hung under the weight of her words. "It was just her, Mom. She was the only one." He raised his head; his pale eyes were pleading, and I found myself squeezing his hand in encouragement. "And her parents never met me either. It was just her, I promise."

Jack finally stepped into the conversation. "Halina went to a lot of trouble to blur you out of the students' memories, to make sure that no one specifically remembered you. That was very foolish of you, Teren."

Teren seemed to crumble at his father's words. I think they crushed him more than his mother's. I put a hand on his chest. He turned his head to me, grateful for the comfort but looking like he felt he didn't deserve it. My own anger gone at his clear repentance, I kind of wanted his parents to ease off. He had made a mistake that thousands of teenagers make every year, and I suppose for all parties, this one had worked out for the best.

Alanna wasn't quite done with her reprimand though. "I will give you time, but she has to be wiped. Especially, since you are such a strong memory to her." She shook her head. "She knows too much, Teren."

"She knows nothing, Mom," he tried again.

Alanna firmly shook her head, not budging on the issue of her family's isolation. "She remembers you, that is too much." Raising an eyebrow, she gazed at him sternly. "What if you run into her in sixty years, Teren? She will be old and frail, but you, you will be the same man she knew, young and strong. What then?"

He frowned. "I was a kid. I look nothing like I did then. I should be allowed to keep my childhood." He frowned, sounding a little petulant. Alanna sighed like she'd had this argument with him before. He bristled at hearing a sigh that he'd probably heard before. "Besides," he said, "she'll be older. She'll assume I'm a grandson or something."

Alanna shook her head. "That would probably work for some…but you've left her with too strong a connection to you. She'll look in your eyes, and see *you* looking back at her, and she will have no doubt about who you really are."

Teren started to speak, but she cut him off when he opened his mouth. "It's part of your nature, Teren. It's part of what makes you a vampire. You have a strong magnetism that humans respond to. In small doses, it's fine…but you bedded this woman, repeatedly." She raised an eyebrow. "You were each other's firsts?" Teren looked embarrassed, but nodded. Alanna nodded in response, like his answer solidified her point.

Alanna glanced at her husband and then back at Teren. She gave him a look that parents give their children when they are about to say something really embarrassing. "Your sexuality is also part of being a vampire; it's more in your vampiric blood than your human blood. It's just a vampire's nature." Teren flicked a quick glance at me. I felt hot all over, just as embarrassed as when I was young, and my mom explained where the "boy" part went. Alanna quickly continued to the finale of her point. "This human, that you've let get so close to you, will always remember you. If that is left unchecked, even ninety and senile she will remember you, Teren." She shrugged. "Your nature…makes you unforgettable."

She smiled and squeezed Jack's hand. Jack looked a little embarrassed too, but he gave his son a look of fatherly support. I tried to ignore the fact that Alanna was basically saying that sex with a vampire was so good, no one would ever forget it. I knew that was true, but I didn't like some strange woman out there also knowing that was true.

Teren hung his head and then finally, nodded. Alanna put a friendly hand on his shoulder and spoke too softly for me to hear. He nodded again and then lifted his head to look at her. "Why don't you take your wife home, dear?" Alanna looked over to me, her eyes sympathetic. "I'm sure you have a lot to discuss."

Teren gave her and then his father a swift hug goodbye, then he took me back to our home. He spent the rest of the evening telling me about his greatest childhood mistake. By the time he was finished with his story, my anger was sapped. I held him and consoled him as I felt the experience through his terrified teenage eyes instead of my own jealous ones. Seeing the situation through Teren's experience, I found I could let the vivid images of them having sex go. I understood his fear, both at the thought of being a father so young, and at having the mother possibly go into hysterics if she ever found out what he was. And she would have, once the baby was born. Now that I was beginning to comprehend just how rare my initial reaction was, I couldn't imagine how frightened and alone young Teren must have been.

I couldn't forgive him for not telling me—that really should have been something he mentioned while we were trying—but I *could* understand why he didn't like talking about it. And after we spent an entire night talking about it, I let it go. Well, I tried to anyway.

Chapter 10 – Of all the Cities, in All the World...

Teren and I didn't talk much about Carrie after that and he didn't meet up with her while she was in town. I think he wanted to; sometimes when we were at home, I'd catch him staring at the door, lost in thought. I think he wanted to see her, just to make sure she was okay, that her life had turned out well. As if he were somehow responsible for every bit of sadness she may have had over the past ten years, because he'd let her remember one tragic event that had happened when they were kids. But he didn't leave my side. Maybe he felt like he'd done enough damage. Maybe he was kissing up to me by not seeking her out. Or maybe he was nervous that she'd notice his changes. Either way, two weeks went by without a sign of her, and while I wasn't sure how long she was in town for, most vacations don't last longer than that.

I relaxed a lot after that second week passed and I was sure she was gone. I knew it wasn't her fault that she had a history with my man, but I didn't exactly want to sit around and compare notes with her. Surprisingly enough though, I was grateful that I had run into her. Teren might never have brought up that part of his history without a little prodding. He could be secretive if he thought he was protecting someone, and he had wanted to avoid hurting me or exposing Carrie to his family.

I was getting a little better with the fact that he hadn't told me. I mean, we really did jump right into this relationship head first. We never sat down to discuss our pasts. And there were certainly a lot of things in my history that he didn't know. For instance, I'd never told him about the guy who'd slipped me a roofie at a party. Nothing happened, thank God. I'd also never mentioned the guy who had become so obsessed with me in college that I'd nearly had to put a restraining order on him. There were a lot of little skeletons in our closets that Teren and I had never had the time to sit down and talk about. He repeatedly assured me that Carrie was the biggest though, the one he'd been trying to hide from his family, so he'd inadvertently hidden her from me as well.

But he couldn't hide her from his family forever, not thanks to my public declaration of their past. Eventually either Alanna or

Imogen did tell Halina. It became immediately apparent when she knew. She showed up on our doorstep, looking hot and fiery—a thoroughly pissed off vampire. I hid out upstairs while Teren and Halina "discussed" the situation that was Carrie. I'm not sure what they said exactly, since most of it, at least from Halina's side, was in heated Russian. I guess being really mad made her revert to her native tongue. Teren responded in English for the most part, but catching just one side of the conversation was frustrating. After a while I stopped listening.

When Halina slammed the door and left, all I'd gotten out of the face off was the fact that Carrie had indeed left town and Halina wanted to know where to find her. Teren didn't know, or wouldn't say, and Halina was on the warpath to find out. She wanted her wiped more than anything, much more than she wanted Ben's memories. I had a feeling that she'd take everything from Carrie, just to teach Teren a lesson. Assuming she ever found her of course.

Not everything in our life was stressful though. Amid the drama of Carrie's surprise visit, Teren and I had the big ultrasound. We walked into the lab where they ran the tests and Teren's nose wrinkled at the antiseptic smell that even I found strong. We sat in padded waiting room chairs and he rubbed my shoulders while we waited. He'd been doing a lot of massaging after our spat. I didn't tell him that it wasn't necessary, that he didn't need to keep buttering me up. He was good at massages, and my body was sore and aching in spots I hadn't expected to ache in. I wasn't about to ask his heaven-sent fingers to stop.

A short, plump woman with platinum hair and raspberry scrubs called my name. After Teren helped me stand up, we walked over to the doorway to greet her. She held her clipboard to her chest as her pale eyes took in our excited faces. "First timers?" she brightly asked.

Eagerly, I nodded, and Teren laughed. While Teren rubbed a spot on my back, we followed the nurse through the door and into a hallway that led to several small exam rooms. We passed other patients in the rooms full of complicated looking equipment. Some were getting tests done that were not nearly as joyous as the reason for my visit. I tried to contain my joy, and not smile at the dour faces.

Sweeping her arm into the room, the chipper nurse said, "Well, we'll take good care of you." I bounced inside and plopped my growing body down onto a flat, padded bed.

Teren walked in before the nurse. Encouraging me to lie down, she shut the door and flicked off the light. The room had no outside windows like my doctor's office did, and the space darkened considerably. Teren froze where he was by the closed door and shut his eyes. He didn't know how dark the room was, didn't know if the odd glow from his eyes would be too bright. The nurse didn't catch his pause. She walked over to me, turned on a couple knobs to warm up the machine, and started going on about how exciting the first pregnancy was. I only partially listened to her as I stared at Teren. He was still standing close to the door, behind her, ready to slip out of the room if his eyes were too perceptible.

It wasn't exactly dark though; a few nightlights cast a soft light and the machine itself had a glow that was brighter the closer you got to it. I held my breath as I watched Teren put a hand in front of his face, then open his eyes to look at it. I could see the glow from where he stood, back in the darkest section of the room. He could see it too. He looked up, tossing a quick glance at the nurse, then me. He was torn; he wanted to stay, but he couldn't if she'd notice.

I felt tears stinging my eyes. I didn't want him to miss this. I found myself reaching my hand out for him. He watched me with a pained expression, even more torn. Then he took a deep breath and came over to me. My heart increased as I watched him walk past the technician. She was busy running through a few steps on the computer, prattling on about the miracle of life, and wasn't paying any attention to the undead man walking past her.

Keeping his head down, he walked around to the far side of the bed and sat on a spinning stool. He shifted the rolling contraption so that he could hold my hand and be closer to the nightlight. Taking another deep breath, he lifted his head to look at me. I swallowed. The glow was still really perceptible. But then again, I knew it was there. I tried to see the whites of his eyes as an outsider would, but I was so used to it, it was a little difficult. I shrugged, not knowing if it was noticeable to others or not.

"Hey, relax, dear. You're all tense." The jolly nurse was stroking my arm and I made myself not worry. She started taking my vitals and asking me if I'd loaded up on water, because apparently having a bladder close to bursting is how they get the best picture. Then she finally looked over at Teren.

She was listening to my heart and I knew it had just started spiking when her eyes locked on Teren's. He immediately shifted his gaze to my face. The nurse frowned and tilted her head, like she could have sworn she had just seen something weird, but she wasn't sure what. Teren's fingers tightened around mine and I was pretty sure he was holding his unnecessary breath.

The tech turned back to me. "You nervous or excited about this, honey? Your heart's all over the place." I let out a nervous chuckle and felt Teren's fingers relax as he lightly laughed as well.

Without looking at Teren again, she squirted some really cold, blue liquid on my stomach and rubbed it around. I had to laugh when the twins started to kick and squirm. The liquid was almost as chilly as Teren's touch, and they were responding, just like they did when he touched me.

"Oh, active aren't they? Well, that will ease up when things start getting tight in there." She took the scanner and rested it on my stomach. As she twisted it around, she shook her head. "Twins. Brave woman. A girlfriend of mine had twins and those two have aged her at least a decade." She laughed, and then looked up from the computer monitor to my face. She seemed a little worried that she'd offended me, or scared me. "I'm sure it won't be like that for you though." Her tone clearly said that she thought it would be *just* as tricky for me, but she didn't want to freak me out.

I smiled and nodded in agreement, like I was sure my children would be perfect angels and nothing like her girlfriend's. I wasn't sure what they'd be like, but I'd love them no matter what. Just as I was busy picturing black-haired, blue-eyed toddlers running around my feet, the nurse pointed to some hazy, gray blob on the screen.

"And there is a good one of a face." I stared at that stupid screen until she shifted it, nodding, like it was the best face I'd ever seen, but really, all I saw was an abstract gray and white swirl of indistinguishable features.

Teren squeezed my hand. Looking back at him, I saw tears in the faint glow of his eyes. He'd seen it, whatever *it* was. He smiled and stroked my hand, and I sighed. Returning my eyes to the screen, I hoped I would see something that resembled a child today. Then the nurse spotted something and focused the image on it. I gasped when I recognized five perfectly distinct digits that were unmistakably a hand. I started to cry and felt Teren's cool hand brushing a tear off my cheek. The nurse smiled at us as she went over other body parts that she and Teren could see. Teren was quiet, listening to her, but not commenting. He didn't want to draw any attention to himself. He squeezed my fingers whenever he saw something though. I never saw anything else that resembled anything other than a gray blob, but that one hand made my day.

At the end of the test, she looked at each of us with a crooked grin. "Do you want to know the sexes?" she asked with a raised eyebrow.

Teren and I looked at each other and then simultaneously shook our heads. That was one thing we'd both agreed upon earlier. We wanted the surprise. It had annoyed my mom to no end when I'd told her that we weren't going to find out. She'd used the excuse that she needed to know if she should buy pink things or blue things, but I'd been firm on my decision; I told her to stick to yellows and greens. Teren and I had decided that some things were just meant to be surprises. Babies were one of those things.

The technician nodded, wiped off my belly, and helped me adjust my clothes. Teren wrapped a cool arm around my waist as I sat up; his slightly glowing eyes were beaming at me. The nurse flicked the lights back on and we both blinked in the suddenly bright room. I exhaled a sigh of relief that we'd gotten through the exam without Teren getting caught, and without caving on the babies' sexes. As the nurse tucked away the machine, she assured us that everything was well within the spectrum of normal, and she saw nothing to worry about. It made me truly happy to hear that my kids looked normal.

When we left the lab it was dark outside. The parking lot was a cheery orange as we walked through it. A happy smile was plastered on my face as I thought about that tiny little hand floating around in my body. I imagined one of the babies sticking its hand into its mouth and sucking on its fingers. I'd read in one of my baby books that they sometimes did that in the womb. Teren was grinning ear to ear as he described the face to me; his vision had seen it in even more perfect detail than the nurse had seen it.

He was describing the tiny, button nose he'd seen, when he suddenly stopped walking. Grabbing my hand, he brought me to a stop as well. I studied him as his concerned face searched the darkness. I looked over the lot to where he was staring. On the other side of the street, a cluster of trees were thick with shadow. Teren made no protective move like he did sometimes, so I thought maybe he was sensing something he knew, like maybe a relative.

"Halina?" I whispered, hoping the vampire hadn't decided to come pick another fight with Teren over Carrie or Hot Ben.

Teren tilted his head, his eyes still glued to the trees. "No, she's not in the city tonight." I nodded, grateful she wasn't around, but curious as to what he was sensing. That was when he moved in front of me, and a low growl came from his chest. Recognizing that move, I stayed safely behind him. I clutched his arm, just in case he got the stupid idea to check out the oddity without me.

"Teren, what is it?"

He straightened and shifted his gaze down the street. Whatever it was, it had apparently run off. Teren turned to look at me behind him. His eyes went to my stomach, and concern was evident in his face. "Nothing, Emma."

Knowing he was lying, I furrowed my brow. "Teren, just tell me."

He shook his head. "I'm not sure, Emma, but..." he looked down and then peered up at me, "I think someone's stalking me."

My eyebrows shot right up my forehead and the icy panic that I'd kept at bay ever since our abduction flooded through my chest. I put a hand over my stomach and searched the darkness. "A hunter?" I whispered, clutching him tight.

I looked back and he shook his head. "I don't know. I keep smelling..." He twisted to put both hands over my arms. "Please don't go out alone anymore." He frantically searched my face.

"Please, I can't lose you, Emma." One hand drifted down to rest over mine on my stomach. "Any of you."

Nodding, I hugged him tight to me. My eyes darted out over the suddenly vast and terrifying world we lived in. I didn't want to lose any of us either. Squeezing him tighter, I tried to block out the irrational fear I felt. It crept in, though. Its icy tendrils snaked around my core as Teren took my hand and led me to the car. He helped me inside and shut the door. A low growl issued from his throat as he took a final look around, and I thought maybe Teren was feeling that icy fear too.

I spent the next few days keeping close to home and close to Teren. Tracey noticed my behavior and asked if everything was all right. I assured her that it was, that I was just exhausted from the pregnancy and wanted to sleep more than anything. Which was true, I just found sleeping difficult. There is nothing quite like your supernatural husband telling you that someone is stalking him, and subsequently you, to make sleeping soundly near impossible. I tossed and turned at night, while Teren whispered in my ear that nothing was around, that I was safe.

I tried to take that to heart. Teren wasn't exactly easy to sneak up on and he'd never let anyone harm me. But he wasn't infallible either. When Hot Ben came over a few nights later, I thought we looked similarly exhausted now. He asked Teren, yet again, to wipe him, and for the first time ever, Teren seemed to think maybe he should. Ben had lost a good ten pounds in his stress and had deep circles under his eyes now. I'd heard that he and Tracey hadn't spoken in nearly a week as his constant fear had put the brakes on their relationship.

I hated that, but I understood Ben's fear. I was constantly looking over my shoulder now too. One night, while Hot Ben was explaining to Teren that he was sure he'd seen something outside move faster than humanly possible, I made the mistake of telling Ben about Teren's worry that someone was watching us. Ben latched on to that, and we spent an entire evening going over what could be hunting us. I was convinced it was another sanctimonious do-gooder with a stake and a vendetta. Hot Ben was convinced it was a werewolf.

As Teren ushered Ben out for the evening, walking him all the way to his car, he whispered to me, "I'll call Halina tomorrow night." I sighed, thankful that at least Ben's life would get back on track. He could probably still repair things with Tracey, although she was still convinced that he was sleeping with Halina. Picturing Hot Ben returning to his normal, easy-going self, I started thinking that maybe Halina could mind wipe me too? Just about the stalker thing, just so I could sleep. But, I knew that hiding from the problem didn't make it any less of a problem, and I should be aware, just so I could be extra cautious. Still, it was a tempting thought, knowing that I didn't necessarily have to remember. Maybe I'd have her take the memory of Carrie too.

The next night Teren and I went out to eat at a nearby restaurant. Well, I ate, Teren watched. But he ordered food for himself so I could snack on it, since I could pack away an impressive amount now. On the way home, we decided to take a detour to the gym to tell Hot Ben the news. Tracey had told me this morning that he was subbing the kickboxing class tonight. She had *not* been excited about that, but she had decided to go anyway, saying she didn't want their estrangement to ruin her routine.

I ran into her in the lobby after class. "Hey, Emma," she asked, surprised to see me. "What are you doing here?"

Knowing she wouldn't like it, I said, "Teren and I are going out with Ben." Tracey looked over at Ben talking to Teren and glared. "Do you want to come with?" I asked, already knowing what she would say.

Returning her eyes to me, she predictably shook her head no. Tracey and Ben hadn't been out together in a while. She had no desire to see him until he could explain some things to her. I gave her a swift hug, hoping that, if anything, at least their relationship would be better after this.

Ben walked in-between us as we made our way to our cars behind the gym. I took in his workout shorts and sweaty hair and sighed. I sort of missed working out; I hadn't been to the gym since my body had seriously started to expand outward. Teren heard my sigh and gave me a small, sad smile. He knew it was time to release this burden from Hot Ben, but he was still reluctant to do it.

Ben stared at our surroundings. He wasn't noticing anything other than the threat that being out in the open posed. His antsy energy as he looked from car to car, from light to tree, from bush to bush, started infecting me. I started looking around too, a little scared that something really was going to jump out at us. Teren's plan was to have Hot Ben follow us to our house and then he would call Halina. I think he hoped that he could take the short time it would take Halina to arrive to convince Ben that knowing was a good thing. That he should consider keeping his memories, and that he really didn't need to be so afraid.

We approached the side parking lot where the employees of the gym parked, and I couldn't help but notice the emptiness of the enclosed space. It was blocked in on three sides by high concrete walls. As we walked into the lot, it started to feel a little claustrophobic. Ben felt it too. He wrapped his light jacket tight around his body, his muscles flexing with tension.

Teren glanced around the area, but didn't appear concerned. It relaxed me that he wasn't. Of all of us, he had the most accurate senses. If he thought the lot was empty, it was. Teren walked Hot Ben to his car, then told him, "I thought we'd do this at my place, if you want to follow us over there."

Ben looked a little disappointed. "Oh, I thought maybe we'd just do it right here." He brightened a bit. "At least it's happening tonight. By tomorrow, things will be back to normal." He sighed in resignation. "I guess that means I'll be seeing Halina again soon."

Teren smiled; it wasn't a happy one. He still didn't really want this to happen. "Sorry, no way around that one. I can't wipe you."

While Teren talked some more with Ben, perhaps prolonging the inevitable, he started listening to something other than Ben; I could tell by the tilt of his head. That worried me some. It worried me even more when he stopped talking mid-sentence and closed his eyes. Alarm shot through my body as I watched him raise his head to the sky and mutter, "Damn it." At the same time, Ben and I asked him what he heard.

Looking annoyed, Teren turned, right as someone effortlessly hopped onto the six-foot wall behind us. Hot Ben scrambled backwards a few steps while I inhaled a quick, scared breath. Teren only sighed and shook his head. "I thought you'd linger by the wharf for a few more hours."

The dark form on the wall, dark except for the faintly glowing eyes, jumped down into a pool of light and I exhaled in relief—Ben did not, and backed up another step. Halina strolled into the lot, her black hair lifting in the breeze. Her short skirt had shifted higher up her thighs from jumping up onto the wall, but she did absolutely nothing to change how much skin she was showing. She languidly approached Teren; her eyes were focused on Ben a few steps behind him though. When Teren put his hands on his hips and stepped in front of Ben, Halina brought her attention back to her great-grandson.

She shrugged nonchalantly. "I finished my meal early. Thought I'd come say hi." I cringed, knowing what her "meal" had consisted of. I watched Hot Ben do the same. His haggard face paled even more as Halina threw him a crooked grin. Directly at Ben she said, "Are you interested to know which lowlife will no longer be bothering your kind?" Ben sputtered and backed up another step as Halina started to walk past Teren to follow him. Grinning ear to ear she told him, "I believe he was on one of your most wanted lists."

Teren grabbed her elbow as she walked past. "That's enough," he whispered in a harsh tone. Halina snapped her eyes back to his. Probably still a little irritated at the whole Carrie thing, she glared at him, but left Ben alone.

Pushing aside the fact that she'd just admitted to killing someone, I walked up to her as genially as I could. She turned her head to me and her gaze softened as her pale eyes rested on my stomach, then flicked up to my face. "We're glad to see you, Halina. We were just going to call you when we got back home. We need you to do something for us."

She cocked her head at me in question while Teren frowned. I gave him an apologetic face. Teren had been secretly hoping that he wouldn't have to call her tonight. He was still hoping Ben would come around. Left to his own devices, I think Teren would "hope" Ben into an early, stress-filled grave.

"Call me? Why? Did you find her?" She immediately grabbed my arm, her eyes intensifying in the orange parking lot lights around us.

I shook my head as I carefully removed her clenched hand from my arm. "No, we haven't heard from Carrie." Truly, we hadn't been looking for her either. Teren was content to let her go, and I was content to never think about her again. Even Tracey had finally stopped asking me if I was okay with her revelation. While Halina's face scrunched in disappointment, I nodded my head at Hot Ben. "For him…he doesn't want to know anymore."

I heard Teren sigh and watched his head slump. Ben took another step back as Halina's gaze fell solely on him again.

"Do you now?" Shrugging free from where Teren still held her, she walked around a suddenly immobile Ben. He stiffened and jutted his chin out in defiance as she walked in a circle around him, lightly trailing a finger over his body. Knowing how intimidating that move could be, I felt some major sympathy for Ben, especially when she leaned in and her hand shifted to his more…private areas. He inhaled and froze, too terrified to do anything else.

"You don't want to remember? Do you realize all the wonderful things we could do together, before I make you forget?" Ben started shaking as her hand gently squeezed. "I could make you scream, and you wouldn't even remember it."

Before I could tell her to knock it off, she was suddenly sitting on her ass. I blinked. I'd missed the move that had gotten her there, but with Teren standing over her body, looking pretty pissed off, it was clear that he'd had enough of her teasing and had finally stepped in. Ben hunched over on his knees. Cupping himself with one hand, he muttered thanks, as he tried to get his breathing back to normal.

Halina looked up at Teren, pure shock on her face. I got the feeling that Teren had never physically stopped her before. I had no idea how she'd react. I knew they loved each other, but I was pretty sure Halina would rip Teren a new one if she felt he needed it, especially without the other vampires there as witnesses. And even though Teren was strong, I knew Halina could throw him through a brick wall without breaking a sweat.

Not knowing what good I could do, and hoping that Halina wouldn't hurt me, or more appropriately, the twins inside me, I took a step towards them.

Keeping her eyes locked on Teren, Halina humanly slow stood up; her youthful face looked like the petulant teenager that she pretended to be. Teren didn't back down from her gaze. Slowly, he spat out, "I said...enough."

While I took another step towards them, Halina started bringing her hands up to Teren's chest. He didn't react, only kept up the stare-down they were having. I was pretty sure that once Halina touched him, Teren was going to end up in the next county. I could just barely discern Teren bracing his body and thought he was probably aware of that too.

I was standing right next to her, when her fingertips brushed his shirt. I heard Ben say Teren's name in warning, and I braced myself to grab the female vampire and stop her from flinging my husband a town over, somehow. My hand was just on her arm, her hands just on his chest, when both vampires suddenly looked over at the wall that separated the gym parking lot from the accountant's parking lot next door. That wall was around five feet high and brick, just like the back wall. I stared at it as well as the vampires, but I couldn't see anything. Whatever had grabbed their attention from the tension-filled fight that had been escalating between the two of them, made the hairs on my neck stick straight out.

That feeling of unease amplified when they moved as one. Halina took a protective position in front of Ben and me. She crouched low for action and a growl rumbled from her throat. Teren stepped a few paces in front of her, also assuming a protective position, only he was protecting all of us. Teren's familiar rumble joined with hers, and I clasped Ben's hand as we hid behind Halina.

They were both intently focused on the edge of the wall and my mind started spinning over what on this earth could have provoked two powerful creatures so much. Was I right about a hunter, or was Ben right about a werewolf? Ben started to shake and I slung an arm around his waist, supporting him. I was terrified too, but only of whatever was out there, not Teren and Halina. Poor Hot Ben was sort of scared of everybody.

A chuckle filled the still air, emanating from behind the wall and I prepared myself to run if needed. Expecting a burly man yielding a chainsaw or something, I blinked in surprise as a short man who kind of looked like the guy who used to do my mom's taxes appeared. I wondered if the guy worked at the accountant's firm next door and had just gotten off work. Maybe he'd heard a fight starting and was foolishly trying to stop it. I reconsidered that since Teren and Halina hadn't eased up their guarding stances.

The middle-aged man had his hands stuffed in his pockets. He walked into the lot lights as casually as if he were taking a stroll through the park on a sunny, Sunday afternoon. But that's when I noticed his eyes, and I realized that this man hadn't been anywhere near a sunny day in quite some time. His eyes had the same faint glow around them that Teren's got in dim lighting. While not noticeable to someone not in the know, it was a neon sign to me, and I clenched Ben's hand, hard.

The accountant making his way over to Teren…was a vampire.

The stranger shook his head. "My money's on the woman." He laughed at that thought. His voice had a southern drawl to it. It didn't match his average height, average looks and plain blue jeans and brown jacket. Added to his dull brown hair and dull dark eyes, this guy's accent was the most interesting thing about him. Oh, that and the fact that he wasn't alive.

Not relaxing his defensive posture, Teren tilted his head at the man. "Who are you?"

The vampire stepped up to Teren and grinned; his fangs were extended as if to show Teren that they were alike. Teren didn't react to the show. I was pretty sure he knew exactly what this man was; his super ears, used to hearing thumping hearts all around him, would instantly pick up on a walking body that was missing one. The teeth did finally clue in Ben though. He cursed and squeezed my hand so hard I heard something pop.

The man extended his hand out in a friendly handshake to Teren. "So sorry, name's Thomas, but you can call me Tommy."

Teren looked at the hand, but made no move to touch it. Shifting slightly so he was still in front of us, Teren inhaled deep. A low growl escaped him before he spoke again. "I recognize your scent. You're the one who has been stalking me. Why?"

Halina hissed at the man after hearing that revelation. Regardless of her irritation at Teren, he was family, and she didn't like hearing about someone watching him. My eyes were huge as the puzzle began to make sense. I'd suspected something much different than a vampire watching us. I wasn't sure if I should feel relieved at the news, or worried.

Tommy looked over at Halina, gave her a suggestive smile and a wink, then shifted his focus back to who he probably deemed was the bigger threat—Teren. "Sorry about that." He tilted his head as he shoved his hand back in his pocket. "I was just so curious. You smell so odd. I've been trying to figure out what you are. You're not like me, but, at the same time, you *are* like me." He leaned in as Teren subtly straightened. "What are you?"

Tommy seemed genuinely intrigued by the mystery that was Teren, and I relaxed. Maybe our stalker had just been trying to piece things together before making a formal introduction. Maybe he meant us no harm. Being a vampire didn't automatically make you evil after all. Teren relaxed his posture as he seemed to realize this too. Halina and Ben did not, and I hoped my hand didn't go numb, since no blood was getting to it anymore.

Giving the man a cautious look, Teren said, "I'm mixed—part human, part vampire—that's probably why I seem odd to you. I was born this way, not turned, and I'm not...hampered by all of the side effects of vampirism, so I don't smell exactly like a pureblood."

Tommy's dark eyes widened as he absorbed Teren's facts. He grinned than let out a low whistle, as he shook his head. "Part human, huh? Fascinating." He pointed at Teren's chest, probably noting the absence of a heartbeat. "Born? But, you're dead?"

Teren nodded. "I recently died. One side effect that even humanity can't overcome for long."

The man shrugged, not too moved by hearing his story. "Ah, well, I would sympathize, but I died over fifty years ago." He grinned and rocked back on his heels. "I've been vampire longer than I'd been human. And being human was no picnic, I was happy to give it up." Teren frowned and I saw some of his defensive posture return. Tommy's eyes shifted back to Halina. A slow smile spread over his face as he took in the wild beauty crouching in front of Ben and me. "You though..." he inhaled deep, taking in her scent as well, "are pure vampire, like me."

Not looking like she was in a friendly mood, Halina hissed again. The man chuckled, then he looked confused, like he didn't understand why Halina and Teren were still in a protective position. Bewilderment passed his face as he looked between Teren and Halina. His finger came out of his pocket and he pointed in my direction. "Are you protecting...humans?" He couldn't have sounded more surprised by that. "I've seen you with these humans several times." He gave Teren an odd look as he gestured with his thumb over his shoulder. "You do know there's an ocean of them out there, don't you?"

He seemed truly baffled as to why two humans would warrant such a strong reaction in his kind. My stomach twisted as I realized he didn't share Teren's views on eating livestock. Ignoring the throb in my hand, I shifted slightly behind Ben. My movement brought Tommy's eyes right to me and I froze.

"Ah, and one with child...my favorite. No blood is sweeter than a woman filled with life." His grin turned into a leer and my heart shifted into triple time. He heard it and smiled wider. That was all the reaction he got a chance to give though.

Teren was on him in a flash. His hand securely wrapped around the man's throat, and his fangs extended. I prayed no one happened to walk past this tension-filled parking lot while the supernaturals were being, well, supernatural. "She's mine," Teren growled.

His strength superior to Teren's mixed blood, Tommy batted Teren's hand away from his neck like he was a child. That made me nervous, but Halina stepped forward to stand closer to him, to back him up if needed, and I relaxed a little. Two-against-one odds were better.

Tommy glanced at her and then back to Teren. "Relax. It was just an observation. It's not like there aren't more like her out tonight."

He rolled his eyes, like he didn't understand why Teren was being so rude. I hated the feeling of being looked at purely as dinner, and I wanted this creature, gone. Teren seemed to share my feelings. "It was nice to meet you, but we have somewhere to be."

Tommy frowned as both he and Teren retracted their fangs. I relaxed again as the sudden tension started dissipating. "Oh, I was hoping we could get to know each other better. I do get bored being on my own all the time." He tilted his head at Teren. "And you…fascinate me."

Teren smiled tightly as Halina stepped up to his side. "Another time perhaps? When it's just you and me."

Since the vampires seemed preoccupied, I pulled Ben's hand and urged him back towards the car. He didn't move though; his perfect face was glued on Tommy's. He was shell-shocked, too scared to do anything. I silently cursed my luck at being glued to him, and whispered his name repeatedly, trying to break him out of his stupor.

Tommy flicked a glance at me, and a disappointed look was clear on his face. "Yeah, all right, since you're busy with your…humans. I was about to get something to eat anyway." His eyes lingered on Ben, contemplative. Pulling his attention back to Teren, he casually asked, "Do you need both of them? Since you seem so partial to the female, can I have the male?"

He'd asked that as if we were nothing more than Thanksgiving turkeys at a store, being divvied up between customers. Ben groaned and finally took a step back with me. As quietly as we could, we started walking backward. Teren tried to distract Tommy by stepping into his line of vision, but Tommy just looked around him as he watched our slow retreat to Teren's car.

Answering Tommy's question, Teren calmly said, "No, the male is ours as well."

Tommy brought his attention to Teren again. He sighed sadly as his dinner skulked away. "Didn't think so. Fine. Like I said," he flung his arm out to indicate the neighborhood, "an ocean of humans awaits."

Fixing his face and his stance, Teren firmly said, "No."

Tommy grinned, like Teren had made a joke, and then he blinked his dark eyes at him. "Excuse me?"

"There is no killing of humans, in or around the city." Teren's voice stayed remarkably steady when he gave his decree. I almost expected Halina to scoff at his remark, but her face was completely serious as she eyed the strange vampire.

Tommy started laughing but he stopped when he saw that Teren was not even remotely joking. Looking between him and Halina he sullenly said, "I'm hungry, I need to eat. What are a few cattle, in a city this size?"

I cringed at his word choice as Ben and I finally backed into Teren's car. I tried the latch of the door behind me, but the stupid thing was, of course, locked. I cursed under my breath while Teren laid down the law for the vampire. Even terrified, I had to admit that his authority was a turn on.

"You are in my territory and you do not have my permission to hunt here. You will leave every...cow...in my city alone."

Tommy scoffed and gave Teren a once over. "Permission? I don't need your permission, boy. And why should I deprive myself of the best meal in town? It's not like they're endangered. They breed like rabbits. They spread over this world like cockroaches. I'm simply doing my part, to thin the herd."

I really hated this guy referring to us as much lower life forms. Teren took a menacing step towards him. He had a good half foot over the short, plain vampire, but I knew that was misleading. A vampire's strength didn't come from his size.

Halina stepped forward as well, her strength equal, if not greater, than Tommy's. I uselessly jiggled the handle of the door as she calmly told him, "This is my city, too, and since I've been a vampire longer than you, that makes me your elder. And you will listen to *me* when I say, back off. Why don't you try farther south? There are some wonderful specimens in Brazil."

Surprise flitted through me that Halina would care if he hunted here. A part of me wondered if he had simply irritated her, and she'd sided with Teren just to piss him off. Or maybe it was just a show of family unity. Either way, she was more imposing than Teren at the moment, and the man paused as he considered the threat in front of him.

"Well..." he sniffed, brought his hands out of his pockets, and flexed them, "maybe you and I could hunt together, little minx?" He eyed her up and down, a little more seductively than he had Teren. "You could...approve my meal choice, and then perhaps we could find a hole to hide up in until dusk?" He leaned toward her and ran a hand up her thigh. "I'm sure you have one, somewhere."

Scoffing, she batted his hand away and crossed her arms over her chest. "I got a more appealing offer from a junky down at the wharf earlier."

Tommy bristled and anger clouded his face. "I think I will go." He glared at Teren and then Halina. "The hospitality here is not what I expected."

Teren stepped back and swished an arm out to his side in a gesture of dismissal. "We're sorry for the rudeness, but this is our home, and we have rules here."

The man made no move to leave, only frowned further at Teren. "You disappoint me, half-breed. I was so hoping we could be friends."

Teren raised his chin as he shook his head. "I have enough friends."

Tommy's lip twitched, and although I couldn't see it, I thought his fangs had dropped down again. I quietly asked Ben if his car was open. I desperately wanted to be behind a sheet of metal instead of standing out here in the open. Ben didn't answer me; he was too caught up in the showdown going on in front of his face. I jabbed him in the ribs, but he still paid me no attention. He only grasped my hand like I was his lifeline.

Tommy heard me whisper to Ben and shot me a glance. I met his eye and froze again. His lips curved up into a cruel smile. It made me think about how a cat about to pounce on a mouse might look, if their faces could show emotion. His eyes gleamed in the orange lights and his body sank down just a fraction of an inch. Halina and Teren looked at each other briefly while Tommy held my gaze. Not looking away from me, he told them, "Fine, I'll be on my way." He tilted his head, his mouth opening wide enough so that I could indeed see his fangs. "But first...maybe a snack."

That line brought Teren's attention back to him, but he was too late. The vampire who looked like an accountant was fast. He moved quicker than I'd ever seen a vampire move, and that was saying a lot. I saw nothing at first. In fact, I was only aware that something had changed, because I felt it. My mind couldn't track him, and I still saw him standing by Teren. But he wasn't. Before anyone else could do anything, I was shoved against Teren's car, and my bulging body was trapped by one as hard and commanding as stone. By the time my brain could comprehend that he had moved, that he was pinning me to the car, my head was tilted so hard to the side that I thought it might break.

Before I could scream, a searing pain burst through my neck. Then all I felt was pain; my entire body burned with it. My vision swam and faded, the orange glow of the parking lot warping and distorting, and I never did see him standing in front of me. The pain intensified to a level that made speech impossible. I was pretty sure no sounds ever even left my body. I felt warmth being pulled from me as fire burned through my head, neck, shoulder—everywhere. I heard muffled shouts, but they were distant, like everyone was suddenly miles away from me, or I was underwater. Then the pain started to fade and my vision dulled, started shifting to a sheet of black, like someone had turned off every light in the city and pulled a blanket over the stars.

As every muscle in my tense body started relaxing, and one long, raspy breath left my body, "*seven seconds*" kept replaying itself in my head. That was how long an experienced killer took to drain a person dry. It felt like the pain had lasted an eternity to me, but I wondered if only a few seconds had ticked by. As my thoughts started getting harder to hold onto, my very last one was, *I love you, Teren.*

Then I felt nothing.

Chapter 11 – Life, Death, and Everything In-Between

I was dead. I was completely sure I was dead. No one survived an attack like that. No one just walked away from a hungry vampire with a point to prove unscathed, not even this, until now, pretty lucky girl. I hated that what a whacked-out maniac had failed to do a few months ago, a lone CPA looking vampire had managed. I also hated that Teren would be devastated. He'd be so upset with himself, like he'd failed me again. I didn't blame him for my death though; fast as he might be, he couldn't have known what was going to happen. I hoped that his family helped him through my demise. I couldn't even imagine how wrenched he was, losing me and the children, all at once like that.

A new horror struck me as I thought of the children. They were gone. We'd struggled so hard to conceive them in time and now they wouldn't even get the chance at life. They'd never know how much we loved them, how excited their father had been to hold them. They'd never know...

As I dwelled, my thoughts turned to my family, and how much pain they were going to be in. My poor sister. I was sure Teren would tell her the truth about what happened. I wondered if she would have a different opinion of vampires now. Maybe she wouldn't want to know the truth anymore. Maybe she'd ask him to wipe her mind of all of them. I hated that Teren would lose her too. He would be so alone.

My mother would have to be told a lie; an animal attack maybe? I couldn't imagine how she would get through burying another family member. That was just too horrific to comprehend. I thought of Tracey and Hot Ben—maybe their grief would bind them. Maybe Halina had wiped him immediately after the incident, so he would never have to know what really happened. I was sure he would have gone mental with terror, if he had watched his biggest fear happen right in front of his face. That was, if the vampire hadn't killed him too.

Speaking of that bastard, I hoped Halina had rammed her hand straight through his chest and ripped out his heart. Drastic, sure, but we were talking about the creature who had taken the lives of my children. No punishment could be grand enough for him. On second thought, I hoped she had taken him to the ranch and staked him out in a field; let the sun burn away his sins.

A little surprised at my dark thoughts, I raised a heavy hand and scratched an itch on my nose. Odd. I wouldn't think a dead person would still have the occasional itch. As my hand thudded down to land on a soft, springy surface, I thought that was pretty odd, too. Why was my afterlife feeling like waking from delirium?

I experimentally inhaled. My lungs expanded and the scent of iodine burned my nostrils. I choked on it and coughed, and that's when the pain hit me. I forced myself to stop coughing. My eyes stung in protest, but that was preferable to the tearing sensation that had seared through my neck. Why had pain followed me into death? Shouldn't I be pain free, lounging with my deceased father and grandmother on some fluffy white cloud, while a window to earth let me keep an eye on the loved ones I'd left behind?

Unless, of course, I had somehow survived? But that just wasn't possible. I'd felt my throat being ripped into, felt the warmth of my life's blood being stolen from me. I'd felt my body give in, and succumb to death. There was just no freaking way I had lived through that!

But I couldn't ignore the painful sensations running through my sore body. My head felt like it might split open. My throat was dry and aching. Even keeping my neck perfectly immobile, I still throbbed where that bastard bit me. But most of all, over all of the tenderness, was an overriding sense that my body was foreign. Maybe that's why death had seemed a more logical conclusion; I almost didn't feel real.

My skin felt stretched tight over limbs that were suddenly too long, muscles that were too sculpted. I felt the air in the room brushing across my flesh, like someone had left a window open. It was a tad icy and a shiver went through me. My eyes felt heavy and lidded, like I couldn't possibly open them, and my mouth felt…full, like my tongue was too big and my teeth had doubled in size.

I carefully stretched my body and felt dull aches and tensions releasing. I opened my jaw and it loudly cracked in my ear. My jaw ached and I brought a hand to the joint and massaged it while I tried to open my eyes. Well, I guessed I wasn't dead. The room was real, nothing ethereal about it. It was dark, nighttime, but light was filtering in from underneath the door, highlighting it in orange. The effort was too much and I closed my eyes again. I hated being in pain and a tiny, tiny speck of me, preferred the idea of me being dead, like I'd originally thought.

Confused as to how I wasn't, I moved my hand to my neck and felt the bandage there. A thick bandage—hospital grade. I wondered vaguely if that's where I was. Had Teren scooped me up and sped me to the local ER? Now that I was sure I was alive, I wanted to see him, and make sure he was okay too. I wondered where he was. For some reason, I felt like he was close by, and I was sure he was. I doubted he'd leave me, knowing I was hurting.

Hurting…

That thought made me immediately bring my hand to my stomach. The skin there was tight too. Worried, I pressed down, first on one side then the other. I was rewarded with a light kick and a jostling bump as the twins responded to my touch. They were alive…I was alive…we were fine. Somehow, we were all fine.

I inhaled deep again. My nose was more prepared for the hospital smell, and I held my breath in for a few seconds before letting it go. Despite the pain, I felt cleaner, more alive than I'd felt in a long time, maybe ever. But I still felt odd. My throat burned and when I swallowed, it was difficult to do. With one hand still protectively resting over my babies, I listened to the sounds around the room.

Everything was muffed at first, like my ears were also waking from delirium, but as I concentrated, clarity filled me. Surprisingly, I could hear Teren's deep voice and in answer to him, a woman's musical one. I knew the female's voice almost immediately, felt instantly connected with it. He was talking to Alanna. I wondered what she was doing here at the hospital and then, for some reason, I knew that all of the vampires were here. I frowned and wondered why they'd come all this way. Knowing that even *I* had thought I'd died, I supposed it had been pretty touch and go for a while. Maybe they'd all come to support Teren. Maybe my mother and sister were here too, all prepared to grieve me with my husband, if I didn't make it. I cringed and held my abdomen tighter. No longer wishing death over pain, gratitude filled me that I hadn't lost them, that my horrible vision of them never seeing their father wasn't going to come true. Tears stung my eyes as I silently thanked the fates for their safety.

Suddenly the questions were too much. I needed someone here to answer them. Maybe someone with pain meds, for the fire burning on my neck, and water, for the fire burning in my throat.

"Teren," was all I could croak out.

It was enough. The door immediately swished open, and I felt the difference in the air current as it swished closed. Air eddied around me and I shivered again with the ice I felt in it. The bed compressed beside me and I felt Teren's presence, even if I couldn't open my eyes yet to look at him.

His cool hands brushed over my face, tucking my hair behind my ears. I was sure I looked atrocious, and I was equally sure Teren didn't care. I felt him lean down to kiss my forehead; his cool lips were comforting on my searing skin.

"Hey, you're awake. It's been a few days. I was so worried…" His voice was strained, like he was overcome with emotion. He must have been really scared for me. I couldn't even imagine how awful waiting around for me to either live or die must have been. I idly wondered what he'd told the doctor.

I forced my heavy lids open and took in his concerned pale eyes, faintly glowing in the darkness of the room. His face was lit in an odd way that I didn't understand, but I was so happy to see him, that I didn't really care. The tears in my eyes threatened to roll down my cheeks as I took in the perfect face that I was so sure I'd never see again. Teren reached over to the lamp on the nightstand and flicked it on. As soft amber light filled the room, I blinked in the harshness of it, and finally noticed that we weren't at a hospital, we were at the ranch.

Careful to keep my aching neck still, I looked around with only my eyes. "Why are we back here?" My voice sounded strange. My tongue still seemed like it didn't fit in my body correctly, and my throat was raspy, like I was a lifelong smoker all of a sudden.

Teren cupped my cheeks. "Do you remember…anything?"

I carefully lifted my hand and placed it over his. My warmth seeped through his coolness; I felt it on my cheek. "Don't be scared, Teren…I'm fine." He tried to adjust his face so that he looked carefree and untroubled, but I saw the lie behind it. I saw the tension in his jaw, the tightness of his eyes; I could almost smell the fear on him. "I remember…a little. I remember being held down and I remember teeth…"

I closed my eyes as the memory of the attack seared through me. I'd thought it was over. I was positive when I'd felt the viciousness and brutality of the bite, nothing like Teren's love nips, that I was done. Teren's cool head came down to rest on mine. "I'm so sorry, Emma. It happened so fast. I didn't see it coming. I didn't know he was going to…"

I switched my hand to his chest and pushed him back so I could look at him. "It's okay, Teren…I'm fine." Dead thirsty and feeling like I was in a possessed body, but fine. I was alive at any rate and so were our children. That equaled fine in my book.

A look passed over his eyes that I swear was guilt, and he looked down at the pillows. Feeling an odd tension building, I jokingly muttered, "Did anyone stake the bastard?"

He looked up at me; a slight, crooked grin was on his lips. "You won't believe me."

Preferring that face to his worried or guilty face, I dropped my hand back to my belly and gave him an odd-feeling smile, or I tried to anyway. "Tell me." Pain seared through my body, but I ignored it. I didn't want Teren to feel bad, and I didn't want him to leave my side just yet to get me painkillers. I'd been too close to losing him once tonight already, when I'd been sure I was dead.

He sighed at the look of restrained pain on my face and he avoided looking me directly in the eyes. He continued with his story though. Maybe he didn't want to leave me yet either. He shook his head as his wry smile returned. "Ben." My brow furrowed and I tried to shake my head, but immediately stopped when a jolt of pain went through me.

Teren bit his lip as he looked over my face, but he explained before I could ask him to. He rolled his eyes as a small grin brightened his otherwise tragic face. "I guess Ben has taken to arming himself when he goes out." His eyes locked onto my neck. "This time…it was warranted." He looked up at me, and I got the feeling he was making himself meet my gaze. "The whole time he was watching the conversation, he was clutching a stake in his pocket. When that vampire moved, he automatically swung." Teren raised an eyebrow and lost what little grin he'd had. "He pierced his heart, through his back." Then the smirk returned and he nodded his head towards the door. "He's still here, downstairs…drinking heavily. He won't leave until he knows that you're okay." He shrugged and sighed. "I think he's just too freaked out to do anything else yet."

My mouth dropped wide open, and I cringed as a wave of pain ran through my shoulder and up to my jaw. Teren averted his eyes. "Ben?" I croaked out, momentarily ignoring my pain in my shock. "Scaredy-cat Ben staked a vamp?" From somewhere, I swear I heard a husky laugh. I also thought I could hear the sounds of people rustling and talking, but I pushed out my imagined hearing as I focused on my husband. Teren peered up at me, an amused smile slipping off his face as he looked me over. I carefully closed my mouth; it felt odd to do so. "You're right, I don't believe you."

Teren's eyes were locked onto my mouth, so I tried to smile for him, to reassure him, since he seemed to be having major guilt over the attack. My mouth still felt odd and thick though, so I gave up the feeble attempt. It didn't appear to be reassuring him anyway. Reaching over, I grabbed his cool hand and laced our fingers together.

He raised his eyes to mine and swallowed. He also tried a brief, reassuring smile, but it quickly fell off of him as his eyes swept over my face. I wasn't sure what he was seeing, but it must have been bad. He bit his lip; he almost looked like he was on the verge of losing it. "Emma…" He stopped and swallowed again. "I…I don't know how to…" His voice trailed off. Sighing, he ran a hand down his face.

I weakly reached out with my other hand and stroked my thumb over his cheek as I pulled him towards me. "I know, Teren." He'd been gone from my arms from too long and I needed him closer. Whatever guilt he was feeling over me being assaulted, he needed to let it go. I needed him. I needed his reassurance. Understanding my need, or maybe needing it, too, his arms went around me and he held me tight. The coolness of his body felt good on my various aches and pains, and I sighed as I relaxed into the comfort of his familiar touch.

No longer able to look at me, Teren buried his head in my uninjured shoulder, and finally found the words he was looking for. "He bit you, Emma...there was so much blood loss. I heard it...I heard it all being taken from you." He made a pained noise, and I clutched at him. I hadn't considered what the attack would have felt and sounded like to Teren. Being so attuned to my blood, he'd probably been aware of exactly how many units I'd been depleted of. He must have been so scared for me, much like the time I'd been terrified for him, during his conversion.

I stroked his back as I comforted him. "It's all okay now, Teren."

His head rested in the crook of my neck and he started lightly shaking it back and forth. "He took so much blood, Emma..." I kissed his head, as best as I could with my mouth that felt full of marbles. I tried to shush him, but he said it again. "He took so much blood. I'm sorry."

There was so much guilt in his voice when he said it, that my nerves shot right through the roof. I suddenly had a horrible feeling that everything was *not* fine. I tried to swallow again, but my throat was on fire. I wanted water...or a milkshake, something thick and creamy. I wanted to ask Teren for something to ease my throat, and for something to help with the fire radiating from my neck, but adrenaline was pouring through me now and I was almost too terrified to speak. *Everything was not fine.*

Somehow, I found the courage to say his name. "Teren?"

He pulled back to look at me and again his eyes flicked over my face. Did I really look so awful to him? Did he really feel so guilty that he'd let a vampire get close enough to nearly drain me dry?

Nearly...

My brows scrunched together while Teren repeated that he was sorry. "Why...what did you do?"

He closed his eyes and I felt like I'd hit the proverbial nail on the head. He wasn't confessing his guilt over the attack, although I was sure he felt a huge amount of guilt over it, especially since he'd sworn over and over that he'd never let anyone harm me—an impossible to keep promise. But that wasn't what was making his eyes fill to the brim with tears. That wasn't what was making it difficult for him to look me directly in the eye. No, he was torturing himself with guilt over something *he'd* done, not the vampire…something after the attack. My mind spun as I tried to understand. I couldn't. We were all alive—surely that was a good thing.

"Emma…" His voice was shaky and a tear finally broke the surface of his beautiful pale eye to splash on the sheet covering my aching body.

My stomach twisted into painful knots while I tried to decipher his mixed messages. He was glad I was alive *and* he felt guilty. Why? "Teren, you're scaring me…"

He closed his eyes and slowly exhaled, gathering his thoughts and his strength. "You lost…a lot of blood. When his body was pulled off of you, even before, I could hear your heart slowing…your pulse slowing." He opened his eyes and they looked aged. For once, he appeared to be what he really was, dead. "You needed more blood…"

He swallowed and ice filled my veins. "What did you do?" I whispered.

He sat up and his hands went to my upper arms, almost like he was afraid that once he told me, I would make a run for it. As if my pain-riddled body could do that right now. I braced myself for whatever he was going to tell me. "I'm so sorry, Emma…I wasn't thinking. You were going to die, all three of you were going to die…I panicked." He shook his head as he repeated, "I panicked. I'm sorry."

Ice and confusion flooded my system. Somehow my voice broke through the pain and dryness of my scratchy throat to find volume. "What did you do!"

He cringed away from the heat in my tone. "I wasn't thinking. I just wanted to save you...like you saved me..." His eyes searched my face; they were still tired and remorseful.

"Teren!" I was on the verge of grabbing him and chucking his dead ass out the window if he didn't tell me exactly what he'd done.

Maybe noticing my patience was virtually gone, he quietly said, "You needed more blood...I gave it to you."

I cocked my head, not understanding what the big deal was. "Yeah, so...like a transfusion or something?"

His twisted his lips. "Or something..."

The look on his face, the guilt in his voice... A past conversation filled my head, shouting through every fiber of my sore body and reverberating through every aching joint. My hand instinctually went to the wound at my neck as my body suddenly felt on fire. Words tumbled through my mind in a never-ending loop:

"...drained of all her blood...replaced by a vampire's. Drained of all her blood...replaced by a vampire's..."

Replaced by a vampire's. A vampire had drained me...or nearly so, close enough that my heart had been beginning to fail, and Teren had replaced the blood...with his, with his vampire blood. Teren was against turning anyone, and he'd turned me? I couldn't comprehend that. I couldn't believe it. Even dying, I couldn't believe he'd do that to me. We'd never talked about me becoming a vampire, nothing beyond him wishing that I could be like him. But that wasn't possible. It didn't work like that. Did he save me, by killing me?

"What did you do to me?" I asked, stupefied. "Am I...?" I brought a hand to the other side of my neck, trying to find my heartbeat. His eyes tracked my movement as I easily found my pulse on my skin. I could even hear its fast pace in the room. Nope, it was definitely still ticking.

He shook his head. "No, no you're still alive. Your heart is still beating. The babies' hearts are still beating."

Now I shook my head. I was rewarded with a surge of fresh pain as my neck protested the movement. I cringed and my voice came out laced with an edge of pain. "But...did it not work then? Was your blood just blood after all?" He cringed and looked away. I felt the guilt come back into the room and I saw it again, all over his features. "Teren...what did you do? What am I?"

He looked back to me and another tear dropped to his cheek. "I don't know, Emma. I'm so sorry."

Before I could say anything else, Alanna and Halina breezed into the room. They left the door open and I could see the familiar hallway of the Adams family home behind them. He'd brought me back to his home after he'd...replenished me.

Alanna held a travel coffee mug out to me and I slurped it down without looking. I was so thirsty...coffee didn't really sound appealing, and I had been staying away from the stuff, but at the moment, I didn't care. It was warm and thick, and tasted better than any latte I'd ever been given. It was sweet, intense in flavor...and a little tangy. My mouth still felt odd, but the warm liquid was soothing. I even felt the pain in my neck subside and thought maybe Alanna had dosed the coffee with painkillers.

I watched them over my cup as I slurped down my drink. They were all looking at me oddly, like I was some science experiment. Teren looked down, the guilt still clear on his face. Alanna only looked thoughtful, and perhaps a little sad. I shifted my gaze to Halina, she looked the most curious of all of them. Their stares were starting to annoy me.

"Quit looking at me like that."

I went back to my soothing drink while Alanna politely looked away. Halina smiled and continued staring. Once I got to the bottom of my drink and was tipping it back for the last of the coffee, Alanna finally spoke. "Would you like some more, Emma?" Her voice had a strange, curious edge to it.

I ignored her tone and nodded. My neck was feeling better already. "Please...I'm still really thirsty and whatever you put in that, it's really helping my neck."

Alanna put a hand on Teren's shoulder and they exchanged a look before she flitted out of the room. Feeling more put together, now that my throat and body weren't aching so badly, I put my hand over Teren's in his lap. He flinched a little at the contact and looked up at me.

I smiled warmly for the first time since he'd walked in here. It still felt odd, but I managed to do it pain free. "Well, it obviously didn't do anything to me, Teren…your blood. I'm fine. Sore and feeling kind of odd, but fine. I'm not undead or anything." I managed a weak laugh. I expected him to laugh with me at my joke, but he didn't, he looked down again. He looked guilty again.

Halina smirked at me and then shook her head. I got an uncomfortable feeling as I looked between the two of them. Eventually Alanna came back with more steaming coffee. Imogen was right behind her. "Is she really…?" Imogen let her sentence trail off as she stared at me on the bed. Her mouth was wide open. God, did I look that bad? I reflexively put my hand over my neck wound.

Alanna handed me the drink and I started gulping down my second cup of joe. As Teren sighed and locked gazes with his mother again, I concentrated on my pain-reducing coffee. The warm, thick treat got easier to swallow with each loud gulp. As wonderful as it was though, I was about to chuck it on Teren if he didn't stop looking so solemn. I was obviously just fine, heart still beating and everything. Something about me seemed to be freaking them all out, I just didn't know what. Maybe they were just surprised that his blood really didn't do anything to me, but save me. Maybe they were just startled that a mixed vampire's blood only acted as some miracle healing potion. Although, it had only kept me alive, the residual pain in my neck assured me that the skin there was still torn, and healing at a normal human pace.

I still couldn't believe what he'd done for me. As I watched him look between Alanna and Imogen, and watched Imogen place a reassuring hand on his shoulder, I pictured what must have happened in that parking lot. After Hot Ben had dispatched the vamp—and I still couldn't wrap my mind around that one—Teren must have blurred to my side and swept me into his arms. I imagined him crying and moaning my name; he was very bereaved in my mental movie. I pictured Halina scanning the area and warning him that they had to leave immediately; she was not so grieved. And I visualized Ben staring at my bloody near-corpse and peeing his pants. Yeah, I was really having trouble seeing him any other way, but terrified.

Then I imagined Teren's fangs coming out and ripping open his own wrist. I imagined him bringing that wrist to my mouth and my almost deceased body automatically swallowing the cool liquid of his foreign blood. In my mind, I imagined Halina and Ben screaming at him to stop, but overwhelmed with grief, he couldn't, and he continued giving me his miraculous blood until his wounded wrist healed. I had no idea why vampire blood being poured into my stomach had kept me alive, or why it kept any vampire "alive" for that matter, but then, there was a lot about vampires that I didn't understand. Hell, there was a lot about the *human* body that I didn't understand. Some things you just have to go with. But it had saved me, and it hadn't changed me. I couldn't see why they weren't all doing a vampire jig.

I closed my eyes for a second, to wipe away the stomach churning image of Teren feeding me his blood, and concentrated even more on the yummy coffee I was drinking. As soon as I finished this cup, I was demanding some answers from the oddly quiet vampires. As I neared the end, a happy noise left my throat. Dang, Alanna made good coffee, so much better than any coffee house I'd ever gone to.

Teren dropped his head into his hands and Alanna put her hand on his shoulder again. "God…Mom…" He spoke something else, but it was in Russian, and I couldn't make it out. Alanna responded in a solemn voice, also in the foreign language. Teren dropped his hands to his lap and shook his head, looking a little defeated.

Irritated by the let's-keep-Emma-out-of-the-loop Russian, I stopped drinking. Feeling a little saucy, since Alanna's miracle coffee had made me feel better, I spat out, "What? Why do you all look like that? I'm fine. In fact, I'm feeling better every second." Giving each vampire a pointed look, I calmly said, "I'm normal. The babies are fine. Teren saved us all…where's the celebration?"

They all shared a glance between each other, but no one spoke again. I sighed in irritation and was about to speak, when Jack and Hot Ben entered the room. Jack looked at me with the same odd, curious reaction that the vampires had, as he walked over to stand beside his wife. As Alanna clenched his hand, a thoughtful look past between them. I couldn't even begin to place it.

My attention was redirected to the door frame when I heard Hot Ben say, "Whoa, Emma." His face was pale and his eyes were wide as he stared at me. He stumbled some and I recalled Teren saying that he'd been spending his idle time drinking. I tried not to take offense at his reaction to my—I'm sure—horrific face. He was probably barely seeing straight at this point.

He looked about to say more as he ran a hand through his highlighted locks, but Teren shot him a glance that had a clear warning in it. Teren obviously didn't want him mocking my appearance right now. Regardless of my irritation at Teren, I squeezed his hand in appreciation as Hot Ben shut his mouth, leaned against the doorframe, and stared at me relentlessly.

Teren looked over at my smiling face. Holding my cup out to him, I said, "This is really helping, can I have some more?"

Teren looked pained and, focusing on his mother, spoke in Russian again.

"No! Stop that, right now!" I was getting used to my odd feeling body and had brought a little heat into that sentence. Damn their secretive language anyway, I was tired of being kept out of conversations that were obviously about me. They all looked my way, clearly a little stunned at my outburst. "What? You are all looking at me like...I don't know. What is it?"

There were long seconds of everyone looking at everyone else before anyone would finally look at me. Just when my patience was about as stretched as it could go, Teren finally sighed and looked at me; resignation was clear on his face. "Emma," he began slowly, like at any moment I was going to lash out at him, "please don't freak out."

Even more irritated, I spat out, "I'm already starting to freak out. You can't ask me to not do something I'm already doing! What the hell is going on?"

Teren sighed, but it was eventually Halina who handed me a small hand mirror from the vanity behind her. Confused, I took it and looked at my reflection. Ugh, I looked as awful as I thought I would. I had deep circles under my eyes and my hair was a wild mess. The bandage on my neck was huge, and although the pain was more manageable than before, some still tugged at me whenever I shifted; maybe I should ask for that pain pill now. But other than that…I looked the same.

"Okay, I don't get what the…"

I stopped talking once a flash of my open mouth showed in the mirror. I stared at myself with a mix of wonder and horror. I couldn't believe what I was seeing, what they had all been staring at, why Teren was having trouble looking directly at me. For one, my tongue was red, blood red, but more importantly than that, *so* much more importantly than that…

I had fangs.

"Holy shit."

Chapter 12 – Sensitivity

Every sound in the room stopped, or maybe, I just stopped listening to them. Either way, I could have suddenly been in space for all the silence in the room. My pain was suddenly gone now too, like my body had shut off all other sensations to focus solely on my vision. More specifically, to focus on the oddity that was my mouth. And that, I could not stop staring at.

I ran a finger down a canine and felt the long tooth that dropped down to a sharp point. It was coated with a slight twinge of red which rubbed off with my finger, leaving a shiny, white surface underneath. It looked new, slightly brighter than the teeth around it, and I had no idea if my old canines had fallen out, to be replaced with these ones, or if these were in fact my old ones, just somehow sharper and noticeably longer. When I got to the end of it, I experimented by pressing the pad of my finger against it. I broke the surface easily, and a dot of fresh blood welled on the tip of my index finger.

Something inside of me wanted to bite down harder, to make more blood ooze from the wound, and I quickly pulled my hand back. Startled at my own reaction, I locked gazes with myself in the mirror. My eyes were a warm, brown color that normally were bright and alive with whatever underlying emotion I was feeling. If I was happy, I was told that they seemed lighter, the flecks of gold in them overpowering the darker shade. If I were angry, well, one ex-boyfriend had said that my eyes darkened to rival the pits of hell. I really didn't like that comparison, or the boy who'd said it. As I stared at my eyes today, the color was the shade of darkly stained oak, sort of in the middle of the two spectrums. But the whites of my eyes were huge, as the shock I felt was evident, even to me.

"Emma?"

Teren's voice brought all sound rushing back to me. It was a sudden cacophony that assaulted my ears. The rustle of everyone moving—Jack and Alanna whispering worried words back and forth to each other, Imogen rushing out the door to get me more coffee, although, by the color of my tongue, I had a horrible feeling that the world's best coffee wasn't what I'd been enjoying. Hot Ben stumbled near the door, and his hand reached out to brace himself on the frame; the sudden movement sounded like a jackhammer in my brain.

It was all too much and I wanted to cry, I could even feel the tears well up. A cool palm touched my flushed face. "Hey, relax. I'm here, Emma." Teren's deep voice pushed away all the other sounds as I focused on it. I dragged my eyes back to him, watching his lips move as he spoke more soothing phrases.

"It's too loud," I whispered.

He nodded and glanced up at his mother. She had heard me as well and ushered Jack to the door. He hadn't heard me or understood, but he followed his wife's lead unerringly, as if he was aware that a vampire had spoken to her from somewhere. I suppose he was used to not being in on all of the conversations. Halina, the only one being stone silent—she wasn't even breathing as she studied me—nodded at Teren and turned to leave the room. She grabbed a clumsy Ben by the arm on her way out the door. I heard him fall and curse on the other side of it, then heard Halina laugh and pick him up, much to his loud dismay. Not used to hearing so much, so quickly, I closed my eyes to try and shut the sound off again.

Teren's lips were cool on my forehead and cheeks as he comforted me and whispered apologies. His lips brushed mine and I stiffened, not ready for that sort of contact. He sighed, but didn't press the issue. Instead he sat back down on his space on the bed. He removed the mirror from my hand, then clasped it.

"You changed me?" I whispered, now understanding why my mouth felt so strange. I was speaking around fangs. I had no idea how to retract them.

I opened my eyes and watched him cringe and give me an apologetic smile. "It would seem so, although, I have no idea why your heart is still beating." He shrugged and shook his head. "I've been waiting for days for it to stop."

He glanced down to my stomach after he said that, and his face aged right in front of me. I suddenly understood his real fear. He thought he'd converted me. While a conversion would be okay for me, in the long run, it most certainly would not be all right for the two lives dependent on my survival. I put a hand on my stomach and one of the twins kicked me, almost as if to let me know they were still there. "You've been waiting around for me to die? For them to die?"

He met my eyes again. "Yes," he whispered. "I was so scared."

Now I was scared. Just because I hadn't died yet, didn't mean I wouldn't. After all, I knew from experience that the human side could only take the strain of vampire blood for so long. Did my twenty-six year stop watch start now, or was I already ticking away, only having the couple months until my birthday, before I literally became just like Teren. "Am I going to die?"

I was pretty sure I knew the answer to that as well as Teren did, but he shrugged and shook his head. "I don't know, Emma."

Fear made my anger resurface. "You don't know?"

He cringed under my tone and shook his head again. "We've never changed anyone, Emma. We just don't know what will happen to you, or even really, what *did* happen to you." His eyes watered as he whispered, "We don't even know if you will convert...if my mixed blood was enough to complete the change, or...if you'll just...die. We don't know, Emma."

My eyes narrowed at his ignorance. What I needed right now was information, and even though a part of me knew I shouldn't blame him for not having any answers, I didn't have anyone else to blame at the moment. "How could you have done that to me, without knowing what would happen? To me, or to them?"

His face turned sad and he looked away from me, like that was something he'd repeatedly asked himself too. He hung his head and said, "You were dying..."

I had no response to that and only continued to unfairly glare at him. He didn't look at me, his guilt kept his head down and his eyes firmly fixed on my stomach, the real question in this whole equation. If it were my time, then it was my time...I guess, but the twins...

Just as a new wave of anger hit me, Alanna quietly stepped into the room. Well, I'm sure to most it was quiet. To my new hearing, that I could only partially get a handle on, when she opened the door and my attention focused on it, every sound muffled behind it became crystal clear. Jack was asking Imogen what would happen to me. Imogen replied that she didn't know. Halina was hoping the children could be spared before I died. She sounded much less concerned over my fate than that of the twins. Hot Ben was throwing up in one of the bathrooms.

Alanna closed the door and apologized for the intrusion. Teren didn't look up at her. I stopped glaring at him and tried to fix my face into impassiveness. Alanna approached the bed and handed me another cup of steaming coffee. I sniffed it this time. My senses could distinguish every delightful thing about it, the headiness, the tangy sweetness, but nothing in it smelled as awful as what I suspected it was. Hoping I was wrong, I stuck my finger in the dark liquid inside the black thermos. Teren sighed as I pulled my finger back. And of course, my entire finger was as darkly red as the pinprick that had been there earlier.

"You gave me blood?" I focused my disgust solely on Teren, even though Alanna had technically given me the mugs.

He flinched and looked up at me. "Your body needs it now. It will help you heal, Emma." He pointed to the wound on my neck. "You even said it was helping."

Not feeling any better about any of this, I yelled, "You gave me blood!"

Alanna reached a hand out and started saying my name at the same time that Teren did. Feeling overwhelmed, tired, and on the verge of an emotional breakdown, I did the only thing that seemed sensible in the heat of the moment. Stubbornly raising my arm to the door, I snapped, "Get out!"

Teren tilted his head and furrowed his brows, probably wondering if I was seriously kicking him out of his family's home. I was. "Get...out," I repeated, my tone seething, as fear, anger and sadness swirled within me.

Teren looked like I'd just told him I never wanted to see him again. Biting back my guilt at making that expression appear on his face, I pointed to the door again. After giving his mom a sad glance, he finally stood and walked over to it. Before he opened it, his eyes came back to mine. "I love you, Emma," he whispered, and then he opened the door.

Like before, the sounds hit me as my concentration shifted with the opening and shutting door. Before the physical barrier redirected my attention to just inside the room, I heard Imogen proclaim, "Did she really just kick him out? Are they through?" Halina answered her by complaining that she couldn't wipe me now, since I had vampire blood in me. Jack insisted that things would be fine once I cooled down, and, somewhere in the house, Hot Ben threw up again.

On the other side of the door, Teren sighed told me he loved me again, and then sped out of the house. I heard one of the outer doors shut behind him and a sob broke out of me, finally.

Alanna sat down in the spot he'd just left, her thick denim jeans rustling as she adjusted herself. She placed a cool hand over my arm as I silently cried. "You should go easy on him, dear. What he did…was very difficult for him."

I looked up at her; her loose, black hair was hazy in my watery vision. I scrunched my brow, not sure what she meant. She smiled and brought a knuckle up to brush aside my tears. Her hand came down to rub my stomach reassuringly as she continued. "He feels horrible about what he's done to you."

As if to emphasize what he'd done to me, I lifted the mug and made myself take a sip. I knew from all the previous cups I'd had, that it would taste good, but my stomach still churned at the thought of chugging it down. As the thick warmth passed my lips, I resisted the urge to both purr in pleasure and vomit in disgust. Alanna watched me with fascination as I took a few large swallows. "He should. He's dead and I'm about to kill him again," I said after drinking a bit of my Mary-less Bloody Mary.

Alanna sighed. Her pale eyes exactly matched her son's, and watching her was like watching a feminine version of Teren. It hurt my heart, knowing that I'd injured him with my angry words. "Emma, he only wanted to save you, you and the children. You mean everything to him."

I paused in my drink as I felt more tears roll down my cheeks; I swear I could hear them slithering down my skin. It was all so overwhelming. Anger was the only thing keeping me sane and I tried to hold onto it. Peeking up at her, I heatedly said, "But what am I now? What will happen to me, to them?"

Alanna looked down. Removing her hand from my belly, she placed it on her lap. Her eyes fixated on her fingers as she answered me. "I'm sorry, Emma, but we don't have those answers for you." She looked over to my stomach and shook her head; pink tears in her eyes fell to her cheeks. Her hand came up and rested on the bulge of the twins again, and she closed her eyes as she listened to them. "This is all new for us too, dear. We just don't know." She opened her eyes. They were just as wet as mine.

I nodded and tried to accept that I couldn't force answers from people who didn't have them. I rested my hand over hers on my stomach, and my hot skin started to warm her chill. She smiled at me, but her youthful face was still sad. Wiping tears off of her own cheeks, she spoke in a low voice. My enhanced hearing easily picked it up though. "What he did wasn't easy for him. It goes against everything we believe." She raised her eyebrows and gave me a serious look. "We don't changeover anyone—not even our own spouses. We don't have Halina bring people into this life that way, as purebloods, forcing them into the shadows for eternity, like her." Her expression softened as her face saddened. "No matter what they mean to us."

I took a long drink of my healing blood as I thought about that. I knew Imogen had watched her beloved husband sicken and die. She had never changed him. I also knew Alanna was watching Jack age every year, and she didn't seem inclined to change him either. I'd known going into this that immortality wasn't my end game, and I'd been fine with that. Really, it was Teren who had to deal with the loss. I'd have a full, happy, natural life with him; he was the one that would have to mourn me for an unnaturally long time. Thinking of his pain had kept me up at night sometimes. I didn't know if I would have the strength, if our roles were reversed. But that was the way of things, the way things were supposed to go down. This was never part of the plan.

Alanna sighed as she watched my shifting emotions. "Teren and I have had several lengthy conversations on how we'd deal with our loved ones dying." I studied her face as she turned her head and looked down through the floor. Following her gaze, I could hear Jack speaking to Ben, asking him if he was all right. She spoke softly while we both listened to her husband. "It's a tricky thing, knowing that you're going to live so much longer than the person who holds your heart, the person you want beside you forever."

I swallowed as a wave of emotions rippled through me. I could barely contain my need to release those emotions in either a sob, or a temper tantrum. Alanna shifted her gaze back to mine. "It's even more difficult for Teren and me, knowing that we could possibly save them from that death with our mixed blood." She frowned and shook her head. "But it *is* only a possibility. We really don't know what our blood does to humans. So we resist the temptation. We let them die naturally, as we're all meant to." She gave me a wry smile. "Immortality isn't all it's cracked up to be anyway."

A small smile lit my lips and she grinned wider at seeing it. I supposed that was the whole point of her comment. Her smile dropped as she shook her head again. "But you…" She looked down for a moment before lifting her eyes to mine again. "He wasn't prepared to lose you so fast. He thought he'd get a lifetime, and he reacted purely on instinct…and love." She put a hand on my cheek as my tears fell freely. "Don't fault him for that, Emma. What would you have done?"

I closed my eyes, squeezing out the last few tears welling. I already knew exactly what I would have done for him. The fact was, I'd done much worse for him already. I'd taken a life to save his. He'd only given me a chance at another one, when mine had been ripped away. Sure, this new life might not stick, and either me or the twins, or all three of us, might die anyway, but…we *were* going to die anyway. He had, at the very least, given us a slim chance at survival. Even if today was all I got, at least I'd get to say goodbye.

No, on the grand scale of things, what Teren had done to save me was nothing compared to what I'd done to spare him. What I'd do again to spare him. I'd move heaven and earth to keep him, and I had to believe he would do the same for me.

As my fear and anger started dissipating, guilt flooded in. I'd had no right to snap at him, he'd done nothing wrong. He'd given me a chance, and without him, I'd be lying in a morgue somewhere, instead of lying on a plush bed at a gorgeous ranch resort, sipping on what could arguably be the best cocktail on earth.

I opened my eyes to find Alanna intently watching me. "I should talk to him. Where did he go?"

She tilted her head at me, curious. "Can't you feel him?"

My brows scrunched. "No. Why would I—"

I stopped speaking as a nagging sense in my head shouted at me to listen. I focused on it and suddenly, I instinctively knew where he was. It wasn't like I could see him in my head, I couldn't, but if I was blindfolded and told to point him out, my finger would unerringly go to exactly where he was. In fact, I could sense the location of every vampire in the house that way. Like some people always know where north is, no matter how many times they're twisted around, I knew where every Adams vampire was. Every single one of them was my true north.

Amazement flooded me as I absorbed this new, odd feeling. "He's in the east pasture, about a quarter mile away." Startled beyond belief, my eyes fixed on hers. "How do I know he's a quarter mile away from me?"

Alanna smiled, her suspicions confirmed. She turned one of my hands over and traced the line of one of my veins from wrist to elbow. "Our family blood now runs through these veins. You'll be able to sense all of us, just as we can sense you. You're connected to our family now, Emma. It's in your blood." She smiled broadly and then reached over to hug me.

I was so surprised by this, I only loosely hugged her back, and that was more out of instinct than anything else. I'd already been low jacked, thanks to the twins, but now I was personally low jacked as well. And this connection wouldn't leave when the twins left me. I'd been connected to the hive, so to speak, and we were blood-bonded for life now, however long that life might be.

Alanna left me still reeling over this new development to go talk to Teren. He'd been too far away to hear any of that conversation, and he wasn't yet aware that my anger had faded. I got a little nervous waiting for him to come back; I hadn't exactly been nice to him, and he *had* saved my life, even if it was only a temporary patch. A slice of fear ran through me at the thought of dying, but I pushed it back. I felt fine right now, well, aside from the slight throb in my neck and the overall strangeness of my newly enhanced body. At any rate, I was fairly certain I wasn't dying today.

Oh boy, didn't I sound *exactly* like Teren used to now?

Actually letting a small laugh escape me, I settled in to finish my drink. I let my ears and eyes open as I sipped my blood. There were dings in the furniture that I'd never noticed before—a gouge missing in the vanity leg, a slight crack in the mirror near the corner of the frame, and faint spider-line breaks in the plaster on the ceiling. While my eyes took in the faint threads of blue running through the gold and cream colored quilt over my body, words floated into my head nonstop.

"Oh good, she wants to talk to him, I'm sure they'll work it out now…oh God, I still feel sick…yes, they can't ever seem to be apart for long…drink some water for a change, you'll be fine…and Teren would be so lonely without her…no, don't pass out by the toilet…right, he'd have to find someone else to scream his name when he—"

I sat up straight in bed, which my neck didn't appreciate. "Halina! You know I can hear you now, right?" I felt my entire body flush with heat over the comment that I knew without a doubt had come from her sultry voice.

I heard her laugh as she replied with, "Yes, I'm aware of that…and?"

I floundered for some snappy comeback, but I couldn't manage to come up with anything other than "shut it." Not wanting to sound like a bratty teenager, I kept my mouth closed and silently fumed instead. I set my empty cup down on the nightstand. Even with its contents gone, and the mug itself a good foot and a half away from me, I could still smell the blood. The air in the room was so heavy with the lingering scent of it, that it was nearly palpable on my skin. I tried to pull my fangs back, but I might as well have tried to retract my fingernails. Nothing happened.

Then I felt every sense in my body focusing on one location—Teren was coming back to the house. There was something about his presence getting closer to me that my body reacted to. I didn't know if it was because of our earlier spat, or if it was because he was directly responsible for changing me, but I was more attuned to him than the others. I felt a slight tingling sensation in the core of my bones. I relaxed back on the cushions and inhaled a deep cleansing breath; the smell of blood mixed with the scent of antiseptic and lilacs. Letting my breath out slowly, I could feel Teren approaching me. Just the act of him drawing nearer gave me goose bumps and my body surged with energy; I felt like I was vibrating.

He paused at the door. Wishing I could see through it, I glared at the stupid obstacle. I didn't know why he had stopped; I couldn't sense his intentions, only his location. It was frustrating to me that I didn't know if he felt this energy too. If he didn't, maybe he was just nervous to be near me. Wanting him to enter either way, I whispered, "Please come in. I need to see you."

He twisted the knob and I focused solely on the sounds coming from him, so I could try and block out the rest of the house. Even though I could still make out Jack helping Ben into a bed, Alanna and Imogen having a tearful conversation about husbands, and Halina tossing out suggestive one-liners, Teren's slight noises helped push them all back into a dull buzz in a corner of my brain. The sound of his strong hand twisting the brass knob, the creak of the wood frame as he pushed the door in, the rustle of his jeans as he stepped forward, the slow, deep breaths that he didn't need to take, but that he faked so often he did it as unconsciously as any living person, and my name, whispered off his tongue as he came into view.

The energy in my body came to a sharp point, and I gasped when I saw him. It was an odd sort of feeling, like how I'd imagine lovers reuniting in an airport terminal after months, or maybe even years of separation must feel. I had no idea if my physical reaction to him was just because of the emotional day and everything we'd gone through already, or if it was the rekindling in the air as I waited to tell him that he'd done nothing wrong and I wasn't angry. Or maybe we were uniquely bonded now, and we'd feel this electricity every time we were together.

Tears stung my eyes as the emotion in the room and the energy in my body mixed. Teren's face had the same sort of surprised, emotional look on it that mine did. He softly closed the door and his eyes, and then inhaled deep, almost like he was savoring the tension of reunion in the air, savoring the smell of us. I could sense it too. Even with all the other smells lingering in the room, like notes of a specific fragrance, I could pick out his. It was unexplainable. It was just a smell unique to him. Nothing on this earth compared. Nothing on this earth smelled as good, not even blood.

I was bristling with the need to touch him by the time he opened his eyes. Nearly ready to jump out of this luxurious-to-the-touch bed, I tossed back the covers at the same time that he blurred to my side. He scooted into the spot I'd just opened up for him. His hands were instantly on my face, his lips were instantly on my mouth.

The energy between us culminated when we connected: fiery, needy, unrestrained. Our heated kisses tapered as the feeling between us finally subsided to a dull roar in the background. It slowly returned to the more normal level of love we felt for each other. His lips eased on mine and it was only then that I noticed that his hand had drifted down my body to curl my leg around his hip, my fingers were locked in his hair, and somewhere along the way, I'd managed to pull my teeth up.

We pulled apart to look at each other and from down in the kitchen, I heard Halina's throaty chuckle. Swallowing, I tried to steady my too-fast breath. Teren's was fast as well as he searched my face. His gaze drifted over the wound on my neck, a wound that, until he'd looked at it, I hadn't even felt. I felt it now, and I rolled onto my back. My leg slid away from his hip as I moved.

He propped up unto an elbow and leaned over me with his brow creased. "I'm sorry, I just needed…to do that."

A laugh escaped me and I sucked in a quick breath as my neck throbbed. He laid a cool hand over the bandage and I sighed as his touch calmed the area. Meeting eyes with him, I gave him a small smile. "Don't be…I needed that too."

He leaned down to kiss my forehead. "I'm so sorry, Emma. Please believe me."

His eyes were down when he pulled back. I sighed, cupped his face, and carefully shook my head. "No, I'm sorry. You did what you had to do, to save us. It may or may not have worked, but you had to try." I gripped his face harder, making him raise his eyes to mine. "I love you so much, for fighting for us." Reaching up, I grabbed his hand from my neck and placed our fingers over my stomach. The twins reacted to our joint touch and we both smiled. "I love you so much, for fighting...for them."

Leaving his hand on my stomach, I stroked his cheek again. "This may not have been the path I expected, but, I want us to be in this together, not pushing each other away." The tears fell freely as the uncertainty of my future loomed ahead of me. "I don't know how much time I have, Teren. I don't want to spend it fighting. I love you too much, for that to be how we end."

The tears in his eyes fell too as he reached up to touch my hand on his cheek. Leaning over me he whispered, "I won't let anything happen to you, Emma. You or them." His voice quavered as the emotion behind it threatened to crush him. "If we don't have the answers, then we'll find those who do." His mouth set in a firm line as determination filled him.

I scrunched my brow, feeling like I was a step behind. "What? Who would know about this? Who would know if I'll be okay?"

"Other mixed vampires." He nodded after his statement, like it was really just as simple as that.

I blinked at him. *Mixed?* Up until that maniac had taken us, the family hadn't even known other mixed vampires existed; they'd thought they were the only ones. His revelation that they weren't, had been quite a shock to them, and their existence was surprising to full vampires, as that bastard who'd created this mess had pointed out. He'd obviously never seen anything like Teren. But somehow...we were supposed to find these secretive vamps in time to save the children's lives and mine? If they even could help us. Or would.

Teren's face didn't lose any of his determination as he watched my reaction. This was his hope. This was what he'd cling to, to save himself from despair. I swallowed. I wouldn't snatch his hope away. I wouldn't tell him he was grasping at straws. He needed this. "Okay," I said quietly. "What do we do?"

He relaxed and even smiled. I think he'd been prepared to have to convince me that this was a completely doable and realistic goal that he'd set for himself. Grabbing my fingers, he interlaced them. His thumb stroked my skin as he animatedly explained. "That man that killed me, Great-Gran kept all of his journals. She wanted to make sure he was working alone, and that no one would come searching for him." My eyes widened; I hadn't realized they'd looked into his life. Teren shook his head. "We can't find anything that says he wasn't, so we're pretty sure he was on his own." I nodded and swallowed again.

Teren automatically returned his hand to my neck and I realized I must have flinched when I'd nodded. He kept detailing his plan; he'd obviously done quite a bit of thinking about this in the past few days, when he'd been waiting around for me to die. "Great-Gran also wanted to know what he'd dosed me with, so she kept anything that looked like research." His eyes brightened along with his smile. "I think I can use his notes to find others." He shook his head, his eyes swimming with hope. "There has to be someone out there, like us, who's tried to turn a human. There just has to be. And I'll find them." He nodded, his jaw set.

I put my hand on his jaw, trying to ease the tension I felt there. "We'll find them, Teren. Together, remember?"

He briefly looked away and then looked back. "No, Emma. I'm sorry, but you have to stay here now."

I laughed, then realized he was serious and stopped. "What? No, I want to go with you. I want us to do this together."

He sighed and ran a hand down my hair. "Emma, baby, it's too dangerous. We don't know…what sort of people we'll find." He looked down. "I'm not risking your life like that. Not when I'm trying to save it."

"Then I don't want you to go. If it's dangerous…" My throat closed up on me and I couldn't finish my thought.

Teren sighed again as he looked over my face. I could see the strain of the last few days in his countenance and hated everything that had happened to our merry family, changing it completely. I suddenly wished our biggest problem was still the ex who remembered too much of him.

Finally, he said, "What choice do I have, Emma? I can't just sit back and not try and save you." I looked about to protest again and he held up his hand, cutting me off. "I won't go alone. I'll take someone with me." From downstairs I heard a flood of Russian and Teren chuckled. Magically knowing Russian wasn't something that was passed along with his blood, unfortunately, and I hadn't caught the comment. Teren smiled as he explained. "Great-Gran just volunteered her services."

I relaxed back into the pillows a bit with that news. Halina was strong, stronger than Teren, and as driven to save my children as we were. Plus she'd fight tooth and nail to keep Teren safe. As far as bodyguards went, she was a pretty good one.

Seeing my silent acceptance, Teren's face brightened. I smiled at seeing the hope there. It didn't ease the strain I saw underneath it, but it lightened the edges of it considerably. I wanted to let myself believe that he'd find our answers, that everything would be okay, but even with the madman's help, finding others like Teren seemed impossible to me. At least finding them in time seemed impossible.

I exhaled in an attempt to distract my mind from my pessimistic thoughts, and felt my teeth stubbornly drop back down. They slid into my lower lip and popped right through the tender skin. "Ow," I muttered, as I carefully sucked on my cut.

Teren gave me an odd, knowing grin as he pushed back a corner of my mouth to look at my tooth. He didn't seem at all weirded out by seeing fangs on me, now that I was clued into the fact that they were there, but I felt a little weirded out by him examining me. He dropped my lip and returned his hand to my stomach. "You need to be careful, those things are sharp."

I gave him as much of a lopsided grin as I could with my mouth that still felt foreign. "Well, I didn't exactly mean to do that. I suppose I'll get used to them. I hope I do okay at work…." I sighed and looked over his suddenly still shape as he lay beside me, propped up on his elbow. "What day is it anyway, Teren? How much work have I missed?"

Watching his reaction carefully, I wondered how angry Clarice was at me for missing even more work. I seriously hoped she didn't take it out on me by inundating me with records room work. My feet were starting to swell in the afternoons, and the thought of standing on them all day made them ache already.

Teren sniffed and looked down, speaking more into the sheets than at me. "It's Sunday. You only missed Friday."

I was relieved by that. The attack was on a Thursday night. If I somehow got through this with only one day missed, she might not can me. Feeling the dull throb at my neck return, I started to wonder how I'd explain the bite. I hadn't looked at it yet, but I was positive the wound was much more than two tiny fang pricks that a turtleneck would easily cover. I was pretty sure that bastard had used every chomper he had. My skin probably looked like a pit-bull had mauled me. Swell.

Teren still wasn't looking at me, and I thought some of his earlier guilt had crept back into his features. A bit of the anxious ice crept back into my stomach. "Teren, please tell me you called in for me on Friday?"

He peeked up at me from the corner of his eye. "I did."

I exhaled again. "Oh, good. I wouldn't want to get fired." I chuckled, but he didn't laugh with me. He bit his lip; that worried me a little. "What did you tell them? What's my story?" I was fairly certain he hadn't told them a creature of the night had bitten me.

Teren looked away again. I had the sudden image of a large hammer slowly lowering through the air. I wasn't sure why, but I was pretty sure I wasn't going to like what he was about to say. He sighed, confirming my suspicions. "I told them you were in a car crash."

I heard a gasp escape my lips as he looked up at me. Car crash seemed a little extreme for a neck wound. I supposed he had been under a lot of strain at the time, and I guess I could hide my neck with a brace. Not exactly flattering, but, effective. Teren looked over my face as he continued with, "I told them the crash put you into premature labor and the doctors were barely able to stop it." My eyes widened even farther as the tale he'd spun grew. I didn't see why he'd felt the need to expand on the lie. Wasn't simpler better? Looking nervous, Teren swallowed and finished his cover story. "I told them…the doctors put you on bed rest until the babies are born."

I felt that imagined hammer land squarely on my head.

"You what?" I yelled that, and my ears started ringing. Teren flinched and I was sure his ears were ringing too. I really I didn't need to be so loud now, but some things can't be helped. "They don't think I'm coming back? Why would you tell them that?" I managed in a more level tone. From where the vampires were still chit-chatting in the kitchen, I heard Halina mutter, "Here we go."

Teren sighed and put a hand on my cheek. "Because you can't go back, Emma. You have to stay here…at the ranch."

His eyes looked sad and sympathetic. He knew I liked my job and had goals of moving up in the company. Being kept from there for months? Well, I wasn't even sure I'd have a job to go back to. It wouldn't be the same one I'd left at any rate. Clarice would most likely replace me. I'd have to start over, in the mail room or something.

Feeling stubborn and childlike, I whispered, "You don't get to decide that for me."

He looked thoughtful for a moment, then said, "I didn't, you did."

Confused, I stared up at the ceiling. I didn't remember a thing over the past few days, and surely I'd remember basically throwing my career away. "I've barely been conscious. When did I agree to that?"

He smiled and a cool finger traced the edge of my cheek before twisting to grab a long piece of my dark hair. With a half-smile he said, "When you told me I was foolish for staying in San Francisco, around all those innocent people." I blinked at him and was about to start in on a response when he lost his small smile and shook his head. "The fact is, Emma, we don't know what's going to happen to you." He gave me a pointed look. "If you convert," he looked down, away from me, "which is what I'm hoping happens, if your body can't handle…"

He didn't finish that thought and looked back up at me. "You'll awake just as hungry as I did. You'll attack anything that moves." His small, wry smile returned as he twirled the lock of hair in his fingers. "And *you* are the one who convinced me that the safest place for a creature about to go through that kind of transformation, was here, at the ranch." His eyes looked beyond the room, as if he were taking in the land outside. "Surrounded by yummy cattle," he murmured.

I pursed my lips, annoyed. I didn't really have an argument for that, since it was sort of my argument in the first place. Me and my big mouth. I never once imagined when I'd first said it, that I'd be referring to my own situation later on down the road. Yeah, the shoe on the other foot thing? Don't like it.

His smile grew at my silence and his fingers trailed down the strand of hair before he let it drop. I could hear the individual fibers sliding over his skin. Teren sighed and his fingers shifted to my face; a light scent of grass was on the tips, like he'd been plucking it outside. "I know, I didn't like it either, but you were right and here is the safest place for you."

Knowing I'd sound foolish objecting, I tried to anyway. "But...I have doctor's appointments to keep and the hospital is so far away now." I knew I was spouting improbabilities. The odds of me surviving until my due date probably weren't that great, but still, I was first and foremost a first time mom, and I was a little worried about the whole "exiting" process. Doctors in white coats, with sterile equipment and vials full of drugs, were a very soothing thought. "I know you drive fast but—"

He tilted his head at me, his brow scrunched. "You...can't see doctors anymore, Emma. I'm sorry, I thought you'd see that right away. Your blood is mixed now, like mine, and it's just too risky. We can't let them examine you too closely. And really...a hospital birth was never going to happen. They would test the children's blood. I'm sorry. I thought you'd see that."

Truthfully, I had made that connection, but I'd pushed it out of my head almost immediately. Denial was a strong thing. And so was fear. "Can't see doctors? Can't go to a hospital? I'm about to have babies, Teren. How do you expect me to do that without doctors?" And loads of pain meds.

He smiled and ran his hand down my hair again in a soothing fashion, like he thought I was on the verge of hyperventilating. I heard supportive encouragement coming from both Alanna and Imogen, but I blocked it out and focused on the stubbled jaw of the man who, quite rightly, was keeping me from my building full of well-trained professionals. "You can do it, sweetheart." His grin turned a little wry. "And you'll do it the same way women have done it for thousands of years."

I was about to roll my eyes and tell him that he couldn't possibly understand the turmoil I was feeling over this new consequence of my attack, but he leaned down to kiss me, and my objection died. "Besides, all the women here have experience in baby delivery. You'll get all the help you need, right here."

I heard Alanna and Imogen agreeing with him, telling me that they'd take the very best care of me. Even Halina said everything would be fine. Of course, her concern was more for the infants in my womb than for my pain level. Thinking about having a child in my luxurious bed with the satin sheets that felt like liquid against my skin, made my chest tighten in anticipation. I was not a "natural" birth sort of girl.

"Can my mom be here? She wanted to be with me for the birth." Not that I was agreeing to any of this yet.

He slid his elbow down the silky sheet to rest his head on his arm. His face was directly in front of mine as I looked over at him. "Emma, I don't know about that. She can visit as often as she wants, of course, but the actual birth, may be…too much for her." I nodded, tears glistening in my eyes. Being like I was now, I had no idea what to expect from childbirth. Assuming I even made it that far. I guessed I really was stuck with vampire midwives.

He kissed my nose. "I haven't called her yet. If I told her you were in an accident, she'd rush right out here, and you needed time to…adjust before you saw her."

I sighed and looked down at his chest. "Oh." I looked back up. "Ashley?"

He nodded. "Ashley knows. I told her the truth. She is dying to come see you, but I asked her to stay away until you called her." I raised my eyebrow and he shook his head. "I didn't mention that you might not make it." He smiled sadly. "I painted it in the best light that I could for her."

I wondered how he'd painted being attacked by a vampire in a good light. He was either very vague or underplayed things a lot. "Does she know you gave me your blood?" I asked.

He shook his head. "I only told her I saved you, I didn't go into details. She didn't ask either, so I'm pretty sure she figured it out." He sighed, then kissed me again.

I swallowed a painful lump. My sister was probably going out of her mind with worry. I should call her right away. I wondered if Ashley had talked to Tracey for me, may be explained about me missing work. Maybe she even told Tracey that Hot Ben had been there, and had been very heroic. Maybe in the story, he had pulled me from the wreckage or something. Either way, Tracey was probably waiting for a phone call too.

I closed my eyes, overwhelmed by all the lies I'd have to tell soon. Eyes shut, I heard words around the house drifting to me. Hot Ben was snoring, sleeping it off. Jack was watching TV while Alanna and Imogen started making dinner. Imogen and Halina were talking about eating outside tonight. My mouth started watering at their detailed conversation. I felt my teeth growing longer and heard my heartbeat quicken in anticipation.

Teren's hand came up to my cheek, returning me to this room, with him. I opened my eyes, surprised to find my breath faster. He was smiling at me, and his eyes were sympathetic. "You'll get used to it," he whispered.

I nodded, both surprised and grossed out over how much my body wanted blood. Apparently my pregnancy hunger had shifted to this kind of nourishment as well. I supposed staying out of the city was a good idea after all. I didn't plan on biting anyone, ever, but the cravings in my body might try and convince me otherwise.

Shutting out as many of my enhanced senses as I could, I focused on Teren's calming, sky blue eyes. I could see flecks of gray in them that I'd never noticed before. As my heart and breath returned to normal, I started relaxing. Feeling at peace, I found I could will my teeth to retract. They moved slowly, and in my awkward mouth, I could hear the canines sliding against my gums and against the teeth next to them. I smiled when they were pulled in as far as I could get them, and I ignored how my jaw ached from having to create space for the new, longer teeth. Teren grinned at my normal smile and kissed me.

Our kiss started picking up a little and I heard Halina's chuckle before she and Imogen left the house. As Teren's tongue swept along mine, and I marveled that some things felt exactly the same, a stray thought pricked my brain. Pulling back, I playfully said, "So, are you sort of my father now? Do I call you Sire?" He grinned and I leaned in for another kiss. "Because that makes this a little creepy," I muttered between our lips.

Teren laughed and gently angled me to kiss me deeper. His cool palms rested on my neck, soothing me. "Husband will be fine," he chuckled.

One of his hands stayed on my wound, while the other trailed down my body. His leg started coming up over one of mine. I sighed and pulled him over, so the top half of him was over the top half of me; the bottom half just had way too much belly in the way for him to lie on. His hand still came down to cup my backside though as he pulled my leg over his hip again. My fingers tangled in his hair, and that earlier connection we'd shared started burning under the surface. I again wondered if that bond was unique to us, or if it was just a remnant of our terrible experience. While I thought about it, his hand traveled over my stomach.

One of the twins reacted to Teren's caress and kicked him so hard we both looked down. He laughed and rested his palm over them. They squirmed to get near him. I found I could hear their movements too. I closed my eyes, tuning out every other sense I had, and concentrated. It took a minute, but then I heard it—the faint, fluttery heartbeats, the same as at the doctor's office. I could hear them without any special equipment. I could hear the life flowing through their veins. It warmed my heart, and tears were in my eyes when I opened them.

Teren was watching me, his hand still on my stomach. "I can hear them," I whispered, a huge smile on my face. Thinking of what

Teren's blood may have done to them, I frowned. "What do you think happened to *them* in all of this? Do you think your blood…altered them in any way?"

Teren's hand rubbed my stomach and he shrugged, his face thoughtful. "I obviously don't know for sure…but I don't see why it would. Unlike you, they were never entirely human in the first place. My blood was already in their veins."

I nodded, feeling relieved by that. He smiled and leaned down to kiss me again. Before his lips touched mine, I whispered, "Take them." He pulled back, confusion clear on his face. I searched his eyes as I explained. "Whatever happens to me, if I die and convert, or die and just…die, take them."

He tilted his head, concern now clear too. "What?"

I reached up and cupped his cheek; a calm peaceful resolve flowed through me as I did. "Take them out of me, and do whatever you can to save them."

He shook his head. "Emma, it's too early. They won't survive and we can't take them to a hospital, not with their blood."

I could see that he didn't want to think about this yet. I needed him too though. We needed every possibility covered, and the chance that I wouldn't make it to full term was too great to ignore. "I know I'm asking you to do something terrifying, something that you know nothing about. And I know it's an exposure risk, for them and for you, if you take them to get help. So all I can ask from you is that you and your family try and save them. I trust whatever you all decide is best, but promise me, that no matter what happens, you'll take them out of me. Promise me that you'll at least try. That's *my* deathbed request." I moved my hand to cover Teren's on my stomach. "Don't let them die inside of me, Teren. Give them a chance…please."

He looked down at our hands resting over the bulge of our children. His eyes were wet when he looked back up at me. "I will, I promise. I love you, wife."

I smiled, knowing that it may not make any difference, they may not make it anyway, none of us might, but at least he would try and save them. "And I love you, husband."

Chapter 13 – Adjustments and Constants

Teren stayed cuddled in bed with me. He pulled me onto his chest and I wrapped my arms underneath his cool body. He tucked one of his hands under my aching neck, soothing me, then he ran the other down my hair, calming me. As we embraced in that plush setting, I tried to forget the many uncertainties in our future and instead I focused on my one constant—him.

Closing my eyes, I memorized all of the markers that made him unique. Most of the ones from my human senses, I already knew—the dark hair, pale eyes, coarse stubble, deep voice, cool skin—but I found that my other senses could pinpoint him even more accurately. Besides the odd sensation of feeling his location in my head even when he was lying directly beneath me, I could also smell the way the world danced across his skin. The different fragrances mixed, mingled, and retreated from his own masculine scent. The cologne smell I'd always associated with him was more distinct as well. I could almost taste the different notes in it. It made my mouth water.

I could hear his slow, easy breath between the deep words he was telling me—words of love and devotion and encouragement. I ignored the words themselves and listened to the timbre, the feeling he inlaid into every syllable. As odd as it sounded, I could feel love, like it was some physical thing and not an intangible object. His words rumbled deep in his chest as he spoke, and the rise and fall of his lungs were a steady rhythm that I found myself matching.

Peeking my eyes open, I looked up at him. I watched the lamps in the room create a band of reflected light in his dark hair, and noticed that the shade was different to me now. I could see the varying degrees of black in it—some of it so dark, it almost crossed into blue, other parts so light, it almost looked brown. It was nothing pure human eyes would ever notice; to them, his hair looked one solid color. It was fascinating. I drifted over his sculpted face, easily seeing the bone structure beneath it. He was strong, masculine, profoundly attractive and, I could see now, perfectly symmetrical. My eyes drifted over his eyes that were watching me as he spoke. The gray flecks I'd noticed before were still there, still clear to me, only now, I could see a pattern in the right one; it sort of looked like a small clover. It was beautiful and I smiled at seeing it.

He smiled as well as he watched me take him in. My eyes drifted down to his lips—full, perfect, one edge curled up into a small smirk, hinting at the playful attitude inside of him. I watched those lips form words and phrases, watched the tongue enunciate sounds that could have been in Russian, for all the attention I was giving them.

He swallowed naturally during a break, and my eyes flicked down at hearing the sound. I glanced over the slight stubble he kept over his jaw line, dark, but lighter than his hair, making him constantly look as if he'd spent a long weekend wrapped in soft sheets, too preoccupied with other things to worry about shaving. It was hot.

He swallowed again and I continued on down to watch his throat move. I took in his neck while he talked, the way he turned and adjusted, the way the air crept up from his lungs, making his throat bob. I could hear the light breath on its journey and I smiled again.

Then I noticed a vein at the base of his neck move. It startled me, and I focused on it. It was a thick vein, full of blood that I had to imagine was as cool as his body. It popped away from his skin, the same as all large veins did on humans, but I was a bit dumbfounded by it all. Experimentally, I took a finger and pressed down on it. It gave way and then bounced back. The room silenced as Teren, maybe curious of my curiosity, stopped speaking.

He shifted his neck and the vein shifted as well, sinking away somewhere deeper in his skin, where I couldn't see it. "What are you doing?" he whispered, running a hand down my hair.

I peeked up at his amused face and then back down to find that vein again. "I never noticed before, but your veins are just like mine."

His body lightly rumbled under mine as he laughed. "No, you probably wouldn't have noticed that. You weren't as focused on blood before." I peeked up at him and he grinned. "Why are you surprised? Of course I still have veins."

I gave him a wry smile and rolled my eyes. "I know that." I looked back down as he shifted again and the vein reappeared.

Gently, I stroked it with my finger. Focusing my senses, I could feel the blood moving under his skin, I even imagined that I could hear it surging through his body. "It's moving," I muttered, mystified.

He laughed again and brought his hand to my back, pulling me into him. "Of course it is. Did you think my blood was stagnant? Just pooling at my feet? Or maybe suspended…like Jell-O?" He laughed again, and I could tell my ignorance on the subject really amused him.

I glared when I looked back up at him. "Well, yeah, actually." I furrowed my brows. "You don't have a pumping heart, how does your blood circulate?"

Smiling, he ran a finger down my cheek. "I'm a vampire, Emma. Don't try and apply the rules of human anatomy to me." I gave him a blank look and he laughed again. "I don't know how. I haven't exactly dissected a vampire to find out. But, something in our blood keeps it moving. We don't need a circulatory system; our blood takes care of its own." He cocked his head, considering. "I think that's one of the problems with being mixed, having that kind of blood along with a heartbeat." He looked at me and shrugged. "The two are constantly battling each other; the vampiric blood wanting to move on its own, at its own fast pace, the rest of the body wanting a slower, more relaxed rhythm."

I grinned at the image that popped into my head. "Like an insolent teenager, battling its parents." I stopped grinning when I realized that my body was fighting with itself now, too.

He sighed as he looked over my changed expression. "Yeah, something like that." He raised my jaw and made me look at him. "But in answer to your implied question, yes, it moves." A thought occurred to him, and he gave me a devilish smile. "How else did you think I could still…perform?"

I blushed and laughed, smacking his chest as I settled down to stare at that fascinating artery again. He laughed underneath me and held me tight.

I pictured that blood, just under the surface and thought of the blood I'd downed earlier. I wondered if Alanna would bring more with the dinner I could hear her finishing up in the kitchen. It surprised me a little that I actually wanted her to. Of course, what happened next surprised me even more.

As I watched that flowing vein under his skin, I found my lips moving towards it. Teren resumed talking, explaining other theories of vampirism that he had, but that vein commanded all of my attention. I brought my lips to his cool skin and felt the flow against my flesh. It didn't pulse like my blood, it was just a constant stream, a river, surging under the surface. A never-ending loop of fresh, cool, refreshing blood. My tongue came out to lightly stroke his skin and he instantly stopped talking again. I think he stopped breathing too, but I was too fascinated to pay close enough attention to know for sure.

I pressed down on the vein with my tongue. Even dead, his skin was still slightly salty to me. The vein popped right back up when I released it. I groaned a little at the pleasing sensation, and my teeth instantly snapped back down into place. My tongue had been in the way this time, and I poked right into it. Wincing in pain, I pulled away from his skin. "Ow, damn it."

Teren rubbed my back, but he didn't laugh at me injuring myself again. Instead he looked at me with an eyebrow raised. His eyes took in my extended fangs and he furrowed his brows.

What?" I asked cautiously, feeling a little stupid that I'd basically been thinking about snacking on him. Hadn't I just sworn I'd never do that?

He seemed to know what I'd been about to do too. "Were you going to bite me?" His voice came out amused and concerned.

I looked down, embarrassed. "No, I don't know…maybe." I looked back up at him. "I wouldn't have, not without asking you." Not that I wanted to, not really anyway.

Teren shook his head, brushing aside my concern. "I heal fast, Emma, you wouldn't have hurt me. I'm just…" He rubbed my back, looking worried.

"What?" I asked again, thinking I'd almost done something really wrong. "Do vampires not feed on each other? Not that I want to," I quickly added.

He shook his head again. "Sometimes they do. Great-Gran on occasion likes a little… But that's not what I'm…" He stopped again and bit his lip.

I felt tears stinging my eyes. I was doing something wrong, I just didn't know what. I wish he'd just tell me what faux-pas I was making. It wasn't really my fault anyway. I'd only had a day to really get used to these cravings. He was born this way, used to it from day one.

Teren's finger lifted my jaw when he noticed the emotion in my eyes. "Hey, you're okay, Emma." He smiled warmly at me. "I'm not angry at you. It's okay if you want to bite me." He raised an eyebrow and gave me a devilish grin. "I think I'd even like it."

I ignored his expression and felt myself pouting. "But you're concerned…why?"

He looked down for a second and then met my eyes again. "Your cravings. They just seem more advanced, like when I was close to…" He stopped talking as his eyes moistened.

I exhaled, understanding. "You think I'm close to a changeover, because of how much blood interests me?" He nodded, swallowing heavily. I looked down, absorbing that. One of the twins jostled me while I was thinking, and I grinned and looked back up at him. "It's them, Teren."

Looking confused, he seemed like he was about to ask who, when he stopped and stared at my stomach. Understanding, he smiled. "All of my cravings have ramped up because of them—ice cream, pasta, hot chocolate…"

"Sex," he interrupted, that grin on his face again.

I rolled my eyes and hit his chest again. "And now, blood," I finished, ignoring him. His smile relaxed into an easy one. "It's not because I'm close to dying, it's just because of them." I said it matter-of-factly, like somehow saying it firmly enough, would make it true. But the truth was, we had no idea. All of this was new territory for the whole family.

Teren nodded and looked reassured, but my new vision could tell that he wasn't. But he only encouraged me to rest against his chest, and continued stroking my hair while he talked to me about things I could do around the ranch so that I didn't get too bored.

This was just something we'd both pretend to believe. It was better than the alternative.

I felt Alanna approaching a while later. Felt her, heard her, and smelled her and the dinner she carried. No more sneaking up on this girl. Out of courtesy, she knocked before entering our room. She smiled at Teren and me, snuggling together in bed, and then set a tray of food—soup and a grilled cheese sandwich, sick person food—on the night stand. The tray also held a glass of milk and right beside it, two tall travel mugs that I knew were full of warm blood. My fangs were still out. They extended a bit more as I watched her pick up the two steaming drinks. She handed one to me while Teren helped me sit upright. Still a little grossed out, but wanting it too much to care anymore, I started downing it immediately. Teren and Alanna both chuckled, and I paused to watch them watch me; Alanna hadn't even gotten around to handing Teren his yet. She smiled and urged me to continue. "It's all right, Emma," she encouraged.

Blushing, I continued drinking, more slowly, and Teren smiled before taking a sip of his. His fangs were out as well now as he thanked his mother. She rumpled his hair before wishing us both a good night. Teren turned back to me and smiled widely around his mug. I didn't know what pleased him more, being with me, or drinking what I now understood to be the best damn stuff on earth with me.

"I can't believe we're drinking blood together." I laughed once and shook my head, noting that my neck felt even better as the blood acted as a natural pain reliever.

He grinned and tilted back his cup. "Think of the possibilities now. When your neck is healed, we could even paint each other's bodies with it, then lick it off." He laughed, so I knew he was joking, but just the thought made me stop and stare at him. His eyes took in my expression and he stopped laughing, he stopped breathing too. That made me giggle as I sipped my drink.

I sighed as I finished my cup. "I can't believe I enjoy this. I can't believe I'm a vampire…sort of."

He regarded me with curious interest as he finished his. "You've never thought about it? Really?"

I sighed wistfully, wishing I had more blood as I handed the cup to him. He put them both on the nightstand, then wrapped an arm around me. I leaned into his side and looked up at him. "Well, of course I've thought about it. I mean, you can't exactly date a vampire and not think about it." He smiled, a little sadly, and I continued. "But, after the way you reacted when I asked for Ashley, I just sort of took it off the table and stopped thinking about it. Plus…I didn't want to be tempted to kill my friends and family. That's not cool."

He let out a hearty laugh as he hugged me. Kissing my hair, he muttered, "I think you can handle it."

I heard Alanna laugh, too, and heard Jack ask her what was funny. While I heard her repeat my comment, I pulled away from Teren to give him a serious look. "I'm sorry about asking you to change my sister. I'm sorry I begged you to bite her, to drain her blood when you didn't want to. That was wrong of me to try and make you do that. It was wrong of me to even ask, and I apologize."

He sighed and shook his head. "You had a right to ask. I'm sorry I overacted. We just…we don't do that…normally."

He looked down, and I put my hand under his chin to bring his gaze back to mine. "I know. I get that now. I love you." He nodded and kissed me. I looked over his face as I pulled back. "Do you want to tell me what happened?"

He understood my vague question about the night he gave me his blood and looking at the sheets, he shook his head. "No, not really."

I sighed and ran a finger down his cheek. "Will you anyway?" I whispered my words, but they were loud and clear to my ears.

He looked over at the tray of food Alanna had brought in. Sighing softly, he reached over and grabbed a plate piled high with grilled cheese sandwich halves. Handing it to me, he started telling me about what was probably the worst night of his life.

"I was by your side before you even made it to the ground." He stared at the sheets again. "But I still wasn't fast enough." I paused in picking up a still-warm sandwich, to put an encouraging hand on his chest. He glanced over at me and sort of smiled. Sighing again, he laid his head back and shifted his gaze to the ceiling. I noted the silence in the house as Alanna listened to her son speak his pain. "Ben had already gotten him. Great-Gran pulled him off of you, and all I saw was blood. So much blood. His, yours. It was awful. Everyone was talking to me at the same time, and everything seemed so loud."

A shudder passed through me as I replayed the event in my head. "Great-Gran was telling me that we had to get rid of the body." He looked over at me. "At first, I didn't know which body she meant. But then I heard your heart—it was so faint. She picked up the vampire and blurred away, telling me to get you out of sight. Ben was yelling for me to get you to a hospital. He kept pulling at me, trying to get me off of you." He shook his head as his eyes watered. "But I was holding in your blood. My hands were on your neck, and I was holding in what little blood was left."

He ran a hand down his face. Food momentarily forgotten, I set my plate on my lap. Kissing his shoulder, I whispered that I loved him. He peeked over at me, seemingly comforted. "You started to shake, so I picked you up and we got into the back of my car. I yelled at Ben to drive and then…"

He paused, like he really didn't want to confess this part. Since I already knew it, had already pictured it in my head, I nodded at him and urged him to continue. He swallowed before he did. "While he drove, your heartbeat started stuttering. All I could think was that my blood heals fast now, maybe it would heal *you*." He shook his head. "I wasn't thinking that it would change you. I just…I wasn't thinking." He swallowed again while a tear ran down my cheek. He must have been so scared.

"It's okay, Teren." I rested my head on his shoulder. "Tell me."

He exhaled a shaky breath, like he was trying not to break down. "I tore my wrist open, put the wound over your lips. You wouldn't drink it at first. It just kept collecting in your mouth. I didn't know what to do. I begged you…and eventually, you swallowed it." He smiled and then frowned as he looked down at my untouched plate of food. "Ben went nuts when he saw what I was doing. He nearly stopped the car, but I…growled at him, told him to drive to the ranch." He pursed his lips. "I may have told him I'd kill him if he didn't." He looked up at me. "But I knew I couldn't take you to a hospital, not with my blood inside of you." I nodded and he looked away.

"I didn't know how much you needed, or if it was even doing anything. I wasn't thinking about anything other than *more*, you needed more." He closed his eyes. "I had to keep reopening my wrist, it kept healing. I was making myself really weak, but I couldn't stop, your neck hadn't healed." I grabbed his hand, his wrist. He opened his eyes and watched me as I examined the skin. It was perfect, flawless. I grabbed the other one, but it was the same. He was completely healed. "I've never been so scared, Emma. Not even when I died. I've never been that scared in my life."

He didn't continue, and I thought that was the end of the story. Then he looked up from where his wrist was resting in my hands. His eyes were wet again. "I fed you the entire way back to the ranch. I only stopped when Mom pried me off of you." He swallowed. "I think if she hadn't, I would have given you every drop I had." Another tear dropped to my cheek at his admission. I wanted to say something, but he interrupted me with a smile. "It was only when Mom picked you up, that I realized your heart was beating steadily again. And when we looked, your neck wasn't healed, but it wasn't bleeding much anymore." A long, languid smile broke over his face. "My blood didn't do what I'd expected it to do, but it kept you alive. It kept you all alive."

His eyes drifted to my stomach, to the twins resting under my plate of cooling food. I smiled and brought a hand to his cheek. "Have I ever told you how amazing you are?"

He grinned and I leaned forward to kiss him for a few long moments. I was glad I was unconscious for that the attack, and didn't have that memory haunting me. I wished someone could take the memory from Teren. I couldn't imagine how scared he'd been. Then again, I'd watched him die, almost twice. Maybe I could imagine his terror all too easily.

After taking a few moments to collect myself, I dug into my human food. My comparatively bland human food. Not that it was bad; it wasn't. Alanna was amazing in the kitchen. But it wasn't what my body really wanted. The human part of me still needed it though, so I ate everything in front of me. Teren sat behind me while I ate, playing with my hair or massaging my shoulders. He didn't seem to want to leave me alone. I understood. I didn't want him to leave me alone either.

But eventually, he had to. Eventually it was Monday morning and he had to go back to work. He knelt by my side of the bed, concern clear in his face. "Hey, I have to go. It's going to take me longer to get to and from work now, but I'll be here, just as soon as I can." I nodded and Teren leaned over to kiss me. "I'm going to swing by the house and get some stuff for us." He looked down, a little worried again. "I need you to talk to your mom today, if you don't mind." Confusion scrunched my expression, and he explained, "I don't know how long we're going to be here, so I thought I'd leave Spike with her." He gave me a wry grin. "Since she loves him so much."

I nodded. Mom would need to know why she was watching the dog for so long. I sighed, not looking forward to that conversation. She'd want to move out here to the ranch when I told her I was on bed rest. That would put a strain on the vampires though. And on me too. I'd have to convince Mom that there were plenty of people waiting on me, and she needed to stay in town for work, and now, the dog. That would brighten the experience for her. I smiled and told Teren I'd call her this afternoon, then let him know what she said. He grinned and kissed me goodbye. He lingered for a much longer kiss than we generally said goodbye with, and I tried to block out the feeling that he was saying "goodbye" with his goodbye…just in case.

After he left, I stretched out on the bed. My body was still a little stiff, and still felt really odd, but overall, I felt better. The ache on my neck was at a manageable level. The human and vampire sides of me were both working together to fix the damaged skin. My fingers went to the wound. The rustling of the bandage was loud in my ear, and I had the sudden desire to shower, dress, and try to appear normal, since I didn't feel normal at all.

Bracing myself, I slowly sat up; the bed compressed a bit under my weight. My head swam for a fraction of a second and then cleared. I heard Jack and Alanna talking quietly downstairs as Alanna made him something to eat. In one of the side buildings, I could hear Hot Ben snoring away. No other noises intruded on me, but I could sense where Halina was tucked away for the day and where Imogen was being deathly silent. I remembered that Teren didn't breathe or move much when he slept, so I figured that was probably what Imogen was doing.

Wanting a shower, I slowly stood up. Well, that was my intention anyway, but my desire to be clean was so strong, since my sensitive skin could feel the layer of grime on it, that I blurred to my feet. I'd never moved at vampiric speed before, and really, I hadn't been expecting that side effect. It completely took me off guard, and not even having time to curse, I overshot my balance and crashed to the ground.

"Emma? Are you all right?" Alanna called from the dining room.

Blushing, and grateful that at least no one had seen that, I muttered, "Yeah, I'm fine…just clumsy."

I carefully sat up on my knees and then stood up. Alanna's concerned voice filtered up to me. "Oh, okay. Be careful. You need to concentrate on how quickly you move. Everything for you will take a concentrated effort for a while, but then it will be natural."

I nodded, then remembering that she couldn't actually see me, I thanked her. Great, just what a pregnant woman with a major case of space-brain needed—to have to concentrate really hard on everything I did. I had a feeling I'd be falling over a lot for a while. With my mind focused on every muscle contraction in my body, I slowly walked into the bathroom.

Alanna's voice followed me. "Are you hungry? I can bring you up some breakfast."

I walked over to the mirror and sighed at my reflection. I had the worst case of bed-head I'd ever seen. My thick, wavy locks were one big snarl. The dark circles under my eyes made it seem like I hadn't slept in days, my lip was swollen from where I'd pierced myself yesterday, and the bandage on my neck was so huge, it was comical. There was a slight red tinge seeping through it, and my stomach growled and my fangs dropped down. Luckily, they didn't pierce anything this time. Staring at my teeth, I focused on pulling them back up. It was more difficult than you'd think. They resisted, but, like purposefully contracting a muscle, I eventually made them hide again.

I sighed as I answered Alanna. "I'm going to attempt a shower, then I'll come down and join you. Wish me luck," I muttered softly.

I heard her faint laughter. "Good luck."

I turned on the shower and adjusted the knob until the temperature was just how I liked it. Walking back to the mirror, I wondered if sunlight would be an issue for me. Teren had told me once that his family had the same reaction to light after their conversions as before. I'd been sequestered in our room here at the ranch for days. I hadn't been in direct sun yet. But I took it as a good sign that I wasn't suddenly Halina's roommate in her lightproof dungeon. Our bedroom had heavy, beaded curtains but it was nowhere near as light-resistant as Halina's pad. Or Imogen's dark room, for that matter. Plus, neither Teren nor Alanna had mentioned anything about the sun. I also took that as a good sign. I didn't know if I could handle never seeing daylight again.

Returning to the mirror, I slowly tore off the bandage covering my wound. It stung where it pulled away from my skin, and I paused. Taking a deep breath, I let my control over my muscles relax and I ripped the material off lightning-quick. I hissed in a sharp breath and clasped my hand over the surge of pain. Finger by finger I removed my palm. The wound was just as horrific as I'd imagined, and it was days old now—red, raw, blood-encrusted skin, with a distinct oval shape that was obviously from a mouth. Twin circular holes were at the top, right over my jugular, but his remaining teeth had gouged deep into my flesh. The top and bottom edges were ripped ragged from where he'd dug in. He'd practically torn out a chunk out of my skin to get to the blood beneath. It had been a grotesque injury. I could see a couple places where someone had sewn me up with a stitch or two. The stitches themselves were pulled out, but the skin was puckered around the area. I knew I'd have a permanent scar there.

Anger surged through me as I ran a finger along the bumpy skin. Prick vampire. In my irritation, I lost control of my teeth and they crashed back down. Too irritated to do anything about it, I left them down. Mad, I jerked off my clothes and stepped into the shower.

The warm water calmed me down and I was able to tuck my fangs away again while I was dressing. With the wounds cleaner, they weren't quite as bad, although they were still not pleasant to look at. I left them uncovered and fluffed out my hair to partially hide them. As I took in my refreshed appearance, I felt a little better, and now I was starving. I moved to the door, but let myself do it a little too fast and stumbled as I ran into the knob. Really grateful that Teren wasn't witnessing my awkwardness, I opened the door and carefully walked down the elaborate staircase that led into the entryway. Not wanting to fall down the stairs, I deliberately focused hard on every single step.

I hit the bottom right as Hot Ben walked into the room. I smelled him before I saw him; he did *not* smell good. I wrinkled my nose at the stench of scotch and vomit wafting from him. He didn't look much better. His eyes were bloodshot, and his highlighted hair was sticking up on one side and flat on the other. His clothes were rumpled. They were obviously the ones he'd fallen asleep in, or passed out in, yesterday. His face, although still sculpted and gorgeous, was pale and slightly green.

He looked up at me when I stepped off the last stair. I was smiling over the fact that I hadn't tumbled down them. "Hey," he whispered.

I wanted to hold my breath at the smell on his. "Hi, Ben. How are you doing?"

He gave me an ironic smile as he pointed at my neck. "Shouldn't I be asking you that?"

I shrugged and hid my wound a little better; I didn't want to freak him out even more. His eyes locked onto my scar though and something in his visage changed. Staring at where I'd nearly been killed made him stand a little taller. His blue eyes shifted back to mine and his entire demeanor seemed more focused than I'd seen in a while.

"I'm really glad you're okay, Emma. I can't imagine if you'd…" He shook his head and swallowed. "I've been sort of handling things…poorly," he looked down and then back up at me, "but that changes, starting now." He tilted his head at me. "I've caught bits and pieces of what's going on. I don't really understand it, but I understand that you're still in danger, and so are your kids." His eyes flashed to my stomach as I automatically put a hand on them. He looked back up at me, his face solemn. "I want to help. Whatever you guys need."

That surprised me. I sort of figured that Ben would have been wiped by now. It was shocking that he hadn't been yet. And now, here he was, offering to remember for even longer. I swallowed and walked over to him. Carefully, so I didn't choke him as my high emotions threatened to bubble over, I put my arms around his neck and gave him a hug. "Thank you, Ben."

Wrapping his arms around me in a friendly way, he held me back. "You're welcome. I only wish I could have stopped…"

He sighed and I pulled back. His grieved eyes were staring at my neck again. "Hey, even Teren wasn't fast enough," I said. Squatting down, so I could make him look me in the eye, I added, "Don't beat yourself up, okay?" Nodding, Ben grinned, and his whole face lightened.

We separated, and I clapped his shoulder so I could use him to slow my footsteps while we walked to the kitchen together. "I can't believe you got him," I said, shaking my head. "You staked a vampire."

Ben looked over at me walking beside him. "I know. Frankly, I can't believe it either." A small, confident smile lit his lips. "It actually feels pretty good to know I can defend myself."

"Good." I gave him a meaningful glance. "Are you done with the drinking then?" He looked down sheepishly and nodded. I laughed, feeling lighter than I had all morning. "Good, because you smell really bad."

He looked up at me, embarrassed. "Sorry."

I teasingly bumped his shoulder as we entered the dining room. A bright ray of sunlight flashed upon my hand and I cringed…but felt nothing. Relaxing, I laughed again. "Don't worry about it." Ben helped me sit in a chair, then took the one beside it. I watched him sit down; a small smile was on his lips as he nodded over the table at Jack. "You know how you could help me the most, Ben?" I said.

He looked over at me with his brow furrowed, but his jaw set. I had the feeling he'd agree to whatever I asked of him. I smiled at my upcoming statement. "You can call Tracey," I said softly.

He looked sheepish again. "Yeah, I know. I owe her...so many explanations." I opened my mouth to warn him, but he quickly shook his head. "I won't tell her about Teren, or you, but I need to explain myself somehow." He shrugged. "I'll come up with something. I'll call her today."

I grinned and rubbed his back. "Good, because she loves you, you know?"

He smiled. "I know." He looked up as Alanna flitted into the room with a plate of food for Jack. "I love her too," he murmured. He tore his gaze away from Alanna kissing her husband and looked back at me. "And now I know I can protect her." His eyes intensified with his words. "I won't let anything touch her."

Smiling, I nodded. Somehow, scaredy-cat Ben now sounded exactly like Teren. Through our bond, I couldn't sense exactly where my husband was, just his general location. He was somewhere to my left. Miles and miles away to my left. It was a surprisingly lonely feeling having him that far from me, and I was a little amazed that I wanted to sense him closer. I almost ached with the need of it, like I wouldn't feel whole again until our bond was more closely connected. I wondered if he felt that way too.

Hot Ben left a little after breakfast, saying he wanted to clean up and surprise Tracey at work by taking her out to lunch. I wished I could be there to see the look on her face when he showed up. I imagined her struggling between tears and anger—things had been tense between them for a while now. But I was pretty sure Tracey would melt like butter for Ben. It would just take a little effort, and a lot of fanciful tales, then their relationship would be back on track. Hot Ben was the only guy Tracey had let herself fall in love with, the only one she hadn't pushed away with superficial excuses. Regardless of the strain lately, she'd take him back simply because she couldn't *not* be with him. I was immensely grateful that Ben was a good guy, and that his secrets were nothing near what Tracey had been afraid of.

I found myself passing the time by being on the phone. I had a surprising number of calls to make. Settling into a comfortable chair in one of the libraries in the main house, I called my doctor's office first, to cancel every appointment I had. I hated to do it, I wanted to go to them, but Teren was right, I couldn't let them test me anymore. I was just going to have to trust that everything was going smoothly. At least I could hear the twins now; I could keep an ear out for any odd changes. Not that I'd be able to do anything about it, if something did go wrong.

Pushing aside my fears, and my abhorrence at the thought of giving birth, literally, the old fashioned way, I told the receptionist that I was having an at home birth at my in-laws place, and I had found a clinic closer to their location. She urged me to come see them before the births, just to be on the safe side, but I reassured the girl that there were a couple of midwifes here and I'd be just fine. When I hung up the phone, Alanna confirmed that I would be well taken care of. I glanced through the wall to where I could sense her in the living room and thanked her. I was not excited about the prospect though.

After the doctor, I called my sister. She interrogated me for fifteen minutes on the details of what had really happened. Apparently, Teren had been really vague when he'd explained things to her. It had taken all of her will power to not rush out and see me; Teren's warning that I needed time to adjust was the only thing that had given her pause. With a heavy sigh and tears in my voice, I proceeded to tell her exactly how I'd nearly died, and exactly how Teren had saved my life.

Only silence answered me. "Ash?"

More silence, but I could hear shifting in the background and thought she was pacing. I could even hear her heart pounding, through the phone. Finally she said, "He made you a vampire?"

I really wasn't sure how to answer that. "Um…well…"

She didn't let me finish. "How could he do that to you, to the kids? How could he condemn you to that life?"

I sighed, momentarily thankful that I'd never mentioned my crazy plan to condemn *her* to that life. "What choice did he have, Ash? Watch us die? You know Teren. He's not capable of just sitting there and watching without trying to help me. Not after everything we've been through." I said that last part quietly and heard my sister sniffle at the memory.

She was silent a moment more and then sighed. "I know. I'm not angry at him. I guess, I just wish that hadn't happened. I mean, what happens to you now?"

Even though she couldn't see it, I shrugged. "We don't know. I'm still mostly human right now, like Teren used to be." I paused, considering. "Actually, I seem to be exactly like Teren was, back when he was alive."

She brightened and I could hear her smile through the phone. "Oh, well that's not so bad. You'll just have to hide the fangs and not suck on any cows around people." She laughed and I heard the rustle of her sitting, her heart started calming too.

I closed my eyes. Part of me wanted to let her keep her fantasy version of my new life, the one where everything about me, pretty much stayed the same. Another part of me didn't want to hold back the awful truth of what I was really facing. Eventually, that part won out. "Ashley, it's not that simple."

She stopped laughing. "What do you mean?"

I hated that I had to cause another person I loved worry. Imogen upstairs offered kind words of encouragement. Alanna told me she loved me. With a deep inhale, I prepared to jolt my sister's world, again. "Do you remember *all* of what Teren went through, how his human body couldn't handle the strain of being mixed...?" I let my voice trail off, hoping my sister understood what I was getting at. I didn't want to have to say it.

She gasped and I heard her heart miss a beat. She understood. "You're going to die?" Her voice hitched as she said it. I was about to tell her everything would be fine, when she repeated louder, "You're going to die!"

Tears were in my eyes as I listened to my sister start to cry. "Ash…don't cry. It will be fine. I'll come back, just like Teren." I really didn't know if that would happen, but I couldn't leave my sister without any hope. I just couldn't do that. She needed to know the truth, but in the broadest sense of the term. She didn't need to worry about the details. There were enough of us worrying already.

My sister saw right to the problem though. "What about the babies? What if you die before they're ready?"

Before I could stop it, a sob escaped me. "I don't know…we just don't know." I sobbed into the phone while Ashley sobbed on her end. I was just wishing I could hold my sister as we both cried, when the library door swished open and Alanna scooped me into her cool embrace. Still clutching the phone to my ear, I hugged her back. Alanna whispered that everything would be fine, that none of them would stop looking for an answer, and I relayed the sentiment to my sister.

With sighs and hiccups and a promise to not let Mom know anything was wrong with me, aside from the doctor-ordered bed rest, we said our goodbyes. I clicked off the phone and continued to hold Alanna, grateful for her comfort. She soothingly stroked my back and kissed my head, then she confessed that Imogen and Halina had spent all last night, pouring over the madman's journals.

I pulled back and blinked away tears. "They did?" Hope filled me that maybe they'd found an answer already.

Alanna sighed and brushed aside a lock of my hair. "Yes. Grandma has looked through it before, but not with the same…intent." She raised an eyebrow at me and I nodded. No, things were much different now. Things were much more serious. Alanna nodded as she watched me, then she frowned. "They haven't found any leads yet." I frowned as well and Alanna brought a palm to my cheek. "We won't stop looking. We'll find something."

I nodded, then Alanna kissed my forehead again. When she left the room, I continued on with my difficult phone calls.

My mother was next and just as I'd suspected, she wanted to spend every long, boring moment sitting in a chair beside my bed. I told her over and over that Imogen and Alanna had experience being midwifes, since they had helped their older sisters deliver children, also part of the cover story. I also told her that they had the free time to wait on me. My mother had a nine-to-five job and bills to pay. She couldn't just drop everything for me. She protested, vehemently, and then I asked if she could help us out by watching Spike. That gave her pause. I told her the girls here were allergic to dogs—since I couldn't exactly tell her that Halina had a sweet tooth for them. Not that she would do that to Teren, but no need to tease her with Spike being under foot all of the time. I begged Mom, telling her it would really help us if we knew he was being taken care of.

After long pauses and exaggerated sighs, Mom finally agreed to take him. Honestly, with Ashley moved out, I think my mom was getting a bit lonely. While she was worried about me, I think my news had just made her day. Mom asked for details on the accident, which I had to have Alanna fill me in on before I could tell her. The story was nothing too dramatic, it mainly involved us getting rear ended hard enough to jumpstart my labor. Mom asked if I'd been hurt, and I told her my neck hurt a bit, which was true. We finally said our goodbyes, and Mom assured me that she'd be up often, especially when I got closer to my due date.

I didn't say anything to that. I couldn't think that far ahead, not without crying, or panicking, or both.

I took a break after that, to have a light, blood-filled lunch with Alanna in the kitchen while Jack took care of ranch stuff out in the fields. She flitted outside to help him throughout the day, but she had to take breaks from the sun if it was too nice out. Today was sunny and bright, a beautiful spring-is-just-around-the-corner day, so she'd been spending a lot of time indoors.

We talked about inconsequential stuff while we ate. Alanna seemed to understand that I'd had enough tough conversations already, and I really didn't want to have any more. I thanked her for the sandwich and the glass of fresh blood, and then I made my way back to the library to make even more hard phone calls.

My next two happened to be to work. Opting for the easier of the two, I called Tracey's direct line first. She picked up on the second ring, her voice light and happy. "Neilson, Sampson and Peterson. This is Tracey."

I blinked in surprise at her tone. She hadn't sounded like that in a while. I could hear her light breath coming through the phone, heard her hair swishing in a repeating pattern, like she was twirling a piece in her fingers. "Hello?" she asked.

I coughed, embarrassed. "Hey, Tracey. It's Emma."

Her voice brightened and I could hear her smile through the other line. "Hey! Missed you Friday. Clarice only scowled when I asked about you. What'd you do to piss her off?"

I exhaled a breath I hadn't realized I'd been holding. It was clear from her ignorance that no one had told her my story yet. I was happy about that; at least she hadn't been worrying about me all weekend. "Well, that's why I'm calling actually…" I went into all the details of the fake story that I could. Alanna supplied the details I still wasn't sure about, whenever I paused mid-sentence.

Tracey's voice was sympathetic, but unworried. "Oh, Em. God, that sucks. I have no idea what I'd do if I was stuck in a bed for months." She started laughing and I knew exactly what she was picturing herself doing, if she was stuck in a bed for months. A thought struck me as I remembered Hot Ben saying he was going to surprise her for lunch. She seemed pretty chipper, compared to how she'd been lately. Maybe it had gone well.

Grateful to talk about something that didn't directly involve me, I smiled and said, "You seem in a much better mood than you have been recently. Something up?"

She started giggling and I heard her hand come up to the receiver, like she was cupping the phone. "Besides the world's best nooner?" She laughed again while I rolled my eyes. From upstairs, I heard Alanna and her mom laugh. I shook my head. I guess things had gone exceedingly well.

"Ben?" I asked, already knowing who had met up with her today.

She laughed again, her hand dropping from the receiver. "Yes, of course Ben." She sighed and I heard her relax back in her chair. "He came into work with a bouquet of flowers, looking hot as hell." Knowing how awful he'd looked this morning, I bit back a laugh. A small, satisfied sound escaped Tracey's throat. "We went to that café around the corner, and he told me that he'd been acting stupid because of some family drama back home, but he'd never meant to push me away. He said he loved me more than anything." She let out a dreamy sigh. "Em, you should have heard him, he was so sweet, and honest, and...regretful. He was so worried that I didn't love him anymore. It was charming. He was almost desperate to get back together with me, like he wanted to be by my side every second now, to watch over me or something." She laughed. "We didn't even make it through our meal before I was pulling him into the bathroom."

I laughed and made a mental note to never use the restroom in that particular café again. "That's great, Tracey. I'm glad you two...worked things out." I laughed again and she laughed with me. I thought over Hot Ben's cover story to her and smiled that he'd basically called Teren and me family. And him not wanting to leave Tracey alone, I knew exactly what that was about.

Tracey sighed, and then a thought that wasn't about Hot Ben seemed to strike her. "Oh, you're on bed rest...you're not coming back, are you?"

I felt the tears sting my eyes as I sighed softly into the phone. "I don't know, Trace." I ran a finger down a canine; my fangs had decided after lunch that they were not going to stay up; they were snapping down every time I stopped thinking about them. It was annoying, and after a while, I'd stopped trying to keep them up. Right now, I didn't see how things would ever return to normal.

Tracey sighed and I heard the quiver in her voice. "I'm gonna miss you, Emma."

She swallowed heavily and I heard her sniffle; it made my barely contained tears flow too. "I'm gonna miss you too, Trace." She sniffled a little more and I struggled to not let my surging hormones run away with me. Struggling to pull myself together, I told her, "Hey, stop that. We'll still see each other. I mean, we're best friends and our guys are best friends, right? We'll still see each other all the time." I didn't mention that we'd *all* be keeping some major secrets from her now.

"You're right. I'm being silly. We'll see each other so much you'll get sick of me." I laughed and she added in a brighter voice, "And besides, I love kids, I can't wait to babysit yours."

That line got to me, and I slapped my hand over my mouth so I didn't openly sob. I just didn't know if they would get the chance to be "babysat" by anyone, much less Tracey, a woman who could never know what they really were. I nodded and squeaked out a "Yep."

Her tone suggestive, Tracey wished me the best of luck breaking in my bed, and promised to come see me soon. Feeling calmer, but still hanging on by a thread, I told her I'd call her often, and then we said our goodbyes.

That left me a worn out, tired mess when I finally called Clarice. I didn't hold back any of my tears with her. I figured she didn't really care either way, and I could at least get the emotional release I needed, while at the same time sounding contrite. Clarice told me that she wasn't holding my spot for me indefinitely, but under company policy, she couldn't fire me. If and when I decided to come back, she'd find a place for me…somewhere. I sighed, knowing that wherever I ended up…would suck. But I also knew that out of everything in my life right now, my job was the least important, so I thanked her for her tutelage over the years and wished her well in finding a replacement. Surprising me, she told me that she'd miss me, and then she curtly hung up the phone, not even waiting for my reply. I blinked into the receiver and then sighed and hung up.

My last call was to Teren, to let him know that Mom was excited to watch Spike for him. "Okay, good. I'll swing by her place after I head home for a little bit. Then I'll head to you," he told me.

I sighed, wishing all his errands were already done, and he was here with me. "I miss you. I hate feeling you so far away."

He made a wistful noise that spoke volumes about how much he missed me too. "I know. I feel the same way." I told him to hurry back to me, and then we said our goodbyes.

After all my calls were done, I headed upstairs. I only slipped once on the top step, when I moved faster than I'd intended and tripped over the lip of the stair. Then I stumbled into bed, threw the blankets over me, and wished the blip on my internal radar that was Teren would hurry up and get closer already.

Chapter 14 – And I Thought I Wanted You Before

I was just starting to feel the pull of sleep when something in my body instantly sprang awake. All the fatigue that I'd been feeling, poured off of me, and was replaced with an icy wash of anticipation. My skin pebbled in response, my breath picked up pace, and I squirmed under the silky sheets of my bed, suddenly restless. Teren was getting closer. I could feel it, and the pull in my body to be near him was growing with every single step he inched towards me. He was still miles away though, and I felt like my skin was crawling with the need to be in his presence. I couldn't stop shifting positions.

I tossed and turned; the dull ache in my neck was practically non-existent as the restlessness took over. He was so far away. I needed him closer. I needed him in my arms. I needed him now. I had no idea what this pulling sensation was, or if it was even normal, but it was driving me crazy, like foreplay without the play part.

As I turned over again, Alanna asked me if I was all right. Sighing, I sat up. My face heated as I explained. "Teren's getting closer."

Alanna blurred upstairs at the sound of my distress. She knocked, then opened the door. "I know, dear." She looked over my heightened breath, my glazed eyes, my extended fangs. She tilted her head. "Your reaction... You seem almost..."

She inhaled and I felt myself blushing. Not wanting to hear her say it, I stood up. "I know. It's like this..." my hands ran over my body, "...this pull. I just need to be near him. Now." She tilted her head at me and scrunched her brows. I frowned at her reaction. I'd sort of been hoping they all felt this way on some level. "You don't feel...weird, when the others get close to you?"

She shook her head. "No, not like this. I might be happy to see them if it's been a while, but certainly not to the degree that you're feeling it." She shrugged. "Of course, my relationship with Teren is much different than yours."

Beyond embarrassed, I sighed and covered my face with my hands. Alanna laughed and removed my hands. She replaced them with her cool ones and they felt nice against my fevered skin. I closed my eyes, but the rest of my body buzzed with energy. "Curious," she muttered. "I wonder if he feels this too, and if it's because you're in love, or because he created you."

I opened my eyes to find her studying me, like a science experiment. "Or maybe this is just on your end," she glanced down at my stomach, "because of them?"

I pulled away from her. My body needed to move as I felt Teren approaching me. It was like waiting for your lover to walk from the bathroom to the bedroom, only the walk Teren was on was much, much longer. The anticipation of reunion was making me stir-crazy. "I need to get out of here." I blurred past her, tripped on the door frame, and nearly crashed to the floor. Her cool arms were securely under me before I could fall.

"Calm down, Emma. He'll be here soon." One of her hands smoothed my hair, and I whimpered and bit my lip. I wanted to run. I wanted to set out on the highway, run blazingly fast, and fly into Teren's arms. I knew enough to know that wasn't a typical reaction, so I nodded and forced myself to walk at a slow, human pace down the elaborate staircase.

Once in the entryway, I made myself stay in the house. It took every amount of willpower that I had. I kept staring at the door and imagining myself running through it. Alanna stood near the fountain and watched me; her eyes were curious and concerned. I supposed I had the frazzled look of a woman who would run out into traffic, if it met her goal.

Teren had gone on a lot of errands after work—going to our house, then dropping off Spike at Mom's. I knew my mom had probably grilled him about the accident, making sure I was really okay, and making sure the women out here could take proper care of me. All of his tasks had taken a while, and the sun finished setting while I was pacing.

Imogen came down the stairs and stood by her daughter. They both curiously watched me. Halina, probably wondering what we were all doing hanging out in the entryway, eventually strolled in and sat on a step. She looked over at Alanna as Jack peeked his head into the room, shook it, and then headed to the living room. "What's her problem?" she asked, amusement in her voice, and a huge grin on her face.

Alanna shrugged as she answered her. "Teren is getting closer to the ranch."

Halina looked confused. "Yeah, and?" Alanna only shrugged again and turned back to watch me pace.

Shoving down my embarrassment, I made an irritated noise of frustration as I ran my hands back through my hair. The restlessness ate away at me as I paced in circles on the marble floor. My hands ran over my body in ways that I really shouldn't have touched myself with everyone watching, but I couldn't help it. My body was on fire. Occasionally I even itched and had to scratch my arms in places. I was pretty sure if this went on too long, I'd develop a nervous tic.

He got even closer, to the point where I could feel him at the end of the super long driveway. I flashed a look at the door again; my chest was heaving as I let out heavy breaths. He was so close now that I imagined I could already smell him. I wanted to burst through the door and go to him, but I knew that was nuts. I made myself stay put, staring at the door as I willed him even closer.

Halina giggled. "This is exciting!" I tossed a glare at her over my shoulder, but she only smiled wider as she looked over at Imogen and Alanna. "I wonder what will happen when he gets here?" She returned her eyes to me, delight clear in her face. "Do you think they'll combust...or just start having sex in the driveway?"

I hissed at her in a way I'd seen her do on several occasions, but she only laughed. Throwing her arms over her knees, her short dress exposing all of her thigh, she rested her head on her hands, like she had a front row seat to the biggest event of the year.

I couldn't focus on her any longer though; Teren was halfway down the drive and approaching fast. My heart surged, my breath picked up even more, and the circle track I'd been pacing became a short back and forth strut, right in front of the door. I couldn't help the image of Spike pacing like this when he'd see Goldie in the backyard and he'd wanted out to chase her down. I wanted a chase too...just a much more satisfying one.

Over Halina's chuckles, I heard Alanna and Imogen talking about how unusual my reaction was. Apparently getting into a fervor over your lover approaching, was not typical vampire behavior. Maybe it was the twins that were ramping up my emotions. Maybe I'd break through the door and Teren would be completely unaffected by coming closer to me. But then again, yesterday he'd been just as eager as me. And that had been a much shorter separation. If he was feeling an ounce of what I was feeling, Halina might not be too far off the mark with her joke.

I heard the crunch of his tires as he pulled up to the house, and I stopped walking. When I heard the engine of the car shut off, I stopped breathing. My body started shaking with uncontainable energy and a rush of longing surged through me. He was so close. So close. I'd be in his arms soon. Soon.

The ache became too much with him right outside, the need to be with him too great. I surged forward, not even trying to hold back my super speed. Alanna just barely streaked to the door and opened it, before I busted right through it. The cooler air temperature prickled my skin and the wind buzzing past my ears was distractingly loud, but neither one did anything to impede my progress. I was just past the huge, ancient timbers supporting the massive overhang of the front door, when a streak came rushing towards me.

He grabbed me, and twirled me in a quick circle. My balance was momentarily thrown off, but before I could fall, my shoulders were pushed back into the supportive log behind me. I ignored the brief pain I felt as Teren's presence collided with mine. The joy of it was too powerful. My breath came back in a groan and my hands reached out to grasp any part of him I could find.

His mouth came down to mine and he let out a low growl as his body pressed carefully, but firmly, into the side of my hip. He was being cautious of my belly, even in the midst of…this. We both moaned as lips, tongues, and in my case, fangs, attacked the other. I tasted blood and I knew I was nicking him, but he never complained, only groaned and pushed his hard body into mine. Wanting to kiss him deeper, and feeling, more than knowing, that my fangs were in the way, I somehow managed to pull them back up. He slipped his tongue into me and I whimpered as I sagged against the beam that was now holding me up.

His breath was heavy as his hands ran over my body. "God, I couldn't get here fast enough," he muttered as his fingers ran down my backside and wrapped my leg around his hip.

He rocked against me and I gasped, then groaned. "I know, I was going crazy." My hands ran through his hair, tangling in the longer pieces and pulling him into me. I wanted to absorb every piece of him into me. I just couldn't get close enough. I heard Halina laughing, and sensed her at the door. She was probably leaning against it, amused, waiting to see if her prediction would come true. Alanna and Imogen had gone into the kitchen to start making dinner. They, at least, were giving Teren and me some privacy in our "reunion."

Teren growled again as his lips shifted to the uninjured part of my neck; his hand ran up my shirt. "I've never felt this...pull before. I need you so much..."

I loved that this wasn't just on my side, that he was overwhelmed by it too. It probably wasn't the twins then. I groaned and felt my fingers sliding down to his pants. I knew Halina was about to be right, and this was about to get really graphic. I also knew that she'd probably watch the whole thing, just to chide me on it later. I knew it—I just didn't care. The sound of his leather belt sliding free of the buckle was loud to me, louder than our fast breaths and occasional sounds of pleasure. "What is this, Teren? What is this feeling?" I managed to get out.

He broke apart from my skin. His cool breath was heavy in my ear as he murmured, "I don't know. It's wonderful though, isn't it?"

"Yes, God, yes."

I inhaled deep after my words; the smell of the world danced across his skin and clothes, entering me. My hands on his slacks paused as I sensed the different flavors running from my nose, to my mouth. It was almost like a roadmap of where he'd been today. While his body continued to furiously attack mine, I started relaxing. I took in the underlying scent of him, and tucked it away as I focused on the new smells—paper and ink from his work, the calla lilies from our entry way, Spike, the perfumed air of my mom's house and then, underneath it all, something that smelled like...engine oil.

He started pushing down the lounge pants I was wearing. I paused; my body was coming back to rationality, now that he was with me. Teren wasn't there yet, or maybe he'd just shifted into a different sort of irrationality. He groaned in a frustrated way. "Please, Emma. I need you."

I put my hand on his cheek and made him stop kissing me, made him look at me. "Teren, calm down. Breathe me."

He swallowed, his eyes were unfocused as desire still led his actions. Then he closed his eyes and took a deep breath. His lips curled into a smile as where I'd been and what I'd been doing leeched off my skin and clothes. He stayed that way for a while, slowly pulling away from me. I heard Halina sigh and felt her speed off to be with the other girls. As Teren relaxed, I heard her tell them that we did nothing. Disappointment was clear in her voice. Imogen and Alanna laughed and then they all started debating about what was going on between us.

When Teren opened his eyes, he seemed more like himself. He removed his hands from my body, and let me step away from the log my back was pressed against. Sheepishly looking down at himself, he re-buckled his belt. When he was finished, he watched me straightening out my own clothes. Then in a casual voice, he said, "Hey."

I laughed and slung my arms around his neck, giving him a moderate hug. "Hey," I said back. He squeezed me tight as the overwhelming urge to consume each other faded away. I sighed as I wondered if it would be like that every time we reunited. Then I looked past Teren, to his car in the driveway.

I stiffened in his embrace and he pulled back to look at me. "What?" he asked, confused.

I shifted my eyes from his car to him. "What happened to the Prius?"

He looked over at the car and frowned. The entire back end of it was scrunched in, like someone *had* actually hit him. It was still drivable, but it was going to cost him a pretty penny to fix it. He sighed as he returned his eyes to mine. "We were in an accident, remember?"

I furrowed my brows; the ache in my neck was starting back up since the energy in my body had dissipated. "No, we...I mean, not really, that was just a story."

He shrugged as his hands loosely rested on my hips. "A story that would obviously be a fake one, if nothing was wrong with my car. I needed something to fix, so I created something to fix." He shrugged again while I shook my head. The never ending charade. How could I forget?

"Are you okay?" I looked him over, but I couldn't see anything even remotely wrong with him. He looked delicious. Even my overeager kissing earlier wasn't apparent on him.

He laughed; the sound came out deep, husky and soothing. Just being in his presence was soothing. "Of course I'm okay, Emma." He kissed my head and started walking us into the house. "I'm fine." He sighed and I thought that maybe he was remembering that technically, I wasn't. I sighed too.

His arm was around my waist, and my head was on his shoulder as we made our way into the dining room. Alanna and Imogen had just finished making a steak dinner. The smell of cooked meat and fresh blood made my mouth water. My fangs dropped back down and I let out an irritable groan before sucking them back up. Halina was scouring over an ancient leather-bound book laid on the table, but she still managed to look up and laugh at me.

Her eyes shifted to Teren. Taking in his rumpled hair and clothes from our "greeting," she gave him a smirk. "Teren, glad you're home. We've been eagerly awaiting your return." She laughed and I again halted the desire to tell her to shut it. It was prudent to not piss off the vampire, whether you were the bearer of miracle twins or not.

Teren ignored her comment. Walking around the table, he hovered over her shoulder. One hand came down to rest on the table as he read the book she was studying. I suddenly realized they were looking over our abductor's journals.

"What did you find?" he asked her, intensity in his voice.

She looked over her shoulder at him and pointed to a section in the book. Reaching over, he shifted the pages closer to him. He muttered something in Russian that I was sure was a nasty curse. Shaking his head, he lifted the book and read the passage over again. Then he started flipping pages. I could smell the grime and dust coming off the paper as he turned them over.

"What is it?" I asked as Imogen flitted into the room. Coming over to me, she examined the wound on my neck. I sighed and closed my eyes as her cool touch soothed the dull ache. Teren looked up to answer me right as she touched me. His eyes locked onto my unbandaged wound and he froze. He hadn't been paying too close attention to the spot in the parking lot—he'd been more focused on the unblemished side—but it certainly had his attention now.

Never taking his eyes from the scar under Imogen's fingers, he whispered, "He killed them all." His eyes came up to mine, moist and haunted. "Entire families. He didn't leave a single member alive...not even the children."

My eyes watered as my hand went to my stomach. I closed them and willed the sudden bile in my throat not to rise. I couldn't even imagine such hatred. I felt Teren blur to my side as Imogen stepped away. Her scent retreated with her as she went to sit by her daughter.

Teren's cool hands cupped my cheeks and I opened my eyes to gaze at him. "We'll keep looking. We'll find someone." I nodded, not knowing what to say.

Teren brushed the hair away from my shoulder as he stood close beside me. He swallowed, bit his lip, then slowly lowered his head. He gently placed his lips over the wound. His touch was tentative, like he didn't want to scare me by moving too quickly. Nothing Teren did frightened me, so I carefully tilted my head to the side, letting him know that I wasn't scarred by the attack. Well, not emotionally anyway. Physically, I was, and probably always would be. But Teren's mouth was welcome anywhere on me. He sighed and placed another kiss there, gentle, but firm. I heard him mutter that he was sorry, but before I could tell him that he had nothing to apologize for, Alanna swept into the room and told everyone to sit as she brought out dinner.

Teren studied his glass all throughout our meal and I could practically see the gears turning in his head. While we sipped our blood, he spoke with Halina and Imogen about every detail of the notes they'd already read. While his eyes never left his blood, he intently listened as they repeated detail after horrible detail. The man had sliced, staked, and burned a path of vampiric destruction across the country. Teren started asking questions about the last few entries. The entries that had led the man to him.

Finally looking up, Teren muttered, "Something's not right about this."

Halina scrunched her brows. "What do you mean? His last entry was a nest in California...us."

Teren shook his head. "His notes make it seem like he'd learned about the nest a while ago." He shook his head again. "He admitted to me that he'd stumbled across me. No one tipped him off, he got lucky." His voice came out sarcastically on the word "lucky."

As meals were finished and Alanna swept the dishes away, Imogen said, "Well, didn't you say he tracked you for a while? The notes could still be about you."

Teren ran a hand through his hair. "I don't know. It would be a hell of a lot easier if he'd just said, Teren Adams, vampire, living in San Francisco." He sighed. "The vague way he talks is driving me crazy."

It was true. From all I'd heard them discuss, he rarely used names or locations. Everything was references and descriptions. *The dark haired one. The blonde. The woman and child. Found a group in the place where the sun never sets.* It was all gibberish that only meant anything to the man who'd written it. I supposed that was a precaution. I mean, the creatures he was stalking were, in the eyes of the law, people. He couldn't exactly keep a hit list on them.

Teren grunted as he stood from the table. "I want to look at the rest. I feel like we're missing something."

Halina nodded. Standing, she beckoned with her finger. Teren moved to follow her and, grabbing his elbow, I stopped him. He looked back at me and I frowned. I knew that once he got his nose in a book that might hold the key to saving me, I'd never see him again.

He ran his hands down my hair. Leaning in, he kissed me before resting his forehead against mine. "I'll be up in a little bit." He kissed me again, then followed Imogen and Halina from the room.

I sighed as I watched them leave. With the bond, I could sense him go into the living room and then down into Halina's room. The three of them stopped there and I stared at the floor, where they were underneath me. The sound of books shuffling and pages flipping met my ears. By the sound of it, there were a lot of journals. Diaries of a madman. That's what we were relying on to save me. Splendid.

Alanna slung her arm around my shoulders and twisted me. "Come on, dear. Jack and I were just about to watch a movie. Won't you join us?"

I looked between her youthful face and Jack's weathered one. He smiled at me as he reached a hand out for his wife. I had a feeling they were on "occupy Emma" duty tonight. I reluctantly nodded and followed them.

I only half watched the movie. I was more listening to Teren's deep voice than anything else. By the expression on Alanna's face as she snuggled into her husband's side, I thought that maybe she was more listening to them too. Her eyes flicked over to me as I sat in a plush chair, rubbing my stomach and trying not to worry. I met her gaze and we both gave each other small, reassuring smiles. All we could do was hope for the best.

When the World War II movie Jack had picked out wrapped up, Teren and the girls were still deep in discussion over a phrase in the book that Teren was convinced had been the man's real target. Teren had it in his head that the man had come to California for someone else, and he'd been sidetracked by Teren. That would mean that the original mixed vampire he'd been stalking was still out there, somewhere. We just had to decipher where.

Getting the feeling that Teren was going to decipher "where" all night long, I yawned and stood up, with Jack's help. "Teren, I'm exhausted," I said at a normal volume.

He paused in speaking to one of the girls and I could tell he was debating what to do—he wanted to stay down there and keep going with his line of thought, he wanted to come to bed with me. When a few seconds of silence ticked by, I sighed and said, "Will you just come tuck me in?"

"Of course."

No sooner had he finished saying it, than he'd blazed into the room and was standing beside me. I'd felt him moving though, so his sudden presence didn't surprise me. I slung my arms around his neck while he smiled down at me. Tired, my head rested against his chest as he scooped me up. Even though I knew he was dying to return to his research, he walked me at normal pace up the stairs to the bedroom. My lids felt heavier with every step he took. He opened the door to our room one-handed, swished us inside, and closed it behind us. I pointed to the bathroom, wanting him to walk me in there too. He laughed, but obliged me.

He set me down on the counter and I smiled as he backed away. With one hand, I grabbed him and clutched his dress shirt just before he could speed away from me. His jaw tightened, but he smiled and stepped towards me. I knew he wanted to leave, but he'd been gone all day and I missed him. Ten minutes wouldn't kill him...or me.

My eyes drifted over him as I thought about our time apart, and more importantly, our time back together. I wondered if our reunions would always be that intense. They did say absence made the heart grow fonder, but I thought we were pushing the limits of decency on that phrase. Meeting up like that could be really embarrassing in the wrong place, like a church or something.

Replaying our hot little encounter, I smiled seductively at him. My teeth spoiled the moment by dropping down. Luckily I didn't slice anything. Irritated, I grunted and focused on pulling them back up. Teren smiled at me while I shot him a glare. "Why can't I get them to stay in place? You don't seem to have as much of a problem with it as me?"

He gave me a sly smile. "Don't I?" He raised an eyebrow and I flushed with heat as I remembered how I'd found out about his little secret in the first place. They'd sort of slipped down when he'd gotten a little too...excited.

I smiled and looked away as I delighted in the memory of his embarrassment. His hand touched my cheek, pulling my gaze back to his. "I've had a long time to get used to it. You will too." I sighed. I'd wanted an instant answer, not an "it-will-get-easier" response. He tilted his head and added, "It may help, if you think of it in a different way."

I scrunched my brow, lost. "Huh?"

He laughed as his thumb stroked my cheek. "I think most people assume that vampires push their fangs down to use them." I frowned; that's how I'd always imagined it. Teren smiled and shook his head. "We don't. We're constantly holding them in."

I tilted my head and tried to feel the pressure on my fangs. I could sort of sense the difference in what he was saying and I experimentally relaxed my mouth. My teeth instantly popped into place. I smiled at him as he nodded at me.

"It's where they naturally want to be. You have to constantly hold them up, like you're sucking in your gut around a cute guy." He smirked while I sighed at the thought of always having to be in control of them.

"What if I can't? I mean, you have to relax sometime?"

He nodded and shifted his hands down to my legs. Rubbing his cool palms over my thighs, he said, "It will get easier. After a while, you won't even think about it. I promise."

I nodded, but it made me tired just thinking about the level of control he must always be using. It was a miracle he didn't slip up more often. "Don't you ever get a break? What about when you sleep?"

His hands ran up to my hips. "Yes, they'll come out when you sleep, as your body relaxes. You'll need to learn to sleep with your mouth closed." He curved his lip into a playful smile. "Or mostly closed. You can still snore if you want to."

I reached out to smack him, but he blurred away from me before I could. From downstairs, I heard Halina laughing. "I do not," I whispered, mortified.

Halfway across the room from me, he grinned and laughed. "If you say so."

I pouted at his amusement, then carefully hopped off the counter. Knowing he didn't really want to be in the bathroom with me, I pointed at the floor with a stern face. *Stay.* He gave me a wry grin as he folded his arms across his chest. He wasn't moving, but he didn't necessarily like being commanded. Smiling, I twisted around to brush my teeth, wash my face and examine the wound at my neck again.

Teren stared at the scar like he thought he could wish it away by glaring at it. Fluffing my hair around my shoulders, hiding it as well as I could, I remembered his earlier apology. He was still staring through my hair at the wound; his perfect vision could probably still see it.

Cautious of my speed, so I didn't bulldoze into him, and cautious of my mouth, testing out this suck-in-your-gut feeling, I slowly walked over to him. His eyes never left my neck as I laced our fingers together.

"Why did you apologize to me earlier?" I whispered.

He pulled his gaze from my neck and glanced at me before staring at the ground. "I failed," he whispered.

I dropped one of his hands, grabbed his chin, and turned his rough, stubbled jaw towards me. "What do you mean, you failed?"

He glanced at my neck and sighed, as he returned his eyes to mine. "I swore I'd never let anything harm you, and…" He shrugged and glanced at my neck again. "I didn't know who was watching me or why. He was so fast, always gone before I could do anything about it, and other than a faint trace of his scent, I never really got a chance to…" He sighed, angry at himself. "I should have tried harder to figure out more. Maybe if I had tracked him, found out what he wanted with me, things would have turned out differently. I just never expected…" He stopped talking, and his eyes glassed over. "When it mattered most, I couldn't protect you. I failed."

I leaned into him, as much as my belly would allow anyway. Still holding his face, I made him kiss me. "You can't protect me from everything, baby," I whispered between our lips. He let out a pained noise, but I pressed harder against him, to distract him. "No one's perfect. I blame him, not you."

I pulled away from his mouth and his sad, pale eyes washed over me. I ran a hand back through his hair and sighed at his remorse. "Please let this go, Teren. I don't want you to feel guilty every time you look at me. I'm fine. We're fine. Please?"

He bit his lip and I knew he was thinking that I might *not* be fine, but he wasn't going to say it, anymore than I was. Finally he nodded and smiled. Wrapping his arms around me, he leaned down for another kiss. Loving that he was still here with me, I grinned into his lips and playfully pushed him backwards. Well, I meant to playfully push him, but I'd forgotten that my body was slightly more enhanced now. I ended up shoving him a good three feet away from me. He took a couple of balancing steps, then cocked his head at me, looking surprised and intrigued over my strength.

"Sorry," I muttered, embarrassed.

Grinning, he held out his hands for me. "Don't be…it's just who you are now." He raised an eyebrow. "You'll have to be careful with me." He laughed after he said it, amused by the idea.

I walked into his hands, amused at him. He helped me change into pajamas, his hands lingering in places that really had nothing to do with changing my clothes, and then he slid me under the covers. As he leaned over me, I slung my arms around his neck and tried to pull him under the covers with me. He went at first, his knee rested on the sheets as our kiss grew heated. The hand that wasn't supporting his weight slid down my back. Cupping my thigh, he pulled my hips towards his, to connect our more…sensitive areas. Just as I was shifting my body into a better position, I heard Halina's voice.

"Teren, we found something that may be referencing a place in California. You should come down and take a look at it…if you're finished tucking Emma in for the night, of course."

He paused in kissing me, looked over my face, and then down at the floor. In a tone I wouldn't have heard before, he told her, "I'll be right there." He returned was gaze to me, and I frowned.

He looked sheepish for a minute when he realized that I'd heard him say that; he was used to being able to speak to them without me knowing. "I really should go see what she found. It could be relevant." He gave me an apologetic smile as his eyes swept down my body.

"Fine," I muttered. My head knew that what he was doing was actually very important, but my hormonal body struggled to remember that. When he leaned in to kiss me a final time, my body struggled even more.

Not playing fair at all, I grabbed his jeans and used my new strength to pull his hips down to me, to finish the connection he'd started. My strength took him by surprise again, and I let out a husky groan as his very-ready body instinctively rocked against mine. He tilted his head to the side and bit his lip as he pressed against me again. Since he couldn't lay on top of me, not with my stomach barrier, he was partially sitting up on his knees. I wrapped my legs around him and tilted my hips up, giving him an even better angle. He closed his eyes. His breath was faster as his fingers trailed over my body, concentrating on my baby-enhanced chest.

Halina's voice, again, ruined our moment. "Not to interrupt the love fest, but you already knocked her up, you can stop trying. We do have work to do."

"Mother, they missed each other. Give them two minutes."

Teren's eyes snapped open at Imogen's words. He twisted his lips in displeasure, but didn't say anything. I tried really hard to not laugh at the "two minute" comment. Not exactly the most flattering thing for a guy to hear, especially from his grandmother. Teren glanced down at my face and frowned deeper as he shook his head. That was too much and I started laughing uncontrollably.

He sat back on his heels and crossed his arms over his chest. "You're just as bad as they are," he muttered, offended.

Twisting around my belly, I sat up and slipped my arms around him. "Oh, I know you have more stamina than that." I laughed again and heard Halina laughing with me while Imogen started stammering apologies, having just then realized that she'd offended him.

Teren ran a hand down his face, then peeked at me through his fingers. "I hope we find a solution to your problem soon." Removing his hand, he leaned over me as I lay back on the bed again. A devilish smile lit his face and I bit my lip at seeing it. "I need a more private place to be alone with you."

My hands went to his chest, then snaked up to his hair while he smiled seductively at me. "Yes, yes you do." Our lips briefly pressed together, and then he sighed and pulled away.

"I really should go." I nodded and he tucked me into the bed, placing a pillow under my stomach as I shifted to my side. He sat on the edge of the mattress and ran a hand down my hair. "I love you. I'll be back in a little bit."

He leaned down and kissed me, then shut the light off as he left the room. Determined to wait up for him, I stared at the ceiling, but exhaustion took me first, and I was fast asleep before he ever made it back to the room.

And I was pretty sure I slept soundlessly. I did *not* snore. Smartass.

Chapter 15 – Reconnecting

The rest of that week started the beginning of a new routine for us. Teren would leave me after dinner to do research with the family. Usually one or two of them would stay upstairs and occupy me, while the rest scoured over the books. I helped on occasion, but Teren liked me to stay away from it. He told me it was terrible stuff, and I shouldn't have to deal with it in my condition, like somehow I'd stress myself to death if I pored over the journals with him. I told him he was being ridiculous, and he told me he could concentrate better if he wasn't worrying about how I was handling the horrors. I sighed and left him to it.

He was right anyway; I never found anything but multiple atrocities in the writings. And I hated reading about any crime that he'd committed against the mixed children…and there were a lot of them. He'd used them as guinea pigs for the "drug" that he'd used to force Teren's conversion. He was curious to see on how young of a child it would work. He'd practiced on a lot of children. He might have been vague with names and places, but he was quite descriptive on all the other horrendous details. Just reading about it had made me throw up.

Teren would take a short break when I got tired, to lay me down in bed for the night. He always reassured me that, while they still hadn't found anything yet, he was sure they were on the path to something. Then he would disappear back downstairs to burn the midnight oil with Halina. He either slipped back into bed when I was unconscious or he stayed up all night, but in the early morning he'd always kiss me goodbye before heading off to the city for his job, where he most likely whipped out his articles lightning-fast and spent the rest of his time surfing the Internet for leads.

After I got up for the day, I would trail Alanna and offer to help at every possible opportunity. She would always say that she had everything under control and I should just rest or call my family.

I usually ended up doing the latter. I missed my family. Even though they weren't that far away, and even though if I were home I wouldn't see them any more than I did now, there was just something about being forced apart from them that was lonely. But I wasn't apart from them for very long.

My sister came by the day after I called her. She blew off school and spent the afternoon with me. She teared up when she saw my scar and laughed when my fangs extended without my permission, mid-sentence. Once I told her that I had to concentrate on keeping them up twenty-four-seven, she spent the next several hours helping me hone my fang-hiding ability. By the time she left for the evening, I'd managed to keep them hidden away for most of the day.

That turned out to be helpful, since my mom came out the next night. While I loved seeing the plump, happy woman, having her there was stressful. For one, I had to wear a brace around my neck. A whiplash strain was a convenient way to hide my healing wound, but it was exceedingly annoying. But not nearly as annoying as never getting out of bed. My mom took bed rest very seriously. If I hadn't protested with all my heart, she would have made me use a bed pan.

But even with those annoyances, it was fear that made her visit stressful. The fear that I'd slip up—that I'd move too fast, or my fangs would pop out, or, I'd forget that my mom couldn't hear Alanna through the walls and I'd answer a question she asked me. By the time my mom left for the night, I was exhausted, and I hoped she stayed away for a few days. I hated thinking that.

Hot Ben came over nearly every night, which surprised the hell out of me. I sort of figured he was done with the whole lot of us, but after a couple of days of sequestering himself with Tracey, he started showing up late in the evening, usually around the time I was headed off to bed. He then headed down with the others to pore over notes and journals.

I couldn't have been more shocked by his turn around. Not too long ago, Ben would have had a mini coronary over the very idea of going down into Halina's rooms, deep under the earth. And from what I could hear before I zonked out, Halina seemed to have shifted her view of him as well. She stopped the seductive, terrifying banter that she used to use on him, and treated him with nothing but respect. The conversations that flowed around that room were all business. And all about me. How to save me. How to save the children. And how to find more mixed like them, in the hopes that someone would have an answer.

When the following week plotted out in much the same way, I began to think I might never see my husband again. I knew he was trying to save me, but in the process, he was seeing less and less of me. Especially when he started getting home later and later, sometimes not making it back until the time I was ready for bed. He'd always call or text me, telling me specifically where he was, since our bond only gave me the general idea of his location. And he was always checking into a lead from the journals.

They'd been able to pinpoint a few places in the state that were cryptically referenced. Nearly two weeks after the attack Teren called me from work and let me know that the right questions, payouts, and from what I'd heard, some of Halina's unique mind control talents, had finally led them to a group of vampires, albeit pureblood vampires, just outside of Santa Rosa. He called around lunch, to let me know that he was checking it out after work, once the sun went down.

"Teren, no, don't go walking into a strange vampire's home alone! Be smart about this, please?"

I scratched my healed, itchy neck as he laughed in a way that was supposed to relax me. My sharper hearing heard the lie behind it, though; he was nervous, even if he'd never admit it. "I'll be fine, Emma. It's no different than going to a human's house. They won't harm me without cause, and I don't plan to give them one. I just need to know what they know about vampires like me."

I sat down on our bed and cradled the phone to my ear, wishing it were him. "Please? Come home first, make love to me, and then go with Halina." I was hoping the sex part might persuade him. I'd been having lonely nights for a while now.

And he did pause as that sunk in. "It will be quicker if I just go after work. Besides, I'm not going alone."

I rubbed a hand over my expanding belly and felt one twin wrestling for space with the other. "Huh?" I could hear Alanna and Imogen talking in Imogen's room, and Halina was sleeping out the remnants of the sun downstairs. I didn't know who he was talking about.

"Ben is coming with me." I unintentionally laughed, partly out of nerves, partly out of disbelief. Hot Ben was his backup…seriously? I swear I could hear Teren frown into the phone. "Why is that funny? Between the two of us, he's the one who has actually staked a vampire before."

I sighed. Confident or not now, all I could picture when I thought of Hot Ben was the guy who had begged me to not let Teren eat him. "He's human, Teren. You're walking in there with a meal? You know how that jerk-off reacted to Ben and me. He didn't see people, he saw a buffet."

Teren sighed, too. "One bad seed doesn't make them all bad. Look, I've met vampires before. On rare occasions, when some have been out traveling or hunting, they've come across our scent and have come out to the ranch to say hello. They are not *all* like him. He was…off." I wanted to protest, but honestly, the only vampires I knew of were Adams vampires. He took my silence as acceptance. "We'll be fine. I'll see you before bed."

"Fine, you better," I sullenly muttered.

He laughed and I closed my eyes, memorizing the sound and sensing his location. He was so incredibly far from me that it felt like the other side of the country. Tears started slipping down my cheeks and I sniffled, just once. "Hey, Emma, don't cry. I'm doing this for you. I love you."

"I know. I just miss my husband." I let myself sniffle again, since he'd already heard it.

He paused and I heard him rustling around. I pictured him running a hand through his hair, torn. "I tell you what, when I get home, we'll go upstairs and I'll stay with you. I'll give you me, for as long as you want. I'll be your husband, over and over again."

Desire shot right through me at hearing his words. Our "reunions" when he got home, had continued to be heated ones, but he always pulled himself away from me. He always let duty clear his mind and calm his body. I wanted, just once, to let this crazy passion we felt run away with us. "No stopping?" I asked.

He laughed and a smile crept into his voice. "Definitely no stopping."

It made me smile that he understood my vague question. I wanted to feel the intensity. My body was already burning with the need for it, but first, he would be doing something possibly really dangerous. "Be careful, be safe. Come home to me."

"I will. I love you."

I repeated his sentiment, and then we hung up. I sighed and sank down to my bed, wishing he was home, not miles away from me and about to get even further. After a couple of long sighs, Alanna asked if I was all right. Not having to elaborate on my mood, since she'd heard that entire conversation, I told her I was. I wasn't as embarrassed about the lack of privacy as I once would have been, probably because I could hear everything too, and in this house, someone was always having an intimate conversation or moment. After a while, you just got used to it.

Later in the day, I smelled the enticing aroma of fresh blood from a recent kill. It compelled me to walk downstairs and into the kitchen, where the scent was the strongest. Alanna smiled and gave me a swift hug as she cleaned herself up. She and Jack had been outside, making a new batch of fresh steaks. Blooding the cow was Alanna's favorite part, for obvious reasons, and she was freezing containers of it for her family. By the number of freezer tight boxes, it had been a big cow.

I momentarily felt bad that I used up so much of their blood, especially since I could eat regular food too, but Alanna brushed off my concerns by telling me that she and the girls ate less and less every year. Halina could even go a few days without even noticing it. She said they'd met older vampires who could go weeks. Teren could only go a few hours before he needed a quick fix.

I sat and talked with Alanna about some of the vampires that had visited the ranch. I wanted to hear about the non-evil kind, so I would stop picturing bad things happening to Teren. She sat a small glass of plasma in front of me, and told me a story about a very nice female couple who had stopped by a few years ago. She laughingly told me that they had been quite taken with Teren, when he'd come up to visit over the weekend while they were there. She started to explain how one of them had tried to bite him and my eyebrows shot up my forehead. I was very concerned over that. Seeing my face, she quickly shook her head and said, "Oh, no she wasn't attacking him, she was…" She stopped talking and bit her lip, as she realized that perhaps her son's wife wouldn't want to hear about this.

I cringed when I understood that she was talking about foreplay. I remembered Teren telling me that vampires did feed off each other sometimes, and I remembered his devilish smile when he'd said he would like it. I knew I was his first bite, but had he been bitten? Curious, I peeked up at Alanna. "Did she? Bite him?"

Alanna busied herself with cleaning up the kitchen; her hands moved blurringly fast. "I don't think so," she said. "Anyway, they left soon after that. Nice couple." She started humming as I narrowed my eyes at her.

Right, she didn't think so. Teren and I were seriously going to have to have the exes talk. I could see that now. Taking my empty glass, she immediately switched over to tales about male guests. The sun went down while she was talking, and Halina sauntered into the room. Sitting on a stool, she delighted in the conversation she'd walked into. She went into graphic detail about a couple of the male vampires that had crossed paths with her. I blushed and studied anything but Halina's face while she told me every outrageous thing that I was afraid Teren had done with that female vampire. Yeah, we definitely needed the talk.

I sighed as I felt his location. It had shifted a few hours ago, when he'd gotten off work and headed to the vampire's home. It unfortunately hadn't shifted any closer to me; he'd headed miles north, towards Santa Rosa. I hadn't felt the distance lengthen or shorten since he had stopped; he was still there. I hated it, knowing where he was but not *how* he was. I wondered if it would just stop if he died. Would the GPS binging in my head vanish the second he was staked, or would it continue to go off until his dead body was disposed of? I closed my eyes. God, I did not want to think about that.

Imogen's cool hand went to my shoulder; she'd come in to join us. "He'll be all right, dear."

Halina stood up and adjusted her short skirt. "Yeah, it's just a vampire nest, a small one even. He and Ben will be fine." She smiled crookedly when she mentioned Ben, and I wondered how she knew all the details. She'd been asleep when he'd called. That could only mean that they'd discussed this plan last night, while I'd been sleeping.

Irritation flowed through me. I hated being left out of loops. "Why aren't you with him? Aren't you the protector? Isn't that your role?" I snapped at Halina. The entire room silenced. No one generally talked to Halina like that.

She cocked her head as she stared at me. I couldn't tell if she would laugh or knock me off my chair. Her hands went to her hips as she leaned into me, and her ageless eyes burned with a sudden anger. "You know nothing about what I am," she coldly said. Then, abruptly, she straightened and smiled. "Besides, he'd be done by the time I got all the way out there." Confused by her sudden mood shift, I watched her turn to leave the room. "It would be a waste of my time," she said before she left.

Still dazed by the display, I turned my eyes back to Alanna. She was watching her grandmother intently. When I felt Halina leave the house and then the property, going for a run apparently, Alanna's eyes came down to mine. "Teren forbid her." She shrugged. "It's sort of a sore point."

Shocked and bewildered, I shook my head. "He...? Why would he do that?"

Alanna bit her lip and looked over at Imogen. Imogen shrugged. She looked a little lost as to how to explain it, but she tried anyway. "Mother...might know these vampires, and they may not...react well, if she showed up."

I was even more confused. "What? Does Teren know them?"

Imogen shook her head and a dark lock of her hair escaped from her loose bun. "No, this was before he was born." I raised my eyebrows, waiting for an explanation, and Imogen eventually sighed. "We think it's this woman vampire, who may or may not have had this mate, who Mother may or may not have slept with, at some point, when the woman and this mate may or may not have still been together." She shrugged again. "It's all very vague, and we're not really sure. Teren just didn't want to start out confrontationally, if it really was the woman we think it is."

I dropped my jaw at the revelation. "He's going to see the scorned woman of his great-grandmother's lover?"

Alanna and Imogen shared a look and then they both shrugged. "Possibly," Alanna answered.

I shook my head, irritated at the little vampiric soap opera playing out before me. "She's going to stake him when she realizes who he is."

Alanna quickly shook her head. "He won't tell her."

I groaned and ran my hands back through my hair. "You all look exactly alike! He's a walking advertisement of Halina's genes! All of you need to start keeping that in mind!" I knew I was ranting, but I was really not a fan of being left out of plans.

Alanna looked at Imogen like she was seeing the resemblance for the first time. I sighed and rolled my eyes. "Hmmm," Alanna muttered. "You do have a point." She turned back to me and smiled a warm, reassuring smile. "It will be fine. The nest was only her and her new mate." She grinned and started making dinner for Jack and me. Looking over her shoulder, she added, "Rumor is, she staked the old one."

I closed my eyes, not feeling any better.

I didn't feel any better during dinner either, as I felt each long minute that he was north of me, tick by. I didn't start to feel better until Alanna was clearing away everyone's dishes. Then I started to feel a lot better. It happened like it always happened. The minute his blip on my internal radar started moving in my direction, I started to feel the pull. It was faint as first, since he was so far from me, and I only closed my eyes and inhaled a deep breath.

Halina, across from me, chuckled and I could feel her eyes on me. She was still wildly amused by my reaction to Teren coming home. "He's on his way," she muttered, laughing a little.

I stayed in my chair, stiff and straight, with my eyes closed. The sensation was still faint, but I knew it would get stronger, and I was preparing myself. This was just what I did whenever Teren came back to me. I found some place to stay very still and practiced my deep breathing. That usually worked...for a while.

He was farther away from me than usual, and I sat in that chair for over an hour as the other vampires went about their evening routines. Alanna and Jack went downstairs with Imogen to look over the books. Halina stayed seated across from me, watching.

Eventually, as Teren got closer, my mouth dropped open and my breaths came in shorter pulls. My hands came up to the table, and I held onto the edge so hard I probably marred it. He was within a mile of me, approaching fast. That's when things really intensified. It was like we were two huge magnets, each fine and fully functioning so long as we were kept apart. But start bringing us closer to each other, and you could practically feel the energy crackle between us. The thought that we weren't going to do anything to stop that unbelievable energy wasn't making my waiting any easier.

As I ran a hand through my hair and down my suddenly dry throat, I heard Halina's curious voice. "It's so fascinating. Just him coming closer to you drives you into a frenzy." I heard her plop her elbows on the table, but I didn't crack my eyes open to look. "And he feels it too, so it's not the pregnancy." She sat back in her chair as she continued to speculate. "It has to be the blood. It has to be because he spawned you."

Nearly panting now, I opened my eyes and looked over at her. She had her head tilted to the side as she watched me struggle for control. "Why...would that...do this?" I got out between shallow breaths.

She shrugged, her brows bunched. "I don't know. I didn't exactly keep my creator around long enough to ask." She gave me a cold grin and I shuddered, remembering that she had ended his life shortly upon him turning her. She'd never wanted this and she'd let him know that.

While I wrestled with controlling the buildup in me, Halina spoke in an oddly serious voice. "I know that I may seem...standoffish to you at times, but I do care about your fate, about the children's fate." My eyes widened at her rare sincerity, especially since it was being shown towards me. Her pale eyes took in my startled expression. She shook her head, her youthful eyes sad. "But...I'm not human anymore, Emma, and I haven't been for a long time. And while the others may share some of my traits, none of them truly understand what being pureblood means. The constant desires I push back. The alieness I feel inside of me..."

Her voice trailed off as she looked away. My body started shifting two different directions, desire and restlessness over Teren approaching, sympathy and compassion for the reluctant vampire in front of me. As my breaths increased even more with my struggle, her eyes slid back to me. "If you make it through this, I pray for your sake, that you end up more like Teren...and less like me."

I thought to reply, but instead, my head snapped around to the hallway leading to the front door; Teren was at the driveway. Before I knew it, I was standing, and my chair was knocked over from where I'd streaked upright. Halina laughed and walked over to fix it. I glanced at her. All trace of her previous comments were gone and she had returned to her sultry self. I quickly tuned her out. The fire in my body was too overwhelming to worry about her anymore.

Whimpering in frustration, I let my hands trail over my body, feebly trying to satisfy the ache. It didn't do anything, but it gave my restless body something else to concentrate on while I waited. This is when it got really bad, when he was super close. I had the feeling that if something or someone detained one of us right now, I would explode. It would not be pretty.

Luckily, none of the vampires here were going to try and halt our connection. They knew better. I streaked to the parking lot when I felt him pull up; Halina darted ahead of me to open the damn door.

I was at the side of the newly repaired Prius before he'd even shut it off. I yanked on the door, accidently pulling a hinge off with my revved up strength, and pulled him out of the car. He was on me in a flash—hands, lips, tongues—I was practically crawling over him as the magnets inside us completed their connection. Our bodies were all the more energized for it.

Knowing he'd promised not to stop this, I started tugging at his clothing. I heard the buttons of his shirt pop off as I ripped it open. A low growl escaped his chest as his hands tangled in my hair.

A few feet away from where we were mauling each other, I heard Teren's other car door open. A foot crunched onto the gravel and the smell of aftershave and body wash hit me. As I was pulling Teren's ruined shirt off his shoulders, I heard a startled voice say, "Um…guys?"

Wanting privacy, I jumped up, swinging my legs over so Teren would catch me in his arms. Luckily for me, he did. "Bed," I muttered, in the one second break between kisses.

He grunted some sort of response and then he was moving, streaking us upstairs, so we could finally relish this heat instead of pushing it away. As the world rushed by, my super hearing heard Hot Ben mutter, "What the hell was that?"

As Teren kicked in our door, breaking the frame, I heard Halina reply with, "That's just how they say hello now."

Teren set me down by the bed and we started ripping off clothes. Panting, I finished tearing off his outfit. Literally. I ruined everything he'd been wearing. Between our erotic noises, I whispered, "She's right, we never say hello anymore."

Finished with peeling off my clothes, his lips attached to my neck. "Hello," he muttered into my skin, before he dragged his tongue up to my ear.

Letting out a husky laugh, I heard Hot Ben enter the house with Halina. He was telling her, "It was weird. You should have seen him in the car, it was like he wanted to tear the seat to pieces, he was so antsy. He wouldn't even talk to me, wouldn't even drive me home."

Teren pressed his naked body against mine and I let out a loud groan. Not loud enough for a still-confused Ben, but loud enough for the others. Halina laughed as she responded to him. "Yes, she's like that too. It's very entertaining."

Teren tossed me down on the bed, not hard enough to hurt our children, but rough enough that I bounced on it. He was beside me in a flash; his cool, hard body along the side of mine, ignited me. "You were gonna rip apart the seats?" I asked him, turned on even more by the image.

His hand slipped down between my thighs, and I groaned again. "You have no idea. I couldn't wait to get home to you. I couldn't get here fast enough." His cool breath in my ear electrified me. His fingers running up and down my slick skin brought me right to the brink.

"Me too," I moaned as his finger dipped inside me. That took me right over the brink, and I cried out as I clutched his hair tight.

As my ecstatic noises died off, I heard Ben ask, "So…what are they doing now?"

Teren's cool mouth darted down to replace his fingers, and another loud cry echoed throughout the room as a second explosion hit me. Halina laughed and told him, "Guess."

Ben laughed as I came down off my second high. Teren flipped me to my side and came up behind me. As my stomach was generally in the way when we faced each other, this was how we could be the closest. His chest rested against my back and I felt the rumble of a growl through my skin. I turned my head to him. My fangs extended as I lost control on them, but he kissed me anyway. Lifting my leg up around his hip, he swept a hand down to my core again, making sure I was ready for him. I was.

He dropped his head to my shoulder; his fangs prickled my skin as he dragged them across me. I panted as he brought me right back to the edge again. It really didn't take much at this point. The energy buzzing between us was intensifying everything we naturally felt for each other. Not really caring about anything but being with him, I let out a loud cry when he removed his fingers and entered me. Then he was plunging deep and hard, grunting with each thrust. He grabbed my hip as he rocked me back and forth, pulling me closer, deeper. I bent forward a bit, away from him, allowing him to go as deep as he could. He gasped and muttered my name.

Careful not to hurt me, but moving against me with a purposeful fury, he let out more erotic noises than he usually did. He was animalistic in his movements, ravaging me with the beast within, not reining in his vampiric nature at all. His unrestraint drove me to madness, and I barely registered Halina telling Ben that we were, "About to bring the house down."

My hand clenched the sheets in front of me as the passion between us escalated. Finally, Teren growled deep and slowed his hips as he reached his climax. Feeling that release and hearing him groan in the most erotic way made me come again too—a particularly hard and particularly long one. Third time's a charm.

We rode out the sensation in tiny hip movements and bursts of staggered breaths. Eventually, Teren stopped moving and sagged against my back. Heart racing, breath heavy, I sagged against him too. Removing himself, he laced his arms around me and buried his head in my neck. "I love you," he muttered.

I could only grunt a series of sounds that sort of sounded like, "I love you too." He chuckled and reached over me for the covers we'd shucked aside in our haste. I sighed as a thick warmth enveloped me, protected me from the chill of his extremities. His core, the part that had been actively rubbing up against me, was quite warm.

As our breaths returned to normal and the intense energy dissipated, I heard an ongoing conversation that I'd managed to block out as things had gotten a little…intense, at the end.

"…so she started chucking things at him! It was hilarious." I heard Hot Ben sigh and Halina laugh.

I twisted my head to look at Teren. "The vampire chucked things at you?"

He kissed my shoulder. "Yeah, she took one look at me and knew exactly who I was." I twisted all the way around to him and he shook his head. "See, Great-Gran knew the vampire's boyfriend—"

I cut him off. Alanna had already explained the dramatics to me. "They told me." I shook my head as I looked over his perfect face, his rumpled hair. "I told them she'd know who you were."

He raised an eyebrow and I heard Halina mumble, "We can't help it if we're unforgettably attractive."

Teren rolled his eyes and looked down at the floor. "Well, she definitely remembered you. You may want to stay out of Santa Rosa for a while…or maybe even the state."

Halina snorted. "She should get over it. I mean, if you think about it, I did the cow a favor."

Teren sighed and snuggled against me. "Right," he muttered, just as Ben asked, "What did you say, Halina?"

I laughed, delighted by the fact that I was now privy to all the secret conversations. Well, the ones I was awake enough to hear anyway. Just as I was about to ask Teren what had happened, and maybe berate him for not telling me the entire situation before he went over there, I heard Hot Ben continue with, "Yeah, she went off on him for like twenty minutes...but then, this big vampire showed up. Things got a little hairy after that."

Teren sighed and rolled onto his back. "What happened?" I asked, my hands running over his chest.

He looked over at me with bunched brows. "He defended his girl's honor, knocked me around a little."

I sat up on an elbow, shocked. From downstairs, I heard a deep growl coming from Halina, and Ben asked her if she was okay. Teren sat up with me. His hand came up to my cheek as he said, "I'm fine. He didn't even leave a mark." He smirked and showed me his bare body. I frowned. Any "mark" on him would have healed by now. Just because his skin was pristine, didn't mean he hadn't been hurt.

Sighing, he rested his head against mine. "I'm fine. Eventually, I got them talking to me, explained what I was looking for." He pulled back, and his pale eyes flicked over my face. His expression was suddenly apologetic as he shook his head. "They didn't know anything." He sighed again and looked down at the floor, at Halina. "Nothing about others like me. They had another name though." He looked back up at me. "Another nest of purebloods. But that's all I got from them."

I exhaled a held breath and pulled him into me for a tight hug. I ran my fingers through his hair, pulling his head into me. I never wanted to let him go. I closed my eyes and bit back the tears, knowing that I had to let him go. I had to, or we'd lose everything.

He sighed and held me tight. "I love you, Emma."

I sighed and nodded. "I love you too."

I heard Halina start to grill Ben over the details of this new nest and heard his startled reply that she knew about that. She didn't tell him that she'd just heard Teren mention it, and I was sure Hot Ben was now wondering if she was a mind reader too. I'd imagine that would freak him out, to think that.

Teren and I relaxed back into the pillows, content to stay with each other while Hot Ben explained the details to the others. He even went downstairs and repeated the news to Alanna and Imogen, who had probably heard it the first time. Then Ben asked for a ride home.

I sighed and snuggled into Teren's cool shoulder, glad that he was with me, even if it was just for one night. In fact, he only left my side to grab a glass of blood from the kitchen. Throwing on some clothes, he cast a sheepish glance at the door as he left the room; it wouldn't close properly anymore. He ran into Ben as he was leaving with Imogen, who'd offered to give him a ride back to his house. I heard laughter and playful ribbing, as Ben chided him on our "reunion" in the parking lot. Ben told Teren that he'd have to get his car fixed again since I'd ruined the door, then Ben muttered that he wanted some hot sex like that and left the house. I grinned, knowing that Ben probably had more adventurous sex on a day to day basis with Tracey than most men got in their entire lifetime.

As quick as he could, Teren was back in bed with me, sipping on a tall, steaming glass and handing me one of my own. Even though I'd gorged myself at dinner, I greedily took the glass and began chugging it down. And once again I felt guilty over how much I drank. Teren laughed at my enthusiasm. His fangs were red and extended as he sat on my side of the bed and placed an arm around my shoulders. I relaxed into his body, loving how deeply we were connected, and hoping it lasted. Hoping *I* lasted.

I felt Teren's eyes on me as we drank, and I turned to see him smiling at me. Tentatively, he reached out and ran his finger down one of my fangs. It was like an instant jolt of electricity though me when he touched it. I half closed my eyes and wondered if my worn body could handle a round two.

"These are beautiful," he whispered, removing his hand.

Opening my eyes, I looked away from him. "You're just saying that to make me feel better about this. I know I look..." I couldn't finish my thought, and a soft sigh escaped me as a hormonal sadness swept over me.

His fingers curled around my jaw, turning me back to him. He opened his mouth wider, showing me his teeth; they were licked cleaned and once again pearly white. "You don't find these attractive?" he asked, as he smiled at me with a self-assuredness that stole my breath.

"You know I do." I grinned and ran my finger down his fang. He shuddered. "These are very sexy," I murmured.

His smile turned devilish, an expression his teeth only emphasized. "I feel the same about yours. I find them equally attractive. " He tilted his head and ran some of his cool fingers back through my hair. "Now, you can take my word on that…" he bit his lip, his fangs still extended, "or I could show you, again, exactly what you do to me?" He raised an eyebrow suggestively and I felt my skin flush.

I bit my lip, carefully, so I didn't actually *bite* my lip, and his eyes tracked the movement. Mine locked onto his teeth. "I believe you," I said softly, replaying our last encounter. Then I shook my head and nestled into his shoulder. "But mine just don't look natural to me yet, not like yours." I sighed as I looked over his smiling, attractive face; his eyes were still focused on my mouth. "Yours are very beautiful too," I said. His eyes flashed up to mine and he gave me a warm smile. I grinned and added, "Some vampires can have thin, reedy teeth, or wide, ugly teeth. Yours are very nicely proportioned."

He laughed at my description and then said, "You're checking out other vampires now?" He took a sip of his blood while I laughed.

"Just on TV."

Grinning, he shook his head and set his empty glass on the nightstand. With a playful twist of his lips, he leaned in to kiss my neck. "Well…my teeth aren't the only beautiful and well-proportioned things about me."

I let out a husky laugh at that, but my breath quickened and my body let me know that, yeah, I could handle a round two…or three, or four… Swallowing as he pulled my glass out of my hands, I muttered, "Beautiful? Really?"

Laughing into my skin, he muttered, "Just going with the theme of the evening."

I started to laugh, but then his mouth and hands were on me and I found that I couldn't focus. I heard him inhale me, inhale my desire for him, and a shaky breath escaped from the both of us. As his fingers brushed over my bare body, I heard Halina mutter, "God, I'm not listening to this again." After that, I felt her leave the house. Good riddance.

My breath sped up as I looked over the desire building in his face. "I want you, fangs or no fangs," he said, as he grinned crookedly. Looking over my desire, he added, "And I think you want me too."

Boy, did I ever.

He pulled my bare body onto his lap and I straddled him, my knees on either side of his hips. Making love with my giant stomach between us wasn't exactly the most romantic thing in the world, but the hormones in my body weren't exactly shouting moonbeams and sonnets, if you know what I mean. I had an acute ache, an ache that was growing larger by the second, and I needed him to fill it. Luckily, he didn't seem to mind the girth between us, and by his breath and face, he was feeling the same ache as me. That thought was confirmed when I lowered my bare hips to his lap—he had a very profound ache.

He sat up with me, stringing his fingers through the hair at the back of my head as he pulled me in for a deep kiss. His tongue matched the pace of my hips as I rocked against him. He groaned in my mouth as he, very carefully, stroked my extended fangs with his tongue. I moaned at the sensation and ground harder into his hips, needing him much deeper.

Suddenly, a loud rumble sounded throughout the room, startling me. I was used to low feral noises from Teren when he got in *that* mood, but these noises were different than the growls I associated with him. These were different, because I could still feel the lingering vibrations along my ribs, along my skin. These were different because they had come from *my* chest, not Teren's. I sat back on his lap, breaking our intense make out session.

"Oh my God, I growled at you!"

He smirked and leaned in for my neck. "I know, it was hot."

I pulled away and twisted my lips at him. "How is me growling at you hot?"

He raised an eyebrow, and I felt myself flushing. I knew what he was going to say—*Isn't it hot when I do it?* And it was. That always got some sort of response from my body; I just wasn't used to being the one making the animal noises. He started to reply but I cut him off with my lips as I leaned into his body.

"Don't say it," I muttered and I could feel him chuckling beneath me.

Chapter 16 – Obsession

After that amazing night of reconnecting over and over again, a feat that eventually also drove Alanna and Imogen from the house, my husband became a ghost. Not literally, but for as much as he was around after that night, he might as well have been a vague spirit in the house—sensed but never seen.

It started the very next night when he followed up on the lead that the scorned vampire had given him. I was worried when he called and told me he that he wouldn't be home until tomorrow. That worried me for several reasons. One was the fact that the nest was so far away that he had to stay overnight somewhere.

Second, I was worried because Teren was anxious. He was too worried that he wouldn't find the nest in time to wait the few hours until sundown when Halina could go with him. He assured me that she would catch up with him when she could, but he wasn't going to wait for her. As it was still daylight out when he left, he couldn't take any of the mixed vampires with him either. Alanna maybe, but even she wouldn't feel good, riding in a sun-filled car for hours. That meant he had to take Hot Ben again. Yeah, I still didn't know what to feel about that, other than worried.

But lastly, I was afraid of him facing more vampires. Maybe that one asshole vampire who had bitten me had put me off on the whole species, but I was filled with anxiety over him going out and knocking on the doors of potentially dangerous people. I mean, as strong as he was, he was a third generation mixed. Strength-wise, that was comparable to a teenager going up against a WWE wrestler. Well, maybe not *that* drastic, Teren was incredibly strong, but he would be outmatched if things turned violent before Halina got there, Hot Ben guardian or no Hot Ben guardian.

And I couldn't help the thought that this scorned vampire had sent him to some biker gang nest or something, to make sure he was ripped to pieces, just to send a message to Halina. I was also pretty sure that if that were the case, Halina would retaliate by frying the woman alive. But who knew, maybe she considered that a risk worth taking. All of it made me nauseous.

So the twins and I muddled around the house, reading, helping Alanna with housework when I begged her for something to do, making phone calls to my friends and family, and having conversations with the vampires while they worked on their research project of saving my life, or more importantly, the twins' lives.

With Teren gone, I pored over the journals with them. My stomach battled itself over whether to feel revulsion over what I was reading, or fear over Teren's overnight trip. Imogen stroked my arm while she read beside me, her pale, youthful eyes occasionally giving me concerned glances. Jack and Alanna talked in the corner over a particularly nasty section in the book that involved eradicating a group of "breeders"—humans, wives and husbands—and I had to put a hand on my stomach. Sighing, I looked over at the stone wall of Halina's room to where my Teren-sense told me he was, miles away from me.

"He'll be fine, dear."

I looked back at Imogen. Noticing her tight smile, I thought maybe she was just as concerned as I was. "I know," I whispered, wanting to comfort her as much as she was trying to comfort me. At least we were all in our fear together.

"He'd better be," I heard Halina growl from the other side of the room. She was pacing as she waited for the final rays of sunlight to fade. "I will hold that bitch personally responsible if she led Teren into a trap." Halina's eyes flashed pure anger as a low growl rumbled from her throat. "And she knows better than to mess with me."

Alanna put a hand on her arm and the teenage-looking vampire straightened and silenced. I nodded, oddly reassured by her threat, and then I continued poring over the lunatic's ramblings. Ten minutes later the sun set, and Halina darted out of the house, and zipped away at a brisk pace.

My eyes closed a few hours before dawn as my head dropped down to the grimy paper.

After hours of looking at horrible acts of cruelty, my sleeping mind replayed a night that I hadn't visited for a while in my dreams. I started having a nightmare of that man and his cruelties towards us. And since it was a nightmare, my mind increased the horrors. Instead of him ruthlessly kicking Teren's shattered shins, I visualized him plunging stakes through them, pinning him to the ground while he screamed. And since being pregnant now felt more natural to me than not being pregnant, I imagined myself swollen with life, chained to that wall beside Teren. While Teren screamed, unable to help me, I watched the man approach with a cruel smile. With a flick of his wrist, he cut a deep slice along my abdomen and viciously ripped the twins out of me. Slumping to the ground in a fog of pain, I saw their perfect, pink faces. Their tiny fangs were just visible on their newborn smiles as he coldly snapped their necks.

I woke up screaming.

Cool hands were on me in an instant, as a tall muscular body slid into bed with me. I vaguely registered that one of the vampires must have carried me back to my room after I'd fallen asleep; good thing they were all strong. "Emma, it's all right, I'm here." Teren's cool breath hit my ear as sobs continued pouring from my mouth.

He pulled me into his chest. His body was shaking as he struggled to contain the energy we usually felt when we were reunited. I'd been asleep during the build-up and wasn't riled up like he was. He was gentlemanly enough to not ravage me while I was so obviously grieved. He only stroked my back and kissed my head. I knew from experience just how much restraint he was using, and I loved him all the more for it.

Knowing I was making that restraint harder for him, but needing his comfort, I clung to every part of him that I could. Through sobs, I muttered, "I'm so glad you're back. I had such a bad dream."

He sighed in a way that sort of sounded like a groan. "It's okay. No one hurt me, I'm fine."

I shook my head against his chest. My nightmare hadn't been about him meeting with vampires. "No, I dreamt that that man had taken us again…and our babies. He…he…" I couldn't even speak the horror out loud, and started sobbing again.

Teren's shaking stopped as he stiffened in my arms. "Did you read the journals last night?" His voice, while not angry, was not pleased.

I bit my lip and peeked up at his face. The room was dark, the early morning rays blocked out by the heavy curtains closed over them, and his eyes glowed at me. I took a moment to absorb his comfort before I answered him. He waited patiently, knowing that he was soothing me, and then I noticed that he was staring at my eyes too, and that his face seemed to be relaxing. Then I noticed that his features were being lit from an odd angle, not from his eyes, but from an outside source. There were no other lights in the dark room and I was horribly confused, until I realized that...*my* eyes were glowing.

I widened them in shock and held a hand in front of my face. Sure enough, I could clearly see that my palm was being highlighted in a way that had nothing to do with Teren's glow. I'd never noticed this before. I hadn't realized I'd gotten this vampiric side effect too. I didn't know why I'd never thought of that. I guessed I'd just had too many other things on my plate to notice.

"My eyes glow now, Teren," I said through hiccups, as my breathing tried to stabilize.

"I know, don't change the subject." His voice was amused, but serious.

I looked back up at him; his brows were bunched as he watched me. I struggled to remember his question. "Um...yes, sorry. I wanted to help," I said, a slight whine to my voice.

He sighed and pulled my head to his. Resting his cheek on my hair, I heard him inhale me, inhale every trace of the world I'd encountered while he'd been gone. I found myself doing the same with him, cringing a bit at the scent of cheap, imitation perfume; the vampire had been a girl again.

"Do you think giving yourself nightmares is helping, Emma?" he said into my hair. I started to object but he pulled back, eyeing me with a serious expression. "I want you mellow, relaxed." His hand came up to lightly stroke my cheek. "Let me worry about finding the mixed. You..." his hand came down to rest on my belly, and a child kicked him in response, "take care of our children." He smiled as he rubbed my stomach. "And stop stressing, please?"

I gave him a half grin and nodded as I relaxed into his side. We were silent for a few moments and then I asked him about the nest.

He sighed and rested his head against mine. "They weren't happy about me barging in on them, asking questions, but they did have an answer for me." I lifted my head to look at him and he shrugged; the glow of his eyes shook with the movement. "It wasn't violent, Emma, I promise."

I nodded and asked, "And?" I hoped he'd tell me that they'd said something like, "Mixed? Oh, yeah, there's a group of them that meet for hot fudge sundaes every Saturday morning at the Ghirardelli Ice Cream shop in the Square."

Teren sighed. "They didn't know anything about me, but they gave me more names, a few this time."

I sighed and slumped down to his chest. I guess my scenario had been a little farfetched. Mixed were rare. We'd be lucky to find one, let alone a group of them. Teren sighed with me and kissed my head. I peeked up at him. "I thought you'd be gone longer. How come you're home? Not that I mind."

I smiled and he smiled in return. "The pull. I found them much faster than I thought I would. Ben and I were done by the time Great-Gran caught up with us." He chuckled. "She was *not* happy about immediately having to turn around and run home to beat the sun, but she didn't want to stay holed up in a strange place for a full day. Ben wanted to go find a motel, since it was so late, but when I turned the car in your direction, I couldn't make myself pull away from the highway. Not when you were calling to me. Not when I had no reason to stay in the city anymore." He grinned at me seductively. "It's a good thing I took Great-Gran's car today. It's much faster than mine."

I laughed and ran my hands down his back to his jeans, pulling him into me. He smiled, as he leaned in to kiss me. "Ben?" I asked, between kisses.

Listening to the sounds of the house, I could hear Jack lightly snoring, Alanna and Imogen talking about my nightmare, since my screaming had woken them both up, and one person downstairs sighing in irritation, muttering about how he was taking his own car next time. I laughed as Teren confirmed that Ben was hanging out in the living room.

Just as I started reveling in the softness of my miraculous man's mouth, he pulled back and gave me a sheepish expression. "Don't take this the wrong way…" I frowned as his guilt increased. "They gave me a lead that I think may have something to do with a nest talked about in the journals. I think they may be connected to a group of mixed that the man already…" He ran a hand through my hair. "I really want to go check it out…"

I sighed when I realized he was asking to leave. "Oh…can't it wait?" I squeezed his body tighter to mine. "At least until morning?"

He leaned down to kiss me. "It *is* morning, Emma."

I peeked at the clock over his shoulder. It was morning in only the vaguest sense of the term; even the sun was probably begrudging the hour. "Barely," I sullenly muttered.

"I need to get on top of this, Em. If they have anything to do with mixed…? If they know about our kind…? I thought I could get it researched enough this afternoon, that Ben, Great-Gran and I could find them tonight." I could hear the turmoil in his voice. He wanted to stay, he wanted to go. I decided to make it easy for him, since he was doing all of this for me anyway, me and the kids.

I pushed away from him, cuddling into my sheets instead. "Fine. I'm still tired anyway, I guess I'll go back to sleep."

He pulled the blankets around me, tucking me in. With a sexy smile, he leaned over to kiss me. "I'll miss you. I love you."

I had to bite my lip to not tell him that he didn't have to miss me, that his entire body could be wrapped around me right now. I didn't place that guilt trip on him, though. This was just something he needed to do. "I love you too."

We both heard Ben sigh in annoyance again, complaining that he'd rather be snuggling up with Tracey than a throw pillow, and we laughed. Teren sighed and ran a hand down my hair. "I probably should run Ben home."

I bit my lip and nodded, hating that he was leaving the house again. The reverse of the pull, while not as drastic as the reuniting, wasn't pleasant. It was a tearing feeling, like a part of me was being stretched away. Never detached though, just stretched. It made the reunion part that much sweeter.

I yawned as he watched me. "I'll probably be asleep when you get back," I sighed in remorse, knowing there was no way I'd be able to stay awake this early after a night of restless slumber.

Teren solemnly nodded. "I'll leave you alone." I knew how difficult that would be for him. A part of me wanted to use that to my advantage, wanted to tell him that he should at least say hello, since I knew I could twist that kinetic energy between us into a break-the-bed love fest, but another part of me didn't want to abuse our connection that way. I didn't want to use sex as a weapon to keep him near me. Not when what he was doing was so vastly important.

I put my hand on my stomach, reminding myself what really mattered, and nodded. "Okay."

When Hot Ben started muttering that Teren should learn to handle his hard-ons the way every other guy did, I started laughing. "Does he remember that we can all hear him?" I chuckled.

Teren frowned at the floor and then looked back at me. "No, I think that's slipped his mind." He sighed. "I should get him home."

He pulled away from me and stood up. I sighed as I studied his lean body highlighted by our glowing eyes. "I still can't believe he willingly goes with you."

Teren smiled as he looked down at me. "He's actually pretty helpful." Delight that he had been able to keep that friendship tight was clear in his face. "He constantly surprises me." He gave me a wry grin. "You'd be very proud of him. Tracey too...if the whole thing wouldn't have her screaming in terror." He laughed at that, then leaned down to kiss me a final time.

Once back downstairs, I heard him surprise Hot Ben in the living room. "I'm done. I'll take you home now."

Ben let out a grateful sigh. "Oh, thank God, you're fast in the bedroom too." I heard the sound of Ben being smacked. "Ow! What? Just saying..." Teren sighed and they both started heading for the door, Ben muttering, "Sorry, no offense or anything. I'm just tired. I want to go home and be super speedy with my girl too."

Both of the guys laughed and I blinked, surprised. In all the chaos, I hadn't realized that Ben and Tracey had moved in together. It irritated me that I was missing out on so much, being quarantined here, but it made me smile that Tracey and Hot Ben were moving in the right direction. Teren was right. Ben had turned out to be very surprising.

And that began the pattern of Teren getting further and further away from me. He'd search out every lead a vampire gave him, but he never found anything more than more names, more nests, more leads. No pureblood vampire he came across seemed to know anything about mixed vampires. Most of them were startled that such a thing was even possible. The one group he'd found that he'd thought was somehow connected to mixed, turned out to be a dead-end. Teren had thought they were connected because of a vague reference in the book that sounded like one of the vampire's last names, but it turned out to just be a coincidence. The purebloods he'd found had nothing to do with the long-dead mixed vampires in the journals.

So far, no vampire he'd met knew anything about his kind, but every vampire gave him the name of another vampire, usually to get his annoying ass off their property. But Teren didn't care how he got a name, so long as he got one. As he was gone more often, taking some of his family with him if the trip was close enough, I started hearing about more frequent fights and scuffles.

And as the weeks went by and my lifespan dwindled, I started hearing about genuine knockouts. I could even see the result of fighting in Teren's clothes, if not his fast-healing body. And, of course, Teren couldn't hide Hot Ben's wounds. When I saw him with a black eye one night, I nearly went ballistic. They both assured me that it was nothing, merely a misunderstanding, but it riled me up, and I demanded that Teren stop this craziness. Obviously, the vampire community knew nothing, and obviously his continual prodding of their nests was starting to piss them off. He was stirring the beehives, so to speak, and as a general rule of thumb, it was a good idea to leave something as dangerous as hornets alone.

But Teren didn't. He couldn't. As we rolled into the beginning of April, and my 28th week, Teren started panicking. He didn't take my upcoming due date as a good sign—that I'd make it, or at least that I would make it close enough so that the babies would be able to live on their own, and everything would be fine. No, he started freaking out because my twenty-sixth birthday was in two weeks. To him, that was it. That was the end of my life, and subsequently, the end of theirs.

I felt sort of stuck, as trapped emotionally as I was physically. I knew I needed to stay at the ranch. For the safety of mankind, I knew I couldn't join Teren on these little outings, in case I died and reanimated. If that happened, and Teren's blood *was* enough to bring me back to life as an undead vampire, I'd go into a bloodbath-frenzy and I'd chow down anything with a pulse. And as much as it pained me to think about it, I wasn't sure if I had the same level of self-control that Teren had shown. I had a terrible feeling in the pit of my stomach, that got exceptionally strong when I was tipping back a bovine beverage, that I wouldn't stop, even if the human in question were family. That realization frightened me enough to stay put.

I also understood why Teren needed to go. I knew I needed to let him do whatever was necessary to try and save the lives inside of me, but I couldn't help the feeling that all he was doing was wasting our precious time. If nothing could be done, and I was going to die anyway, then we were wasting weeks that we could have been spending in each other's arms.

A phone call from Tracey a couple of nights later only emphasized the unease I felt about Teren's increasingly volatile meetings. She'd called me right after I'd hung up the phone with my mother. Mom was worried about how bored I was, which I wasn't, since I could get up and move around just fine. She was also delighted about all the time she was getting to spend with her four-legged grandchild.

Hearing Alanna humming while she worked just outside the front door, I answered the home phone when it rang. I'd hoped it was Teren. It wasn't. "Hi, can I talk to Emma?"

Recognizing Tracey's voice, I merrily exclaimed, "Hey, Trace, it's me."

She didn't respond right away and I felt tension curl into the line. I also heard her heartbeat surging, even through the phone.

When she spoke, her voice was tight. "Is Teren trying to get Ben killed?"

Panic flooded my body. My heartbeat accelerated so fast and so suddenly, that I knew my revved up vamp blood was taking over. Not wanting shock to start my conversion, I exhaled in a long, slow breath, trying to ease my body back to normalcy. From outside, Alanna stopped humming and asked if I was okay. I whispered that I was, just before I finally answered Tracey.

"Uh, what do you mean?" I crossed my fingers, hoping Tracey was still oblivious to what her boyfriend's true extracurricular activities were. I didn't relish sending Halina to her doorstep.

She exhaled with clear irritation. "The fighting, Emma. You know, the training stuff." I heard clicking and pictured Tracey's long, high-heeled legs pacing back and forth in her kitchen. Before I could ask her what she was talking about, she sighed and continued. "You should see his body, Emma. Yeah, he's even more ripped than before, but the black and blue patches are not attractive…and it can't be good for him." Her voice trembled as her true concern showed.

"Oh, well, Teren…" I trailed off, since I really wasn't sure what Ben and Teren's cover story to her was. I kicked myself for not listening to those conversations better, not that Teren had been around much to share them with me.

Tracey sighed again, her voice quavering. "And his face…did you see his black eye?"

I sighed. Yeah, I had seen that. "Sorry, Trace. I'll talk to Teren." I wasn't sure what I was talking to him about, but I'd definitely try talking to him again.

She plopped down somewhere, her clothes rustling. I heard the sounds of shoes being slipped off and thought maybe she'd gone to her room. Her voice relaxed as well as her heart. "Yeah, okay, thanks." She exhaled again and I heard a mattress compressing as she lied down. "I don't know how he ever talked me into this, Emma. I mean, really, it's sort of ridiculous."

I leaned back in my favorite plush chair in the library, one hand stroking my belly as I pulled my feet up. Outside, I heard Alanna continue her humming. Upstairs, Imogen clacked away, knitting. "I know, Trace. Men," I harrumphed. I still didn't know what they'd told her, but condemning the male species was usually a proper response to any female conversation.

Apparently it was. She laughed and I heard her roll over on the bed. I could even hear her feet banging together. "Right. I mean, UFC fighting? Seriously?" She laughed again, a little condescendingly. "I know he teaches kickboxing at the gym sometimes and works pretty regularly at that dojo in Chinatown, but Ultimate Fighting?" She laughed again, heartier. "Who does he think he is now, Bruce Lee?"

I closed my eyes and cursed my husband. Not for their ridiculous cover story, but for the fact that they knew Hot Ben might get tossed around enough that he'd need a violent cover story. This was really getting out of control. "Yeah, Trace...kind of absurd." I wondered how far they'd take the story. Was Hot Ben actually going to try out?

Tracey snorted. "Yeah, and Teren sparring with him. Who knew the metrosexual was so aggressive in the ring?" She quickly added, "Uh, no offense or anything."

I laughed at her analysis of Teren. I'd sort of accused him of the same thing once. He was just very put together, for a guy. But that wasn't what made me laugh. No, it was Tracey, the girl whose boyfriend could shoot Calvin Klein ads, calling my boyfriend metrosexual. She laughed with me when she realized I wasn't mad at her comment. My laughter died as what they'd told her sunk in.

I sighed and she did too. I heard her sit up on her bed. "I know they're both really into this, Em, but maybe you could ask Teren to ease up?" She sighed again as concern filled her. "You know, I just don't like to see him hurt. And I'm sure you don't like seeing Teren hurt either."

I sighed, remembering Teren's ripped clothing, the dried blood that I knew had come from his already-healed body. "No, I don't. I'll talk to him again, Trace. I promise."

Her tone brightened and she stood up, I could hear her feet padding across her carpet. "Good! Maybe if you do, I can see a bit more of my boyfriend." I heard her walk into the bathroom as I mentally agreed with her—I'd love to see more of my guy too. She started running water and I heard her giggle. "Did I mention we moved in together?"

Laughing a little myself, I let my tension disappear, if just for a moment. "No, I had to hear it from Ben." I relaxed back into my chair, wishing I had some blood to sip, and smiled at Tracey through the phone. "Spill."

Tracey giggled as she got ready for her bath. Then she proceeded to tell me all about it. As she went into the details of Ben asking her to live with him in the middle of one of their adventurous sex acts, I felt the stress slide off of me, and let myself just be a girlfriend. I laughed along with her story, commented in all the right places, and silently thanked Tracey for unknowingly easing my mind. Sometimes, I wished I could tell her how often she did that.

I could have used Tracey's easing powers that Saturday afternoon, when Teren, after being gone for most of the week and all of that morning, rushed home with Ben following as close on his heels as a human could. Having felt him approach, I was waiting in the entryway, clutching the naked woman statue to stop myself from blurring to the parking lot and destroying his car again. He haltingly walked into the room; restraint was clear in his features as he took jerky steps towards me.

We were trying to control the strong pull we felt towards each other when we were reunited. It was a constant struggle, something we had to contain, much like I always had to contain my teeth from popping down.

At human speed he walked over to me. His movements didn't look natural and breezy, they were more like a bad stop-motion movie, halting and restarting. I smelled the outside world on his clothes as he got close enough. Using that to control myself, I closed my eyes and took in long inhales. I also used the lingering anger in my belly, from the fact that he was gone so often. The smell of the bay danced on his skin, along with the unmistakable smell of fish. He'd been on the wharf today.

I heard Ben enter the house, muttering something about how weird that was, before turning to walk down a hallway that led to one of the side buildings. I tried to listen to Ben for as long as I could, grounding myself, but eventually the pull of Teren was too strong and I ignored him. I ignored everyone—Imogen and Alanna talking upstairs, Jack working on one of the cars in the driveway, and Halina's stone-silent sleeping presence—everyone.

No one existed but Teren. My anger faded as my breathing increased. I could hear his increase as well as the draw pulled him closer to me. When we were a few inches apart, we both lost control. Then it was much like it always was when we got together; our restraint dissolved as the tension became unbearable. It was nothing but searching hands, probing tongues, small gasps and heavy groans. He pressed his hard body against mine as my fingers tangled into his dark hair. A rush of desire burst through me, and in my mind I begged him to take me. And it could be anywhere, right here on the rim of the fountain would be fine, just…take me.

Then duty and obligation calmed his breath and he gently, but firmly, pushed me away. Panting, I opened my eyes and stared up at him. I was both disappointed *and* grateful for his level of control. His lips inched away from mine, minutely coming forward before pulling back again. His eyes struggled with the conflicting desires in his body.

I did what I could to help; I still didn't want to abuse this amazing draw. Stepping back from him, I removed my hands from his body and held them at my sides. Every fiber of my soul screamed at me to touch him. Containing a whimper of frustration, I ignored the sensation as I bit my lip. I knew this feeling would pass, but it was torture to not give in. Especially with the memories of the few times we had caved filling my head. In this state, climax was effortless and easily repeatable. My body was yearning for it.

He closed his eyes and inhaled deep. I knew he was trying to ground himself too, but I also knew he could smell my desire in the air. That really wasn't helping anything. He started shaking. "Emma," he said, his voice shaky as well. "I have to…help Ben. We have a lead with a very short window." He opened his eyes, they were pained. "There's a chance that they're leaving their nest at nightfall, and it will take hours to get to them. I'm sorry, but I need to reach them before they leave. I don't have time for this."

My eyes flared as anger cooled my desire. "You never have time."

He straightened in front of me, his body coming under control as my tone irritated him. "You know why I have to do this." His eyes flashed down to my stomach and I felt myself heating in embarrassment and frustration.

Yes, I knew why. I was reminded why with every kick, squirm, and thumping heartbeat. I couldn't escape the reasons—they were with me constantly. But I missed him...and I worried for him. He took a step back from me while I struggled for something to say. Not having anything, I watched him turn away and follow where Hot Ben had gone.

I turned from the sight of his muscular back leaving me. I felt him exit the main building and enter a side wing. I knew exactly which room he'd gone into—it was at the far end of the ranch. I stared at the crying woman fountain, feeling tears spring into my own eyes. It wasn't fair. He'd promised me when he'd proposed to me that he'd never take a single second together for granted, and here we were, just a few months later, and quite possibly the last few months I had left, and he couldn't spare twenty minutes to ravage me into oblivion.

A part of me knew I was being petty. A part of me knew being together wasn't as important as what he was doing. But the majority of me was pregnant, hormonal, and sexually frustrated.

Feeling a low growl growing in my chest, I twisted my head to where I could sense him through the structure of the home. "Screw this," I muttered.

I blurred to the room he was in and busted open the door, cracking the frame. Hot Ben jumped about a foot in the air and squeaked, startled. Teren had already been looking at the door; he'd sensed me coming. His brows furrowed, his face was not happy. Mine wasn't either.

"I'm coming with you," I stated matter-of-factly.

He straightened, shook his head and walked across the room to me. "No, you're not, Emma."

He stepped up to me as I put my hands on my hips. "Yes, I am. We were supposed to do this together, Teren. That was the deal, remember? That we'd look for the mixed together." I looked up and down his lean body. Mine was responding in conflicting ways—angry and aroused. "It's the only way to spend time with you, anyway."

He sighed in frustration, sensing my two moods but not knowing what to do with either of them. He put his hands on my upper arms as he squatted to search my eyes. His pale ones looked tired. "Well, things changed, Emma, and now you can't. I can't risk you coming with me. You have to stay here, where you're safe."

I raised my chin, feeling childish *and* empowered. "You're not the boss of me, Teren. It's my decision to make and if I want to go, I'll go."

He gave me a look that parents give insolent children, and I narrowed my eyes at seeing it. His tone matched his expression as he used logic against me. "I am the boss of you when it comes to this, when it comes to your safety, and the safety of every human you may come across, if you convert in the field."

Internally, I cringed. I knew he was right. Irritated, I jerked away from his body and snapped, "That's not fair." Damn male logic.

He shrugged, straightening. "No, it isn't, but it's true and you know it. And that's why you'll stay here."

My hormonally revved up body heated to a boiling point, and again, I said something that sounded rather childish. "Sometimes I hate you."

He looked up at the ceiling, like he was exasperated with me. After a supercharged second he looked back down and crossed his arms over his chest. "I'm going to believe that that's the hormones talking, and not you."

I crossed my arms as well. "Believe whatever the hell you want." Oh yeah, I was definitely crossing into pre-teen territory. In fact, I'd had a similar argument with my mother about going to a boy/girl slumber party in the eighth grade.

Really not liking my tone, he ran a hand through his hair. "I can't have you around me, Emma." He flung his fingers out to indicate my body. "You're too distracting."

My jaw tightened in annoyance. "Well, get a grip on it, Teren. I'm coming."

Hot Ben cleared his throat and resumed shoving things into a green duffel bag. I tuned him out as I concentrated on my suddenly chauvinistic husband. He ran his hands down his face, looking like he just wanted to order me to stay, and have that be the end of it. He knew me well enough to know that it wouldn't be that simple—not this time. I was done waiting around.

"Emma." His voice was strained. "I can't protect you out there. It's too dangerous."

Stepping up to him, I grabbed his face with my hands. His stubbled skin was coarse against my sensitive fingers. It sort of matched my mood. "That's exactly why you shouldn't be going. What you're doing, provoking vampires—it's too dangerous!" My eyes shifted over to Hot Ben, his hurt eye socket was a horrid mix of black, blue and yellow. "Look what you're doing to Ben!"

Recalling my phone conversation with Tracey, I leaned around Teren to snap at him, "UFC, Ben? Really?"

Ben stopped shoving objects in his bag and shrugged at me, his model face sheepish. "What? It seemed like a good excuse. I've always wanted to…" He didn't finish explaining, just ran a hand through his highlighted hair. That was when I noticed what was in his hands, what he'd been shoving into the bag.

Stakes. Handfuls of sharp, six-inch long stakes—some wood, some silver and some, a hard plastic.

Fear washed over me as I looked back at Teren. He stiffened when he realized I'd finally noticed. "What the hell are you doing?" I backed away from him. My hand automatically went to my stomach as my horrible dream of that man staking Teren's shins was suddenly fresh in my mind. Incredulous, I gaped at him. "What…are you guys some sort of…vampire hunters now?" I looked between the both of them, noting the other objects that Ben was packing—silver knives, one of the journals, a short sword, and a gun, most likely containing silver bullets. They looked like they were going to war. I focused on Teren. "Have you gone mad?"

Teren lifted his jaw and clenched it. His eyes were both worried and infuriated. He obviously didn't want me to see this part of his "meetings." He raised his hands as he shook his head. "Vampires are starting to hear about us. They've been…resistant." He shrugged nonchalantly, like it was all no big deal. "We make them talk, that's all."

"You make them…" I didn't even want to think about what that meant. I didn't want to think about him turning into a crazed torturer, just like our abductor. Panic clenched me at the thought of the two of them walking into a potentially deadly nest of vampires who might be expecting him, who might have *heard* of him. I clutched his upper arms tight, my new strength making my grip hard enough that Teren actually flinched. "Don't do this. Are you crazy? They could kill you, both of you."

He jerked out of my grip and pushed my hands away. "We'll be fine, Emma. Please don't str—"

I cut him off. "Do *not* tell me not to be stressed about this. This is dangerous and stupid, and I'm going to stress as much as I damn well want to stress!"

Hot Ben, behind Teren, sighed and I glanced over to see him running a hand through his hair. "He's right, Em. We'll be fine."

I gaped at him. "Well, aren't you a far cry from the man who begged me to not let my fiancé *eat* him!"

Ben flushed with color and turned away. I turned back to Teren; my panic increased my irritation. "I never see you anymore. You're always out tracking down some farfetched lead that some random vampire gave you. You're becoming this person I don't even know. This isn't like you. You're obsessed!" I hissed.

Furious, he leaned down and put his face right in mine. "Of course I'm obsessed!" His hands flashed down to me and I actually took a half-step away from him. His fingers rested on my stomach and a twin jostled under his touch. "They are my children! My *life*! And I will do anything to protect them—to protect you!" His eyes searched mine, heated and impassioned. I barely recognized him. "I will do anything to keep you alive! *Anything*!"

As I backed away from him, fear and anger took over my mouth. "Maybe you should have thought about that before you pissed off a hungry vampire!"

He stepped away like I'd slapped him in the face. His expression was almost tortured, and his eyes started to glisten. I saw *my* Teren in that look of betrayal and I felt my own tears stinging. "Teren…I…"

He took a step back from me, shaking his head, and then he blurred from the room. I felt him leave the house, then felt him leave the property. I thought he might decide to run all the way back to the city, or wherever they were going.

I dropped my head to my hands, not even believing I'd just said that to him. Of all the awful, hurtful comments I could have made— that was the worst. I knew he felt guilty. I knew he hated to even look at the scar on my neck. And I knew he thought all of this was his fault. I'd just sliced him open and dumped a trailer load of salt in his wounds. I hated myself.

Hot Ben walked up to me as he slung his bulging duffle bag over his shoulder. More calmly than I ever would have thought possible, he placed a hand on my shoulder and said, "I'll watch over him, Emma. We'll be all right. I'll bring him home."

I looked up at his confident blue eyes. He was so different from the man who'd clutched my hand in terror in that fateful parking lot. I wished I had his assurance, but in my head, I imagined that Teren would be the one most likely keeping Ben alive today, and maybe not even succeeding in that. I numbly nodded at him, appreciating his sentiment, since I couldn't quite believe his promise. He patted me on the shoulder and then headed out after Teren.

Chapter 17 – The Breaking Point of a Good Man

Almost immediately upon feeling Teren leave the property, Alanna darted after him. I supposed she had heard our entire argument and had some thoughts on the matter too. Imogen confirmed that for me, by repeating over and over that she had no idea he would resort to such extremes to get what he wanted. She couldn't believe he was being so reckless and foolish. Like me, she was convinced that he'd only get himself killed. And also like me, she seemed to be surprised by Teren and Ben's method of "interviewing."

Feeling Teren and Alanna's lives zipping away from me, I sank to the floor. It looked like an office in here, but smelled musty, like it hadn't been used in years. As I crouched onto my knees and started to cry, I noticed that there were tons of maps in this room. Some were scrolled and tucked up in bookshelves. Others were tacked up on the walls. A large one of North America was taking a place of prominence next to a wide, sunny window. That map had several pinpricks in it—the little pins, with red balls on the end. Tracker pins. As tears slid down my face, I absentmindedly thought that it was probably a map of everywhere the Adams vamps had lived or visited over the years. If Teren and I made it out of this mess in one piece, I wondered if I would visit any of those pinpricks.

I sensed when Teren shifted his direction away from his mother; he obviously wasn't in the mood to talk. But I had to give it to the determined woman, she wasn't about to let him go, and she was fast, even a smidge quicker than he was. She gained on him inch-by-inch until finally, after what felt like an eternity to me, both of their presences stopped.

I held my breath, my hand covering my mouth to hold in my grief. I felt like I was going into shock. I couldn't move off the floor, couldn't run to my husband, couldn't beg for his forgiveness, or plead with him to stay. I couldn't even comfort Imogen, who was actively cursing the sun that was keeping her a prisoner in the house. I was immobile with pain. All I could do was wait on my knees on the floor, and pray that Alanna could do what I had failed to do so miserably—talk some reason back into Teren.

My knees started to ache as I waited. My breath came back in stuttered pulls and my body started to shake with tension. I wanted to know what was going on. I wanted to be able to hear Alanna's heartfelt pleading and I wanted to hear Teren agree with her. I wanted to feel the pull in my body of him returning. The desire to feel it ached worse than my stiff knees. But after what felt like an eternity, I eventually felt Alanna's presence returning to the house.

That was when I broke down in sobs. Because Teren didn't return with her. He never even turned back in my direction. As Alanna shifted to me, he shifted away, off to madly chase after vampires with his human companion, who was probably picking him up right now and driving him away from me.

Imogen began to cry in her room too, as Teren got farther and farther away. As my head dropped to my hands and I felt each individual tear splash onto my skin, I wondered if they would still let me stay with them if Teren got himself killed today because of me. That thought only made my sobs come out in a tortured wail.

Then Alanna's soothing arms were around me and she was picking me up. The woman was no bigger than me. With my pregnant girth, she was actually much smaller, size-wise, but she easily lifted me. She cradled me in her arms as I mercilessly cried on her shoulder.

My breath hitching around my words, I managed to get out, "You couldn't get him back?"

She swallowed; her eyes were heavy with pink tears. Kissing my forehead, she muttered into my hair, "I needed to get out of the sun. I kept him from leaving, but I couldn't block him forever. He stayed an arm's length from me and waited it out. He knew I only had so long to get him back." She rested her cheek on my hair and sighed brokenly. "The entire time we were talking, he kept telling me that he had to go, that he was running out of time. He just kept repeating it over and over again." She lifted her head and stared straight in front of her as a pink tear dropped to her cheek. "I've never seen him look like that, Emma. He was almost…unhinged."

I clutched her as we walked through a covered breezeway. The difference in the air temperature was blazingly apparent on my sensitive skin. I hiccupped through my sobs as she walked me upstairs to Imogen's room. A second set of hands were on me then, and I was carefully laid out on Imogen's bed and tucked in like a child. With neither woman saying anything, they both silently comforted me with tender strokes.

Eventually my grief ended enough that I was able to take in the young faces watching me. My enhanced eyes could more easily see the differences between them than my regular eyes could—Alanna's hair was a shade lighter, Imogen's eyes were a touch bluer. In the dark, candlelit room, all of our eyes glowed softly, and I noticed that even that phosphorescence was a slightly different shade. We were each our own persons, but we shared a common heartache—Teren.

I eyed his mother. She was trying hard to keep serenity on her face, but her jaw was tight and her free hand was clenching the edge of her jeans, twisting them in her tension. I shifted my gaze to her mother. She was turned away from me, staring through the walls of the home, towards the direction where I could feel Teren getting farther and farther away from us.

"Will he be okay?" I whispered.

Imogen looked back to me. Her eyes were red with unshed tears of almost pure blood, her cheeks were stained with ones that had already fallen. She didn't say anything, only shrugged as a thick tear dropped to her cheek.

Alanna, on my other side, watched her mother and then started to cry. It only took a half-second for Imogen to switch positions; her body flashed to the other side of the bed and her arms went around Alanna in comfort. I watched them and my tears resurfaced. I'd done this. This pain was all because of me. This was supposed to be the most joyous time of our lives—the impending birth of Teren's children—but instead, it had gotten twisted into something painful and dangerous and just plain…awful.

My sobs resurfacing, I managed to choke out, "I'm so sorry."

They both twisted back to me, shaking their heads and telling me that it wasn't my fault. Looking desolate, Alanna muttered, "If anything, this is my fault. He's my child. I should have seen this coming." She looked back at me, tears dripping down her cheeks. "I just didn't realize the extent of what he and Ben have been up to.

And lately, he's been asking mother and me to stay away, to help out here with researching all of the new leads, and with helping you. He asked us to let him handle the meetings."

She shook her head, and her long, black hair settled around her shoulders. Her face was a picture of frustration and regret. "I didn't think he was in a lot of danger. I mean, vampires aren't necessarily evil. Just like humans, they come with all kinds of personalities. He was only supposed to be politely asking them if they knew anything, and then leaving if they didn't. That was our agreement when we started this."

Alanna looked back at her mother for a moment before twisting back to me. "I knew he was getting into some scuffles, but he always assured me that he was being careful, that the fights were nothing serious, just a couple of misinterpreted actions, he'd say. I had no idea he was starting to…go this far." She shrugged her shoulders as fresh tears fell on her cheeks. "I didn't think he'd ever start purposefully provoking them. And forcing information from them? Making them talk? I don't even know what that means." She hung her head and Imogen brought her hand to her shoulder.

Uselessly wiping my cheeks, I shook my head. "What about Halina? She'd never let him get away with this?"

Imogen sighed and stared at the floor, to where I could feel Halina sleeping. "Mother told me that he's recently started conducting these meetings before full sunset, bursting in on still sluggish, quarantined-by-the-sun vampires. By the time she gets there, he's already…interviewing them, sometimes heatedly. She told me she broke up a pretty decent fight a couple of nights ago, one that left poor Ben black and blue. She assumed the vampires were angry at being intruded upon." She looked up at me, and her eyes were bloody. "I'm sure she didn't realize what he has really been up to."

Blinking back tears, she sighed and rubbed her daughter's back. "I tried to talk to him about it, to convince him that running in uninvited on drowsy vampires was a dangerous game, and that he should always wait for mother." She shrugged. "But he said it was fine and the scuffles were blown out of proportion. When I told him I was coming with next time, he sighed and said he'd wait for mother." She raised an eyebrow at me. "I should have taken that as a warning." She shook her head. "I knew he was getting desperate, but I never thought he'd do this…"

The room was silent for a moment as we all felt him drift even farther. "What did he say outside to you?" I asked Alanna weakly, still suffering from shock and sniffles.

She shook her head. "He was upset, angry, but he looked like he'd been crying too, after…your argument." I wanted to apologize again, but she spoke over my words. "He was rambling, Emma. I don't think he even knew what he was saying. He kept repeating that he didn't have a choice, that they were leaving, and he had to get to them before they did. He told me that they could be *the ones*. They could be the nest that knew about mixed vampires, and he couldn't risk them disappearing. The last thing he said to me, before I had to leave him, was that he wouldn't start a fight…but they *would* tell him what he wanted to know. As long as he got a name, nothing else mattered."

An ominous silence hung in the air. None of us really knew what that meant. None of us were sure how far a terrified-to-lose-me Teren would go, if he had to.

Alanna let out a dreary sigh. "He's been getting so manic about this in the past week or so. We really should have gone with him anyway, to make sure he was okay. But…we had a reason to stay, too…"

She swallowed and looked over me in such a way that I knew she meant me. I suddenly understood the real reason why Alanna and Imogen rarely left my side. They were afraid I'd convert any day, any moment. And if I did, someone had to be here to help me when I woke up, assuming I did wake up. Conversions were the deadliest part of an undead vampire's life. I knew that from experience with Teren's. As Alanna's eyes drifted down to my stomach, I remembered asking Teren to take the twins from me. From the look in Alanna's eye, she was also sticking close by to honor my request. If and when I keeled over, she was ready to take them, if Teren wasn't around to.

I felt horrible. In a way, I had made them choose between their son and grandson, and me and the twins. But none of us could have anticipated just how far Teren would take this. Time was running out and Imogen was right, he *was* getting desperate. And knowing that his family would never approve of his methods, he'd found ways around them. Secretive and stubborn as always, if it meant protecting someone he loved. And ultimately, that was what he was trying to do…protect me, save me.

We all three stayed in bed for most of the afternoon, alternating between bouts of crying and worrying. At times Imogen and Alanna both got up to run to him. Then one would convince the other that making the attempt in daylight was futile. It would be better to let Halina get him at nightfall. She was faster and stronger than both of them. Imogen accepted it more readily than Alanna; she didn't have as much of a tolerance for sunlight as her diluted daughter. Alanna looked ready to charge out into the sun anyway, to bring her child back to the ranch. But she stayed, knowing that, just like before, she would only make it so far before she'd have to find an enclosed place to hide.

And me? There was more than one occasion when they both had to hold me down from flying unimpeded by the sun to his side. But I'd already hurt him once today, and I was scared of what another showdown between us might bring. Especially if it happened in the middle of an agitated vampire nest. I was already scared that he was going to make a stupid, fatal mistake because of our argument. I didn't want to show up and have him be so thrown off by me that someone got the drop on him. Especially with how distracting our bond was. Especially if he was…unhinged.

Maybe sensing the heavy quiet in the house, Jack came in and found us all lying in bed. Alanna and Imogen solemnly told him what had happened. He closed his eyes and slowly reopened them to gaze at his wife. They shared a brief, pain-filled hug, and then Jack discretely wiped his eyes and walked back outside. I supposed, like us, Jack wanted to rush to him too, but it would do no good if he did. Teren was still moving, still on his way to the nest. By the time Jack drove to him, it would be too late; he'd be among the vampires. And if Alanna couldn't get her stressed son to stay, I didn't see how the comparatively weaker Jack would, especially if Teren was in sight of what he wanted—possible answers.

We listened to the sounds of Jack puttering around outside, keeping his mind occupied with manual labor, so he didn't have to think about the possibility of losing his son. My eyes were so dry I couldn't even blink them, my head was throbbing in repeated patterns, and my stomach rumbled from the lack of food. I thought maybe Jack's way of handling the stress was healthier, or at least, more productive. By early evening, when I figured Teren was just approaching the nest that he had traveled to, Halina woke up.

I heard her moving around downstairs, sighing, stirring, possibly dressing, and I looked at Alanna and Imogen. "When do we tell her?"

"Tell me what?" Halina automatically responded. I sighed. I had forgotten just how good their ears were.

I replayed the fight, and what I'd caught Teren doing— essentially packing for a battle. Imogen sighed and Alanna sniffled. Halina cursed and responded with what sounded like stone crashing through stone. I thought that she might have just punched a hole in the wall.

"Stupid child," she muttered, pacing her room as she waited for the last of the sun's rays to die. "I will skin him alive, if they don't."

I sat up in bed; my head was woozy from nearly nothing in my stomach. "What are you going to do Halina? He's too far away…" Wherever he'd gone, it had taken him a good chunk of the afternoon to get there before nightfall. She couldn't run that far, and return before sunup.

She growled and when she spoke, her voice warbled, like she was holding back her own tears. "I will dig a hole in the desert if I have to, but I'm not letting him continue this foolishness without me." I heard her resume pacing, all the while muttering, "Supposed to wait…stupid…foolish…idiot…did I teach him *nothing*…men…"

I fell back to the pillows, exhausted. My stomach grumbled loudly and Alanna blurred to standing. "Oh, Emma. I'm so sorry," Her face couldn't have looked any more apologetic. "I forgot to make you and Jack something to eat. I'm so sorry."

She blurred from the room but I called after her. "It's okay, Alanna, you don't need to wait on me. Besides, I really couldn't have handled food today anyway."

I knew the second the sun set, and not because Imogen grabbed my hand and walked with me down the stairs to the kitchen. No, I knew because Halina hauled ass out of the house. She was gone so fast, I stumbled with my step. The sense of her blurring away that quickly was disorienting. She streaked towards where our senses pointed out Teren. And she was letting it out, running faster than I'd ever felt her move.

Feeling somewhat better, now that he had a more substantial backup on the way than Hot Ben, someone who could stop him from doing anything too stupid—and hopefully get there before anyone did anything to him—I relaxed and sat down to a huge, refreshing cup of blood and a huge plate of pasta. Well, I slightly relaxed. I didn't completely relax until the next morning.

I wasn't sure what time it was, but I knew it was early in the morning, a few hours after dawn maybe. I'd had trouble falling asleep last night and had stared at the ceiling, watching my eyes highlight strange shapes in the textures. I'd considered studying my glow in a mirror, to see if I could hypnotize myself into a mellow state. I'd passed out some time later, well after the witching hour.

I woke up with a start when I smelled him. It hit me so hard, that it shocked me into awareness. I turned my head, sat up, and stared at the door. Teren was standing in the open doorframe, gripping the sides of it, to stop himself from hurling himself on me. I'd slept through the build-up again and wasn't feeling the pull he was. But he was resisting, shaking with restraint as he gripped the wood.

I twisted around to face him. Putting my feet on the floor, I wanted to hurl myself on him too. Not because of the pull, but because I'd missed him, because I'd been terrified, and now relief was washing through me, cleansing away every bad thought I'd had in the past several hours.

But he only continued to shake as he stared at me from the doorway. I wondered if maybe he was still angry at me. I'd said some pretty nasty things before he left. I slowly stood up, not sure what to do. His eyes tracked my movement, and his shaking increased the closer I got to him. I tilted my head as I held a hand out for him. He looked at it, but he still didn't move or speak.

Fighting tears, I took a deep breath. I savored the smell that was purely him, but registered the smell of other people on him…and the chalky smell of drywall dust mixed with the tangy smell of blood. There had been violence.

My eyes widened and my heartbeat increased as I took another step towards him. I searched his clothes, but I didn't see anything that even remotely looked like fresh blood. There were some holes in his shirt and a snag in his jeans, but those could have been from a previous fight or from natural wear and tear. Teren had been letting things like new clothes slip by the wayside lately.

Just as I was about to rush into his arms and beg him to forgive me, beg him to talk to me, he bit his lip. And when I say "bit his lip," I mean he literally bit his lip. He clenched down so hard, he sliced right through the skin. A deep, dark trail of blood oozed from the wound and dripped off his chin.

He did nothing to wipe it away or stop it from falling, and it dripped right onto his shirt. The stain it caused was ominous and startling and sent me right back into terror. I froze, my eyes wide and my heart pounding. I knew being this stressed wasn't good for me, but I couldn't calm down, not when he was being so odd and still. His shaking was his only real movement.

"Teren?" I said quietly, my voice trembling and echoing around the empty space between us.

My voice seemed to wreck him. His shaking increased as he released the doorframe, and dropped to his knees right in front of me. The shaking, that I'd assumed was from his attempt to resist the pull, shifted to sobs as he dropped his head into his hands. Confused and alarmed, I carefully kneeled in front of him. My hands slid over his cool shoulders, shaking from sobs now. I pulled his head into my chest. "Teren, you're scaring me," I whispered.

I felt Alanna approaching, also woken from sleep by the return of her son. She stopped a few steps behind him in the hallway, just on the other side of the door, and watched us. I held my hand up to her, wanting a minute with my distraught husband. She paused, waiting. Her body was tense with the desire to comfort her child, but she seemed resolved to give that responsibility over to another woman. I imagined that was a pretty hard thing for her to do.

Teren let a stuttered cry escape him and finally spoke to me. "Emma..." His arms slipped around my waist. "Oh, God..."

Terrified, I ran my fingers back through his hair. "What, baby? What happened? Please...talk to me."

He shifted, so that he was still kneeling before me, but his head was resting on my stomach. His hands came up to cup my belly, and he began placing tender kisses along my stretched skin, the sleeping children inside only gently stirred at his caress. "I'm sorry, I'm so sorry..." he repeated over and over.

The blood on his chin transferred to the white t-shirt I'd slept in. The contrast was startling, even in the pale light of our glowing eyes. I clutched his head to my stomach, not sure if he was apologizing for our fight or if something had happened. I reached out my senses, but Halina wasn't in the house. She was miles away, nowhere near the property. A streak of terror flashed through me; maybe she hadn't made it, and I was sensing her corpse. Or maybe Ben...

"Teren...please, what happened? Are you okay? Is...everyone okay?"

He raised his head. His eyes were wet and pained, his body was still shaking. His fingers cradled our children as he gazed at me and finally nodded. "Yes, we're fine."

Grateful that at least no one was hurt, I crawled into his lap. He laid his head on my shoulder as he pulled me as tight to his body as he safely could. Alanna, behind him, exhaled in relief. Nodding once at me, she turned and left us alone. I had to imagine that her level of control right there—walking away from her stricken son—rivaled Teren's control when he'd been thirsting for blood and had restrained himself from taking mine.

He started crying as he held me and I stroked my fingers down his back. I wanted to help him in some way. I just didn't know what was wrong. "Baby, is this because of what I said?" I pulled back to search his eyes. Tears were dripping off my cheeks now. "Because, I didn't mean it. I was just mad...I'm so sorry." My voice warbled after I said it, and Teren immediately began shaking his head and kissing me.

"No, oh, no, baby. I know you were mad. I'm not…I'm okay." He sniffled, more tears falling as he struggled for control. My hands ran over his face, brushing the cool tears aside as I tried to understand.

"Then…?" I shrugged, emotion closing my throat.

Exhaling a steadying breath, he pulled back. With renewed moisture in his eyes, he whispered, "You were right." He choked and swallowed. "You were so right." He shook his head. "This isn't the way." He broke down and leaned his head against my shoulder again.

Rubbing his back, I closed my eyes as his despair washed into me. "Teren…talk to me."

He sniffled as he brought his emotions under control, but he didn't lift his head to look at me again. "I got…nothing. They told me…nothing."

I grabbed his face in my hands. "It's okay, baby. You have other leads, right?" I kissed his cheeks, a little surprised that I wanted him to keep looking, keep digging. I guess I just didn't want to ever see this level of pain on him again.

He grabbed my wrists and pulled them away from his face. "No, I can't…" He shook his head; his eyes were older than I'd ever seen them. "You were right. I'm turning into something…I don't even recognize. I'm obsessed," he whispered.

I shook my head and fought against his grip so I could hold his face again. He held me tight, though. "No, I was wrong, petty…"

He cut me off, his gaze and voice hollow. "I almost staked a woman tonight." I froze in his lap. My legs straddling his stiffened with tension. He looked over my reaction, and when he spoke again, his voice was overflowing with so much emotion that it came out numb. "I almost plunged a rod of pure silver through her heart, because she wouldn't tell me what I wanted to know."

His grip on me hardened as he shook his head, and tears sprang back to his eyes. "I can't even say it was self-defense." He shrugged. "It wasn't, she never even tried to touch me." His eyes searched my face. I couldn't even imagine what he saw there. "But…I knew she knew something—a name, a nest—something."

Seemingly disgusted with himself, he looked away from me. His grip on me got even harder. "She was the only one left in the nest when we found it. Ben and I kept her cornered for hours, but she still wouldn't tell me anything. Then I took a silver stake and dragged it over her skin. She screamed..." He closed his eyes and bit his lip. He pierced the flesh again and a trail of blood rolled off of him. His lip healed immediately, right before my eyes.

"I can still hear the screams..." He opened his eyes and a tear rolled off his cheek and dropped onto his chin, following the trail of blood. "I pierced her skin and told her I would shove it through her chest if she didn't tell me what I wanted to hear."

He relaxed his tight grasp on my wrists and I inhaled a quick breath as feeling returned to my hands. He dropped his head into palms. Between his fingers, he mumbled, "She still wouldn't tell me. She said she'd rather die, than give up her mate."

As he gave into grief, I wrapped my hands around his body and drew him into me. I tried to comfort him, but he shook his head and peeked up at me. "God, I almost killed her, Emma, and she was only trying to protect...well...her version of you." He cupped my cheeks. "She was protecting him from another madman." He raised his eyebrows and shook his head. "Only this time, it was me."

I rested my head against his. "Baby..."

He shook his forehead against mine. "I don't know who I am anymore, Emma." He crumpled in my arms, his head resting on my stomach as he broke down. "I don't know what I'm capable of anymore...what lengths I'll go to, to protect you." He peered up at me. "If Great-Gran hadn't..." He swallowed and brought his hands around me as he nestled his head into my abdomen. "Oh, God, Emma, I can't do this anymore. This isn't me. I'm not being me..."

I exhaled brokenly as tears coursed down my cheeks. Whispering his name, I laid my head on his back and tried to be as comforting as I could.

He shifted and looked up at me, his face panicked. "I'm so scared, Emma. I don't know what to do. You're dying, they're dying, and I don't know what to do." His voice tore me, and I swallowed back the grief welling in me. His hands came up to grasp my face again. "What do I do? Tell me what to do." His eyes searched mine, pleading.

Absorbing the smell of him, absorbing the sense of him, absorbing the undeniable love between us, I closed my eyes. Knowing this was no way to live, for either of us, I made a choice. It was the hardest choice of my life, but it was the only choice left to us. He couldn't continue on this path he'd started. He was right, that path would lead him to be the same sort of madman who had kidnapped and tortured us. I could see it—I could see pain and fear leading him that way. He had to stop this insanity. He had to accept that there was nothing we could do...but have faith.

Opening my eyes, I placed my palms against his cheeks. "You stop, Teren. You stay here with me...and you stop."

He cocked his head, looking about to protest. "No, I know. I may die. They may die, but..." I bit my lip and shook my head. "I can't let you become *this*, to try and save me." Kissing him, I whispered, "It's not worth it. I'm not worth it." He pulled back, sputtering for a response, and I hardened my expression. "If this is all we get, Teren, then don't waste a second with me." I rested my head against his. "You promised me that you would spend every moment we had, trying to make me happy." I indicated the emotional wreckage that used to be my strong, confident husband. "This isn't making me happy. Spend all the time you can with me, with us, and then, if the fates decide my time is done...then you love me, and remember me with *good* memories, for the rest of your eternal life."

When I pulled back, tears were dropping to my cheeks. "That— that is what you can do."

He opened and closed his mouth several times. Then he closed it and stared at me. I felt his body calming as he did. I felt my body calming, my heart returning to its normal, steady beat. His eyes never leaving mine, he quietly whispered, "I love you. I'll always love you."

I nodded and hugged him tight.

We shucked off our clothes, and I uselessly examined every square inch of him for injuries. I knew I wouldn't find any, and he knew I wouldn't find any, but I had to see for myself. Standing still with his head down, he let me. His face was...glum, but once I had him slipped under the covers with me, I did my best to make him feel better, if only for a moment.

He fell asleep afterwards. His breath stopped, his face stilled, and all emotion momentarily slid away from him. I kissed his forehead, grateful that he could find peace somewhere, even if it was just in slumber. I watched him for hours, not wanting to fall asleep or leave his side. Just wanting to be near him, to cherish every second we had.

I was gently rubbing his back when I felt Alanna approaching. I knew from the strong rays seeping through the cracks in our heavy curtains, that it was well into morning and she was headed downstairs for her ritual of making human food for those who could eat it. I wasn't sure if I could today.

She paused at our door and I whispered that it was okay, that he was sleeping. I watched the brass knob on the recently repaired door twist, and then her dark head peeked into the room. Her eyes immediately went to her son's bare back. I rested my head on his arm, where he was stretched out to me, facing me.

Alanna searched him with her eyes. "How is he?" she asked quietly.

I made myself not blush as I watched the concern flit over her face. She didn't care about the intimate moment we'd had earlier, she cared about how upset he'd been when he first came home. Feeling tears in my eyes as I watched her step into the room and put a few fingers on his shoulder, I shrugged and whispered, "I don't know." My eyes returned to his stone face. His mouth was just slightly parted and because I was looking for it, I saw the tip of a fang. He was right, they extended while we slept.

Brushing a knuckle over his cheek I said, "It's so difficult for him, not knowing what to do. He tries so hard…"

I felt Alanna's fingers on my arm and looked up at her. "It's hard for all of us, dear." She gave me a warm smile and I returned it.

Putting my hand over his back, I nestled into him and I whispered, "I think he'll be okay. If he stops…I think he'll be okay."

She patted my hand on his back and nodded. Pulling away she asked, "Are you hungry, dear? I was just about to make breakfast."

I paused and my stomach rumbled. Looking torn, I didn't answer her. I didn't want to eat, I wanted to stay by his side, but my stomach had other plans. Seeing my indecision, Alanna smiled and answered for me. "Stay with him. I'll bring you something."

I exhaled gratefully and nodded. It wasn't a hard decision, but I was tired of thinking, and having someone else do it for just a moment was a welcome relief. Alanna looked over the two of us, smiled, and then twisted to leave. Before she streaked away, I sat up on my elbow.

"Halina?" I asked hesitantly.

She turned back with her hand on the doorframe. "She's all right. Probably just holed up somewhere, until nightfall." She grinned and I could tell she was just humoring me, she didn't really know. "She's going to be very angry. She hates sleeping in the ground."

Before I could respond, she streaked away. "Thank you," I muttered as I settled back down to Teren's cool skin. He didn't shift in his sleep like a human would. He was in the exact same position that he'd fallen asleep in, and I knew from experience that he'd stay that way until he woke up. His rapidly self-flowing vampire blood didn't have the same circulatory problems that human blood did. Teren's limbs didn't ever go numb.

"No, thank *you*, Emma," Alanna responded from downstairs.

I smiled and went back to Teren-watching.

He woke up at the same time that I heard a car pulling up the driveway. I was listening to the crunch of tire on gravel and wasn't paying attention to him. We were still naked in bed, draped around each other under the covers. He was still in the same position, but I'd twisted and turned, trying to get comfortable with the massive belly that impeded me from resting in my favorite position—on my stomach. I was also getting an ache from where a child was repeatedly kicking a rib.

I was staring at the ceiling, listening and rubbing my side, when Teren's cool fingers pushed mine aside and rested over my sore spot. I smiled and looked over at him. Alanna had opened the curtains for me and he was bathed in a warm, cheery light. His face was haggard, tired, but he smiled at me.

"Hey," he whispered.

I twisted to face him. "Hey," I whispered back, running a hand through his hair. He closed his eyes and inhaled, drinking me in. When he opened his eyes, his brows furrowed. "Who's here?"

I listened to a door opening with my head cocked. Then I stood up, blurringly fast, and stumbled. Teren shot up right after me, steadying me as I adjusted to the odd feeling of moving faster than my mind could follow. I started to say thanks, but instead I stared at his bare body and then my own. Looking back up at him, I cringed. "My mom's here."

He tilted his head, listening, and then, hearing what I'd heard, my mom chatting with Ashley as they walked to the front door, he nodded and swept me into his arms.

Confused, I actually struggled for a bit. I thought he might try and fit in a super quickie before they entered the house. But I stopped trying to get away when he walked me over to a wide walk-in closet. There were enough maternity clothes in there for about three pregnant women; Teren had emptied our closet at home, and Alanna and Imogen were always bringing me something new to wear. A little retail therapy.

I smiled and held him close when he set me down. Looking at me adoringly, he ran a thumb over my cheek. His eyes watered as he stared at me, and I knew he was replaying our conversation from last night. I shook my head and grabbed his face. "Don't stress," I whispered, as the rarely used doorbell chimed throughout the house.

He grinned at hearing his oft-repeated phrase repeated back to him, then he sighed and gave me a soft kiss. Teren and I quickly got dressed while Alanna greeted Mom at the door. She feigned surprise and gave them apologies at taking a few moments. She told them she'd been in the back and hadn't heard them. Uh-huh.

She kept them busy for a few minutes downstairs while Teren and I "prepped" our room. He tucked me into bed and then zipped around upstairs, finding magazines, books, water, movies and candy. Everything a pregnant woman confined to a bed would need to entertain herself. As he left to go greet my mom, I started popping gummy bears. Might as well play the part.

As my group of visitors started trudging up the staircase, I started to worry about the one vampire who wasn't safely tucked into the house with us. A little surprised that I was actually concerned for the vixen, I paused in my sugary treat and to ask Teren, "Is Halina okay? Where is she?"

Teren was currently walking up the steps with my mother. She was thanking him for offering his arm as her leg was starting to go out on her every once and a while. To her, he said, "It's the least I can do for a beautiful woman." My mom tittered while she told him that he was very sweet and I was a lucky girl. That I was.

To me, he imperceptibly whispered, "She's fine. The nest was empty when I left...she was going to stay there." He laughed at Mom's comment after speaking to me, but his voice sounded tight. I wanted to ask him more, but Ashley asked him how I was doing, and he started filling her in. I decided to not interrupt his conversation. Besides, just knowing Halina was fine relaxed me in such a way that the smile on my face was genuine when Mom finally came through the door.

She immediately smiled and flew around the bed to get to me. She was holding a box of chocolates and a small bouquet of flowers. The combination of those smells and the lingering scent of Spike on her made me a little nauseous. I hadn't felt that way in a while. For a moment, I actually would have preferred that she'd had a baggy of blood on her to chocolate. Knowing that the twins were largely responsible for my hemoglobin cravings, I laughed and hugged my mom tight.

She sat on the edge of the bed, rubbing my arms before switching to rub my stomach. A twin kicked her and she giggled. Ashley sat on the other side. Kicking off her shoes, she ducked under the covers to snuggle into my side. I threw an arm around my sister and contained a sigh; the two of them were probably planning on spending the afternoon with me.

Teren stared at the three of us on the bed, and that realization was on his face too. He bit his lip, carefully this time, and stared at the ground. He shifted back and forth, somewhat antsy, and I could tell that he didn't want to be in this room. Mom was oblivious to his odd behavior as she regaled me on the adventures of her grand-pup.

I smiled and nodded at her while I watched Teren from the corner of my eye. He looked out the window, maybe mentally counting down the remaining hours of daylight. I knew what he wanted. He wanted to leave here and find vampires. He wanted to question them on what they knew of mixed breeds, and beat them into submission if they refused to answer his questions. He desperately wanted someone to have a clue where he could find vampires like himself, all in the hopes that one of those rare persons would have an answer for him on the huge question mark that was my fate. Was I set to die in a couple weeks? Would the twins die with me? I would just be hitting my thirtieth week. Would they be far enough along to survive without me?

His eyes flashed back to me; they were moist. I knew this was killing him. I knew he, at the very least, wanted to be doing research, but I also knew he needed to stay. Nothing out there would help me, and Teren was turning into something...well, monstrous.

Turning my full attention to him, I held out my hand. He stared at it, torn between staying and leaving. "Teren, that's not the way," I mumbled under my breath.

He looked down and nodded while my mom asked me if I'd said something. Still focused on Teren, I said nothing to her. Noticing the tension in the room, she eventually silenced. My sister stiffened, and I felt her staring at Teren too.

He looked up at me and his eyes were dangerously close to shedding a tear. I didn't know how we'd explain that if he did. As it was, I could feel curiosity pouring out of Mom.

Finally, Teren smiled and strode over to the bed. He sat on the corner and took my hand. The tension broke with his movement, and Mom shrugged and continued on with tales of her life. Ashley, more clued into our situation, looked between the two of us. She squeezed my leg under the covers and I knew that she was aware that something was going on that she didn't know about, and she wanted to know about it.

I couldn't tell her with mom in the room though, so I only gave her a warm smile before I refocused on Teren. He smiled at me with a tight jaw and an unwavering gaze. He was forcing himself to stay, forcing himself to not run out and try to save us. I loved him so much, for both staying *and* wanting to leave.

I whispered that to him, and he sighed and nodded. "You're right, that's not the way." He tilted his head at me and spoke under his breath while my mom continued jabbering. "We'll find another."

Smiling brightly, I nodded.

Chapter 18 – Surprise, Surprise

The basis of our new plan was to try and save the children. Teren was coming to terms with the fact that I might or might not survive the shift, but with every day that passed, there was a greater chance that we could save the twins. He stopped doing research from a madman's diary, and started doing research from medical journals. He spent every second he could poring over premature deliveries—how to incubate and preserve children that were only the size of small heads of cabbage.

The lungs were the biggest issue. If I made it to thirty weeks, keeping them breathing would be the hardest part. I eagerly pored over this research with him. Unlike his previous research, I found it fascinating and hopeful, not terrifying and nightmare-inducing.

His manic need to save me, shifted to this as well, and it didn't take long before he was "interviewing" doctors and specialists, although in a much nicer fashion than he had the vampires. It was all done in the guise that he was writing an article on preemies for the magazine he worked for. It was the first time that his career had proved a useful cover story. He gloated a bit about that. Hot Ben helped him with this too. It made me smile that at least he wasn't coming home with black eyes anymore.

The rest of the family eagerly helped out as well. They ordered all the supplies that we would need. And I was sure Halina compelled people to give us stuff too; I had a sneaking suspicion the medical equipment wasn't purchased. Pretty soon, a room right next to ours was set up as a nursery. Sort of. It also resembled a hospital room, thanks to the incubators, heart rate monitors, and vials and vials of different medicines. I wasn't sure if any of the vampires knew what any of the stuff really did, but, they were going to try their best. It was the only option left to us.

Teren told me late one night, a week before my birthday, that he'd bring in a doctor. Worst case scenario, if nothing he did was going to save them, then he'd rush to a clinic, kidnap someone, and bring them out to the ranch. Then he'd have Halina wipe them, once the children were out of the woods. He'd do it as many times as necessary to keep them alive.

I smiled, kissed him, and told him to ask the doctor nicely first, before he just confiscated him. Teren gave me a sheepish smile and promised that he would. Once it seemed that my children might actually survive this, a part of me relaxed. Now, the only real question was, would I?

Halina shocked the hell out of me by saying that she would give me her blood, if I wanted. I stared at her, dumbfounded—she didn't do that, ever. She was firmly against the idea of turning anyone. She had certain resentments over her life and wouldn't restrict someone else with her affliction. She'd even admitted that she hoped I didn't end up like her. And if I had her blood in me, I'd be sentenced to a life of never-ending night, forced to dig a hole in the ground if I had to, to escape the day. But, it was better than being dead, I supposed.

I already had v-juice in me, though, and none of us knew if I could be turned twice. Here's where knowing another mixed would come in handy, especially one who had tried to turn someone. But, Halina promised she'd try. If I didn't come around, she'd try. She reasoned that I was already a vampire, and either way, I was dying. She said that in the end, my being like her would be preferable to my not being around anymore. She followed that with, "You're far too entertaining to just let die."

But, like I said, we weren't sure what would happen to me, and finding mixed hadn't been going well. And now, I was pretty sure we were done with rustling up vampire nests. Teren was done, anyway. Even if he hadn't admitted that he couldn't handle it anymore, Halina had made it quite clear that his method of "interviewing" was over. She'd ripped him a new one when she'd come home from her overnight trip.

It had been late the following evening when she'd rushed back to the ranch. She'd woken us both up and berated him for a good hour and a half on his foolish behavior. The rest of the family had woken up and occasionally interjected their concerns as well. Teren sheepishly looked at my lap, while I sat beside him on our bed, and absorbed their chastisement without complaint. Halina had arrived at the nest just as he'd been about to end that poor woman's undead life. Ben had been trying to get Teren to back down, but he'd been set on his course of action and had ignored Ben pulling on his arm. He couldn't ignore Halina though.

She'd torn in there, called his name, and then pushed him into a wall when he hadn't responded to her. From the way she told the story, he'd gone straight through the wall and into another room. The terrified vampire had blurred out of there after that, probably to go join up with the love she'd been protecting.

From there, things had gotten a little hairy. Teren had been furious that Halina had let her get away and had actually charged his great-grandmother. Halina had tossed him through another wall. At this point, Teren said, Ben disappeared on him, muttering that he hadn't signed up for torture. Halina towering over him and Ben's comment had snapped Teren out of it. He hadn't seen it that way, until that very moment.

Still avoiding looking directly at Halina, Teren buried his head in my neck when he admitted that to me. Halina went on to tell me that after she'd finally gotten Teren to leave the nest, she had stayed. She'd searched the countryside for the female, since she hadn't had time to run home. Teren looked up at her, curious and hopeful. She glared at him. "No, I didn't find her, but you can bet that her boyfriend now has a huge score to settle with you."

He hung his head again as his arms tightened around me. I clutched him back and looked up at Halina. Her slight body was still in a scolding position. Then her expression changed and a sly smile lit her lips. "A different male came to the nest shortly before dawn. He looked around the remains of his house and was naturally curious, so I filled him in." She grinned in such a way that I had no doubt he'd done a little "filling in" as well.

I shook my head and looked away from her. Teren lifted his hopeful eyes. "Did he...?"

He didn't finish his question, but Halina shot him a look. "No, Teren. No more questions. You are done." She lifted her head and an air of authority seemed to shimmer around her. It reminded me that this woman was the true head of the Adams clan, regardless of impressions. Teren knew this too and dropped his head again. "I will check out the name he gave me...and any other name I get from that."

His head still down, he gave her a small, compliant nod. Sighing, Halina walked over to him. She put a hand under his jaw and lifted it. He avoided eye contact for a moment, but then looked at her. Her face softened and she murmured low, fast Russian phrases. Teren swallowed, his eyes misting, then he nodded. Halina finished with "I love you," and then left us in the room to go soak in a bath before she had to hide away for the day.

Teren was subdued after that, embarrassed by his actions and mortified by his commitment to killing someone, if he had thought it was necessary to help me. We spent a lot of time talking about it. He spent a lot of time feeling guilty about it. His need to protect me, already ramped up from our abduction months ago, had driven him nearly over the edge. There can be such a fine line between right and wrong. That gray realm gets a little larger with every hard decision we make over the years. I knew from experience what being in that realm felt like, and I knew the torment Teren felt. But falling into the black side wasn't an option for him; I wouldn't let it be. And if that meant pulling back a bit and letting someone slightly less emotionally attached take over, then so be it. If it would save his soul, so be it.

And so we stopped focusing on me and started focusing on the children.

It was a brilliant, beautiful spring day, just a couple days before my birthday, and Ashley and I were distracting ourselves from that fact by painting the nursery. Well, nursery/hospital room. We had a can of pale yellow and a can of pale green, since we still didn't know if I was having boys, girls, or one of each. The fumes from the open cans burned my sensitive nostrils, but I ignored it. And even though I detested painting, I cherished the moment, cherished the connection I felt with my children as I did it.

Ash painstakingly slid her green roller over a section of one of the walls while I laughingly blurred over mine. "That's not fair, Em," she chuckled, going back to her humanly slow method of painting. Hers was even slower than most, since her joints were a little stiff where the scars on her body were thick.

I laughed at her and continued painting at a normal speed. I wanted to savor this bonding moment with my sister. Teren was at work, but Alanna looked in on us periodically to check our progress and offer us snacks. Even Jack poked his head in. He slung an arm around each of us, and an expression of fatherly pride was on his face as he examined our work. "It's beautiful, girls," he said, squeezing me tight as he looked over one of the two-toned walls we'd completed.

"Thank you," I replied, leaning into his side and taking in the scent of him that was so similar to Teren's. Teren was so much like Alanna and the girls looks-wise, that it sometimes slipped my mind that this burly ranch man was a part of him too.

When I slung my arm around his waist and laid my head on his shoulder, he flushed and looked a little embarrassed by the display. He quickly kissed my head, and then darted out of the room. I heard him sniffle in the hallway, and I felt my eyes water. He might try to hide it, but he was worried about me too.

As Ashley was going over what details she knew of premature babies, having studied more about human anatomy during her nursing classes than anyone else in the house, I heard the sound of tires crunching up gravel. I paused in painting, and a growl burrowed up from my chest. Ashley paused mid-sentence, her eyes wide. She'd never heard me growl before; that was generally something I reserved for Teren.

I stared through her, to the world beyond the walls. I wasn't sure why, but I was having a reaction to whomever was approaching. It wasn't Teren, he was still miles away in San Francisco, and it wasn't my mom or Tracey, they were both at their jobs. I supposed it could be Hot Ben, but something inside of me knew that it wasn't.

I closed my eyes, listening intently, but other than Jack asking Alanna what was wrong, Ashley breathing heavily, and the two fast and fluttery heartbeats inside of me, blending with my own, the house was deadly quiet; all of the awake vampires were listening just as hard as I was.

When the tires stopped and the car shut off, I set down my roller. The harsh smell of paint mixed unpleasantly with Ashley's fear. "What is it, Emma?" She looked around the room, like something creepy was going to come through the walls. For a second, I wondered if that had been how I'd looked to Teren, when he'd heard strange noises I couldn't hear.

I tried to throw on a casual smile, to ease her panicking. "Someone's here. I'm sure it's just Peter or a friend of Jack's." Ashley nodded and set down her roller. She knew that the ranch had help come in sometimes, and she'd met Peter at my wedding. The family had been holding off on bringing anyone here until my situation was resolved, but Ashley didn't need to know that.

Look at me, being the secretive one for a change.

Swallowing, I tried to push away my discomfort at not being completely honest with my sister. True, I wasn't sure who was here, but my body knew it was a potential threat, and that sort of ruled out any ranch hand.

As calmly as I could, I walked to the door. Ashley was close behind me. I paused in the doorway and looked down to the other end of the hall, where Alanna was similarly paused at Imogen's door. Imogen behind her was blinking in the faded, hazy light of the hallway. Even those weak rays caused her pain. Jack stepped past the two of them and held his hand out for his wife. As Alanna took it, Imogen whispered that she wanted to see who was here, but Alanna told her to stay in her room, that we would check it out. I nodded at Alanna and started down the hallway towards her and Jack.

Ashley behind me, not having heard any of that, grabbed my arm. She slung hers around mine as we walked together. Hearing one set of light footsteps outside, casually strolling up to the door at an unhurried pace, I looked down at Ashley attached to my arm. "You should stay up here with Imogen," I told her.

Ashley gave me a blank look. "I thought it was just a friend." I bit my lip, having caught my error too late. Ashley noted my reaction and stiffened her stance as we reached the stairs. "I'm with you, Emma." She shook her head. The hair on the half of it dangled around her shoulders. "I'm not leaving your side."

I sighed and then stopped as Alanna caught up to us. Locking eyes with my sister, I realized it was pointless to argue with her. She was a Taylor after all, and we had a tendency to be...stubborn. Sighing again, I nodded over at Alanna and Jack. "Stay behind us, then."

Ashley nodded and we all started walking down the stairs. Outside, I could hear someone calmly standing in front of the door, waiting. I could even hear their smooth, steady heartbeat. I knew, it being broad daylight and all, that they would be human, but still, the thumping rhythm was reassuring.

Shifting her stance so she was holding my hand, Ashley stepped down to the front door with me, right behind Jack and Alanna. Not sure who was here, my tension got the better of me and my fangs dropped down. Ashley's eyes widened at seeing them; the image was still a little shocking to her. Breathing out slowly, I gained control and retracted them. The human outside might or might not know about us. I didn't want to accidently tip off a could-be hunter.

The person silently waited, still not even knocking, and Alanna closed her eyes for a brief moment. Slapping on a farm boy smile, Jack stepped forward to open the door. I held my breath after the warmer outside air hit my skin; the smell of the ranch had come with it. Even with all that was going on, my body could sense blood in the air. Somewhere out there, a cow was bleeding. Sickeningly, my hormonally revved up body desired it. Desired it so strongly, that I had to clench Ashley's hand to stop myself from blazing across the fields to find the wounded beast. I clamped my mouth shut, fearing that I'd lose control on my teeth while I fought off the urge.

Seeing the person who had managed to rile up a house of vampires, helped diminish my desire.It was a short, tan, blonde, Valley girl, or so I'd imagine. She had a shaggy crop of ridiculously over-styled hair, and sunglasses so dark and round they sort of resembled bug eyes. She started smacking on a piece of gum as she smiled brightly at us; the smell nearly pushed me back a step. Dressed in high heels and a designer dress, she looked very out of place here. Clutching her Prada bag to her side, she extended a hand to Jack before he could even say hello.

"Hi-ya, I hear you're looking for me." She said that chipperly as well, her voice saccharine-sweet.

Jack opened and closed his mouth, not sure what this woman who was manicured head-to-toe and had clearly never shoveled cow poop in her life, wanted with him. As he mumbled an, "Excuse me?" Alanna stepped around him to stand outside with the girl.

Still smacking her gum like the cows smacked on grass blades, she turned her head to Alanna; the gum chewing was loud to my sensitive ears, and annoying. I wished it would stop. The girl calmly took her glasses off and shoved them in her pricey bag. Shifting onto a hip, her gaze locked onto Alanna's, and it was clear that she wasn't here for Jack.

Bright and cheery, she said to her, "You've been causing quite a stir looking for me, so I thought I'd come find out why."

She turned to me as Ashley and I stepped down to stand on her other side. Her eyes were a blue-green, and seemed older than the twenty-something she appeared to be. As I scrunched my face, confused, Ashley whispered, "Who is she, Emma?"

The woman dropped her smile and stopped smacking on her gum. Her entire demeanor changed as she stared at me. Tilting her head, she narrowed her blue-green eyes. "What do you want with me?"

Confused by the sudden viciousness in her tone, I sputtered, "I don't know. I don't even know who you are."

The woman sighed and looked exasperated. "Well, God, with the stories I've heard, you've knocked on every nest, in every state in the southwest, looking for me." She gave me a crooked smile and put her hands on her hips. "I was expecting to be expected."

My already wide eyes opened comically wider and Ashley, beside me, gasped. I vaguely registered Alanna muttering something to her mother and Jack saying, "I don't believe it," but I could only gape. The tiny debutante in front of me had a pair of perfectly white, dainty fangs, just visible inside her wry smile.

I stupidly looked up at the sky, at the sun. She laughed at my maneuver, finding great humor in my surprise. "Yes, I'm mixed…just like you," she looked over at Alanna when she said that.

My eyes watered and I nearly wanted to hug the girl in my relief. We'd been looking for mixed vampires for so long, Teren had risked so much, and now, here was one just showing up on our doorstep. A hand flew to my mouth as I held in a cry. Ashley slung her arms around me, and I heard her sniffle.

The stranger seemed confused as to why we were so emotional over her arrival. I wasn't sure what Teren had been telling the vamps he'd run into, but this woman didn't seem to realize who I was, and what we needed from her. She only seemed to sense that the heartbeatless Alanna was a mixed vampire. She didn't know I was too…for now.

Cocking a pale eyebrow at me, she repeated, "What do you want with me?"

I reached out for her arm and she hissed and backed away. I paused; she might be playing at being casual, but she was wary of this group of vampires, knocking on purebloods' doors to find her. I didn't blame her, I would be too. I held my hands up, in a gesture of peace. "We just want to talk to you. To know…if you know how to help me. I've been changed, a few weeks ago."

As I said that, I rested my hands on my stomach, outlining my pregnancy. Then I relaxed the hold on my teeth. They dropped into place and this time, her eyes widened. "Holy hell," she exclaimed. Turning to Alanna, her face flushed, she bit out, "Why would you try and turn a pregnant woman." She stepped up to a startled Alanna and put a hand on her cool arm. "Don't you know how dangerous that is? Were you trying to kill them all?"

Relief that she seemed to know something about this won out over caution, and I released myself from Ashley, grabbed the girl's shoulders, and twisted her to face me. Her eyes widened at my proximity, but she looked more pissed off than scared. "She didn't do this. I was attacked." I shifted my head so my dark hair fell away from the scar on my neck. "My husband tried to save me…by doing this."

Her eyes locked onto my scar, and her face softened in sympathy. She glanced back up at me as I relaxed the grip on her arms. Tears in my eyes again, I whispered, "I'm going to die soon…and if I do, they do. Can you help us?" My voice warbled as the tears finally fell down my cheeks.

She sighed as she looked over my face. Finally pulling back from my grasp, she extended a hand out to me. "My name is Starla." She cocked an eyebrow at me. "I think I should meet your husband."

I bobbed my head, excited that she hadn't just flat-out told us no. "Of course, yes. He's in town, working, but I can take you to him. He's so eager to meet you." My smile was so wide I was sure I looked slightly medicated; I hadn't even retracted my fangs yet.

Her face fell into a disgruntled expression. "Yes, I know."

My sister came up and grabbed my hand again as she watched Starla curiously. Jack moved over to stand beside Alanna; both of them seemed unsure if this was a welcome development or not. Remembering everything Teren had been doing lately, I dropped my head at Starla's words. My sweet, generally gentlemanly husband had been acting anything but gentlemanly lately. All to protect me of course, but to an outsider, that was of small significance.

When I was about to apologize for his behavior, Starla continued, "The last nest I heard about, happened to be the home of an acquaintance of mine." She tilted her head as I peeked up at her. The last nest Teren had gone to had involved him almost shoving a stake through a woman's heart. "If my friend hadn't had nice things to say about the pure vampire in your midst, our meeting today would be a much different one."

Her blue-green eyes turned to ice and, for a moment, the Valley girl looked quite menacing. I felt a growl rumbling up in my throat, but I forcefully shut it off. She had a point. I exhaled and pulled my teeth back up as I nodded. "He's been under a lot of stress lately. He's very sorry for hurting your friend."

She started smacking on her gum again, looking calm and casual as she flicked her hand dismissively. "One of the guys was my friend." Spinning on her high heel, she turned to head back to her car. Over her shoulder she added, "The girl was a snotty little bitch. He *should* have staked her."

As she sauntered back to her vehicle, I clenched my muscles to stop myself from speeding off after her. She might be mixed, like most of my new family, but I still didn't know her. Looking over at Alanna and Jack, I watched as Alanna shifted in the sun; she was already uncomfortable and needing a break from it. She looked over at me with heartbroken eyes, "Emma, I can't go with you." Jack squeezed her waist, urging her to go back inside the house.

She walked up to me instead, her cool fingers sliding over my cheek. "Be careful." I nodded as her hand came down to rest on my stomach. A brief second of hope flickered across her face as she glanced at Starla, checking her watch as she leaned against her BMW. She gave me a quick kiss on the cheek and then Jack ushered her back in the house.

Once he'd closed the door on her, he walked up to me. Looking unsure about the whole situation he told me, "I can come with, if you like."

As I watched him peek at the door behind him, I knew he really wanted to stay with Alanna. They didn't like to be apart, and I knew he would worry about her if he left her behind. Understanding, I patted his arm. "Teren will be with us soon. It's okay, if you want to stay here."

He relaxed, but he also looked a little embarrassed that he wasn't going to come with. Giving both Ashley and I a warm hug, he stepped into the house with Alanna. Imogen and her daughter both counseled me to be cautious and then apologized for not being able to go.

I shook my head at the closed door. "It's okay. Tell Halina about this when she wakes up…if we're not back yet. Then…have her come find us." I heard them agreeing and promising that they would. I suddenly felt tremendous relief over being LoJacked. Even if Teren and I got separated, someone could find me.

Ashley was staring at me with an eyebrow cocked as I turned back around to her; she'd only caught my half of that conversation. I heard Starla sigh and ask if I was coming, but I focused my attention on Ashley. Her curious expression eased as I put a hand on her shoulder. "Stay here, Ash."

She immediately shook her head, and her hand clenched over mine. "No, I'm by your side until the end, Emma. We're blood." Starla snorted, but my eyes watered, and I nodded my head. She was right. My blood might be all wonky now, but before all this craziness, Ashley and I were blood. If the situation had been reversed, someone would have had to physically separate me from her.

I pulled her tight to me. The faint smell of paint that was lingering on our skin and clothes briefly overwhelmed my acute senses, and I let myself feel just a sliver of hope that maybe that beautiful nursery would indeed get to be filled.

Starla was examining her manicure when we approached her car; she was still chomping away on that sickeningly sweet bubble gum. With a bored expression, she muttered, "Finally," and then she opened her door and got inside. Ashley and I walked around to the other side, and I helped her get into the back seat. I wanted her as far away from this strange vampire as possible. Hoping I was doing the right thing, I shut my door. Then Starla started the car and we pulled away from the Adams ranch.

Alanna and Jack reappeared at the door as I watched in the rearview mirror. They both looked hopeful, regretful, and very, very worried. I stuck my hand out the window and waved, wanting to ease their minds, and maybe my own as well.

As we approached the end of the driveway, an idling car pulled in behind us. It was pitch black with black tinted windows. The girl didn't react to the person following us, so I figured they were together. "Friend of yours?" I casually asked.

Starla looked over at me with a wry smile on her lips. "Did you really think I'd come out to a strange nest alone?" She scanned the road as she pulled out onto the highway. "I'm not an idiot," she muttered.

I wanted to ask more about the car trailing behind us, but as her car sped down the road, on its way back to the city, my Teren-pull kicked in. It started faintly at first, but I knew it would increase exponentially, the closer we got to him. I'd never been on the "moving" end of the pull. I was usually the one waiting around for Teren to come to me. There was a slightly different edge to being the one heading towards the other. It gave me a rush.

Practicing my calming technique, I settled into her bucket seat, closed my eyes, and breathed slowly and deeply. Starla's gum smacking stopped and I heard her shift to look at me. "Huh, I guess you were telling the truth. You are bonded to your husband."

I peeked my eyes opened and looked over at the well put together woman. She stepped on the gas and the car surged forward. I inhaled a quick breath and dropped my head onto the seat as the draw to him spiked. My breathing heavier, I asked, "You know what this is?"

She resumed her chomping and I resisted the urge to snap at her to stop that annoying habit. With a short laugh, she shrugged. "I've seen it before. It's the blood bond between a creator and his or her createe." She looked over at me. The pieces of her shaggy hair were so spritzed with an overpowering, floral hairspray, that I was sure even a hurricane wouldn't move a strand. The scent was nauseating, and I started to worry that my morning sickness might come back. "It's designed to keep them close to each other. Being new is the most critical time for a vampire. The bond helps to ensure that the Sire won't stray far from his child." She grinned after she said that.

I groaned, partly because of how fast we were getting closer to Teren, and partly because of what she'd said. "Please don't call me his child. It's creepy." She laughed, amused at my comment and my discomfort. Sighing as my agitation grew, I said, "So, it all comes down to blood, doesn't it?"

She blew a quick bubble, then noisily popped it. "We're vampires, honey. Everything comes down to blood."

I tried to relax back into my seat, to force the draw to Teren from my mind, but that was pointless and impossible. Gripping the seat as the pull increased, I asked, "Does it go away?"

She glanced at my white, straining fingers. "Well, it's different for everyone. For some, it's only a mild recognition of each other, but it can be a lot stronger, especially if there was a connection pre-turning."

I laughed, in a tittering, agitated sort of way, and started squirming in my seat. My entire body wanted to be miles ahead of where we were. The waiting was torturous. "As I said, we were married." A groan escaped me, and not because of any comment she'd made.

She sighed. "This should be fun. Do you two have any level of control, or is he going to rip your clothes off right in front of his coworkers?"

Her tone was irritatingly sarcastic, and I glared at her. "We can handle this. He'll be fine." My words came out between pants, and even I didn't believe them. I pictured Teren in his office, gripping his desk to restrain himself from blurring to me. I knew that sensation—feeling him approaching but not able to do anything about it. That was torturous too.

Starla shook her head and turned back to the road. "Yeah, I can see that. Well, regardless, in most of the cases I've heard of, it usually eases up after the first year...or so."

Almost immediately after she said that, my sister started ringing. Okay, it wasn't her, it was the cell phone in her pocket, but my revved up hormones only registered a loud sound coming from her body. I glanced back at her, eager for a distraction, any distraction. Furrowing her brow, she dug in her pocket and pulled out the tiny flip-phone.

"Hello," she said quietly, the number on the phone not registering with her. Her eyes widened and then she looked up at me. Without saying anything, she handed me the phone.

My breath fast, I clenched the thing and put it to my ear. Before I could speak, words filled my head. "Why did you leave the ranch? Why are you coming to the city? Where is your phone?" Teren's voice in my ear was fast and breathy. He was definitely feeling this.

"Oh," I sighed, squirming in my seat again. "Well, I left so fast, I guess I forgot it." I was reacting to just his voice, so I ended up answering his most inconsequential question first.

"Emma," he groaned. "Why are you coming to me? Is everything okay?" I heard something that sort of sounded like wood splintering.

"Yes," I sighed again. My voice was husky and strained, and it didn't really sound like I was answering a question, if you know what I mean.

Starla let out an exasperated noise as she snatched the phone away. "Good God, you two have no control whatsoever. I'm not just gonna sit here and listen to you have phone sex." Putting the cell to her ear, she chipperly said. "Hey there, vamp boy." I could hear Teren's low growl and I gripped the seat even tighter as a growl of my own escaped my chest.

Starla rolled her eyes at me and spoke to Teren before he could start questioning her. "Your girl and I are coming to get you. Clear your schedule for the day. There is someone who I think you should meet, someone who will be very interested in speaking with the both of you. Someone I think you'll be interested in speaking with, too."

Straightening, I tilted my head at her; she hadn't mentioned this before. "Who?" I could hear Teren ask. His voice seemed slightly calmer.

Starla smirked into the phone. "Now, I wouldn't want to spoil the surprise. We'll be to you soon…which, I'm sure you're perfectly aware of."

Silence on Teren's end and then, "Who are you?"

She smiled brightly. "Name's Starla. See you soon." With that, she snapped the phone shut and handed it back to my sister. Grinning over at me, she noisily smacked her gum as her blue-green eyes sparkled in the sunshine. "Curious now, aren't ya?"

I could only gape at her and shake my head.

Chapter 19 – Mixed

When we entered the city, the pull got deliciously stronger, and I couldn't think about my odd traveling companion anymore. I squirmed in my seat, my breath embarrassingly strained, and pointed her in the direction where I felt him. Looking annoyed that I had no apparent self-control, she rolled her eyes. I wanted to snap at her, "Back off! Have you ever felt this? Didn't think so! I'm doing the best I can!" But I couldn't focus long enough to put that many words together.

As the office building housing Gate Magazine came into view, I clutched the console, anything to keep me in the car. The building had an underground parking lot, and with vague grunts and directives, I got Starla into it. As she put the car in park, I felt Teren coming towards me. Fast. That's when I lost it.

I hopped out of the car before she even turned it off. I had only taken three steps in the dimly lit underground before I was engulfed in cool arms and devoured by cool lips. My fingers locked in his dark hair, holding him securely to me, even though he was making no effort to get away. His hands clenched and unclenched my body, like he really wanted to tear off the loose sweats I was wearing. We panted in each other's mouths as the draw completed its connection. We were, once again, how our nature wanted us to be—together.

A low growl rumbled up my throat, and as Teren's cool hands slid over my backside, I heard an irritated throat clearing behind me. With a concentrated effort, Teren pulled his mouth from mine. Breathing heavily, and resisting the desire to return to my lips, he looked over my shoulder. When he spotted Starla, I saw his control instantly snap into place. Mine wasn't quite there yet. While he straightened and stared her down, my lips attached to his collarbone and my hand traveled down the front of his slacks. Hey, I wasn't just fighting the pull. I was a seven month pregnant chick with a hot husband and an acute desire.

I heard my sister giggle nervously while Starla muttered, "God." Teren luckily stopped my fingers from slipping inside his slacks. Looking down at me, he gently pushed me away. "Emma," he whispered, his hands coming up to cup my cheeks.

My breath eventually evened as his slightly glowing eyes enveloped me. Swallowing, I nodded that I was better. From behind me, I could hear Starla resume her cow-like gum smacking. Saucily she murmured, "Yeah, I can tell you guys have the bond *well* under control."

I turned to face her, about to tell her where to go, when suddenly the door leading to the stairwell burst open. Hot Ben came striding out, panting and holding his stomach like he'd just run a marathon. Striding over to us, he shook his head. "God you're fast, Teren."

I blinked at seeing him, surprised. Teren answered my unasked question. "I called him. I wasn't sure what was going on." He furrowed his brow as he looked back at Starla, then over to my sister. Ashley waved as she stood at the back of Starla's car.

Teren shifted his attention back to Starla while Hot Ben sidled around to his other side and asked him what was going on. Not answering Ben, Teren narrowed his eyes at the stranger in front of him. Starla's blue-green eyes were faintly glowing in the dim lights. To a human, the glow would have hardly been noticeable, and easy to dismiss if you didn't realize what you were looking at. To a partial vampire however, the glow was unmistakable. Teren's mouth dropped wide open.

"You're…"

She extended a hand to him. "Part human, part vampire…and I hear you've been looking for me."

Hot Ben gasped beside Teren and stared at Starla with a look of complete wonder on his face. Teren's face matched Ben's as he stared at her too. For a moment, he was even too stunned to take her hand. She waggled it in front of his face, her lips twisting in annoyance at being ignored, and Teren finally woke up from his daze and grasped it.

Both of his hands closed around hers and his eyes moistened. I bit my lip to not start hormonally crying at the image in front of me. Teren had waited so long for this moment. "It's…amazing to meet you. Thank you for finding me." His voice was nearly reverent, and I momentarily hoped that this tiny blonde vampire didn't let Teren down. He'd built up meeting more of his kind in his head, and so far, she hadn't been what *I'd* been expecting.

A little taken aback by his reaction, Starla pulled her hand away. "Yeah, well, you've been causing quite a stir, poking your finger into every vampire nest you could find." She raised an eyebrow. "That sort of thing doesn't go unnoticed."

Teren straightened his stance as he shook his head. "I had good reason."

Starla's eyes flicked to my stomach. "Yes, I've been brought up to speed on that."

Teren stepped towards her, arms outstretched like he was going to grab her. His fingers barely brushed her arms, and that was as close as he got to her. He was suddenly shoved back. And by shoved back, I mean he was pushed thirty feet in the air. Landing on his back, he smacked his head to the pavement with a sickening crunch. Hot Ben immediately pulled a stake from his pocket and moved into a defensive crouch. My sister screamed and backed up a step. I teetered on my feet, not sure if I should run to Teren's side or run to my sister's. Indecision held me in place.

A part of me wanted to smack Starla for pushing Teren. Only, it wasn't Starla who'd tossed him back. Distracted by the draw of our blood bond, I'd completely forgotten that Starla wasn't alone. Teren's aggressive move had drawn the attention of her bodyguard. Ben and I warily eyed the imposing man. Having blurred into a battering ram the moment Teren had stepped up to Starla, he was now standing in the space where Teren had been. He was taller than Teren and wider too. His hair was a light brown that matched his slightly glowing brown eyes, and he was dressed in head-to-toe black, like he thought that was an inconspicuous outfit or something. His fangs were dropped and a low growl broke the sudden silence of the room as he crouched down in a protective stance in front of Starla.

Starla's "muscle" was a mixed vampire too then, albeit it, an undead one. There was no thumping heart to be heard in his barrel-sized chest. But he had to be a partial vampire, if he was protecting her during daylight hours.

Teren popped up from where he'd been tossed aside. He zipped back to the man, and I speedily moved to block him from leaping on the vampire. It took quite a bit of effort on my part to hold Teren back, since he was a little revved up. Hot Ben came over and helped me, holding back his other arm.

Teren eventually calmed down as Starla sighed and walked around her protection. Thumping his chest with her hand, she muttered, "Down, boy." Coming up to Teren, she shrugged her shoulders. "Sorry, he doesn't like me being touched." Her turquoise eyes flicked to me, then back to Teren. "You can understand?"

Teren shot the man a hard look and then focused again on Starla. Ashley came up beside me and clutched my arm. I clutched hers back, both glad she was here and wishing she was far away. When Teren spoke, his voice came out irritated, but with a forced patience to it. "I was just going to ask if you can help us?" He looked over at me, then back to Starla, and his voice softened. "Can you help her?"

Starla looked between the two of us as her bodyguard crossed his arms over his chest. She sighed and shook her head. "Not me, but you should speak with Father. He sent me here, curious about what you wanted with us. But seeing what you've done," she disdainfully shook her perfect head, "he will definitely be interested in your situation."

Teren eagerly nodded. The thought of getting some answers, far outweighed his irritation at being thrown across the room. As Starla chomped on her gum and indicated her car with her head, I looked over Teren's body. He seemed fine, but that had to have hurt. "You all right?" I asked, while Starla got back in her car.

Teren eyed the big man zipping back to his car on the other side of the lot. "Yeah, I'm fine." He returned his eyes to mine; they sparkled with hope. "I'm great, Emma."

Over Teren's shoulder, I watched Hot Ben casually put his stake back in his pocket. I had the feeling he was always armed with one now. Twisting, I watched my sister eyeing where the big vampire had gone. She was fine with Teren, and fine with the tiny, unassuming blonde vampire, but that big guy had freaked her out. I could smell the fear on her.

When Ben moved to his car, presumably to follow us, I blurred over and stopped him. He paused and blinked in shock at me suddenly standing in front of him. I rarely moved blindingly fast in front of him. I was just glad I hadn't tripped along the way. Putting my hands on his chest, I searched his blue eyes. "Teren and I can handle this." He immediately began shaking his head and objecting. I forcefully shook mine, digging my fingers into his skin. "No, please...take Ashley home."

I glanced over his shoulder at my brave but terrified sister. She was determined to see this through with me, no matter how much the whole thing scared her. Ben looked over at her too; his body slumped as he did. Ben had always been very gracious around my sister, never making her feel self-conscious about her appearance, never treating her any different than he did other friends. His eyes took in her small frame, slightly shaking as she stood with her hands clutching her elbows, her arms locked tight around her body. She noticed us looking, and smiled—it was a forced one.

Hot Ben glanced over at Teren. Having heard the entire conversation, Teren nodded, and Ben turned back to me. "All right, Em," he said. Surprising me, he wrapped me in a swift hug. In my ear he whispered, "Be careful...both of you."

We stepped apart, and I nodded at him, tears in my eyes again. He moved back from me and nodded, his chiseled face determined. I had the feeling he would take his assignment with all seriousness, protecting Ashley from every bad thing in the city. He might even stay by her side all night long, just in case. For the millionth time, I could have kissed Hot Ben.

Teren held out his hand for me while I heard Starla sigh in exasperation, and mutter that we were worse than her pampered princess of a sister. Ignoring her, I took Teren's hand. His cool fingers gave me strength as I walked up to the car. Noting that it was time to go, Ashley walked up to the car as well. I gently put my hand on her shoulder as she moved to open a door.

"No, Ash. Not this time."

She sputtered and shook her head at me, and I dropped Teren's hand to grab her shoulders. "I love you, Ashley, and I know you love me. You don't need to do this to prove it to me." She started to say she wasn't, when I interrupted her. "I know, and if I were in your shoes, you'd have to pry me away."

Pulling back, I placed my fingers on her wet cheeks and lovingly stroked the roughness of her scars. "This is something Teren and I need to do together, alone." Leaning in close, I rested my head on hers. "I love you, but I can't have you there with me. I need to know you're safe…" My voice trailed away as emotion cut it off. I felt Teren's hand come up to my shoulder, and I suddenly had a much greater respect for him always wanting to keep me away, to keep me safe. Having someone you love in danger was harder than having yourself in danger.

Ashley started to cry in earnest, but eventually nodded. Pulling away from her, I wiped the tears off my cheeks and told her I loved her. As Teren and I got into the car, I watched Hot Ben come up to her and put his arms around her in comfort and camaraderie. She held him tight and he stroked her back as he watched us through the window. His jaw was clenched as he nodded at Teren.

Starla started the car and snorted. "God," she muttered. "Overdramatic lot, aren't you? You'd think I was driving the two of you to certain death." She started to laugh as she drove away, and Teren and I gave each other uneasy glances in the backseat.

Once it was clear we weren't staying in the city, Teren leaned forward in his seat. Clutching my hand tight, he asked her, "Where *are* you taking us?"

Starla popped a bubble and glanced at him in the rearview mirror. "L.A.," she casually said.

Teren nodded and sat back in his seat; his cool side edged right up to mine. Starla reached into her purse on the passenger's seat, dug out her bug-like sunglasses, and turned the radio up. Some pop hit boomed through her speakers and I figured she was discouraging us from asking any further questions.

I sighed and leaned into Teren, happy that, for once, we were having an adventure together instead of apart. Teren sighed as well and kissed my head before leaning his cheek on it. A twin nudged against a sore spot and, trying to get comfortable, I adjusted how I was sitting. Los Angeles? That was several hours from San Francisco.

Settling in for a long drive, I was grateful that Halina would blaze her way to us when the sun set. She wouldn't have time to run back to the ranch, but Teren and I could find somewhere for her to hide. It would just be nice to have our "muscle" with us.

After a few silent miles, Teren shifted to look at me. I pulled away from his side and gazed up at him. The afternoon sunlight streamed through the window, highlighting his eyes that matched this sunny Californian spring day. "You smell like paint," he said, a corner of his lip lifting.

I smiled and subconsciously rubbed my belly. "Ashley and I were working on the nursery. You should see it…it's beautiful." My eyes watered at the thought. I wasn't sure why. Maybe from the thrill of preparing to see my babies, or maybe from the fear that I might never meet them.

His hand came up to cup my cheek and his thumb grazed over the surface. I could hear his skin sliding across mine, even over the music, and I could smell some sort of grease, lingering on his fingers. "You smell like…the underside of a car."

Starla snorted and popped another bubble. Teren ignored her as he smiled down at me. "It's chain grease. I went home and got my bike this morning." He dropped his hand from my face and looked down. "I just needed to work off some energy."

Grabbing his hand, I laced our fingers. "Did it help?" I asked, knowing his workout was more to relieve stress than to exercise, much like my art project today.

He looked up at me with a crooked smile. "Not really." I leaned in to kiss him. Ignoring an annoyed sigh from Starla, who turned the music up even louder, we kissed for a few moments in the backseat. During a break, Teren pulled back and whispered, "I'm sorry I didn't tell you about Carrie."

I pulled back, surprised at the road he'd decided to take our conversation down. I noticed Starla stop smacking her mouth and slightly turn the music down. Apparently listening to gossip was better than listening to us make out. Teren's eyes were remorseful as I shook my head. "That? Of all the things to be sorry for lately…you pick that?" My lips lifted at the corners as I looked over his face.

He smiled at seeing the humor in my mouth and shook his head, too. "I just felt like that one was still lingering between us." He shrugged. "I don't want to walk into this with anything…between us." His face turned serious.

I cocked my head, then nodded. He continued when he saw that I understood his reason for bringing this up again. Sighing, he ran a finger through my hair and pulled out a fleck of paint. "I should have told you, but everything with us just happened so fast. We never really had the 'exes' speech, and it was such a long time ago," he said.

I smiled, having had that same thought myself. "I know." I mentally added that we still needed to have that talk—I had a few questions, especially about him and "visiting" female vampires—but I didn't want to have that conversation with Starla listening. And I was more confident than Teren was about us getting out of this unharmed.

I stroked his arm as he stared at my stomach. Perhaps he was thinking of the woman who had briefly carried his child before me. Trying to push back my jealousy, I asked, "Why did you let her remember? Why didn't you tell your family what happened?" My hand went up to touch his cool cheek and his eyes lifted to mine. "I'm sure they would have understood."

His eyes rapidly flicked between mine. "I…I just…" His voice trailed off as he shifted his vision over my shoulder, to the window. We were out of the city now, speeding down the interstate on our way to the largest city in the state, where the elusive group of mixed vampires were hiding out. Blocking his view with my head, I raised my eyebrows and waited for a response.

His eyes came back to mine and he shrugged. "I knew Great-Gran would take everything…and she was the first girl who loved me, the first girl I loved." He swallowed, like he hated telling me this. I smiled reassuringly, and he continued. "If it were up to me…they'd all have their memories. That was Gran and Great-Gran—protect the family. Of course, now, I can see the logic in that, but back then, I'd have preferred if they all remembered me…like I actually did exist." He swallowed again, his eyes watering. "With Carrie…I just wanted someone out there to remember that they loved me once. I just wanted *one* person to remember me."

I swallowed the emotion building in me at the look on his face. "I remember you. I'll always remember you," I whispered.

"I love you so much, Emma," he said, his lips immediately lowering to mine.

After a brief kiss, I pulled back. "I know why your family wanted Carrie wiped, and why some of the girls had to be…altered, but why does Halina take it all? Can't she leave some of the good parts? The beginning at least?"

He looked down, a small smile on his lips. "You know how they feel about loose ends." He shrugged. "They don't want us running into people who will notice that we don't change. Plus…" His voice trailed off and I lowered my head to meet his gaze again.

With a sheepish smile, he shrugged. "It was easier. If they didn't know me, then they wouldn't try and rekindle the romance." He shook his head as he relaxed back into the seat. Starla, in the front seat, snorted again and resumed her gum smacking. Teren glanced at her and frowned. "And, one way or another, they had all proven that they couldn't handle the truth. There was no future with any of them."

I leaned back in my seat. "All of them?" Overlooking his condition had been pretty simple for me, in the beginning, before I'd learned how serious it was. That had taken a bit longer to accept, but I'd done it. It was a little surprising to me that other women hadn't been able to see past the species to the amazing man underneath.

He smiled and leaned into my shoulder. "Until you." He tilted his head as he regarded me. "You truly don't understand how rare you are."

I bit my lip before kissing him again. Their loss…my gain. Sighing, I pulled away. "I can see why that would make you reluctant to share things about your life. I suppose you've just been conditioned to be secretive."

He smiled. "Do you forgive me then, for not telling you about her?"

I grinned as the last lingering remnants of jealousy completely faded from me. His past didn't matter. My past didn't matter. Even our futures were vague, grayish blobs of uncertainty. What mattered was today. What mattered was riding in this car with him, and a strange eavesdropping woman, and feeling the love that flowed so easily between us. I still had questions, as he probably did about me, but all of the questions in my head were just to learn more about this unbelievable man who'd married me. There would be no anger, jealousy, or resentments in my questioning. Not when he was so completely mine, and I was so completely his.

That coy smile still on my face, I murmured. "Maybe in a few years."

Starla let out a dramatic groan as she turned the radio up to an earsplitting level. Over the music she loudly said, "You guys are worse than a Hallmark movie. Good God." Shaking her head, she started singing along to a top forty hit as she drummed her fingers on the steering wheel, tuning out our love fest. I laughed and rested my head on Teren's shoulder.

Under the music, Teren told me, "I don't know where Carrie is, but once we get past this…speed bump, we'll track her down and I'll have Great-Gran erase her memories."

I pulled back to look at him, surprised that he'd concede to her memory being taken. I found myself nodding as I looked at the determination on his face. He smiled in return and whispered, "You're the only one I need to remember me, anyway."

Starla groaned again as Teren and I kissed.

The drive to L.A. was not a short one, especially with two tiny people pressing on my bladder. After the fifth pit stop so I could pee, Starla finally got irritated about my condition. Her earlier compassion was all but gone. I very politely informed her that I could just relieve myself on her hand stitched leather seats instead. She stopped complaining after that.

Teren made the almost eight hour drive as comfortable for me as possible. He rubbed my shoulders, encouraged me to take a nap on his lap, and made me drink a couple of packets of blood that Starla had in her car. Quite ingeniously, her group of mixed had designed portable blood packets. They were in silver pouches that you poked a straw through, reminding me of kids' juice boxes. They were cold though, and didn't have the same bite as the warm stuff. I drank it anyway, not even daring to ask what sort of animal it was from. My stomach just couldn't handle it if the answer was one I didn't want to hear.

Just when I was about to forcibly rip the gum out of Starla's mouth, my last tired, sore, and uncomfortable nerve used up, we entered the outskirts of Los Angeles.

I'd taken family trips down here as a kid, back when my dad was alive. We'd done all the touristy stuff people do in L.A.—Disneyland, Knott's Berry Farm, Universal Studios, La Brea Tar Pits, counted the stars of the Walk of Fame. You name it, we'd probably done it over the multiple summers we'd vacationed here. But I hadn't been here in years, not since Dad had died, not since the fire.

I found myself taking in the prepackaged beauty of the city. The sun had set on the long drive over and the lights of the miles-wide metropolis lit the sky with an orange glow. We wouldn't need to worry about our eyes in this place. Feeling Halina racing towards us, I started spacing out and let memories of happier times with my family flood into me. Then Teren asked Starla, "What part of Los Angeles do you live in?"

Starla brightened in clear adoration for her favorite city. "The only part of L.A. that matters—Hollywood." Her face turned a little smug as she bragged about her zip code. I resisted rolling my eyes.

Teren didn't bother. He even laughed at her a little. "Hollywood...seriously?"

She sniffed, offended by his reaction. "You know a better place to look eternally youthful?" Teren twisted his lips and sank back into his seat. Looking over at me, he shrugged. She did have a point.

We started weaving our way through palm tree lined streets, heading towards the nicer and nicer neighborhoods. As the houses started getting larger, security started getting tighter. Every house we passed had high walls and gates with intercoms and security cameras watching every movement. I started missing our place in San Francisco. It was cozy, warm and inviting. I couldn't wait until I could go back there.

After another ten or fifteen minutes, we stopped before a gate at the crest of a steep-sided hill. Shrubbery lined either side of the fence around the gate and the house contained within wasn't visible. Nerves started attacking me as Starla drove up to a box, pushed the button on the intercom and said, "I'm back, brought a pair of mixed with me." The gate started rolling open, the metal scream loud to my sensitive ears. Starla pulled inside, and the black car of her bodyguard followed close behind.

She pulled up to the front of what looked like a seven-car garage, parked the BMW, and immediately stepped out if it. I noted that she left the keys in the ignition and figured that she'd never had to put her car away in her life. As Teren helped me out of the back seat, a couple twenty-something vampires approached us. I couldn't tell if they were mixed or pure, not with it being night now, and them not having heartbeats. Although they had a certain scent to them, something that was familiar...comforting.

They eyed Starla for injuries, before examining me. Their expressions were surprised when they noticed my stomach, but they quickly returned to normalcy. Ignoring me, they shifted their attentions to Teren, clearly the threat.

Starla adjusted her dress and tossed her hand out to one of the guys. "This is Jacen," she flicked her hand at the other one, "...and Jordan. They're mixed too."

Jacen stiffly nodded at us. He was sort of short for a guy, but had the same shade of blonde hair as Starla; it was also meticulously over-styled. I couldn't help but think that these were not vampires who went camping. His eyes were the same blue-green mix as Starla's, and I thought that maybe they were related in some way.

The man beside him, Jordan, didn't nod at us, only eyed Teren warily. He was the opposite of Jacen, tall, lean, and dark everything—hair, eyes, skin. He blended into the background of night around him and the whites of his eyes seem to glow at me more than the others.

Teren nodded politely to both of them. A small, excited smile was on his lips. "I'm Teren Adams. This is my wife, Emma." His smile broke into a wide one. "We're very happy to meet you."

The men glanced at each other and then back to Teren. Jordan finally spoke. "We know who you are." He glanced at Starla again, still looking like he was making sure she was okay, and then he returned his gaze to Teren. "We also know what you've been doing, and we're more...cautious...than happy, to meet you."

Teren nodded, his smile fading. I grabbed his hand and stretched out my aching joints as Starla's bodyguard parked his car and got out to stand behind us. The nervous energy in me tripled. I could hear my heart rate spike; I could even smell my own fear in the air. I couldn't help my reaction, though. We were surrounded in a strange, sealed-off location.

Teren whispered in my ear that everything would be okay, and I nodded as I clenched his hand even harder. Jordan nodded towards the house and our group started moving that way. Starla sighed. She already looked bored as she clutched her Prada bag and examined her nails. They looked perfect to me, but maybe she thought she'd scratched one on the long drive here.

As we followed the tall, dark mixed vampire walking beside the short, blonde mixed vampire, Starla eyed us and muttered, "I suppose your pureblood is flying down to you as we speak?"

Teren glanced at her. He looked like he didn't want to tip her off to that fact, but then, seeing where we were, and the sort of precarious situation we were in, he changed his mind and nodded at her. I supposed that was smart. Surprising them with an unannounced arrival might not be the best idea. Starla nodded, like she was well aware of Halina's progress. Resuming that damn gum smacking, she calmly said, "We have full vampires too."

I had no idea if she was stating a fact, or if she was implying a threat. My heart sped up even more. Hearing it, Jacen turned his blonde head to me. "Calm down, no one here is going to hurt you." Not letting me respond, he shifted his head to Starla. "Will you spit that damn stuff out? Do you have any idea how loud that is?"

She twisted her lips and put a hand on her hip. "Shut it, Jace."

He rolled his eyes and twisted to the front door we were approaching. As he grumbled that she resembled a cow, I felt myself relaxing. As scary as these strangers seemed, underneath it all, they were a family, much like the one I'd left behind at the ranch. That made me feel a little better as we walked through the front door of the compound.

I say compound because of its size. Much like the Adams vamps, this group liked space. There were one or two smaller, side buildings in a basic one level design, but the main building was an impressive one to three story dwelling. It varied in height, shape and dimension, so that the building almost seemed alive. Everything was all curves and arches and roundness, as if Dr. Seuss had designed the house. But underneath that odd architecture was a layer of opulence that made Teren's family seem thrifty.

Waterford Crystal vases held flowers that smelled completely fresh and new. I was pretty sure they were rotated daily. The foyer had an actual Oriental rug. My eyes could see the intricately woven patterns. I thought it was a little gaudy, but it definitely screamed money. The ground not covered by the expensive rug was cool, polished granite and the ivory walls were filled with original works of art.

As I stared at the crystal chandelier hanging over my head, I wondered if there was such a thing as a poor vampire.

Starla harshly tossed her designer bag onto an intricately carved purpleheart wood entryway table. Sighing in irritation, she smacked Jacen's shoulder. He glowered as he looked back at her. Smacking her gum on purpose, she gave Teren and me a wry glance as the bodyguard shut the door behind us all. With her thumb, she indicated Jacen. "Did you know that before he died, Jacen here attempted to be a stage actor?"

Jacen tilted his head at her; his face was not amused. He crossed his arms over his chest as she continued. "Yeah, he even got a small part in a play. Wanna guess what his role was?"

She gleefully raised her eyebrows while Jacen growled low in his chest. Teren and I looked at each other and shook our heads. Teren started tuning them out, looking around the room like he could somehow find an answer to our all questions in one of the many paintings hanging on the walls. I could tell he was getting antsy, being so close to what he'd wanted for so long.

Starla laughed as she smacked Jacen's shoulder again. "A vampire. The dork actually got a role as a vampire." Jacen told her to shut up, but she started laughing almost uncontrollably. As Jordan rolled his eyes and disappeared into the house, Starla managed to spit out around fits of laughter, "The director fired him...because he wasn't convincing enough."

She bent over, clearly delighted by this fact. Jacen straightened and glared at her. He could be imposing in a way, but he was still barely bigger than her. "Bite me, Starla."

She smirked and popped a bubble in his face. "Anytime, Jace." Smiling, she flashed a fang at him.

My eyes darted between the both of them. I wasn't sure what to do with any of that exchange. Teren, beside me, had finally had enough though. Dropping my hand, he stepped forward. That got everyone's attention. The relaxed mood in the room vanished as Jacen and the bodyguard bared their fangs at him. Starla was fine. She'd spent quite a bit of time with us, and wasn't nearly as wary as she had been upon our first introduction.

She put a calming hand on Jacen's shoulder while Teren shook his head and raised his hands in the air. Taking a step back to stand by me again, he irritably tossed out, "Why did you bring us here? For stories?" Sighing in frustration, he ran a hand back through his dark hair. "You said we should talk to your father...can we see him now, please?"

Just then, Jordan came back to the room with another vampire, also appearing to be in his twenties. I figured he was a mixed too. Jordan looked between Jacen and Starla, his dark eyes disapproving. "Do you two ever stop acting like children?"

As one, they both turned to him and stuck their tongues out. The new vampire cleared his throat authoritatively and they both immediately stopped goofing off. As Teren grabbed my hand again, Starla skipped over to the new arrival.

"Hello, Father," she said, throwing her arms around him and kissing his cheek. "I brought back the vampire causing all the problems. Seems he tried to turn his human."

Her father smiled down at her. His face was smooth, lineless and intrinsically beautiful. He had completely green eyes and sandy brown hair, but looking at him gazing at his daughter, I thought I could see the resemblance. "I'm glad you've returned safely, Starla." He glanced up at her bodyguard and briefly nodded. The big, silent man nodded back and left the room. I exhaled with relief when he did.

Looking over at the two of us, the man slung his arm around his daughter and kissed her head. While never removing his eyes from us, he said, "It's Teren, isn't it?"

Still holding my hand, Teren extended his other to the man. "Yes, sir."

The man smiled with one side of his mouth. "Please, call me Gabriel. And this one here is your mate?" Gabriel smiled at me as he extended his hand in my direction.

I took it, noting the coolness of undead skin, and gave him my greeting. At the same time, Teren answered with, "She's my wife, Emma." He emphasized the word *wife*. To Teren, that word carried greater weight.

Gabriel took in my obvious condition and frowned. None of them seemed to realize what Teren had wanted with the mixed. None of them seemed to have expected a pregnant girl to turn up. Turning his head to Teren, Gabriel raised his eyebrows at him. "You tried to turn her? While pregnant? I can see your dilemma now. That was very foolish and quite a risk. Why would you do that to someone you obviously care about?"

Teren took that as his opening. "She was dying. Another vampire bit her. I tried to save her. Can you help her? Do you know what I've done to her? Do you know if she'll convert? Can you save the children before she does?"

Gabriel laughed. Releasing Starla, he gripped Teren's shoulder. "Are you always this anxious?" Extending an arm down a hallway, he calmly said. "You and I have some things to discuss, don't we? Come, first I have something to show you."

Teren sighed, frustrated to not have his questions answered immediately. Then he nodded, and stepped where Gabriel indicated.

Chapter 20 – Gabriel

We walked down hallways lined with gold-fringed tapestries. A lot of the pictures were scenic, but some were actually of vampires. It was discreet of course, one merely being a man kissing a woman's neck, but my enhanced eyes could see the slight shadow of a fang on the woman's neck as the vampire leaned in to drink from his meal. Sadly, the picture made me hungry.

Teren clutched my hand hard as we walked behind Gabriel and Starla. Glancing at him, I could see that his jaw was tight. He was nervous, excited and most of all, struggling with impatience. My upcoming birthday was like a death knoll, gonging in his head. Rubbing my stomach with my free hand, I checked my physical state. Aside from swollen feet and a mild case of heartburn, I felt fine. Not about to have a heart attack or anything.

I leaned into Teren's side, and he looked down on me; concern replaced the anxiousness in his pale eyes. I smiled encouragingly, and he gave me a nervous smile in return.

Jacen, from behind us, snorted. "You two act like we're marching you to the gallows. Stop being so dramatic."

Teren frowned at him, but Gabriel in the lead, stopped and looked back. Clear displeasure was on his striking face. Starla laughed and smacked her gum. I heard Jacen swallow, but my attention was all on Gabriel.

Narrowing his eyes, he calmly said, "I expect immaturity from Starla, she is only twenty-two, after all." Starla beside him harrumphed. I almost expected her to stomp her pricey high heels too, but she refrained. Ignoring her, Gabriel continued. "You, Jacen, are over one hundred twenty." He raised his eyebrows. "Start acting like it."

From behind us, I heard Jacen sigh and slump. "Sorry, Father."

My head swung around to stare at Jacen after he said that. *Father?* Jacen was staring at his shoes, admonished under his father's stern gaze. Confused, I looked back at Starla. She'd called him father as well, but he'd also just said she was twenty-two. I didn't understand how he'd had children one hundred years apart? I was under the impression that that wasn't possible.

"Teren, how did he...?" I didn't know how to finish my sentence, so I didn't try. I didn't need to either. Gabriel swung his green eyes back to me and smiled.

Understanding my vague question, he answered with, "They are not my blood children." He glanced at Starla attached to his arm, and then at Jacen and Jordan behind us. "The title is honorific, I suppose." He shrugged and indicated for us to keep walking. As we approached a marble staircase, leading down into even more levels, he continued with his speech. I was grateful for it. His deep voice was a soothing distraction from the feeling that we were headed towards the dungeons.

"All of my actual children have converted and moved on to start their own nests around the world. I miss them, but I can sense them through the bloodline, and take comfort in that." He looked down at Starla, fatherly pride on his face. "As for my new family, well, I take in what mixed I can, giving them a home and a safe place to changeover, if they still need to. They are free to come and go as they like, but many have decided to stay here with me. Safety in numbers." He looked back at Teren and me. "They gave me the appellation out of respect."

Starla grinned back at us as she blew a big bubble. With a slight clearing of his throat, Gabriel held his hand out to her. Pouting like a child being unfairly reprimanded by a parent, she spit her gum in his hand. Jacen laughed and Starla shot him a glare. While not technically related, the two sure acted like squabbling siblings.

As we descended to a hallway, deep under the main level we'd started out on, I noticed that the luxuries continued even down here. Plush carpet replaced the granite flooring from upstairs, and I nearly wanted to shuck off my shoes and let my aching toes sink into the fibers. The hallway we were walking down had several closed doors in it, almost like a dorm. I wondered if we'd traveled down into the living area of the mixed. I wondered if the full vampires stayed here too, but then thought not. While dark and underground, it wasn't as lightproof as Halina's rooms. Maybe they were the next floor down. As we padded along, Starla still pouting, Teren stepped up to walk beside Gabriel. There was enough room in that hallway that I was able to stay beside him, and the four of us walked along.

With a mixture of wonder and respect in his tone, Teren asked, "If I may, sir, how old are you?" I widened my eyes in curiosity. If Jacen was over one-twenty, and deferred to this man, he must be even older.

Gabriel smiled. There was a calm wisdom in his emerald eyes that only decades of experience can give you. It was still odd to me, to see so much life experience in the eyes of someone who looked younger than me. With a shrug he stated, "Six hundred eleven."

Shock ran through me, and a low whistle escaped my lips before I could stop it. Wow. He'd been around for the actual medieval times. I couldn't even begin to comprehend everything he'd seen.

He smiled softly, and for just a moment, I saw the weariness behind his eyes. Wisdom came with a price. As Alanna had told me once, immortality wasn't all it was cracked up to be.

"Oh," Teren said, looking like he was trying to process that as well. Nearly in a whisper he added, "I wasn't even sure if we could live that long." He looked down, like his ignorance on his own kind embarrassed him.

Gabriel put a hand on his shoulder. "There is much that you don't know." Gabriel sighed, almost regretfully and Teren looked up at him. "I blame myself for that." Teren scrunched his face, confused by his statement. Gabriel sighed again. "Your nest came to my attention years ago." I was so surprised by that, that my teeth embarrassingly popped out. Only Starla noticed. She giggled at me as I pulled them back in.

Gabriel continued, looking chagrined at Teren's surprise. "You all looked so peaceful and content at your little ranch. A blissfully ignorant little family." He smiled and shook his head. "I didn't want to interfere."

Teren started sputtering and ran a hand through his hair. "We didn't know...we thought we were alone. Why...? How...?" Calming himself, he took a deep breath and exhaled slowly. "We would have been honored to meet you. You should have come by."

We approached a T in the hallway and Gabriel turned the group to the right. Behind us, I could hear Jacen and Jordan silently following. They listened, but didn't interrupt their master. I had no idea what they felt about the matter. Starla seemed...bored. She had released herself from Gabriel's side and was examining her nails again, buffing out a spot with her thumb while we continued down yet another long hallway.

Gabriel glanced over at Teren with the corner of his eye. "Well, you all seemed to have everything under control." He flicked his eyes over to me, then my stomach. "Until you started knocking over every vampire nest you could find, that is." His eyes went back to Teren's. "Annoying our brethren is not a good way to remain unnoticed, or alive."

Teren glanced at the floor for a second before raising his eyes back to Gabriel. An almost defiant look was on his face. "I had no choice. I didn't know how else to find you."

Gabriel smirked, then nodded. We finally approached the end of the hall. Looking behind us, behind Jacen and Jordan, I could see that the hallway we'd been walking down wasn't a straight one, it had angled some, and I could no longer see much of where we'd been. That thought didn't exactly please me.

Twisting back to the front, I saw a set of double doors before us. The handles were gold, with gold inlay around the trim that highlighted a red octagonal pattern set into each panel. Teren swallowed as Gabriel smiled and pulled down the handle. I wasn't sure what we were walking into, but I was sure it held the answers we were looking for. I clutched Teren's arm, attaching myself to his side.

Gabriel swung the door open and we looked into a room that was set up like...well, a laboratory. Confused, Teren and I entered the odd room. It was straight out of a horror movie, and I even found myself looking around for the mad scientist. All I found was Gabriel, walking up to some steaming beakers and sniffing them. Smiling, he turned down a burner under one. Jordan walked into the room and joined Gabriel. He examined a batch of some pinkish fluid resting in vials under a heat lamp. Jordan seemed to eye the room with the casual air of someone who came down here a lot. Jordan probably assisted the ancient mixed vampire…in whatever they were doing down here.

Jacen stepped into the room and shut the door behind him. Instantly, I felt the difference. Teren and I glanced at each other, and I could tell he sensed it, too. This room was soundproof. And not just any sort of soundproof, this room was vampire-soundproof. That was saying something. As the background noise of people rustling, talking, moving, watching TV, and clacking keyboards, instantly silenced, my nerves spiked. The smell of chemicals, steam, propane, and the faint sweetness of blood suddenly seemed cloying.

Having heard my reaction, Gabriel looked up from a pot of liquid. "Don't fret, child. I find that the silence helps me think." He smiled, looking tired again. "Sometimes, a little quiet is nice."

I nodded and tried to relax. Jacen looked around the room after closing the door. He didn't look like he came down here very often. He seemed interested, but obviously confused; he didn't know what this stuff was anymore than I did. Starla seemed to have a better idea.

She walked up to Gabriel and sat on a stool in front of him. Lifting her arm, she exposed the inside of her elbow to him. Teren and I walked up to them, still confused. Gabriel held his hand out to Jordan, who gave him a pink vial. The stuff looked vaguely familiar to me, but I wasn't sure why. We watched in silent awe as Gabriel stuck a syringe in the vial, extracted a small amount, and then injected it into Starla's arm. She flinched, but didn't seem overly concerned.

"What was that?" Teren asked. There was a strange edge of apprehension in his voice.

Gabriel handed the empty syringe to Jordan and patted Starla's arm as she hopped off the stool. Not directly answering Teren, he said, "When my heart was still beating, my human wife and I had three children." He smiled, looking at the floor for a moment. "Our two girls grew up, had children of their own, converted, and then left my care." His reminiscent smile evaporated as he raised his eyes to Teren's. "My son…" He swallowed and I could clearly see the ancient sadness bubbling in him. "He didn't survive the conversion. The hunger consumed him…"

I swallowed and clutched Teren's arm tighter. I could see Teren's jaw was tight. He'd nearly been consumed by that hunger too. Picking up a full vial, Gabriel began shifting it back and forth in his hand; the liquid inside sloshed from one side to the other. "After my wife passed, I spent the next five hundred years, trying to find a way to stop the conversion."

His eyes left the liquid to look back at Teren. "To stop the human side of our kind from prematurely dying. To let the vampire have a choice in when and where, they go through their conversion. I want them to have children when they want to, to have a heartbeat as long as they want to, to enjoy humanity for as long as they want to. I want to give our kind a choice—to be reborn as an undead creature, or to live and die a purely human life. A choice my son...never had."

Teren took an excited step forward. I could tell he was itching with the restraint to not scream questions at this man. Gabriel held the vial up to him as he took another step forward. Teren released my hand and grabbed the vial. He held it like it was somehow sacred. Gabriel continued, while Teren and I looked confused. "I concocted this. It's a derivative of our mixed blood." In a whisper, he said, "Among other things, it slows the vampiric blood inside us, eases the strain placed on the human heart, allowing it to beat for much longer than normal."

Teren's eyes snapped up. "Does it work?"

Gabriel glanced over at Starla, now standing beside him. "I haven't been able to test it on as many living-mixed as I'd like, but Starla here has been taking it for the past six months or so." She grinned at Gabriel's affectionate look and leaned back on her hip; her posture was a little smug.

I frowned. "But she's only twenty two. You won't really know if it works on her for years." Starla frowned at me for bursting her prideful bubble.

Gabriel smiled, but didn't answer me. He turned to Jordan and in a low voice said, "Bring Samuel here."

Jordan nodded and blurred from the room. Teren and I watched him leave, our brows still scrunched. Finally Teren shook his head.

"This…may save her?" His eyes were glistening; there was so much hope in them.

Gabriel sighed. "To be honest, I don't know. The treatment doesn't take for everyone." He raised an eyebrow at me as my shoulders slumped. "But, then again, you lived through a vampire attack." He pointed at the telltale scar on my neck. "The fact that you are not dead and gone is quite astounding, my dear."

I smiled wryly as Teren and I exchanged a brief glance. Teren smiled just as the door to the lab opened again. Amid the rush of noises reentering the room, I heard a definite heartbeat being added to mine and Starla's. Curious, I looked over. My jaw dropped straight to the floor. Tall and dark Jordan was walking into the room with a man who was clearly older, approaching his forties, if not already there. The smell of the man, foreign, yet with a familiar note that I was coming to associate with partial vampires, filled me, and I stared at him in awe.

Teren gaped as well. Walking over to see him more closely, he stared at him like the sound of his still-beating heart was mystifying. And it was. I'd been so used to twenty-something mixed vampires, that the sight of an aged man with graying hair, heartbeat, and fangs was stunning.

Teren twisted back to Gabriel; his smile was glorious. "It works," he breathed.

Gabriel smiled and nodded at Samuel, indicating the stool. Samuel obediently walked over and lifted his arm in the same way Starla did. As Jordan prepared a second vial, Gabriel nodded at Teren. "In the ones that take to it, it has worked exceedingly well."

He frowned, his lips twisting in displeasure as he injected the fluid into Samuel's arm. "The first batch I created…did not." He was silent for a second, then he fixed his face into a clinical expression, as he explained. "Conversions are an interesting process in mixed. In pure vampires, it happens when they are created. When a mixed is born, the element that completes the transformation from living to undead stays dormant. But eventually, the strain of our free-flowing blood is too much, and somewhere between twenty-one and twenty-six, depending on the family history of the vampire, an event is triggered, and that element activates. The blood then accelerates to a point where the vampire's human body can no longer handle it. The heart burns out, the human side dies and the vampiric blood takes over, reanimating the creature."

I watched, fascinated, as he finished injecting Samuel and handed the empty syringe to Jordan. He glanced at our curious faces. "You see, the process of conversion isn't just the human side dying, it's also the vampiric side awakening. Kill a mixed vampire before that trait has a chance to awaken, and you kill the vampire as surely as you would kill a human. That genetic marker in the blood is the key to vampirism." He sighed and shook his head. "The first batch I created accidentally triggered that dormant element in the blood— revved it up and burnt out the heart within hours, jump-starting the process, regardless of the vampire's age." He shrugged and looked very sad while Samuel rubbed the injection site on his arm. "I accidentally converted quite a few vampires, much too soon." He shook his head and I gasped.

He flicked his eyes to mine, seemingly concerned at my alarmed reaction. "I stopped. Once I realized what it was doing, that it was never going to work, I destroyed all of the samples and locked up my research. Don't worry, I have considerably adjusted the formula." His eyes took on the look of a scientist as he said that—emotionally detached from what he'd done. Of course, he probably didn't understand the extent of what he'd actually done.

Teren gasped as well as he looked back at me. Locking eyes, we understood each other. Teren returned his eyes to Gabriel. "I think you may have missed some." His voice was rough, hard with anger.

Gabriel blinked at hearing it. My eyes stung as I found Teren's hand. That man who'd kidnapped us had injected Teren with something that had killed him. It had revved up his blood and given him a heart attack. He'd claimed it as his own creation at the time, but it hadn't been. Somehow, he'd gotten a hold of Gabriel's samples, and had pawned it off as his own. I always suspected that the bastard hadn't been smart enough to come up with something like that. But I couldn't believe a mixed vampire had come up with it. I wondered if Gabriel knew that a hunter had been out there, killing other mixed with his creation. By the look of shock on his face as Teren described what had happened to him, I didn't think he'd known. As Samuel stood from the stool, Gabriel heavily sat down onto it.

"That's not possible...the only person who could have..." His voice trailed off as he left that thought unfinished.

Anger still in his voice, Teren cocked his head, and asked, "Who?"

Gabriel, still stunned, shook his head and looked up at Teren. His face slowly regained its ancient composer as he smiled. "A family matter. Thank you for bringing it to my attention, but I will take it from here." Standing up, he cast a significant look at Jordan. He nodded once, then left the room. I had a feeling that someone was in a world of trouble.

Returning his eyes to Teren, he calmly asked. "Has the hunter been dealt with?"

Teren smiled with an edge of his mouth as he nodded. "He didn't survive *my* conversion." I knew for a fact that that knowledge actually bothered Teren, but he wasn't about to show a hint of weakness amongst this house of supernaturally strong strangers.

Gabriel raised an eyebrow and smiled at Teren. "Well, I can't say I'm sorry about that."

Teren raised his eyebrows, looking like he'd just mentally assembled some puzzle pieces in his head. "He must have come to California for you." Gabriel gave him a curious expression, and Teren shook his head. "The hunter left journals. They actually helped lead us to vampires. I think your nest was referenced in them. I think he was here for you, but he made a pit stop when he stumbled across me."

Gabriel stared at Teren for long moments. "Interesting. It would seem that our lives started entwining before today." He frowned and shook his head. "I am terribly sorry for what happened to the both of you." He nodded at Teren, solemnly. "Because of you, he can no longer use my creation to harm anyone else. You have my gratitude for that."

He looked down and regret filled his ancient eyes. "As you were a mixed that had not converted yet, I *was* planning on coming out to your ranch, to offer you the shot, if you were interested." He peeked up at Teren. "I was obviously…too late." He shrugged. "When I had the time to come visit with you, word got back to me that you'd already converted. I didn't think anything of the circumstances surrounding your conversion. I regretted that I'd lost the chance to study you, but I moved on to other prospects." He stood and extended a hand to Teren. "You have my deepest apologies that I was in any way involved in your…unfortunate situation."

Teren and I looked at each other. If Gabriel had offered Teren the shot, and it had worked on him, we would have had all the time in the world to conceive our children. Even now, Teren's heart could have been beating. I let that thought tumble through me, then tumble right out of me. What-ifs were all well and good, but it hadn't happened like that, and Teren was what he was now, and we were fine. My hand idly rubbed my stomach. We'd even managed the conception part in time. Now, we just needed to make it to the giving birth to them part.

Gabriel turned and started packing several vials into a leather briefcase. He filled another one, then handed them both to Jacen, who looked happy that he finally had an important task to do. Starla sighed and started twirling empty vials on the counter. Gabriel grinned at his "daughter" and then indicated the vial still in Teren's hand. "I've provided enough to get her through the pregnancy. Give her 4cc a day, every day. Don't give her more than that, don't give her less, and don't miss a day. It has to be exact for it to work."

Teren stared at the vial, then his hand clenched around it. "How will we know if it's going to work on her?"

Gabriel stared at the ground, before looking back up. "Unfortunately, some things from the first batch have still carried over." Teren and I looked at each other, confused. Gabriel sighed, then explained. "If it is not going to work on her, it will almost immediately awaken the dormant trait within the vampiric blood. Her heart will stop, much like yours did. But while your body took hours to die after your shot, on her newly-exposed body, it will happen fast. If her heart does not give out within several minutes of the first dose…you'll know it worked."

His face conflicted, Teren turned and stared at me. I felt my breathing stop as my face paled. So that was it, all or nothing.

Gabriel's voice snapped us out of our stupor. "I'm sorry there is not a gentler way. I'm assuming she's close to conversion? You seemed desperate to find me."

Teren nodded, still numbly staring at me. "We have no choice, I guess." His jaw tightened and I nodded at him. Yes, we had no choice. My heart would give out if we did nothing. If there was a chance to prolong the conversion until after the birth, to save the children, then we had to take it.

Looking back at Gabriel, Teren whispered, "If it doesn't work, and she starts the conversion…will she finish it? Will she survive? Is my mixed blood enough to fully change her?"

Gabriel looked at Teren for long seconds. I thought I could see the debate in his eyes, like he was judging whether being honest with Teren would drive him over the edge or not. Finally, and without ever removing his eyes from Teren, he spoke to Starla, who was spinning on the stool in her boredom. "Starla, please help Jacen load the vials into your car."

Starla straightened, her perfectly painted lips turning down into a pout. "My car? Do I have to drive them back, Father? They live so far away…and do you have any idea how annoyingly lovey-dovey they are?"

Gabriel looked at her from the corner of his eye, and I heard Jacen suppress a laugh. Starla immediately looked down and replied with, "Yes, Father."

She and Jacen twisted to leave the room. Starla smacked Jacen across the back as he sniggered. "Shut it, Jace," she muttered as she opened the door to leave. The sounds of the house rushed in on me, and I swear, somewhere in the home, I heard what sounded like a muffled cry.

Samuel also seemed to hear it. "Father, I should get back to…that other situation."

Gabriel looked over at Samuel; he was cautiously eyeing us. I wasn't quite sure what situation he was referring to. Maybe Jordan had found the culprit already. Gabriel nodded at Samuel. "Please, make sure the vampires stay back. Zane needs it, not them. He is the one completing his conversion tonight." Samuel nodded, then left through the open door, closing it behind him.

Once again encased in silence, I forgot our original conversation, and curiously asked, "You have someone here, converting?" Stepping forward to grab Teren's hand, I turned back to Gabriel.

Gabriel gave me a sideways glance, also looking cautious. He straightened and his eyes were emotionally detached again. "Yes. He chose to let his human side die. He should be awakening at any moment actually." Gabriel looked through the walls of the home, to where the seemingly dead person was changing. "I should be there for that." When he looked back at us, his face had switched back to concern for his "family." "I always try to be there, to help the new ones." His eyes shifted to Teren, and I clenched Teren's hand tighter. "That first moment can be quite...terrifying."

"What will he eat?" Teren asked.

Pieces of the conversation fell into place, and I felt a little nauseous. Twisting his lips, Gabriel cocked his head at Teren. "You are not the only one that has come across hunters." Gabriel sighed as he came over to stand in front of us. Sitting on the edge of a table, he crossed his arms over his chest. "We found one a few nights ago, trying to...remove one of my children." A hard edge was in his voice and my face paled.

"He's here, alive?" A shiver went through me, remembering the muffled cry I'd heard.

Gabriel shifted his cool, green eyes to me and nodded. "For a little while longer."

Knowing I sounded hypocritical, I sputtered, "You can't just feed him to a vampire. That's murder."

Gabriel stood and walked over to me. Tilting his head, his ageless, attractive face said, "If you found a predator at your ranch, picking off your cattle, what would you do with it?"

I shook my head. "It's not the same..." My voice was small and weak. I knew I was condemning him for something I'd actually done myself.

Gabriel, not knowing that part of our story, shook his head. "To us, it is. The people here rely on me to protect them. I can't do that if I let him live. He could spread the word, tell others where we are." Walking up to me, he ran a finger through my hair. Teren stiffened, but did nothing to stop this powerful man who had agreed to help us. "I'm sorry if you don't approve of our methods, but our survival depends on secrecy."

"You have full vampires. You could wipe him? Take everything?" I tried again. I wasn't sure why I was fighting for the human. Maybe to atone for my own sins, or maybe because I still saw myself as human and I was campaigning for my species. But honestly, the man had chosen his own fate when he'd started a fight with these people.

Gabriel shook his head. "I have hungry mouths to feed." He shrugged his shoulders and dropped his hand from my hair. His eyes rested on my stomach. "I'm...killing two birds with one stone." He looked up at me, a slight grin on his face.

Not entirely comfortable with this situation, I swallowed at seeing it. Teren finally took back the conversation. Pulling me behind him, he quietly said, "What you do with hunters...is your own business. We won't interfere." He squeezed my hand after he said that, non-verbally telling me to drop this. I bit my lip. I didn't want to drop it, but I didn't want to upset the man who might have saved the lives of my children.

I squeezed his hand back to let him know I would be good, and he continued, "What will happen to Emma? Have you ever tried to change someone?"

Gabriel shook his head and walked over to another table, where closed vials of pure red blood waited. He lifted one and my eyes tracked the movement of the sloshing liquid inside. Even though I'd had a pick-me-up in Starla's car, staring at a clear vial of the stuff amped up the vampire in me.

Not able to help myself, I dropped Teren's hand and stepped forward; a low growl left my chest.

Gabriel paused from examining the container and peeked up at me. With a tiny smile he said, "She *is* close, isn't she?" His smile dropped as he looked over at Teren. "I wouldn't wait too long to give her that first dose." He cocked his head as I stopped moving, stopped breathing. "We could do it now, here?"

My breathing started again, faster, and my heart matched its pace. I wasn't ready. I wasn't ready to possibly die. I twisted to look at Teren, pleading in my eyes. He swallowed, torn between wanting to help and not wanting to accidentally kill me. His eyes not leaving mine, he whispered. "We'll wait." In a calmer voice, he added, "We'll do it at home…with *our* family."

My heart and breath relaxed, and I nodded. Teren turned back to Gabriel, who was still thoughtfully holding a container of blood. "You still haven't answered my question." I could hear some of that impatience creep back into Teren's voice. I held my hand out to him, silently encouraging him to relax. He exhaled as his cool hand clenched mine. I nearly sighed with relief; his impatience had gotten us into enough trouble lately.

Gabriel smirked at Teren's restraint, then finally answered him. "I have not done it myself, but I have seen it done." He sighed and raised the vial of blood to his eye. "Some mixed try and turn their spouses, try to keep their loved ones for eternity."

"And?" Teren whispered, taking a step towards the man who had all our answers.

Gabriel lowered the vial. "It almost always leads to their loved one's death." His ancient eyes lost their detachment and he seemed genuinely sad. "I have held many a vampire who inadvertently destroyed their mate." He held the vial up to Teren, holding the top and bottom with his fingers. Controlling myself, I fought back another growl. My body really wanted that stuff he was holding.

With a cocked eyebrow, Gabriel said, "It is so rare for a human to be able to accept our blood." He lowered the vial and smiled at me. "As I said before, it is a miracle that you are even alive, my dear. A mixed successfully turning someone is not common." His focus shifted from me to Teren. "Especially from your blood." Gabriel raised an eyebrow. "What generation are you? Third at least, correct?" Teren feebly nodded, looking stunned and still a little confused. Gabriel's eyes came back to mine, his beautiful face still shining. "You are very rare, indeed."

"So I keep hearing," I muttered, still not sure what my fate was.

Gabriel tilted his head, and the scientific detachment returned to his expression. Completely serious, he said, "I'd love to study you."

My eyes widened, and Teren shifted his stance to stand in front of me. With his brow furrowed, he ignored Gabriel's comment. "So, what happened to her doesn't happen to most. But...what *did* happen to her?"

Gabriel set the blood-filled vial back down into a tray containing other, similar vials. He faced Teren. "Fascinating creatures, mixed vampires. Not quite human, not quite vampire, we exist almost as a species all our own." He raised an eyebrow at Teren. "If you are interested, I could explain to you the difference between what happens when a pureblood vampire changes someone—how their blood completely eradicates every human cell and takes over." Gabriel smiled and extended his hand to indicate Teren's body. "I could explain to you how a mixed vampire's blood works in a completely different way—bonding with any human cells left in the body, working in conjunction with whatever trace amounts of human genes are left."

He continued smiling as I stared at him with what had to be a blank expression; my hormonal brain was too busy absorbing the distinction between the two seemingly similar species. Teren nodded, looking interested, but also impatient; more than a vampire biology lesson, he wanted to know my fate.

Gabriel's emerald eyes on mine, he said in that scientific voice, "I could go into an intricate amount of detail on how mixed blood needs the perfect balance of human blood left behind to work properly." He raised his hand and indicated a small amount with his finger and thumb. "Too little left leaves it with nothing to attach to, and too much," he opened his fingers and splayed his hands wide, "dilutes it to a point where the vampirism is ineffectual, and does nothing." He swished his fingers, miming nothingness.

While Teren looked like he was replaying the night of my attack, mentally recalling how much blood had been left in me, Gabriel crossed his arms over his chest. Looking like a teacher tutoring a couple of students after class, he continued, since we hadn't interrupted. "I could explain all of this and so much more. How intricate and fascinating the fine line is for mixed turnings. As I already mentioned, how rare it is when a human has the genetic disposition to even accept the foreign blood entering it." He nodded his head at me, indicating my body, "You have to be the ultimate universal receiver." His hand flashed out from his chest to indicate Teren again. "I could tell you all about how the chances of a conversion happening are better, the closer to pure the mixed vampire is. The third generation is about the last that can do it, and even then, rarely."

His voice took on a tone of wonder as he gestured in the air with his hand. "Like a masterful, complicated surgery, the act of a mixed vampire successfully changing over a human…is full of the potential for disaster. And it usually is." He shrugged.

I rubbed my temple. I felt like I was back in human anatomy, only now all the rules had changed. Gabriel smiled at Teren and me, his captivated students, and continued. "I could explain all of that in excruciating detail…but…" He glanced at me. I could tell my brows were drawn into sharp bewildered points; this was a lot for my already strained pregnancy brain to try and take in all at once. Gabriel smiled wider. "I wouldn't want to confuse you anymore today than you probably already are."

He crossed both arms over his chest again, looking elegant and undeniably intelligent. "Just know that a mixed turning creates what could easily be classified as another mixed. When a list of specific conditions are met, the new, nearly symbiotic blood, keeps the human body alive. That human then, for as much as you need to concern yourself with, becomes a near carbon copy of the mixed who created it."

I nodded, finally feeling like I was understanding something. It usually didn't work…got it. When it did, a mixed created another mixed…got it. Gabriel smiled at my comprehension, then frowned. "But, exactly like a mixed who was born into the world, the human side will wear down from the strain." His eyes turned sympathetic. "However, unlike born mixed, this will happen much, much faster for you. A pure human just hasn't had a lifetime to be conditioned to the strain, like a vampire born into it. As a result, their body wears out, and that dormant trait awakens, within a few months."

He redirected his gaze to Teren. "To my knowledge, most convert within a month or two of the initial blood transfer. I've yet to hear of one making it to three."

I felt ill as I mentally calculated how much time had gone by since Teren had given me his blood. It had been a while. I'd been secretly hoping that my stopwatch had started that night, that my body could handle the strain for a full twenty-six years. But it would seem that Teren was closer to the truth, and my birthday really was my end game, since it was pretty close to two months after the attack. And he'd said "maybe." I guessed I was pretty lucky that my heart was still beating. Hoping I'd make it to three months was probably pushing the limits of my "rareness."

Gabriel looked over my pallor and smiled. Turning back to Teren, he shrugged and said, "But, to answer your original question, if she has made it this far, I see no problems with your blood being enough to complete her conversion process."

Teren slumped down as relief washed over him. I could smell the fear evaporate as he covered his face with his hands. I watched his body vibrate, and I knew he was struggling to not break down. I smiled as my own relief filled me. It was like a shot of cold water to the face, suddenly believing that I might actually make it through this. I placed a hand on Teren's back, and he instantly turned and swept me into his arms. He grabbed my face and rested our heads together. Tears dripped off my cheeks as I watched his eyes fill to the brim. "You're going to live, Emma."

The anxiety leaving my body came out in a nervous laugh. "Once I die," I added to his comment.

He chuckled, then leaned in to kiss me.

Chapter 21 – Hope

Gabriel laughed as he walked up to us. We stopped kissing when he put a hand on my shoulder; his was as chilly as any other undead vampire that had ever touched me. "You two really are quite lovey-dovey."

Starla's words coming from his ancient mouth made me laugh. I held onto Teren, not wanting to separate yet. His arms slung around me too and his hand came down to rest on my stomach, comforting our children. They squirmed and wriggled at his touch; one kicked me in a sore rib.

Gabriel smiled at hearing them. "Twins among our kind are exceedingly rare." He smirked at me. "Rarer even than you, my dear." With a technical demeanor, he said, "If they survive this, I'd be very interested in watching their development."

Teren's hand firmed on my stomach. His jaw tightened, and I could see the protective instinct flaring up inside him. It flared up in me too. I was very grateful to Gabriel for giving us hope, for giving our family a chance, but I didn't exactly want him poking and prodding our kids like tiny little science experiments. Before I could say anything in rebuttal, Teren responded with, "We are extremely thankful for everything you've done for us. We will never forget…your friendship."

His tone was tight and I knew he was having the same thoughts I was—*you'll never get so much as a drop of blood from our babies.* He couldn't be that blatantly rude to this ancient, well-connected vampire though. We needed him to be firmly on our side, especially if we ever needed more life-giving vials of his miraculous medicine.

Gabriel didn't seem to take any offense to Teren's words or tone. With a smile, he indicated the exit. As we left the soundproof lab, the sounds of dozens of bustling people filled my ears. I didn't know how many I was hearing, or what species they all were—mixed or pure—but there was a harmonic quality to the cacophony and I found myself smiling. Being in that room had been too quiet. Considering how I used to wonder how Teren could stand all of his extra abilities, it was pretty interesting to me that I'd already adapted to mine.

Occasionally, the human hunter's cry would hit my sharp ears. I did my best to ignore him, but every wail and plea for help only made me feel worse. We walked back up the hallway and passed a few mixed vampires, along with a couple who I thought were purebloods. Now that I was surrounded by so many vampires, I was beginning to notice a very faint difference in the smell between the two. As we trudged along, I tried to remember that the hunter being served up as dinner had brought this upon himself.

That really didn't excuse what they were doing, but Teren and I weren't strong enough to take on a house of vampires to save this guy. Teren was right with his non-verbal warning—this was something I was going to have to let go. I just wished I could block out the pleading.

Teren squeezed my hand as we walked back into the main portion of the house. Looking up at his face, I could see the haunted expression in his pale eyes. He was hearing it too, and it bothered him as well. He glanced down at me, smiled briefly, then looked over at Gabriel. "Emma's conversion...you said she was basically a carbon copy of me. Does that mean that she will she come out like me?" I knew he'd said that out of curiosity, and also to distract us with something pleasant to think about.

We walked through a set of glass doors into an arboretum. A few more vampires nodded at Gabriel, before leaving us to our privacy. A couple of them cast hard looks at Teren, and I thought maybe he'd pissed off people they knew. Marble paths laced through raised, barked gardens, which held just about every medium to small-sized tree I'd ever seen. The air was warm in here, and I could feel my feet swelling even more. As Gabriel walked us to a stone bench, I noticed a few more sets of full vampires. They seemed to like the tropical air.

Gabriel plucked a deep red flower with a dark, black stamen and gave it to me. I took the flower as we all sat down, and marveled at the botanical beauty around us, enclosed under a huge glass roof that showed the pitch black night outside.

Sitting on the other side of Teren, Gabriel smiled. "She has your blood. She will share all of your attributes and weaknesses." He grinned. "Or lack thereof."

I inhaled a quick breath, surprised. As I did, the smell of hundreds of flowers assaulted me, making me a little dizzy. I'd sort of not let myself hope that I'd come out of this like my husband. Really, I'd sort of figured I wouldn't be getting out of this. It was pretty shocking to learn that I probably would, and that I'd be at the same level of normalcy as Teren. That just seemed too much to hope for. "I'll get to be in the sun?" I whispered, stunned.

Gabriel looked around Teren, who was also looking a little stunned. As his beautiful eyes swept over me, he asked, "You have no issues with it now, I'm assuming, since you made the trip okay?"

I nodded as my darn eyes watered again. All of this new hope wasn't mixing well with my pregnancy hormones. Gabriel smiled at my reaction. "Then yes, you should be able to endure sunlight, among other things."

Feeling overwhelmed, I needed an answer to our children's outcome too. Putting a hand on my stomach, I quietly asked, "And them? Did changing me do anything to them?"

Gabriel looked at my stomach, then me, then Teren. "They are your children?" he asked clinically. Teren clenched his jaw, but nodded. Gabriel smiled and looked back at me. "Then they were already mixed vampires. Teren's blood is the same as what's already in their veins, if slightly more potent, as he is third generation and they are fourth. Being exposed to more of his blood should not have affected them. As far as we know, vampires cannot be turned twice." He shrugged. "I foresee their limitations to be roughly equal to yours."

I smiled, relieved. I felt a child kick me, almost as if they were relieved too. "And the shot won't hurt them?"

Gabriel shook his head. "No, my dear, they are not close enough to their conversion for it to have any true effect on them." He smiled warmly, and a small laugh escaped me.

Teren smiled at my happiness and shook his head. With a soft laugh he twisted back to Gabriel. "You're over six hundred years old.

You must have seen quite a few of our kind. Have you ever seen the trait dilute out? Have you ever met a vampire's child who was purely human?" Curiosity overtook Teren's expression as he waited for the wise man's answer. Teren's family had lofty ideals of eventually seeing their line return to humanity.

Gabriel twisted his head and took in the paradise around him. Somewhere in the room bursting with life, I heard a nocturnal bird calling to its kind. The sound was odd to hear in a house, but comforting, on a basic, one-with-nature level. It spoke to the foreignness within me. I might not have the sharpness of Teren's "deceased" senses, but I already felt more connected to the world.

Pausing another moment to watch a teenaged mixed, clearly with child, walk into the room, Gabriel turned back to Teren and spoke. "All of the mixed that I have seen...have had, at the bare minimum, fangs and a mild interest in blood. But I've seen very few beyond fifth or sixth generation." His eyes got a faraway look as he thought through the tons of vampiric knowledge he must have in his head. "Having studied the blood for as long as I have, I believe dilution of that level, would take several generations. Perhaps dozens." He smiled wryly. "But who knows, our kind have been around for as long as our cousins, it is entirely possible that some humans in this world *are* descendants of mixed vampires, and they just don't know it."

I pursed my lips as I considered that possibility. "Descendents...that sure would explain some of the nearly impossible things some athletes can do." I shrugged as Teren grinned and nodded. Sure, some people were enhanced through drugs, but there were stories of "miraculous" feats every year, each seemingly more impressive than the next. Some of those people just had to be enhanced in a different way.

As Teren and I started talking about that possibility, a loud growl broke the relative silence. It sent goose bumps down my spine, and my teeth automatically dropped down into a defensive position. Not knowing what was going on, I left them down. Teren, fangless, twisted to stare at Gabriel. Gabriel wasn't looking at our reactions; his eyes were studying the double doors we'd entered as he focused on the sound that had ripped through the night.

I held my breath, and the dizzying scent of various species of flowers stopped. Gabriel flicked a quick glance at us. "Please, excuse me." With that, he blurred out of the room.

My hand found Teren's and I clutched him, hard. The vampire going through his conversion had just awoken—hungry.

I closed my eyes as the sounds of shuffling and shouting entered my brain. The growl intensified, and the shouting and pleading intensified as well. Teren dropped my hand and brought his over my ears, to try and block out the sounds of the hunter screaming for mercy. He only succeeded in muffling them. I started to cry as Teren pulled my head to his chest. Kissing me, he held me tight. To block out the muffled screams and growls that I could still hear, I started going over baby names in my head. I started at A, and made up two boy names and two girl names with every letter of the alphabet, all while inhaling the calming scent of Teren under my nose.

As I reached "L" and Lauren and Libby for girls' names, Teren pulled his hands away. His eyes were closed and his face was solemn. He'd heard everything, crystal-clear. The night was relatively silent again, and my tears flowed even harder. Knowing that the man had brought this disaster on himself, knowing that the man would have killed each of us without a second thought, and knowing that he would have stopped at nothing to take the life of my children, really didn't stop the horror I felt at listening to him die.

I swallowed a huge lump in my throat. "I'm ready to go home, Teren."

As conversations and rustling noises started filling the home again, I noticed that the birds started making noises again, too. An owl hooted at me from somewhere, and I felt myself relaxing. Even nature was moving on. Teren stroked my cheeks, murmuring that everything would be fine and that we'd leave here once Halina safely arrived. I could feel that she had markedly closed the distance between us. She must have been hauling ass to get as far as she had so quickly. I could only imagine that when she got here, she was gonna be pissed that we'd gone off with a group of strange, potentially dangerous partial vampires without her.

As I pulled away from Teren, Gabriel swished back into the room. He stood in front of our stone bench, and his face was apologetic, yet pleased too.

"I do apologize if that was…unpleasant for you." The beauty of his face intensified as he broke out into a wide smile. "But Zane is doing wonderfully, and should be fully recovered within a few hours." He put his hands in the pockets of his jeans, looking genuinely happy that a member of his family had survived, no matter the cost. A shudder went through me.

Teren stood, holding his hand out to help me up. "Is there somewhere where Emma can rest, before we head back home?" he politely asked as he pulled me to my feet.

Gabriel glanced at my stomach and then back to Teren. "You mean, until your vampire gets here?"

Teren looked away for a second before looking back. "Yes. She's wearing herself out getting here so fast. She won't have enough energy to return with us. I won't leave here until I know…" He paused, looking unsure if he should second-guess our savior's hospitality.

Gabriel grinned. "None of you has anything to fear from me. Your vampire will be treated as an honored guest, and will be allowed to stay in the basement levels for as long as she likes." He raised an eyebrow at Teren and me. "You may stay as long as you like as well. It is approaching the middle of the night. The two of you must be tired."

I blinked, not realizing how much time had passed. It had flown by once we'd gotten here. But we'd traveled a bit after the sun had set, and walking through this place took forever, and I suppose we had been in the lab for a while. It hadn't seemed that long at the time, but as Gabriel pointed out how late it was, I suddenly felt it in my body. I slumped against Teren and a yawn escaped me. Teren looked at me with a clear question on his face, but I shook my head. I didn't want to spend the night here. I wanted to be home with my comforts, my safeties, and my husband.

Teren looked back at Gabriel. "No, thank you for the generous offer, but once my great-grandmother arrives and is brought up to speed, we'd like to head home."

Gabriel nodded and extended his hand to the glass doors exiting the room. "Of course. We have several spare rooms at your disposal."

With one hand protectively on my back, Teren and I followed Gabriel as he led us to a rather bland staircase. It led up into one of the house's strange levels. Strange because we went up two flights of stairs, through a tunnel, down a set of stairs, and then back up another set. I was even more tired when we finally got to the room. Besides cursing the architect who had designed this place, I had no complaints left in me when Teren scooped me into his arms and carried me down the seemingly endless hallway to where our guest room was.

I was semi-asleep before we even got there. I heard Teren and Gabriel exchange some sort of parting, then heard the door open and felt the chill of the little-used room. Since I was snuggling against Teren's cool chest, the chill felt normal and I didn't even shiver. Teren clutched me close to him as I swam in and out of alertness. I felt him lay me on something soft, a bed, and then felt his body lie behind me. His arms curled around me and he buried his head in my hair.

He exhaled softly. The sweetness of his scent made me smile, even in my sleep-haze. "We made it, Emma," he whispered. Not able to respond past a grunt, I loosely squeezed his hand. Relief and exhaustion overtook me, and the last thing I heard before I succumbed to sleep was him telling me that he loved me.

I dreamt of our children. I dreamt of holding them, playing with them, watching them sleep. I dreamt of watching Teren play with them, watching him make playful fanged faces for them. I listened to their imagined laughter as they tried to copy him, and watched their little fingers touch his beautiful face.

I couldn't believe that after all of this, I might actually get to have that dream. I just had to survive the shot.

I woke up with a start, uneasy. Teren's cool arms were still around my body, and he stirred when I stirred. "It's okay, Emma," he slurred sleepily.

Confused, I blinked at a stream of sunlight hitting my eyes. For a moment, I had no idea where I was. I twisted uncomfortably. My children were telling me that I'd better find a bathroom soon. Scooting over to the edge of the bed, I looked around the foreign room. Alarmed, I turned back to Teren, still dozing on the bed. "We're still here?" I said, kind of at the top of my voice.

He cringed and peeked at me. "Em, not so loud."

Not enjoying his casualness, I repeated, "We're still here, Teren. Why? I thought we were going home."

He sat up, rubbing his eyes. "Well…"

Standing, I frowned as I rubbed a sore spot in my back. "Well what? You could have woken me up."

Teren stood and walked over to me with a sigh. "I'm…under orders to stay until nightfall." He said that glumly as he stared at the floor.

That's when I felt it. I stared at the floor too, at the exact point in the lower house where I could feel Halina sleeping, several feet below us. I peeked up at him. "Halina…forbade you to leave?"

He sighed again as he rolled his eyes. "Yeah. She wasn't pleased that we'd headed out without her." He frowned. "She sort of ripped into me, right in front of Gabriel and Starla." He rolled his eyes again, looking sheepish.

I couldn't help but smile at the thought of that conversation. Starla had probably laughed her ass off. Then I frowned, thinking of what Gabriel had said about the length of time mixed-turnings took to convert. "He said it happens in the first couple of months, Teren. It's been a couple of months. Maybe we shouldn't wait to go home…" I couldn't meet his eyes after I said that.

His fingers came to my chin, urging me to look at him. "We could dose you here, Emma."

I immediately shook my head. "I won't eat a person, hunter or not, and who knows if they have another 'bird' to kill. I won't be their pawn."

My eyes were wide with confliction. Teren studied me for a moment before sighing and nodding. I was glad he understood. If the dose wasn't going to work for me, it would start the conversion. I had no idea whether or not Gabriel had any other prisoners in this massive complex. Maybe someone was passed out, or asleep, or near death. I couldn't take the chance that he would offer me up a blood-pumping human, right when I was at my weakest. I wasn't sure if I had Teren's restraint, and I didn't want to find out if I did or not. I didn't want that guilt on my conscience, not when the family had plenty of blood sources readily available. Teren understood not wanting that guilt.

"We'll leave as soon as we get you some food." His knuckle gently stroked the soft spot under my eye. At his words, my stomach grumbled loudly and my fangs almost dropped at the thought of food. I noticed the sunken look of Teren's face and realized he hadn't eaten anything since the tiny blood packet in Starla's car. As a fairly new vampire, he still needed to eat pretty often.

"You're starving, Teren." I frowned.

Having heard my stomach, he grinned. "I'm not the only one." He kissed my nose. "And I'm not starving, just mildly uncomfortable."

I nodded and slumped against him. He picked me up and prepared to walk me through this maze of hallways, but before he could, I whispered into his wrinkled dress shirt, "I need a restroom."

He laughed. The lightness of it had been gone for so long that I found myself laughing in response. "Right, forgot about that."

I grinned, looking up at him. "Well, you haven't had to worry about that for a while, Mr. I-no-longer-have-a-functioning-digestive-system." He brilliantly smiled, and I reveled in the joy in his face. I hadn't seen that in a long time either.

As he walked me out of the room, in search of facilities, my hand went to his cheek. "Do you think this will work, Teren? Do you think I'll live, and we'll all make it through this?"

He looked down at me after finding the room in question. "I think you're a miracle, Emma. And if anyone could survive this, it would be you." He grinned again, and we kissed for a moment, until my bladder said enough was enough, and I speedily used that restroom.

A little later, Teren set me down in the entryway. Tall and dark Jordan approached us. With a cool professionalism, he led us into the dining room. Apparently, we'd woken up just in time for breakfast. My stomach growled again as the smell of pancakes hit me. Starla and a few other alive-mixed were already in the room, helping themselves to the buffet style table of food.

Teren looked around, but there weren't any steaming carafes. I didn't smell any blood mixed in with the pancakes and syrup either. He frowned as Starla turned to us. Having heard my stomach, she grumbled, "Great. Preggers is gonna eat all the chow." She smirked at me, and I scowled at her.

Jordan had disappeared upon leading us into the room, zooming back to wherever he'd come from, so Teren only continued to frown as he searched the area for his food. Jacen suddenly approached as I was getting my plate of carbs. Smacking Teren on the back, he pointed to a door leading outside. "Our grub's that way." He raised his eyebrows at him. "We prefer our food fresh here."

Jacen turned to leave as Starla muttered, "Neanderthal." Jacen shot her a glare, then headed outside.

Teren sighed and looked back at me. "Guess I'm hunting after all." Grabbing a Styrofoam cup off a table, he muttered, "I'll bring you back some." I gave him a sympathetic frown, then smiled at his thoughtfulness. Teren really didn't enjoy hunting. I had a feeling that I wasn't going to be a hunter either.

I sat down next to Starla to eat my meal, since she was the only person I knew in the room. She chatted my ear off about the amazing shopping trip she wanted to take me on. She eyed my tacky sweats and baggy t-shirt with open disdain. I took in her fitted designer dress and contained a sigh. I sort of missed my body. I'd have filled out her tight dress nicely a few months ago. But as my twins kicked me, I let it go. I had something vastly more important than an hourglass figure. I was happy to give it up, to bring Teren's children into the world. For a while at least.

Teren was coming back into the room just as I was filling up my second plate. I felt him approaching and my hands started shaking. He hadn't been too far away from me, so the pull of him returning wasn't that bad, but I still closed my eyes and took a couple deep breaths. Starla laughed at me as she left the room to go outside.

Teren walked over to me with forced slowness. A smile crept onto my face at his control. What he really wanted to do was throw himself on me. I knew that, because that's what *I* really wanted to do. Our nature demanded it. But we fought the instinct and calmly met in the middle of the room. Bending over, he gave me an appropriately small kiss. "Missed you," he whispered, his voice a little husky.

"Missed you too," I whispered back, forcing myself to sit down instead of leaning back in for another kiss.

Teren sat beside me and the bond eventually evened out. Grabbing my free hand while I started in on my second helping, he placed a cup of deep red blood in front of me. I stared at it. With concerned eyes, I looked back at him, and he understood.

"It's a puma. Found it up the hillside." I grabbed the cup and immediately started chugging it. Puma wasn't cow, but it was better than human. Conscience-wise anyway. I noted the slight difference in taste as Teren continued. "They've fenced in a large portion of the hill, trapping the wild animals inside. Many here only eat animal, but not all..."

His voice drifted off and I peeked over at him out of the corner of my eye; my fangs were slightly digging through the Styrofoam cup. He looked over my face and sighed. "They've got a house with people...willing to..." He shook his head. "They give them drugs, money or...sex...and the humans let them bite them." He shrugged as I pulled the cup away in surprise. "They don't kill them, but they have the purebloods wipe them when they are done with them."

"How do they find people willing to do that?"

Teren shrugged as he looked out over the room that was listening to us. A voice from behind him answered my question. "We place ads, in the personals." I twisted to look at Gabriel standing behind us. "We don't mention exactly what we are looking for, but you'd be surprised how many are more than happy to do it." He smiled as my surprise shifted to shock. "For the right price, of course," he added.

"Oh," was all I could squeak out.

I took in the leader of this group of mixed and pure vampires behind me, authoritative, yet welcoming, all at the same time. A bright shaft of sunlight was lighting him from the side, lightening his sandy brown hair to almost blonde and making his green eyes exceptionally emerald. He had power, money, charm, and the looks to go along with it. This man was the sort of person who could change the world, if he so chose. But his life mission had been to save Teren's kind. Well, my kind in a way now, too. I was thankful that he was on our side.

He cringed and moved away from the sun. To me, that meant he wasn't in Teren's generation. Maybe Alanna's? He indicated the seat beside Teren, and Teren nodded. Gabriel fluidly sat down and watched me sip my cup of blood that Teren had brought back for me.

"What flavor?" he asked politely.

Teren answered before I could. "Puma, found one on the hill." Gabriel raised an eyebrow at Teren and smiled.

"Those are popular. Our supply has dwindled a bit. Finding one now is quite impressive." His grin widened. "I'd love to hunt with you some time?"

Not wanting to be rude by telling the man how much he didn't like it, Teren smiled and said, "Another time, maybe. We're going to head home after Emma is full."

I smiled around my cup-o-blood. I might never actually get full again while these two fuel burners were inside of me, but I'd be good in a couple minutes. Gabriel looked over at me; a slight frown was on his face. "If you must leave, you may." Bringing his eyes back to Teren, the barest hint of a devilish smile lit the corners. "Your great-grandmother will be very displeased that you disobeyed her order."

Teren looked down, a sheepish smile on his face. "Yeah, well, I *am* an adult. She'll just have to deal with it." He looked up at Gabriel; there was a slight smirk on the ancient vampire's lips as he watched Teren. "Besides, my wife is my priority now, and we don't have time to wait around for sunset."

Teren's voice lost its impishness as determination filled him. If anyone could wish an outcome into existence by sheer will power, it would be Teren. Gabriel eyed him speculatively before shifting his gaze to me. "You won't consider taking the dosage here?"

Not having words for this imposing man, I only shook my head, no. He smiled and nodded, not looking surprised. "I'll have Starla get ready to drive you home."

Teren nodded, and Gabriel started to stand up. He paused halfway to smile down at Teren. "Your great-grandmother is…an extraordinary woman."

Teren's eyes widened fractionally as Gabriel fully stood. "I have immensely enjoyed her visit." I clamped my mouth shut to not laugh. By the slightly dazed, amazed look on Gabriel's face, I was pretty sure he knew Halina in the most intimate way a man could know a woman. Teren's mouth lowered a bit, and I was sure he was aware of that too. Gabriel put a cool hand on his shoulder, smiling down on him as a father figure would. "Your family is welcome here, anytime."

With a slight twist of his lip, Gabriel turned and left us at the table, staring after him in wonder.

Less than an hour later, we were flying down the interstate. Starla grumpily clutched the wheel as she chomped on a fresh piece of gum. It was apple flavored this time, but no less sickeningly sweet. Teren was letting me lie down on his lap as he sat beside me in the backseat. Well, as much as I could lie down in the cramped area. Adjusting the seat belt around my stomach, I listened to the sounds of the liquid vials in the trunk sloshing in time to the thumping music pouring out from the speakers. I hoped that stuff worked better than the dose Teren had been forced to take. Although, I supposed that had worked exactly as intended. I was just hoping for the opposite effect.

As Teren stroked my hair, he watched Starla, singing along to the current hit playing on the radio. "Why do you take the shot?" he asked her. She paused mid-chorus and looked at him in the rearview mirror. Her eyes narrowed as he added, "You don't want to be eternally young?" His gaze flicked over her manicured nails, her over-styled hair, and her expensive dress. Teren did have a point. She seemed like the type that had been trying Botox by fourteen. Now that he had brought my attention to it, I was curious too.

Her jaw tightened and her narrowed eyes turned into a nasty glare. "Don't presume to know me."

Teren blinked, surprised at the harshness in her voice. I was too. "I'm sorry. I meant no offense by that." He shrugged. "I was just curious."

Her face relaxed and she started chomping on her gum again. Her eyes drifting to mine, she let out a quick sigh. "The conversion took my mother and my sister." Her eyes flicked back to Teren's; they were moister now than before. "There is something in our bloodline, that won't complete the changeover. We're faulty, hardwired wrong. I'm the last of my family, and that would have been my fate too, if Father hadn't found me." She shook her head and her voice dropped to a whisper. "I have to take it...it's the only chance I've got."

I stared at her, surprised by her admission. I glanced at Teren. He looked equally shocked. Starla watched us in the mirror before focusing back on the road. "Anyway, that's why I figured Father could help you. I knew that I'd be dead in a few years if he hadn't helped me. Dead-dead, I mean." She smiled as she glanced at us again. "But now, I help Father." Her eyes flicked over to Teren before shifting back to the freeway. "He studies me, studies my blood. He's changed the formula a few times since meeting me, learning what works, from the junk in my blood."

She smiled, pride obvious in her features. "I'm helping him perfect it. The mixed seem to take to it better now, or so Father says. He's tried it out on five in the last several months, and three of those didn't auto-convert." She glanced at us again, while I mentally tried to figure out what percentage rate of success that equaled. She grinned as she watched me try to puzzle that out. "The weird thing in my blood just may be what saves your children. Chew on that." Then she blasted the radio, driving all conversation from the car. Teren and I looked at each other, and he gave me a soft, reassuring smile.

Teren called his family on the way there. Not to let them know we were headed home, they knew that, but to let them know what we'd discovered. Or rather, what had discovered us. I could hear Alanna's relieved sobs through the phone. After that, he handed me his cell and I called my sister.

She berated me for not calling her earlier, and I heard her whisper that we were okay to someone in the room with her. When I recognized the male voice answering her, I blinked. "Hot Ben's still with you?"

I cringed when I realized my pet name for him had slipped out of my mouth. Oops, pregnancy brain. Probably shouldn't have said that right in front of my husband. As I sat up in the seat, Teren frowned down at me with an eyebrow raised. Starla laughed while I lamely shrugged. Appropriate or not, it was true. He *was* hot.

Through the phone, my sister started giggling. "Hot? I suppose he is…" She paused for a moment and I knew she was checking him out. I heard Ben say, "What?" and then my sister responded to my question. "Yeah, he wouldn't leave my house until he heard that everything was cool from Teren." She paused again. "So, is everything…cool?"

With a laugh and a shake of my head at Ben's dedication to his task, I filled my sister in on exactly what had gone down in L.A.

After several pit stops, traffic jams, exasperated sighs from Starla, and backrubs from Teren, we finally arrived back at the ranch. I'd never been so happy to see the river-rock encased beauty. The red roof tiles gleamed at me in greeting as we zipped up the bumpy drive. It was late afternoon, a few hours before dark, and only Alanna and Jack waited for us in the parking lot—Alanna had tears in her eyes.

Whispering how worried she had been, she swept her son into a firm embrace. He returned it just as eagerly, lifting her up a little in his happiness. Then he released her and reached back into the car to help my bulky body exit. He got me standing and then Alanna's cool arms were around me, hugging me as fiercely as she dared. She couldn't even speak through her tears, and my exhausted hormones matched her reaction. We cried in each other's arms for a good five minutes.

Starla groaned and laid her head back on the seat; she was obviously anxious to head back home. She didn't even shut the car off. While Jack and Teren retrieved the suitcases of vials from the trunk, Alanna and I finally separated. Wiping my eyes, I turned back to the car and thanked Starla for coming all this way to get us.

"Yep. No prob," she muttered. She took off the moment Teren closed the back door. He yelled a goodbye at her car as she flew away from us, dirt and gravel highlighting her retreat.

Teren shook his head, amused. "Definitely not a country girl."

I laughed and slung my arms around his waist. He smiled at me as I watched Starla leave. I heard her car squeal onto the highway and wondered if I'd ever see that prissy vampire again.

Looking up at Teren, I sighed contently.

"Ready?" he asked.

My sigh caught in my throat. I knew what he was asking. My heart started beating faster and I clenched a hand over my stomach. No, I wasn't ready. How could you ever really be ready to possibly die? I exhaled slowly, letting the air escaping my body calm me. Without speaking, I nodded. I was as ready as I was going to be.

Alanna put a cool hand on my shoulder as she and Teren walked me towards the kitchen. I inhaled deep as we walked through the home. The smell of freesia from the hallway upstairs hit me, the scent wonderfully reminding me of home, comfort and family. Feeling more at ease, I followed Teren into the dining room. He and Jack set the suitcases up on the table. Teren popped one open and grabbed a small pink vial.

"What is it?" Alanna asked, studying the vial.

Teren shook his head. "Hopefully, it's what will save our children." He grabbed a syringe in the case and prepared exactly 4cc. When it was ready, he faced me and exhaled in one short burst. "Ready?" he asked again.

My heartbeat tripled. I shook my head no, but said, "Yes." We had no more time to wait. It was surprising I hadn't died already. A few more days was all the time this body had. Gabriel had pretty much confirmed that. I was fated to die…one way or another.

Teren squatted down in front of me. "I love you, Emma," he whispered.

Alanna started crying as Jack held her. Imogen blurred into the room, fighting against the strain of sunlight. Instantly, windows were covered to accommodate her, and, shaking in pain, she waited next to her daughter. I didn't reprimand her for coming down. She wanted to be here, and she was willing to take the pain to support me. Tears filled my eyes as I nodded at the loving family behind me. Twisting back to Teren, I said, "I love you too."

He grabbed my arm and adjusted it so he could see my inner elbow. His hand was trembling as he brought the tip of the needle to my bare skin. Just as he was about to stick me, I whispered, "Don't forget to take them." Pausing, he looked up at me. "If I don't make it, if my heart stops, you cut them out of me." I shook my head, my tears falling. "They are thirty weeks now, they've got a real shot." I cupped his cheek. "You get your ass to a doctor and get someone here to save them. Promise me."

A tear dropped to his cheek as he stared at me. "Promise me," I repeated.

He swallowed and his voice came out thick with emotion. "I promise, Emma."

I nodded, then bent down to kiss him. He stuck me while our mouths moved together. I gasped at the brief pain, at the minute smell of fresh blood, and at the warmth rushing up my arm. Teren pulled the needle out, his lips insistent as he continued to pour his love into his kiss. His hands came up to cup my cheeks and I could hear sniffles from the group watching this.

As my hands ran through his hair, I felt the warmth spread through my entire body. I felt myself relaxing as his tongue found mine. I felt my heart slowing as our frantic kiss settled into something languid and lustful. As my heart slowed to calmness, my breath started to pick up.

Teren broke apart from me, his pale eyes concerned. "Are you okay? What do you feel?"

Aching with the loss of his retreat, I leaned forward to find his lips again. "Fine, I feel fine." We met again, and a slight groan escaped me.

Teren pulled away again, his breath faster too. "What do you mean, you feel fine?" His eyes searched mine, the passion there buried under layers of concern.

I smiled, feeling the warmth from the injection circulating through every cell. It gave me a light, airy feeling, like everything about me had slowed down. Everything but my breath. That picked up as I glanced over Teren's face. "I think it worked," I said huskily, finding his mouth again.

He pulled back and cupped my face. The room silenced as every vampire, including me, held their breath. Only Jack's low, deep breathing remained. Teren's eyes moved down to my chest, to my heart. He stared, like he could stare straight through me. I listened with him, as I let out a soft exhale. My breathing returned to a normal, slow pace. I cherished the steady thumping I heard; it was pleasantly mixing with the two fast, fluttery beats underneath it. The entire room listened to those harmonic beats for a solid ten minutes.

Time finally seemed to convince Teren that I wasn't going to keel over. His eyes flicked back up to mine. "You're alive. Oh my God, you're alive." His lips were back on me then, no longer holding back.

I heard Alanna, Imogen and Jack all start to exclaim as they made joyous noises of celebration. Then I felt Imogen slip from the room and offer her congratulations and support from her darker bedroom environment. Alanna and Jack tried to offer their supportive comments, but Teren and I were letting our relief spill out physically; we couldn't even pry ourselves away from each other long enough to acknowledge them.

Finally, Alanna leaned over our making out bodies and said, "Would you mind taking that upstairs, dears? Your father eats here."

I could clearly hear the humor in her voice and I chuckled in Teren's mouth. He wasn't feeling quite as humorous. He only grunted, lifted me up, and blurred me to our bedroom here at the ranch. The room where our children were going to be born...when they were ready to be.

Chapter 22 – And Then There Were Four

Relief, exhaustion and stress finally took its toll, and we fell into a deep sleep after our celebratory reunion. A sleep that I was sure would have lasted for a solid twenty-four hours. Would have, except just before dawn, the door to our bedroom burst open. Stalking into the room, Halina glared at our naked, tangled bodies, barely covered in loose quilts. Ignoring my squeals of protest, she blurred over to Teren, grabbed him around the throat, and lifted him, one-handed, off the bed.

"You disobeyed me…again," she snarled.

She was holding him in the air with one arm, and his feet didn't quite touch the floor. Ignoring the fact that he wasn't wearing anything, she glared at him. She also ignored my plea for her to let him go. Teren struggled against her, looking more embarrassed than hurt. Finally prying her fingers away from his airway, so he could speak, he bit out, "I'm no longer a child, Halina, and I don't need your permission."

Her eyes narrowed at the use of her name and she lifted him a little higher. He squirmed, pried her fingers loose again, then added, "Emma couldn't wait. She needed the shot."

Halina seemed to remember that I was in the room at that point. She glanced over at me, and I clutched the sheets around my body, like she could somehow see me through them. She ignored my nakedness as assuredly as she was ignoring her great-grandson's. She tilted her head as she listened to my heartbeat. "It worked?" she asked.

She twisted back to Teren, and he nodded, or tried to anyway. She was still clenching his throat. Loosening her fingers, he squeaked out, "Can I get dressed now?"

She looked down, finally noticing that he was buck-naked. She smirked as she lowered him to the floor. "I've been changing your diapers since the day you were born. It's nothing I haven't seen before." Teren rolled his eyes before blurring away to the closet.

While he dressed, Halina came around to me. A soft smile on her lips, she reached out and placed a cool palm on my stomach. The twins inside squirmed at her touch, one kicking my bladder. She smiled at them, her teenage face full of wonder. I ignored my desire to be dressed, as I watched her. "Amazing man, that Gabriel. He assured me it would work on you." Her eyes flicked up to mine. "He was right."

She was still smiling at me as Teren came back dressed in gray lounge pants and a basic white tee. She glanced at him as he slid back into bed with me. Straightening, she said to Teren, "Interesting house of vampires down there." She raised one corner of her lip. "I may need to visit again."

Teren slid his arms around me, covering my bare body with more of the sheets. "Yes, I heard you and Gabriel...got along well."

She grinned and sat back on a hip. "Repeatedly."

I groaned and lowered my head into my hands while Teren chuckled and kissed my head. "Can we go back to bed now, Halina?" I peeked at her through my fingers. "You can ream Teren out tomorrow night, okay?"

She smirked at me, then frowned and raised an eyebrow. "Don't think I won't." Abruptly her frown shifted to a soft smile. "I'm really glad you are okay, Emma." Then she blurred from the room. I heard her swish into her daughter's room, waking her up. Then the giggling started as she relayed her trip to the woman who seemed more like a best friend to Halina than her flesh and blood. Both of them were laughing as Halina went over horribly graphic details of her encounter with Gabriel. They had apparently spent several hours of the dawn in a lightproof room downstairs, "getting to know each other." I groaned, as I held my hands over my ears and wished I hadn't inherited Teren's super sense of hearing.

Teren chuckled again and whispered, "Welcome to my world."

We celebrated my birthday with gusto. Mom, Ashley, Hot Ben, and Tracey all came out to help the poor, pregnant, bed-ridden woman celebrate turning twenty-six. We laughed and talked around my bed while they showered me with gifts, many of which were for the upcoming babies, although, Teren did surprise me with a beautiful, antique heart locket. The intricately detailed gold pendant folded out into four small pictures, and he'd already placed tiny ones of him and me inside. He'd left the other two blank and my eyes watered at the thought of filling them. Kissing him, I marveled at how amazing my man was at jewelry shopping. Again, the benefit of being raised by three strong women.

Mom massaged my swollen feet while Ashley laid her head on my stomach, trying to hear the beats I could hear more clearly all the time. Alanna brought us some cake and everyone who was still eating, enjoyed the rich, chocolate dessert.

While Mom stuck a large forkful of cake into her mouth, she indicated where Teren was sitting, and not eating, and asked how his allergies were going. Immediately after the wedding, we'd convinced Mom that he'd developed a severe allergic reaction to certain foods, and, until we could narrow down which foods were toxic to him, he was sticking to a strict home-based diet. But since he joined us for meals anyway, he scored great husband points with my mom. Whenever we'd eaten and he hadn't, Mom had questioned him on what foods he thought might be causing the problem. Teren, having researched it, gave her thoughtful and insightful answers. It made me grin every time I listened to them talk about it, since every answer he gave her was correct—*every* food was toxic to him.

That cover story had worked better than we'd hoped and Mom never thought it odd that he didn't share meals with us. Smiling at her concern, even after all this time, Teren assured her that his doctors were still narrowing it down, but she shouldn't worry, he was getting enough to eat. Hot Ben laughed when he said that, earning himself a strange look from Tracey.

Halina and my sister went over Russian baby names while I relaxed in my mammoth bed, warmed that everything really was going to be okay. I wasn't sure how I felt about not entirely being human anymore, but at the moment, it didn't matter. Our kids were going to have a shot at making it full term—that was all that mattered. Of course, I still wasn't excited over the whole "exiting" process, but I pushed it out of my mind, for now.

When my friends and family grudgingly left me, the vampires broke out some fresh blood and we had a celebratory toast to me successfully getting older than Teren. I reminded them that technically he would always be older than me, even if he had stopped "aging." They all thought that was funny, and we laughed away the last few months of tension.

As the weeks started going by, my body started doubling, and I swear, tripling. I went past the cute, obviously pregnant stage, straight to the I-swallowed-a-house stage. Teren told me I was adorable, and I tried to feel that way, but mainly, I felt stretched. My vampire sensitivity felt every centimeter of my tight skin. But I relished the life inside of me, and didn't begrudge the loss of my trim figure. Teren could help me get that back anyway.

He injected me with Gabriel's formula every day. We did it right before bed, and he watched me anxiously for a few minutes, every time he did it. After the third straight week, I tried to ease his mind, telling him that it was working and my heart wasn't going to suddenly stop. He worried anyway. Worry was a big part of love.

Gabriel checked on my progress, calling me on his cell phone. That was shocking to me at first. He was so old, it was a little startling that he'd adapted to technology; I hadn't even been able to get my grandmother to use an answering machine when she was alive. But Gabriel had a vampiric mind, self-healing, and surging with a free-flowing supply of brain cell enriching blood. I supposed he'd always have his mental faculties, and he'd already proven that he was smart; me being alive proved that.

He was always interested in the state of the twins when he called. I had a feeling he was keeping notes on me and my progress, and we were being discreetly studied. I hoped his inquisitiveness didn't become a problem after they were born. Teren didn't want them treated as science experiments. Neither did I.

After a month of injections, Teren finally let me leave the ranch again. Feeling assured that I wouldn't convert during dinner, he took me out to a nice restaurant. He ordered a plate for himself, for show, but let me eat it. We stayed out of San Francisco, just in case we ran into someone who we'd told the cover story to—I shouldn't exactly be out and about if I was on bed rest. He took me to a small town nearby the ranch and we ate, went for a short stroll, and talked about trivial things. It felt wonderful, like we were a normal couple again.

With no more fear over their fate, we finalized our baby names and guessed what sexes we thought they'd be. We discussed what we thought they'd look like. Teren assured me that they wouldn't necessarily be carbon copies of him. We laughed, flirted and kissed in the moonlight. It was disgustingly romantic, and I cherished it.

Not being able to see doctors anymore, I relied on the women of the house, since they had all successfully carried children before. They listened, felt my body, and assured me that everything was going just as it should. I smiled, trusting their abilities and experience, but still wishing I could have another ultrasound, just so I could see for myself. I even considered asking one of them to steal a machine for me. I didn't, though.

Mid-May, I was done with being pregnant. I was done with being huger than really seemed physically possible. I was done with my back aching. I was done with not being able to get truly comfortable at night, even with Teren's cooling arms. I wanted to be able to bend over again. I was tired of aching, swollen feet. I was tired of not being able to go home. I was anxious to see our creations, and I was ready to be a mom.

I might have started to get a little snippy. I really didn't think I could be faulted for that—I had so many hormones flooding through my mixed blood. But even so, after snapping at Imogen for waking me up in the middle of the night, when she and Halina were laughing downstairs about another rendezvous Halina had with Gabriel, I cried afterwards, I felt so bad. And of course, Halina found my emotional mood swings hilarious.

By the end of May, I started cursing Teren and his defying-the-odds super sperm. I let him know on several occasions that my physical torture was completely his fault. He would smile at me, a little smugly, and with a look of pride on his face. He only once replied with, "It takes two, you know." I pelted him with every object I could find after he said that, so he never said it again.

He started appeasing me with ice cream drizzled with blood. I know that sounds disgusting, but trust me, it was unbelievable. It worked really well too, and my moods started calming back down with the cold, creamy treat.

When June started, I was sure I was going to be pregnant forever. It was the second week in when I started to think that maybe being pregnant forever was okay. Because, in the second week of June, I started having contractions. At first it was mild, just an ache in my low back, not much different than the aches I'd been having for the last few weeks. Maybe just a little stronger. Then those started shifting into painful throbs that had me sitting down and breathing steadily through my mouth. It first happened when Teren was at work. I'd wanted to call him, to have him rush home so he wouldn't miss anything, but Alanna waved her hand and assured me that they weren't consistent enough to be the real thing.

When I gave her a blank look, she explained that when I was truly in labor, the pains would be longer, stronger and closer together. With a smile, she patted my belly and assured me that I would have no doubt when those started. I was not in the least bit happy that I was being treated to fake labor pains. The universe had a twisted sense of humor.

But Alanna was right. They lasted on and off for a few more days. And when they were over, I would have given anything to have felt them again.

It was morning, one week before my due date, when the first true contraction hit me. I was in bed, kissing Teren goodbye for work, when the pain wrapped around my entire abdomen. I breathed through it while Teren asked me what was wrong. Shaking my head, I told him it was another fake contraction. Sensing something that I couldn't, Teren called into work and let them know he was staying by my side today. I tried to convince him that wasn't necessary, but then another one hit me. Clenching his hand, I decided he was right, he should stay.

Those uncomfortable squeezing sensations lasted all afternoon long. At first I thought it was just another false alarm, but then, right around dusk, I knew my body wasn't joking. The vampires could sense it too, and before I had much say in the matter, I was in a loose nightshirt, propped up in my bed, with Imogen feeling around my lady parts. Caring more about the approaching event than my modesty, she assured me that I was nearly ready and the babies were in the right position. Trusting her, I lay back in the bed and waited for the next round of pain.

Alanna gave me a cup of small cubes of blood that she'd frozen. I sucked on those, grateful for the way my body felt slightly relieved, like blood was a natural vampiric endorphin releaser; even the tiniest amount somewhat relieved my pain. The coolness on my scorching mouth helped too. My fangs dropped down, but I ignored it as another burst of pain took my focus instead.

As the rounds started coming closer together, and even my inexperienced mind knew I was really, really close, I asked Teren to call my mother and sister. He looked over my pained expression, my forehead already slick with sweat, and nodded. I was a little surprised; I thought he'd argue.

I heard him in the hallway calling them, heard my mom's excited reaction and her oath that I'd better wait until she got there. I laughed at that, until more pain hit me. Then I stopped laughing and focused on breathing through the pain condensing my core.

Teren came back a moment later and crawled into bed with me. He scooted behind me and placed his knees on either side. I clutched them, grateful for something to hold on to. Placing a light kiss on the back of my neck, he began rubbing my lower back. His cool hands combined with his vampiric strength was a godsend. I nearly wept with relief.

My water broke about twenty minutes later, making me panic at first. There was nothing quite like that feeling to let you know this was absolutely happening—there was no going back. Alanna assured me it was all right and Teren rubbed my shoulders, soothing me. I felt a little bad for getting their bed all messy, but none of the vampires seemed to care as they went about prepping for the delivery. Halina and Imogen began setting up an area for the newborns, to clean and examine them, and the smell of antiseptic hit me. I dropped my head back on Teren's shoulder and prayed for strength.

I felt something deep in my body, just as I heard tires in the driveway. Every vampire turned to look at the door. Mom had just shown up. I started to hyperventilate. My fangs were out. I was too distracted to keep them in. I just couldn't do it...she'd see.

Alanna swished to my side. "Jack will let them in, dear. You focus on the babies. That's all you need to care about right now."

She stroked her hand down my cheek and I nodded.

Imogen checked me again as I heard excited exclamations from downstairs. I pushed aside my fear at Mom seeing me like this, and struggled with the new sensation in my body. Under my breath, I muttered, "I want to push."

I felt Imogen's cool hands, checking to see if my body was ready for what it wanted. Pulling back, she smiled up at me. "Go ahead, Emma. If you want to, you're ready."

Teren squeezed me, whispering encouragement. "You can do this, Emma." I hesitated, fighting the building sensation. I could hear my mom approaching; I could hear her fast footsteps. I didn't know what to do, but the choice wasn't really up to me. My body was going to push, whether I wanted it to or not.

Leaning back into Teren, a contraction hit me and the desire was irresistible. Using every muscle in my core, I pushed down as hard as I could. I could feel the movement, and I could feel the pain. Babies weren't exactly the same size as the area they came out of. I squeezed Teren's arm and paused, momentarily spent. Imogen encouraged me to try again, right as my mom walked into the room.

I was tired, but fear made me look over at her. Her eyes were wide and shiny, excited for her daughter about to give birth to her first grandchild. Then her eyes locked onto my mouth. They widened as she took in the new, unnatural element on me. I wanted to cry and explain, but the urge to push hit me again and I bore down. Ashley went to wait in the corner, being respectfully quiet. Mom rushed to my side.

"What's wrong with her?" Too focused on pushing, I ignored her. I heard her address Teren. "What's going on? Why are her teeth like that?"

Teren sputtered and could only say, "We'll explain later."

A cry escaped me as the baby shifted positions. Imogen called for another push and I ignored my mother asking for more details. As the baby was squeezed farther down, the head nearly ready to come out, the pain intensified. I contained a scream as the pain ripped right through me. Nothing could possibly hurt this bad. I'd rather be knocked out again. I'd rather have my neck ripped open again. I'd rather be doing almost anything, than having my body torn from the inside out. Teren brought his arms around me in an attempt to sooth me. It didn't help, it was excruciating, and I needed relief.

Since the thing I really needed was right there, I made myself forget that my mother was standing a foot away from me. I grabbed Teren's arm and clamped down on the tender, inner area; my extended fangs sliced right through his skin. He flinched as my teeth tore through his flesh. He hissed, but didn't remove his arm from my teeth. The blood welled in my mouth, heavy and heavenly. I sucked down the tangy coolness, letting the heady feeling of drinking steal my mind away from the pain ripping through me. Teren didn't pull away from my attack; he let me drink as long as I needed. In fact, he let me drink so long that his arm started trembling. He still didn't pull away, though, and I didn't stop. He left his arm in front of my face and let me drain him. He even whispered encouragement into my ear as I began the final push.

My mother, on the other hand, went ballistic. She grabbed Teren's arm and tried to pry it from my mouth. I think I may have growled at her, but before Teren or I could do anything about it, Halina pushed her way from us.

"She is vampire, as are we all, and she needs this. Either deal with it right now or leave this room." Her voice was commanding and intimidating. I had to imagine that she'd dropped her fangs as well, to emphasize her point. Even in my turmoil, I was a little surprised that Halina was giving Mom a choice. If she truly wished, the pureblood vampire could compel my mother to sit quietly in a corner, or quack like a duck. Sometimes it was intimidating to think of just how much power that teenage vampire had.

I heard my mother sputter a few times, then she came around, sat next to me, and held my free hand.

I didn't have any more time to worry about it; the baby was coming out. I sucked deep on the already free-flowing blood as I pushed hard. Imogen's cool hands pried the shoulders loose and Alanna helped slide the baby out the rest of the way. Teren's arm started to obviously shake, but he still left it in my mouth, letting me take in his cool, endorphin-releasing blood. I wasn't too worried about harming him. He was already dead; I couldn't kill him by overdrinking. It would only make him a little weak, and if my southern "area" had to be ripped to shreds, then he could suffer through a little bit of weakness.

I smelled the baby first. Something unmistakable hit the air. The scent of new life. The scent of me, mixed with Teren. Even under the haze of all the blood in the room and in my mouth, I could smell it. I released Teren as the relief of not having to push anymore hit me. He shook his arm out, and since my teeth were no longer in the way, the skin healed right before my eyes. Kissing my head, he laughed in happy relief. I ignored the sensation of blood dribbling down my chin, and I ignored my mother muttering, "My God, Emma." Instead, my tired eyes watched the bundle in Alanna's arms as she and Halina cleaned up the child. A tiny, insistent cry filled my ears. It did odd, protective things to my body. I could just make out a thick patch of dark hair on a small, blood-smeared body, but that was it. Just when I was going to ask if I could see the baby, another round of instinct hit me.

Imogen, still playing the part of doctor, patted my knee and told me the second baby was ready. I nearly sobbed. I had forgotten in my thrill of seeing my firstborn, that I had another one coming.

Feeling too tired to do it, I shook my head. Tears running down my cheeks, I muttered, "I can't. I'm sorry." It was like running a marathon and then having the judge tell you that they'd extended the race another six miles and you had to keep going.

Teren massaged my shoulders, then wiped the hair away from my sweaty face. "You can, Emma. You're the strongest person I know. If anyone can do this, it's you."

My mother, stunned into silence at my side, squeezed my hand. I weakly looked over at her, and more tears ran down my face. She smiled, a little nervously, and finally spoke. "One more, sweetheart. I know it's hard, but one more…and then you're done."

I swallowed, my resolve refortifying. Mom didn't understand yet that I was literally done with one more. This was the only chance Teren and I had to have kids, and I wouldn't selfishly risk the life of one by refusing to push. Not that it was really my choice anyway. My body would evacuate these kids one way or another. Gritting my teeth, I pushed.

The second one came out easier, since my body was pretty much stretched to the limits it needed to be. But I still cried out at the last painful push to get the shoulders out. And then, thankfully, a second healthy cry filled the air. I collapsed back into Teren, too exhausted for words.

He was lightly crying into my shoulder, telling me that I did great. I closed my eyes, mumbling some sort of response to that. While Alanna wiped the sweat and blood off of my face, and Imogen tended to my body, I heard Halina and Ashley cooing over my babies. My mother was still silent as she held my hand. I had so many desires happening, that I didn't know which one to tend to first. I wanted to sleep. I wanted to tell my mother I was fine, and that everything was going to be okay. I wanted more blood. And I wanted to see my children.

That desire rose over everything else, and I opened my heavy lids. Ashley was holding one bundle of blankets while Halina held the other. Teren, behind me, kissed my head and told me they were beautiful and perfect. I didn't know how he knew that, since all I saw was fleece, but his senses were more advanced than mine.

"Can I hold them?" I whispered. Ashley didn't hear me in her cooing, but Halina immediately twisted to me.

Her face beaming, she brought over her bundle. Ashley noticed and followed her. My mother, oddly quiet again, released my hand and patted my knee. Ignoring the tugging sensation in my lower area, as Imogen presumably repaired the damage done in the birthing process, I held my arms out for my baby.

"It's a boy," Halina whispered, as she laid the bundle in my arms.

I stared down at the most angelic face I'd ever seen, a face I'd seen countless times. It was as if all of Teren's features had been softened and miniaturized. Looking at his son was like looking at a baby picture of Teren. He was perfect. Shocking, dark hair peeked out of the top of the blanket. It was a jet-black shade that matched all of the vampires. His eyes were closed in slumber, but I could see them shifting behind the pale lids. He had pudgy, healthy cheeks, full pink lips, and the cutest little nose. One hand was out, clutching the warm blanket he was nestled in, and I rubbed a tiny digit. His skin was unrealistically soft, like nothing I'd ever felt before. Perfect skin, untouched by the harshness of the world. As my finger moved over the tiniest fingernail you could imagine, that little hand reached out and grabbed my finger.

My entire world shifted in that exact moment.

I sobbed and kissed his forehead, and my tears dripped onto his perfect skin. Teren sniffled and reached around with his good arm to run a finger down his cheek. "He's perfect, Emma. You did great," he whispered, his voice breaking.

I looked behind me, at his tear-filled eyes. "*We* did great." I kissed him briefly, before shifting my attention back to my son. Ashley, standing at the edge of the bed beside my silent mom, startled to giggle as she looked him over. "He looks just like Teren, Em." She glanced down at the bundle in her arms. "I think she looks more like you."

As what she said hit me, my mouth dropped open. "She?" Ashley looked up at me and nodded, then she held out her bundle for me to take. Shifting one child, I took the other on my other side. I felt like I was moving in slow motion. Even though they'd been jostling around in my body for a while, they seemed so fragile, like the tiniest wrong movement would break them.

Ash laid my daughter in my arms and I stared at her, amazed. She was right, she did look more like me. She had a light splattering of brown hair; she seemed almost blonde next to her brother. I knew that hair would eventually darken into a shade that matched my own though. Her eyes were open, as she examined this strange world around her, and they were clearly dark, clearly going to be brown, like mine. I nuzzled her face and she opened her mouth, like she wanted to suck on my nose.

Teren shifted his hand to stroke her head. His finger gently passed over the tender spot of her skull. The bone there wasn't fully formed yet and the skin pulsed with her heartbeat. He left his finger there, feeling the pulse of life. Outside of my body, her heart was louder, perfectly matching the rhythm under Teren's finger. "She does look like you, baby." His voice came out wondrous, like he really hadn't been expecting that.

I sobbed again, and squeezed them tighter. All the pain and discomfort from giving birth to them was gone. After a few moments of familial bonding, my mother finally cleared her throat. I looked up at her, my eyes watery from my tears. Her eyes locked onto my mouth and I realized my fangs were still out. Popping them back up, I bit my lip. "Mom...?"

Her eyes glistened as she shook her head. "Can I...can I hold them?" She finally spoke.

I nodded, and more tears splashed onto my cheeks. I handed her the miniature version of Teren and her face melted. I thought that at that exact moment, she could have cared less that she was in a room full of mythical creatures. At that moment, I didn't think she was even aware that anyone besides her and her grandchildren were in the room. She laughed and stroked his cheek. His little head moved back and forth as he grunted and squirmed.

Laughing, I handed her my daughter. She lightly kissed her pink cheek and I swear my little girl smiled. Relief flooded through me, and I sank back into Teren's arms. He wrapped himself around me; his coolness felt wonderful on my tired body. Imogen and Alanna finished tending to me, removing some blankets and towels that they'd placed down, that I could clearly smell were soaked with blood, then they modestly covered me. Alanna left to get Jack, since the gross part was over with, and I smiled and closed my eyes as exhaustion overwhelmed me.

Amid the chorus of, "they're beautiful, they're perfect, they're so tiny," I heard a pair of perfectly strong heartbeats. I nestled into Teren's back as I listened to those beats. So many times I'd been afraid I'd never get to hear them, and I relished every wet, steady thump. I smiled into Teren's skin as he gently swayed me back and forth. A deep chuckle came up his throat as he watched our families welcoming the new lives.

"I love you, husband," I whispered, too low for the humans to hear.

He kissed my forehead. "I love you too, wife."

I sleepily peeked up at him as Jack entered the room. He was instantly handed a child. "Are you disappointed?" I asked Teren.

Teren looked away from where his father was congratulating us. He peeked down at me, confused. "Disappointed? Why would I be that?"

I sighed. "You told me once that you never wanted me to change." I shook my head and dropped my mouth open, slightly extending a fang. "I changed."

He smiled with one side of his mouth, and his hand came up to cup my cheek. "I've been told my entire life that if I ever fell in love with a human, I'd have to one day let her go." His eyes watered again. "I came into this relationship, never thinking I'd get to keep you. I can't tell you how *not* disappointed I am right now."

A tear slid down my cheek and across his fingers. Smiling, I leaned up and kissed him. Our brief moment of connection was interrupted by my beaming-with-happiness mother.

"Do these little miracles have names yet?" she asked, twisting away from Ashley to gaze at me on the bed. I smiled. Teren and I had talked about names all throughout the pregnancy. Well, actually, we'd stopped when we weren't sure if they'd make it. We'd put everything on hold during that scary time, but afterwards, we'd picked up again. Wanting it to be a surprise, we hadn't mentioned anything to anyone. Since we hadn't known the sexes, we'd picked out multiple sets of names, one for every scenario. We'd already decided on the boy/girl set. I glanced over at Teren and he nodded, willing to let me make the announcement.

My eyes swept the room. Focusing on Halina, who was cooing at my daughter, I met her eye. "Her name...is Nika Alexis, in honor of Nicolis." Halina's mouth dropped open, and her eyes quickly filled with blood-red tears. They dripped down her cheek as she looked back at Nika. Nicolis had been her husband, the husband she'd inadvertently killed after her conversion. She mourned him daily.

Smiling at her reaction, I turned to my mother; her eyes were transfixed on Halina's bloody tears. Clearing my throat brought her attention back to me. Watching her pale face, I softly said, "His name…is Julian Nathaniel." My mother had much the same reaction as Halina. My sister too, for that matter. Julian was my father's name. My father who had sacrificed his own life to save my sister's. It was the one male name that Teren and I had never wavered on.

With tears dripping down her face, my mother stared at me in awe. I didn't know if she was overwhelmed by what we'd done, or what we were. I hoped that she'd be okay with the latter. I didn't really want Halina to have to wipe all of this from her mind. I had a feeling that in the next several years, learning how to raise children, let alone vampire children, I'd need my mother. And really, I had no idea how to hide what they were from her. Not forever. Not when their teeth came in and they started experimentally biting people. How would I explain that to someone who didn't understand the reason?

Timidly, I tried to start the conversation with her. "Mom, I should explain…" I could hear the reluctance in my voice, could feel Teren minutely squeeze me in support. Halina's eyes shifted to my mom, ready to move in on her, if needed.

My mom immediately started shaking her head. "Are you happy, Emma?"

The largest smile possible spread over my face, and tears sprung into my eyes. "Yes," I whispered.

She swayed Julian back and forth in her arms, and smiled peacefully at me. "Then I don't need to hear it right now. Whatever is going on with you…" her eyes flicked over to the other vampires in the room, "with all of you…" Her gaze came back to me. "All I care about is your happiness."

A sob broke out of me that my mother might accept my strange new family, that she might accept me. Until just then, I hadn't realized how much I'd wanted her to know. Seeing the emotion breaking over me, she quickly came over to sit on the bed beside me, Julian still clutched in her arms. "I love you, Emma, whatever you are." She gave me a kiss on the cheek and then she placed kisses all over Julian. "Besides, these are the most perfect children I've ever seen."

Being one of her children, I tried to not take offense to that as I laughed and leaned into her shoulder. She laughed as well and kissed my head. I felt Teren shift out from behind me, to lie over on the other side of me in our massive bed. Mom helped me lie back on the pillows and then placed Julian in the crook of my arm. I cooed at him and kissed his soft cheek. Mom kissed my head again and then exclaimed, "I'm going to go call my girlfriends and tell them I'm a grandma!"

I grabbed her arm as she rose and she looked down on me. Seeing my concerned face, she added, "I'm going to tell them that I'm a grandma to two perfectly normal, regular, healthy, and beautiful children." I nodded at her that she understood. That what we were, what *they* were, needed to be kept secret. She nodded back, and then flitted from the room to go off and brag about them.

Ashley walked up next, giving Julian and me a kiss. She looked over my shoulder at Teren and then back to me. "You guys did great. You were amazing, Emma." She giggled and added, "And I'm never having children. That was disgusting." I laughed and smacked her arm. She laughed and gave me another kiss on the cheek. "I'm going to go call Tracey and Ben." I nodded and watched her leave.

Imogen swished from the room and came back moments later with handmade knitted blankets in blue and pink. Looking sheepish she said, "I couldn't help but make a whole bunch in different colors." Smiling, she swaddled Julian in blue and Nika in pink. "I was really hoping for one of each," she added.

Taking Nika from Halina, Imogen placed her in the crook of my other arm. Halina looked at her longingly, not seeming to want to let her go. With a sigh, she did though, and backed away from the bed. She stared at Teren and me and our children, then looked at her daughter and grand-daughter. "Well girls, how about a celebratory drink? I know I could use it."

Alanna and Imogen smiled and nodded. Alanna turned to me as Imogen and Halina left the room. "We'll be downstairs, dear." Her eyes flicked down my body. "Holler, if you need anything."

I smiled, knowing that I knew exactly where they were in this house, and I knew they'd hear me if I casually asked for anything. Alanna's comments were sweet though. As she and Jack left hand in hand, I sighed and settled into Teren's side, sort of happy to finally be alone with our new foursome.

Teren's arm went under my shoulders, holding me close in the beautiful bed where I'd birthed our children. His pale eyes locked onto mine as a soft, peaceful smile settled on his face. We stared at each other for several quiet minutes before he spoke. "You know, now that they are safely out of you, you could stop taking the injections, if you wanted."

I stared down at the two bundles in my arms, one a mass of cotton-candy pink with light-blondish, fuzzy hair poking out the top, the other, a sea of powder blue, with a patch of thick blackness at the head. I kissed each soft, warm tuft of hair, then closed my eyes and reached out with my new senses. In the distance, I could hear Jack and Alanna quietly talking in the kitchen. I tuned them out. In the dining room, I could hear Imogen and Halina laughing as they clinked their glasses and sipped their blood cocktails. I tuned that out. I heard Ashley on her phone, talking to Hot Ben, who said he was hopping in his car now and he'd be here soon. I heard Mom on her phone, gloating over how her grandchildren were perfect angels, and one of them bore her late husband's name. Next to me, I could hear Teren softly mimic breathing, waiting for my response. I tuned them all out.

Pinpointing my abilities, I listened for the two tiniest beings in the room. Their breath was faint, but I could hear it. They hiccupped and sighed, stopped and started with their breathing, still getting the hang of it. I squeezed them just a smidge tighter and listened for their hearts. Like a musical symphony, the beats filled my ears. The longer I concentrated on only hearing those specific sounds, the louder they became. I let my own heartbeat fill my ears and smiled as the three of us fell into a similar pattern as they lay near my chest. My heartbeat was slower, one of mine equaling two of theirs, but the rhythm was perfectly in sync.

Opening my eyes to Teren, I sighed softly, contently. "Not just yet. I want to stay like them for a while longer." He nodded, his eyes as content as mine. As he reached out and stroked a dark clump of Julian's hair with his finger, I whispered, "Are you okay with that?"

His eyes snapped up to mine. "Of course, Emma." His finger traveled up to my cheek. "I will stand behind any decision you make on this. It's your body, your choice." Leaning in, he gave me a soft kiss. "And, as I've always said, I'll take you any way that I can get you." He leaned back and gazed at me; his face was still pale from the amount of blood I'd taken from him. "If I get you young and beautiful or old and elegant, I'm happy." He smiled, his eyes brightening. "Because, either way, I get you forever, and I never thought I'd get that."

I smiled, my eyes watering again. "I didn't either. I love you so much."

He crooked a grin at me. "I would say I love you too, but I think I've gone too far past that, so I'll just say…" his grin turned serious, "you make eternity something to look forward to."

I gave up on trying to contain the tears after that. Darn emotional vampires.

The End

About the Author

S.C. Stephens is a *New York Times* and *USA Today* bestselling author who enjoys spending every free moment she has creating stories that are packed with emotion and heavy on romance.

Her debut novel, Thoughtless, an angst-filled love triangle charged with insurmountable passion and the unforgettable Kellan Kyle, took the literary world by storm. Amazed and surprised by the response to the release of Thoughtless in 2009, more stories were quick to follow. Stephens has been writing nonstop ever since.

In addition to writing, Stephens enjoys spending lazy afternoons in the sun reading fabulous novels, loading up her iPod with writer's block reducing music, heading out to the movies, and spending quality time with her friends and family. She currently resides in the beautiful Pacific Northwest with her two equally beautiful children.

Titles currently available for purchase:

The Thoughtless Series (Published by Gallery Books):
Thoughtless
Effortless
Reckless

Collision Course (Published by S.C. Stephens)

The Conversion Trilogy (Published by S.C. Stephens):
Conversion
Bloodlines
'Til Death

Connect with S.C. Stephens

Email: ThoughtlessRomantic@gmail.com

Facebook: https://www.facebook.com/SCStephensAuthor

Twitter: https://twitter.com/SC_Stephens

Website: authorscstephens.com

CPSIA information can be obtained
at www.ICGtesting.com
Printed in the USA
LVOW01s1033050317

526180LV00009B/698/P